Praise for Jennifer Egan's

A Visit from the Goon Squad

"A rich and unforgettable novel about decay and endurance, about individuals in a world as it changes around them. . . . [Egan] is one of the most talented writers today."
—*The New York Review of Books*

"Wildly ambitious. . . . A tour de force. . . . Music is both subject and metaphor as Egan explores the mutability of time, destiny, and individual accountability post-technology."
—*O, The Oprah Magazine*

"A spiky, shape-shifting new book. . . . A display of Egan's extreme virtuosity." —*The New York Times*

"It ends in the same place it starts, except that everything has changed, including you, the reader." —*The New Republic*

"Egan's bravura fifth book samples from different eras (the glory days of punk; a slick, socially networked future) and styles (sly satire, moving tragedy, even PowerPoint) to explore the interplay between music and the rough rhythms of life."
—*Vogue*

"Told with both affection and intensity, *Goon Squad* stands as a brilliant, all-absorbing novel for the beach, the woods, the air-conditioned apartment or the city stoop while wearing your iPod."
—Alan Cheuse, NPR's *All Things Considered*

"Brilliant, inventive. . . . Emboldening. It cracks the world open afresh. . . . Would that Marcel Proust could receive [a copy]. It would blow his considerable mind."
—*The Plain Dealer*

"Frequently dazzling. . . . Egan's expert flaying of human foibles has the compulsive allure of poking at a sore tooth: excruciating but exhilarating too." —*Entertainment Weekly*

"Audacious, extraordinary. . . . Egan uses the pop-music business as a prism to examine the heedless pace of modern life."
—*The Philadelphia Inquirer*

"If Egan is our reward for living through the self-conscious gimmicks and ironic claptrap of postmodernism, then it was all worthwhile. . . . [A] triumph of technical bravado and tender sympathy."
—*The Washington Post*

JENNIFER EGAN

A Visit from the Goon Squad

Jennifer Egan is the author of *The Keep*, *Look at Me*, *The Invisible Circus*, and the story collection *Emerald City*. Her stories have been published in *The New Yorker*, *Harper's Magazine*, *GQ*, *Zoetrope: All-Story*, and *Ploughshares*, and her nonfiction appears frequently in *The New York Times Magazine*. She lives with her husband and sons in Brooklyn.

www.jenniferegan.com

Jennifer Egan is available for lectures and readings. For information regarding her availability, please visit www.rhspeakers.com or call 212-572-2013.

ALSO BY JENNIFER EGAN

The Keep

Look at Me

Emerald City and Other Stories

The Invisible Circus

A Visit from the Goon Squad

A Visit from the Goon Squad

JENNIFER EGAN

The International

2012

IMPAC
Dublin
Literary Award

Anchor Books
A Division of Random House, Inc.
New York

FIRST ANCHOR BOOKS OPEN-MARKET EDITION,
SEPTEMBER 2011

The Library of Congress has cataloged the Knopf edition as follows:
Egan, Jennifer.
A visit from the goon squad / Jennifer Egan. — 1st ed.
p. cm.
1. Punk rock musicians — Fiction.
2. Sound recording executives and producers — Fiction.
3. Older men — Fiction. 4. Young women — Fiction. 5. Psychological fiction.
I. Title.
PS3555.G292V57 2010
813'.54 — dc22 2009046496

Anchor ISBN: 978-0-307-94835-9

Book design by Virginia Tan

www.anchorbooks.com

Printed in the United States of America

10 9 8 7 6 5 4

For Peter M.,
with gratitude

"Poets claim that we recapture for a moment the self that we were long ago when we enter some house or garden in which we used to live in our youth. But these are most hazardous pilgrimages, which end as often in disappointment as in success. It is in ourselves that we should rather seek to find those fixed places, contemporaneous with different years."

"The unknown element in the lives of other people is like that of nature, which each fresh scientific discovery merely reduces but does not abolish."

—Marcel Proust, *In Search of Lost Time*

1

Found Objects

It began the usual way, in the bathroom of the Lassimo Hotel. Sasha was adjusting her yellow eye shadow in the mirror when she noticed a bag on the floor beside the sink that must have belonged to the woman whose peeing she could faintly hear through the vaultlike door of a toilet stall. Inside the rim of the bag, barely visible, was a wallet made of pale green leather. It was easy for Sasha to recognize, looking back, that the peeing woman's blind trust had provoked her: *We live in a city where people will steal the hair off your head if you give them half a chance, but you leave your stuff lying in plain sight and expect it to be waiting for you when you come back?* It made her want to teach the woman a lesson. But this wish only camouflaged the deeper feeling Sasha always had: that fat, tender wallet, offering itself to her hand—

it seemed so dull, so life-as-usual to just leave it there rather than seize the moment, accept the challenge, take the leap, fly the coop, throw caution to the wind, live dangerously ("I get it," Coz, her therapist, said), and *take* the fucking thing.

"You mean steal it."

He was trying to get Sasha to use that word, which was harder to avoid in the case of a wallet than with a lot of the things she'd lifted over the past year, when her condition (as Coz referred to it) had begun to accelerate: five sets of keys, fourteen pairs of sunglasses, a child's striped scarf, binoculars, a cheese grater, a pocketknife, twenty-eight bars of soap, and eighty-five pens, ranging from cheap ballpoints she'd used to sign debit-card slips to the aubergine Visconti that cost two hundred sixty dollars online, which she'd lifted from her former boss's lawyer during a contracts meeting. Sasha no longer took anything from stores—their cold, inert goods didn't tempt her. Only from people.

"Okay," she said. "Steal it."

Sasha and Coz had dubbed that feeling she got the "personal challenge," as in: taking the wallet was a way for Sasha to assert her toughness, her individuality. What they needed to do was switch things around in her head so that the challenge became not taking the wallet but *leaving* it. That would be the cure, although Coz never used words like "cure." He wore funky sweaters and let her call him Coz, but he was old school inscrutable, to the point where Sasha couldn't tell if he was gay or straight, if he'd written famous books, or if (as she sometimes suspected) he was one of those escaped cons who impersonate surgeons and wind up leaving their operating tools inside people's skulls. Of course, these questions could have been resolved on Google in less than a minute, but they were useful questions (according to Coz), and so far, Sasha had resisted.

The couch where she lay in his office was blue leather and very soft. Coz liked the couch, he'd told her, because it relieved them both of the burden of eye contact. "You don't like eye contact?" Sasha had asked. It seemed like a weird thing for a therapist to admit.

"I find it tiring," he'd said. "This way, we can both look where we want."

"Where will you look?"

He smiled. "You can see my options."

"Where do you usually look? When people are on the couch."

"Around the room," Coz said. "At the ceiling. Into space."

"Do you ever sleep?"

"No."

Sasha usually looked at the window, which faced the street, and tonight, as she continued her story, was rippled with rain. She'd glimpsed the wallet, tender and overripe as a peach. She'd plucked it from the woman's bag and slipped it into her own small handbag, which she'd zipped shut before the sound of peeing had stopped. She'd flicked open the bathroom door and floated back through the lobby to the bar. She and the wallet's owner had never seen each other.

Prewallet, Sasha had been in the grip of a dire evening: lame date (yet another) brooding behind dark bangs, sometimes glancing at the flat-screen TV, where a Jets game seemed to interest him more than Sasha's admittedly overhandled tales of Bennie Salazar, her old boss, who was famous for founding the Sow's Ear record label and who also (Sasha happened to know) sprinkled gold flakes into his coffee—as an aphrodisiac, she suspected—and sprayed pesticide in his armpits.

Postwallet, however, the scene tingled with mirthful possibility. Sasha felt the waiters eyeing her as she sidled back to the table holding her handbag with its secret weight. She sat down and took a sip of her Melon Madness Martini and cocked her head at Alex. She smiled her yes/no smile. "Hello," she said.

The yes/no smile was amazingly effective.

"You're happy," Alex said.

"I'm always happy," Sasha said. "Sometimes I just forget."

Alex had paid the bill while she was in the bathroom—clear proof that he'd been on the verge of aborting their date. Now he studied her. "You feel like going somewhere else?"

They stood. Alex wore black cords and a white button-up shirt. He was a legal secretary. On e-mail he'd been fanciful, almost goofy, but in person he seemed simultaneously anxious and bored. She could tell that he was in excellent shape, not from going to the gym but from being young enough that his body was still imprinted with whatever sports he'd played in high school and college. Sasha, who was thirty-five, had passed that point. Still, not even Coz knew her real age. The closest anyone had come to guessing it was thirty-one, and most put her in her twenties. She worked out daily and avoided the sun. Her online profiles all listed her as twenty-eight.

As she followed Alex from the bar, she couldn't resist unzipping her purse and touching the fat green wallet just for a second, for the contraction it made her feel around her heart.

"You're aware of how the theft makes *you* feel," Coz said. "To the point where you remind yourself of it to improve your mood. But do you think about how it makes the other person feel?"

Sasha tipped back her head to look at him. She made a point of doing this now and then, just to remind Coz that she wasn't an idiot—she knew the question had a right answer. She and Coz were collaborators, writing a story whose end had already been determined: she would get well. She would stop stealing from people and start caring again about the things that had once guided her: music; the network of friends she'd made when she first came to New York; a set of goals she'd scrawled on a big sheet of newsprint and taped to the walls of her early apartments:

> Find a band to manage
> Understand the news
> Study Japanese
> Practice the harp

"I don't think about the people," Sasha said.

"But it isn't that you lack empathy," Coz said. "We know that, because of the plumber."

Sasha sighed. She'd told Coz the plumber story about a month ago, and he'd found a way to bring it up at almost every session since. The plumber was an old man, sent by Sasha's landlord to investigate a leak in the apartment below hers. He'd appeared in Sasha's doorway, tufts of gray on his head, and within a minute—*boom*—he'd hit the floor and crawled under her bathtub like an animal fumbling its way into a familiar hole. The fingers he'd groped toward the bolts behind the tub were grimed to cigar stubs, and reaching made his sweatshirt hike up, exposing a soft white back. Sasha turned away, stricken by the old man's abasement, anxious to leave for her temp job, except that the plumber was talking to her, asking about the length and frequency of her showers. "I never use it," she told him curtly. "I shower at the gym." He nodded without acknowledging her rudeness, apparently used to it. Sasha's nose began to prickle; she shut her eyes and pushed hard on both temples.

Opening her eyes, she saw the plumber's tool belt lying on the floor at her feet. It had a beautiful screwdriver in it, the orange translucent handle gleaming like a lollipop in its worn leather loop, the silvery shaft sculpted, sparkling. Sasha felt herself contract around the object in a single yawn of appetite; she needed to hold the screwdriver, just for a minute. She bent her knees and plucked it noiselessly from the belt. Not a bangle jangled; her bony hands were spastic at most things, but she was good at this—*made for it*, she often thought, in the first drifty moments after lifting something. And once the screwdriver was in her hand, she felt instant relief from the pain of having an old soft-backed man snuffling under her tub, and then something more than relief: a blessed indifference, as if the very idea of feeling pain over such a thing were baffling.

"And what about after he'd gone?" Coz had asked when Sasha told him the story. "How did the screwdriver look to you then?"

There was a pause. "Normal," she said.

"Really. Not special anymore?"

"Like any screwdriver."

Sasha had heard Coz shift behind her and felt something happen in the room: the screwdriver, which she'd placed on the table (recently supplemented with a second table) where she kept the things she'd lifted, and which she'd barely looked at since, seemed to hang in the air of Coz's office. It floated between them: a symbol.

"And how did you feel?" Coz asked quietly. "About having taken it from the plumber you pitied?"

How did she feel? *How did she feel?* There was a right answer, of course. At times Sasha had to fight the urge to lie simply as a way of depriving Coz of it.

"Bad," she said. "Okay? I felt bad. Shit, I'm bankrupting myself to pay for you—obviously I get that this isn't a great way to live."

More than once, Coz had tried to connect the plumber to Sasha's father, who had disappeared when she was six. She was careful not to indulge this line of thinking. "I don't remember him," she told Coz. "I have nothing to say." She did this for Coz's protection and her own—they were writing a story of redemption, of fresh beginnings and second chances. But in that direction lay only sorrow.

Sasha and Alex crossed the lobby of the Lassimo Hotel in the direction of the street. Sasha hugged her purse to her shoulder, the warm ball of wallet snuggled in her armpit. As they passed the angular budded branches by the big glass doors to the street, a woman zigzagged into their path. "Wait," she said. "You haven't seen—I'm desperate."

Sasha felt a twang of terror. It was the woman whose wallet she'd taken—she knew this instantly, although the person before her had nothing in common with the blithe, raven-haired wallet owner she'd pictured. This woman had vulnerable brown eyes and flat pointy shoes that clicked too loudly on the marble floor. There was plenty of gray in her frizzy brown hair.

Sasha took Alex's arm, trying to steer him through the doors. She felt his pulse of surprise at her touch, but he stayed put. "Have we seen what?" he said.

"Someone stole my wallet. My ID is gone, and I have to catch a plane tomorrow morning. I'm just desperate!" She stared beseechingly at both of them. It was the sort of frank need that New Yorkers quickly learn how to hide, and Sasha recoiled. It had never occurred to her that the woman was from out of town.

"Have you called the police?" Alex asked.

"The concierge said he would call. But I'm also wondering—could it have fallen out somewhere?" She looked helplessly at the marble floor around their feet. Sasha relaxed slightly. This woman was the type who annoyed people without meaning to; apology shadowed her movements even now, as she followed Alex to the concierge desk. Sasha trailed behind.

"Is someone helping this person?" she heard Alex ask.

The concierge was young and spiky haired. "We've called the police," he said defensively.

Alex turned to the woman. "Where did this happen?"

"In the ladies' room. I think."

"Who else was there?"

"No one."

"It was empty?"

"There might have been someone, but I didn't see her."

Alex swung around to Sasha. "You were just in the bathroom," he said. "Did you see anyone?"

"No," she managed to say. She had Xanax in her purse, but she couldn't open her purse. Even with it zipped, she feared that the wallet would blurt into view in some way that she couldn't control, unleashing a cascade of horrors: arrest, shame, poverty, death.

Alex turned to the concierge. "How come I'm asking these questions instead of you?" he said. "Someone just got robbed in your hotel. Don't you have, like, security?"

The words "robbed" and "security" managed to pierce the soothing backbeat that pumped through not just the Lassimo but every hotel like it in New York City. There was a mild ripple of interest from the lobby.

"I've called security," the concierge said, adjusting his neck. "I'll call them again."

Sasha glanced at Alex. He was angry, and the anger made him recognizable in a way that an hour of aimless chatter (mostly hers, it was true) had not: he was new to New York. He came from someplace smaller. He had a thing or two to prove about how people should treat one another.

Two security guys showed up, the same on TV and in life: beefy guys whose scrupulous politeness was somehow

linked to their willingness to crack skulls. They dispersed
to search the bar. Sasha wished feverishly that she'd left the
wallet there, as if this were an impulse she'd barely resisted.

"I'll check the bathroom," she told Alex, and forced herself to walk slowly around the elevator bank. The bathroom
was empty. Sasha opened her purse, took out the wallet,
unearthed her vial of Xanax, and popped one between her
teeth. They worked faster if you chewed them. As the caus-
tic taste flooded her mouth, she scanned the room, trying
to decide where to ditch the wallet: In the stall? Under the
sink? The decision paralyzed her. She had to do this right,
to emerge unscathed, and if she could, if she did—she had a
frenzied sense of making a promise to Coz.

The bathroom door opened, and the woman walked in.
Her frantic eyes met Sasha's in the bathroom mirror: narrow, green, equally frantic. There was a pause, during which
Sasha felt that she was being confronted; the woman knew,
had known all along. Sasha handed her the wallet. She saw,
from the woman's stunned expression, that she was wrong.

"I'm sorry," Sasha said quickly. "It's a problem I have."

The woman opened the wallet. Her physical relief at having it back coursed through Sasha in a warm rush, as if their
bodies had fused. "Everything's there, I swear," she said. "I
didn't even open it. It's this problem I have, but I'm getting
help. I just—please don't tell. I'm hanging on by a thread."

The woman glanced up, her soft brown eyes moving over
Sasha's face. What did she see? Sasha wished that she could
turn and peer in the mirror again, as if something about herself might at last be revealed—some lost thing. But she didn't
turn. She held still and let the woman look. It struck her

that the woman was close to her own age—her real age. She probably had children at home.

"Okay," the woman said, looking down. "It's between us."

"Thank you," Sasha said. "Thank you, thank you." Relief and the first gentle waves of Xanax made her feel faint, and she leaned against the wall. She sensed the woman's eagerness to get away. She longed to slide to the floor.

There was a rap on the door, a man's voice: "Any luck?"

Sasha and Alex left the hotel and stepped into desolate, windy Tribeca. She'd suggested the Lassimo out of habit; it was near Sow's Ear Records, where she'd worked for twelve years as Bennie Salazar's assistant. But she hated the neighborhood at night without the World Trade Center, whose blazing freeways of light had always filled her with hope. She was tired of Alex. In a mere twenty minutes, they'd blown past the desired point of meaningful-connection-through-shared-experience into the less appealing state of knowing-each-other-too-well. Alex wore a knit cap pulled over his forehead. His eyelashes were long and black. "That was weird," he said finally.

"Yeah," Sasha said. Then, after a pause, "You mean, finding it?"

"The whole thing. But yeah." He turned to her. "Was it, like, concealed from view?"

"It was lying on the floor. In the corner. Kind of behind a planter." The utterance of this lie caused pinpricks of sweat to emerge on Sasha's Xanax-soothed skull. She considered saying, *Actually, there was no planter,* but managed not to.

"It's almost like she did it on purpose," Alex said. "For attention or something."

"She didn't seem like that type."

"You can't tell. That's something I'm learning, here in N.Y.C.: you have no fucking idea what people are really like. They're not even two-faced—they're, like, multiple personalities."

"She wasn't from New York," Sasha said, irked by his obliviousness even as she strove to preserve it. "Remember? She was getting on a plane?"

"True," Alex said. He paused and cocked his head, regarding Sasha across the ill-lit sidewalk. "But you know what I'm talking about? That thing about people?"

"I do know," she said carefully. "But I think you get used to it."

"I'd rather just go somewhere else."

It took Sasha a moment to understand. "There is nowhere else," she said.

Alex turned to her, startled. Then he grinned. Sasha grinned back—not the yes/no smile, but related.

"That's ridiculous," Alex said.

They took a cab and climbed the four flights to Sasha's Lower East Side walk-up. She'd lived there six years. The place smelled of scented candles, and there was a velvet throw cloth on her sofa bed and lots of pillows, and an old color TV with a very good picture, and an array of souvenirs from her travels lining the windowsills: a white seashell, a pair of red dice, a small canister of Tiger Balm from China, now dried to the texture of rubber, a tiny bonsai tree that she watered faithfully.

"Look at this," Alex said. "You've got a tub in the kitchen! I've heard of that—I mean I've read about it, but I wasn't sure there were any left. The shower thing is new, right? This is a bathtub-in-the-kitchen apartment, right?"

"Yup," Sasha said. "But I almost never use it. I shower at the gym."

The tub was covered with a fitted board where Sasha stacked her plates. Alex ran his hands under the rim of the bath and examined its clawed feet. Sasha lit her candles, took a bottle of grappa from the kitchen cupboard and filled two small glasses.

"I love this place," Alex said. "It feels like old New York. You know this stuff is around, but how do you find it?"

Sasha leaned against the tub beside him and took a tiny sip of grappa. It tasted like Xanax. She was trying to remember Alex's age on his profile. Twenty-eight, she thought, but he seemed younger than that, maybe a lot younger. She saw her apartment as he must see it—a bit of local color that would fade almost instantly into the tumble of adventures that everyone has on first coming to New York. It jarred Sasha to think of herself as a glint in the hazy memories that Alex would struggle to organize a year or two from now: *Where was that place with the bathtub? Who was that girl?*

He left the tub to explore the rest of the apartment. To one side of the kitchen was Sasha's bedroom. On the other side, facing the street, was her living room–den–office, which contained two upholstered chairs and the desk she reserved for projects outside of work—publicity for bands she believed in, short reviews for *Vibe* and *Spin*—although these had fallen off sharply in recent years. In fact the whole apartment, which six years ago had seemed like a way station to some better place, had ended up solidifying around Sasha, gathering mass and weight, until she felt both mired in it and lucky to have it—as if she not only couldn't move on but didn't want to.

Alex leaned over to peer at the tiny collection on her windowsills. He paused at the picture of Rob, Sasha's friend who had drowned in college, but made no comment. He hadn't noticed the tables where she kept the pile of things she'd stolen: the pens, the binoculars, the keys, the child's scarf, which she'd lifted simply by not returning it when it dropped from a little girl's neck as her mother led her by the hand from a Starbucks. Sasha was already seeing Coz by then, so she recognized the litany of excuses even as they throbbed through her head: winter is almost over; children grow so fast; kids hate scarves; it's too late, they're out the door; I'm embarrassed to return it; I could easily not have seen it fall— in fact I didn't, I'm just noticing it now: *Look, a scarf! A kid's bright yellow scarf with pink stripes—too bad, who could it belong to? Well, I'll just pick it up and hold it for a minute. . . .* At home she'd washed the scarf by hand and folded it neatly. It was one of the things she liked best.

"What's all this?" Alex asked.

He'd discovered the tables now and was staring at the pile. It looked like the work of a miniaturist beaver: a heap of objects that was illegible yet clearly not random. To Sasha's eye, it almost shook under its load of embarrassments and close shaves and little triumphs and moments of pure exhilaration. It contained years of her life compressed. The screw-driver was at the outer edge. Sasha moved closer to Alex, drawn to the sight of him taking everything in.

"And how did you feel, standing with Alex in front of all those things you'd stolen?" Coz asked.

Sasha turned her face into the blue couch because her cheeks were heating up and she hated that. She didn't want to explain to Coz the mix of feelings she'd had, standing there with Alex: the pride she took in these objects, a ten-derness that was only heightened by the shame of their ac-quisition. She'd risked everything, and here was the result: the raw, warped core of her life. Watching Alex move his eyes over the pile of objects stirred something in Sasha. She put her arms around him from behind, and he turned, sur-prised, but willing. She kissed him full on the mouth, then undid his zipper and kicked off her boots. Alex tried to lead her toward the other room, where they could lie down on the sofa bed, but Sasha dropped to her knees beside the ta-bles and pulled him down, the Persian carpet prickling her back, street light falling through the window onto his hun-gry, hopeful face, his bare white thighs.

Afterward, they lay on the rug for a long time. The can-dles started to sputter. Sasha saw the prickly shape of the bonsai silhouetted against the window near her head. All her excitement had seeped away, leaving behind a terrible sad-ness, an emptiness that felt violent, as if she'd been gouged. She tottered to her feet, hoping Alex would leave soon. He still had his shirt on.

"You know what I feel like doing?" he said, standing up. "Taking a bath in that tub."

"You can," Sasha said dully. "It works. The plumber was just here."

She pulled up her jeans and collapsed onto a chair. Alex went to the tub, carefully removed the plates from the wood cover, and lifted it off. Water gushed from the faucet. Its force had always startled Sasha, the few times she'd used it.

Alex's black pants were crumpled on the floor at Sasha's feet. The square of his wallet had worn away the corduroy from one of the back pockets, as if he often wore these pants, and always with the wallet in that place. Sasha glanced over at him. Steam rose from the tub as he dipped in a hand to test the water. Then he came back to the pile of objects and leaned close, as if looking for something specific. Sasha watched him, hoping for a tremor of the excitement she'd felt before, but it was gone.

"Can I put some of these in?" He was holding up a packet of bath salts Sasha had taken from her best friend, Lizzie, a couple of years ago, before they'd stopped speaking. The salts were still in their polka-dot wrapping. They'd been deep in the middle of the pile, which had collapsed a little from the extraction. How had Alex even seen them?

Sasha hesitated. She and Coz had talked at length about why she kept the stolen objects separate from the rest of her life: because using them would imply greed or self-interest; because leaving them untouched made it seem as if she might one day give them back; because piling them in a heap kept their power from leaking away.

"I guess," she said. "I guess you can." She was aware of having made a move in the story she and Coz were writing, taken a symbolic step. But toward the happy ending, or away from it?

She felt Alex's hand on the back of her head, stroking her hair. "You like it hot?" he asked. "Or medium."

"Hot," she said. "Really, really hot."

"Me too." He went back to the tub and fiddled with the knobs and shook in some of the salts, and the room instantly filled with a steamy plantlike odor that was deeply familiar to Sasha: the smell of Lizzie's bathroom, from the days when Sasha used to shower there after she and Lizzie went running together in Central Park.

"Where are your towels?" Alex called.

She kept them folded in a basket in the bathroom. Alex went to get them, then shut the bathroom door. Sasha heard him starting to pee. She knelt on the floor and slipped his wallet from his pants pocket and opened it, her heart firing with a sudden pressure. It was a plain black wallet, worn to gray along the edges. Rapidly she flicked through its contents: a debit card, a work ID, a gym card. In a side pocket, a faded picture of two boys and a girl in braces, squinting on a beach. A sports team in yellow uniforms, heads so small she couldn't tell if one of them belonged to Alex. From among these dog-eared photos, a scrap of binder paper dropped into Sasha's lap. It looked very old, the edges torn, the pale blue lines rubbed almost away. Sasha unfolded it and saw written, in blunt pencil, *I BELIEVE IN YOU*. She froze, staring at the words. They seemed to tunnel toward her from their meager scrap, bringing a flush of embarrassment for Alex, who'd kept this disintegrating tribute in his disintegrating wallet, and then shame at herself for having looked at it. She was faintly aware of the sink taps being turned on, and of the need to move quickly. Hastily, mechanically, she reassembled the wallet, keeping the slip of paper in her hand. I'm just going to hold this, she was aware of telling herself as she tucked the wallet back into Alex's pocket. I'll put it back later; he probably doesn't remember it's in there; I'll actually be doing him a favor by getting it out of the way before someone finds it. I'll say, *Hey, I noticed this on the rug, is it yours?* And he'll say, *That? I've never seen it before—it must be yours, Sasha.* And maybe that's true. Maybe someone gave it to me years ago, and I forgot.

"And did you? Put it back?" Coz asked.

"I didn't have a chance. He came out of the bathroom."

"And what about later? After the bath. Or the next time you saw him."

"After the bath he put on his pants and left. I haven't talked to him since."

There was a pause, during which Sasha was keenly aware of Coz behind her, waiting. She wanted badly to please him, to say something like *It was a turning point; everything feels different now,* or *I called Lizzie and we made up finally,* or *I've picked up the harp again,* or just *I'm changing I'm changing I'm changing: I've changed!* Redemption, transformation— God how she wanted these things. Every day, every minute. Didn't everyone?

"Please," she told Coz. "Don't ask me how I feel."

"All right," he said quietly.

They sat in silence, the longest silence that ever had passed between them. Sasha looked at the windowpane, rinsed continually with rain, smearing lights in the falling dark. She lay with her body tensed, claiming the couch, her spot in this room, her view of the window and the walls, the faint hum that was always there when she listened, and these minutes of Coz's time: another, then another, then one more.

2

The Gold Cure

The shame memories began early that day for Bennie, during the morning meeting, while he listened to one of his senior executives make a case for pulling the plug on Stop/Go, a sister band Bennie had signed to a three-record deal a couple of years back. Then, Stop/Go had seemed like an excellent bet; the sisters were young and adorable, their sound was gritty and simple and catchy ("Cyndi Lauper meets Chrissie Hynde" had been Bennie's line early on), with a big gulping bass and some fun percussion—he recalled a cowbell. Plus they'd written decent songs; hell, they'd sold twelve thousand CDs off the stage before Bennie ever heard them play. A little time to develop potential singles, some clever marketing, and a decent video could put them over the top.

But the sisters were pushing thirty, his executive producer, Collette, informed Bennie now, and no longer credible as recent high school grads, especially since one of them had a nine-year-old daughter. Their band members were in law school. They'd fired two producers, and a third had quit. Still no album.

"Who's managing them?" Bennie asked.

"Their father. I've got their new rough mix," Collette said. "The vocals are buried under seven layers of guitar."

It was then that the memory overcame Bennie (had the word "sisters" brought it on?): himself, squatting behind a nunnery in Westchester at sunrise after a night of partying— twenty years ago was it? More? Hearing waves of pure, ringing, spooky-sweet sound waft into the paling sky: cloistered nuns who saw no one but one another, who'd taken vows of silence, singing the Mass. Wet grass under his knees, its iridescence pulsing against his exhausted eyeballs. Even now, Bennie could hear the unearthly sweetness of those nuns' voices echoing deep in his ears.

He'd set up a meeting with their Mother Superior—the only nun you could talk to—brought along a couple of girls from the office for camouflage, and waited in a kind of anteroom until the Mother Superior appeared behind a square opening in the wall like a window without glass. She wore all white, a cloth tightly encircling her face. Bennie remembered her laughing a lot, rosy cheeks lifting into swags, maybe from joy at the thought of bringing God into millions of homes, maybe at the novelty of an A and R guy in purple corduroy making his pitch. The deal was done in a matter of minutes.

He'd approached the cutout square to say good-bye (here

Bennie thrashed in his conference room chair, anticipating the moment it was all leading up to). The Mother Superior leaned forward slightly, tilting her head in a way that must have triggered something in Bennie, because he lurched across the sill and kissed her on the mouth: velvety skin-fuzz, an intimate, baby powder smell in the half second before the nun cried out and jerked away. Then pulling back, grinning through his dread, seeing her appalled, injured face.

"Bennie?" Collette was standing in front of a console, holding the Stop/Go CD. Everyone seemed to be waiting. "You want to hear this?"

But Bennie was caught in a loop from twenty years ago: lunging over the sill toward the Mother Superior like some haywire figure on a clock, again. Again. Again.

"No," he groaned. He turned his sweating face into the rivery breeze that gusted through the windows of the old Tribeca coffee factory where Sow's Ear Records had moved six years ago and now occupied two floors. He'd never recorded the nuns. By the time he'd returned from the convent, a message had been waiting.

"I don't," he told Collette. "I don't want to hear the mix." He felt shaken, soiled. Bennie dropped artists all the time, sometimes three in a week, but now his own shame tinged the Stop/Go sisters' failure, as if *he* were to blame. And that feeling was followed by a restless, opposing need to recall what had first excited him about the sisters—to feel that excitement again. "Why don't I visit them?" he said suddenly.

Collette looked startled, then suspicious, then worried, a succession that would have amused Bennie if he hadn't been so rattled. "Really?" she asked.

"Sure. I'll do it today, after I see my kid."

Bennie's assistant, Sasha, brought him coffee: cream and two sugars. He shimmied a tiny red enameled box from his pocket, popped the tricky latch, pinched a few gold flakes between his trembling fingers, and released them into his cup. He'd begun this regimen two months ago, after reading in a book on Aztec medicine that gold and coffee together were believed to ensure sexual potency. Bennie's goal was more basic than potency: sex *drive*, his own having mysteriously expired. He wasn't sure quite when or quite why this had happened: The divorce from Stephanie? The battle over Christopher? Having recently turned forty-four? The tender, circular burns on his left forearm, sustained at "The Party," a recent debacle engineered by none other than Stephanie's former boss, who was now doing jail time?

The gold landed on the coffee's milky surface and spun wildly. Bennie was mesmerized by this spinning, which he took as evidence of the explosive gold-coffee chemistry. A frenzy of activity that had mostly led him in circles: wasn't that a fairly accurate description of lust? At times Bennie didn't even mind its disappearance; it was sort of a relief not to be constantly wanting to fuck someone. The world was unquestionably a more peaceful place without the half hard-on that had been his constant companion since the age of thirteen, but did Bennie want to live in such a world? He sipped his gold-inflected coffee and glanced at Sasha's breasts, which had become the litmus test he used to gauge his improvement. He'd lusted after her for most of the years she'd worked for him, first as an intern, then a receptionist, finally his assistant (where she'd remained, oddly reluctant

to become an executive in her own right)—and she'd somehow managed to elude that lust without ever saying no,
or hurting Bennie's feelings, or pissing him off. And now:
Sasha's breasts in a thin yellow sweater, and Bennie felt
nothing. Not a shiver of harmless excitement. Could he even
get it up if he wanted to?

Driving to pick up his son, Bennie alternated between the
Sleepers and the Dead Kennedys, San Francisco bands
he'd grown up with. He listened for muddiness, the sense
of actual musicians playing actual instruments in an actual
room. Nowadays that quality (if it existed at all) was usually
an effect of analogue signaling rather than bona fide tape—
everything was an effect in the bloodless constructions Bennie and his peers were churning out. He worked tirelessly,
feverishly, to get things right, stay on top, make songs that
people would love and buy and download as ring tones (and
steal, of course)—above all, to satisfy the multinational
crude-oil extractors he'd sold his label to five years ago. But
Bennie knew that what he was bringing into the world was
shit. Too clear, too clean. The problem was precision, perfection; the problem was *digitization*, which sucked the life
out of everything that got smeared through its microscopic
mesh. Film, photography, music: dead. *An aesthetic holo-
caust!* Bennie knew better than to say this stuff aloud.

But the deep thrill of these old songs lay, for Bennie, in
the rapturous surges of sixteen-year-old-ness they induced;
Bennie and his high school gang—Scotty and Alice, Jocelyn
and Rhea—none of whom he'd seen in decades (except for

a disturbing encounter with Scotty in his office years ago), yet still half believed he'd find waiting in line outside the Mabuhay Gardens (long defunct), in San Francisco, green-haired and safety-pinned, if he happened to show up there one Saturday night.

And then, as Jello Biafra was thrashing his way through "Too Drunk to Fuck," Bennie's mind drifted to an awards ceremony a few years ago where he'd tried to introduce a jazz pianist as "incomparable" and ended up calling her "incompetent" before an audience of twenty-five hundred. He should never have tried for "incomparable"—wasn't his word, too fancy; it stuck in his mouth every time he'd practiced his speech for Stephanie. But it suited the pianist, who had miles of shiny gold hair and had also (she'd let slip) graduated from Harvard. Bennie had cherished a rash dream of getting her into bed, feeling that hair sliding over his shoulders and chest.

He idled now in front of Christopher's school, waiting for the memory spasm to pass. Driving in, he'd glimpsed his son crossing the athletic field with his friends. Chris had been skipping a little—actually skipping—tossing a ball in the air, but by the time he slumped into Bennie's yellow Porsche, any inkling of lightness was gone. Why? Did Chris somehow know about the botched awards ceremony? Bennie told himself this was nuts, yet was moved by an urge to confess the malapropism to his fourth grader. The Will to Divulge, Dr. Beet called this impulse, and had exhorted Bennie to write down the things he wanted to confide, rather than burden his son with them. Bennie did this now, scribbling *incompetent* on the back of a parking ticket he'd received the day before. Then, recalling the earlier humiliation, he added to the list *kissing Mother Superior.*

"So, boss," he said. "Whatcha feel like doing?"

"Don't know."

"Any particular wishes?"

"Not really."

Bennie looked helplessly out the window. A couple of months ago, Chris had asked if they could skip their weekly appointment with Dr. Beet and spend the afternoon "doing whatever" instead. They hadn't gone back, a decision that Bennie now regretted; "doing whatever" had led to desultory afternoons, often cut short by Chris's announcement that he had homework.

"How about some coffee?" Bennie suggested.

A spark of smile. "Can I get a Frappuccino?"

"Don't tell your mother."

Stephanie didn't approve of Chris drinking coffee— reasonable, given that the kid was nine—but Bennie couldn't resist the exquisite connection that came of defying his ex-wife in unison. Betrayal Bonding, Dr. Beet called this, and like the Will to Divulge, it was on the list of no-no's.

They got their coffees and returned to the Porsche to drink them. Chris sucked greedily at his Frappuccino. Bennie took out his red enameled box, pinched a few gold flakes, and slipped them under the plastic lid of his cup.

"What's that?" Chris asked.

Bennie started. The gold was becoming so routine that he'd stopped being clandestine about it. "Medicine," he said, after a moment.

"For what?"

"Some symptoms I've been having." *Or not having*, he added mentally.

"What symptoms?"

Was this the Frappuccino kicking in? Chris had shifted out of his slump and now sat upright, regarding Bennie with his wide, dark, frankly beautiful eyes. "Headaches," Bennie said.

"Can I see it?" Chris asked. "The medicine? In that red thing?"

Bennie handed over the tiny box. Within a couple of seconds, the kid had figured out the tricky latch and popped it open. "Whoa, Dad," he said. "What is this stuff?"

"I told you."

"It looks like gold. Flakes of gold."

"It has a flaky consistency."

"Can I taste one?"

"Son. You don't—"

"Just one?"

Bennie sighed. "One."

The boy carefully removed a gold flake and placed it on his tongue. "What does it taste like?" Bennie couldn't help asking. He'd only consumed the gold in his coffee, where it had no discernible flavor.

"Like metal," Chris said. "It's awesome. Can I have another one?"

Bennie started the car. Was there something obviously sham about the medicine story? Clearly the kid wasn't buying it. "One more," he said. "And that's it."

His son took a fat pinch of gold flakes and put them on his tongue. Bennie tried not to think of the money. The truth was, he'd spent eight thousand dollars on gold in the past two months. A coke habit would have cost him less.

Chris sucked on the gold and closed his eyes. "Dad," he said. "It's, like, waking me up from the inside."

"Interesting," Bennie mused. "That's exactly what it's supposed to do."

"Is it working?"

"Sounds like it is."

"But on you," Chris said.

Bennie was fairly certain his son had asked him more questions in the past ten minutes than in the prior year and a half since he and Stephanie had split. Could this be a side effect of the gold: curiosity?

"I've still got the headaches," he said.

He was driving aimlessly among the Crandale mansions ("doing whatever" involved a lot of aimless driving), every one of which seemed to have four or five blond children in Ralph Lauren playing out front. Seeing these kids, it was clearer than ever to Bennie that he hadn't had a chance of lasting in this place, swarthy and unkempt-looking as he was even when freshly showered and shaved. Stephanie, meanwhile, had ascended to the club's number one doubles team.

"Chris," Bennie said. "There's a musical group I need to visit—a pair of young sisters. Well, youngish sisters. I was planning to go later on, but if you're interested, we could—"

"Sure."

"Really?"

"Yeah."

Did "sure" and "yeah" mean that Chris was giving in to please Bennie, as Dr. Beet had noted he often did? Or had the gold-incited curiosity extended to a new interest in Bennie's work? Chris had grown up around rock groups, of course, but he was part of the postpiracy generation, for whom things like "copyright" and "creative ownership" didn't exist. Bennie didn't *blame* Chris, of course; the dismantlers who had murdered the music business were a generation beyond his son, adults now. Still, he'd heeded Dr. Beet's advice to stop hectoring (Beet's word) Chris about the industry's decline and focus instead on enjoying music they both liked—Pearl Jam, for example, which Bennie blasted all the way to Mount Vernon.

The Stop/Go sisters still lived with their parents in a sprawling, run-down house under bushy suburban trees. Bennie had been here two or three years ago when he'd first discovered them, before he'd entrusted the sisters to the first in a series of executives who had failed to accomplish a blessed thing. As he and Chris left the car, the memory of his last visit provoked a convulsion of anger in Bennie that made heat roll up toward his head—why the fuck hadn't anything happened in all this time?

He found Sasha waiting at the door; she'd caught the train at Grand Central after Bennie called and had somehow beaten him here.

"Hiya Crisco," Sasha said, mussing his son's hair. She had known Chris all his life; she'd run out to Duane Reade to buy him pacifiers and diapers. Bennie glanced at her breasts; nothing. Or nothing sexual—he did feel a swell of gratitude and appreciation for his assistant, as opposed to the murderous rage he felt toward the rest of his staff.

There was a pause. Yellow light scissored through the leaves. Bennie lifted his gaze from Sasha's breasts to her face. She had high cheekbones and narrow green eyes, wavy hair that ranged from reddish to purplish, depending on the month. Today it was red. She was smiling at Chris, but Bennie detected worry somewhere in the smile. He rarely thought of Sasha as an independent person, and beyond a vague awareness of boyfriends coming and going (vague first out of respect for her privacy, lately out of indifference), he knew few specifics of her life. But seeing her outside this family home, Bennie experienced a flare of curiosity: Sasha had still been at NYU when he'd first met her at a Conduits gig at the Pyramid Club; that put her in her thirties now. Why hadn't she married? Did she want kids? She seemed suddenly older, or was it just that Bennie seldom looked directly at her face?

"What," she said, feeling his stare.

"Nothing."

"You okay?"

"Better than okay," Bennie said, and gave the door a sharp knock.

The sisters looked fantastic—if not right out of high school, then at least right out of college, especially if they'd taken a year or two off or maybe transferred a couple of times. They wore their dark hair pulled back from their faces, and their eyes were glittering, and they had a whole fucking book full of new material—*look at this!* Bennie's fury at his team intensified, but it was pleasurable, motivating fury. The sisters' nervous excitement jittered up the house; they knew his visit was their last, best hope. Chandra was the older one, Louisa the younger. Louisa's daughter, Olivia, had been riding a trike in the driveway on Bennie's last visit, but now she wore skintight jeans and a jeweled tiara that seemed to be a fashion choice, not a costume. Bennie felt Chris snap to attention when Olivia entered the room, as if a charmed snake had risen from its basket inside him.

They went single file down a narrow flight of stairs to the sisters' basement recording studio. Their father had built it for them years ago. It was tiny, with orange shag covering the floor, ceiling, and walls. Bennie took the only seat, noting with approval a cowbell by the keyboard.

"Coffee?" Sasha asked him. Chandra led her upstairs to make it. Louisa sat at the keyboard teasing out melodies. Olivia took up a set of bongo drums and began loosely accompanying her mother. She handed Chris a tambourine, and to Bennie's astonishment, his son settled in beating the thing in perfect time. Nice, he thought. Very nice. The day had swerved unexpectedly into good. The almost-teenage daughter wasn't a problem, he decided; she could join the group as a younger sister or a cousin, strengthen the tween angle. Maybe Chris could be part of it, too, although he and Olivia would have to switch instruments. A boy on a tambourine . . .

Sasha brought his coffee, and Bennie took out his red enameled box and dropped in a pinch of flakes. As he sipped, a sensation of pleasure filled his whole torso the way a snowfall fills up a sky. Jesus, he felt good. He'd been delegating too much. Hearing the music get *made*, that was the thing: people and instruments and beaten-looking equipment aligning abruptly into a single structure of sound, flexible and alive. The sisters were at the keyboard arranging their music, and Bennie experienced a bump of anticipation; something was going to happen here. He knew it. Felt it pricking his arms and chest.

"You've got Pro Tools on there, right?" he asked, indicating the laptop on a table amid the instruments. "Is everything miked? Can we lay down some tracks right now?"

The sisters nodded and checked the laptop; they were ready to record. "Vocals, too?" Chandra asked.

"Absolutely," Bennie said. "Let's do it all at once. Let's blow the roof off your fucking house."

Sasha was standing to Bennie's right. So many bodies had heated up the little room, lifting off her skin a perfume she'd been wearing for years—or was it a lotion?—that smelled like apricots; not just the sweet part but that slight bitterness around the pit. And as Bennie breathed in Sasha's lotion smell, his prick roused itself suddenly like an old hound getting a swift kick. He almost jumped out of his seat in startled amazement, but he kept his cool. Don't push things, just let it happen. Don't scare it away.

Then the sisters began to sing. Oh, the raw, almost-threadbare sound of their voices mixed with the clash of instruments—these sensations met with a faculty deeper in Bennie than judgment or even pleasure; they communed directly with his body, whose shivering, bursting reply made him dizzy. And here was his first erection in months— prompted by Sasha, who had been too near Bennie all these years for him to really *see* her, like in those nineteenth-century novels he'd read in secret because only girls were supposed to like them. He seized the cowbell and stick and began whacking at it with zealous blows. He felt the music in his mouth, his ears, his ribs—or was that his own pulse? He was on fire!

And from this zenith of lusty, devouring joy, he recalled opening an e-mail he'd been inadvertently copied on between two colleagues and finding himself referred to as a "hairball." God, what a feeling of liquid shame had pooled in Bennie when he'd read that word. He hadn't been sure what it meant: That he was hairy? (True.) Unclean? (False!) Or was it literal, as in: he clogged people's throats and made them gag, the way Stephanie's cat, Sylph, occasionally vomited hair onto the carpet? Bennie had gone for a haircut that very day and seriously considered having his back and upper arms waxed, until Stephanie talked him out of it, running her cool hands over his shoulders that night in bed, telling him she loved him hairy—that the last thing the world needed was another waxed guy.

Music. Bennie was listening to music. The sisters were screaming, the tiny room imploding from their sound, and Bennie tried to find again the deep contentment he'd felt just a minute ago. But "hairball" had unsettled him. The room felt uncomfortably small. Bennie set down his cowbell and slipped the parking ticket from his pocket. He scribbled *hairball* in hopes of exorcising the memory. He took a slow inhale and rested his eyes on Chris, who was flailing the tambourine trying to match the sisters' erratic tempo, and right away it happened again: taking his son for a haircut a couple of years ago, having his longtime barber, Stu, put down his scissors and pull Bennie aside. "There's a problem with your son's hair," he'd said.

"A problem!"

Stu walked Bennie over to Chris in the chair and parted his hair to reveal some tan little creatures the size of poppy seeds moving around on his scalp. Bennie felt himself grow faint. "Lice," the barber whispered. "They get it at school."

"But he goes to private school!" Bennie had blurted. "In Crandale, New York!"

Chris's eyes had gone wide with fear: "What is it, Daddy?" Other people were staring, and Bennie had felt responsible, with his own riotous head of hair, to the point where he sprayed OFF! in his armpits every morning to this day, and kept an extra can at the office—crazy! He knew it! Getting their coats while everyone watched, Bennie with a burning face; God, it hurt him to think of this now—hurt him physically, as if the memory were raking over him and leaving gashes. He hid his face in his hands. He wanted to cover his ears, block out the cacophony of Stop/Go, but he concentrated on Sasha, just to his right, her sweet-bitter smell, and found himself remembering a girl he'd chased at a party when he first came to New York and was selling vinyl on the Lower East Side a hundred years ago, some delicious blonde—Abby, was it? In the course of keeping tabs on Abby, Bennie had done several lines of coke and been stricken with a severe instantaneous need to empty his bowels. He'd been relieving himself on the can in what must have been (although Bennie's brain ached to recall this) a miasma of annihilating stink, when the unlockable bathroom door had jumped open, and there was Abby, staring down at him.

There'd been a horrible, bottomless instant when their eyes met; then she'd shut the door.

Bennie had left the party with someone else—there was always someone else—and their night of fun, which he felt comfortable presuming, had erased the confrontation with Abby. But now it was back—oh, it was back, bringing waves of shame so immense they seemed to engulf whole parts of Bennie's life and drag them away: achievements, successes, moments of pride, all of it razed to the point where there was nothing—*he* was nothing—a guy on a john looking up at the nauseated face of a woman he'd wanted to impress.

Bennie leaped from his stool, squashing the cowbell under one foot. Sweat stung his eyes. His hair engaged palpably with the ceiling shag.

"You okay?" Sasha asked, alarmed.

"I'm sorry," Bennie panted, mopping his brow. "I'm sorry. I'm sorry. I'm sorry."

Back upstairs, he stood outside the front door, pulling fresh air into his lungs. The Stop/Go sisters and daughter clustered around him, apologizing for the airlessness of the recording studio, their father's ongoing failure to vent it properly, reminding one another in spirited tones of the many times they themselves had grown faint, trying to work there.

"We can hum the tunes," they said, and they did, in harmony, Olivia too, all of them standing not far from Bennie's face, desperation quivering their smiles. A gray cat made a figure eight around Bennie's shins, nudging him rapturously with its bony head. It was a relief to get back in the car.

He was driving Sasha to the city, but he had to get Chris home first. His son hunched in the backseat, facing the open window. It seemed to Bennie that his lark of an idea for the afternoon had gone awry. He fended off the longing to look at Sasha's breasts, waiting to calm down, regain his equilibrium before putting himself to the test. Finally, at a red light, he glanced slowly, casually in her direction, not even focusing at first, then peering intently. Nothing. He was clobbered by loss so severe that it took physical effort not to howl. He'd had it, *he'd had it*! But where had it gone?

"Dad, green light," Chris said.

Driving again, Bennie forced himself to ask his son, "So, boss. What did you think?"

The kid didn't answer. Maybe he was pretending not to hear, or maybe the wind was too loud in his face. Bennie glanced at Sasha. "What about you?"

"Oh," she said, "they're awful."

Bennie blinked, stung. He felt a gust of anger at Sasha that passed a few seconds later, leaving odd relief. Of course. They were awful. That was the problem.

"Unlistenable," Sasha went on. "No wonder you were having a heart attack."

"I don't get it," Bennie said.

"What?"

"Two years ago they sounded . . . different."

Sasha gave him a quizzical look. "It wasn't two years," she said. "It was five."

"Why so sure?"

"Because last time, I came to their house after a meeting at Windows on the World."

It took Bennie a minute to comprehend this. "Oh," he finally said. "How close to—"

"Four days."

"Wow. I never knew that." He waited out a respectful pause, then continued, "Still, two years, five years—"

Sasha turned and stared at him. She looked angry. "Who am I talking to?" she asked. "You're Bennie Salazar! This is the music business. 'Five years is five *hundred* years'—your words."

Bennie didn't answer. They were approaching his former house, as he thought of it. He couldn't say "old house," but he also couldn't say "house" anymore, although he'd certainly paid for it. His former house was withdrawn from the street on a grassy slope, a gleaming white Colonial that had filled him with awe every time he'd taken a key from his pocket to open the front door. Bennie stopped at the curb and killed the engine. He couldn't bring himself to drive up the driveway.

Chris was leaning forward from the backseat, his head between Bennie and Sasha. Bennie wasn't sure how long he'd been there. "I think you need some of your medicine, Dad," he said.

"Good idea," Bennie said. He began tapping his pockets, but the little red box was nowhere to be found.

"Here, I've got it," Sasha said. "You dropped it coming out of the recording room."

She was doing that more and more, finding things he'd misplaced—sometimes before Bennie even knew they were missing. It added to the almost trancelike dependence he felt on her. "Thanks, Sash," he said.

He opened the box. God the flakes were shiny. Gold didn't tarnish, that was the thing. The flakes would look the same in five years as they did right now.

"Should I put some on my tongue, like you did?" he asked his son.

"Yeah. But I get some too."

"Sasha, you want to try a little medicine?" Bennie asked.

"Um, okay," she said. "What's it supposed to do?"

"Solve your problems," Bennie said. "I mean, headaches. Not that you have any."

"Never," Sasha said, with that same wary smile.

They each took a pinch of gold flakes and placed them on their tongues. Bennie tried not to calculate the dollar value of what was inside their mouths. He concentrated on the taste: Was it metallic, or was that just his expectation? Coffee, or was that what was left in his mouth? He tongued the gold in a tight knot and sucked the juice from within it; sour, he thought. Bitter. Sweet? Each one seemed true for a second, but in the end Bennie had an impression of something mineral, like stone. Even earth. And then the lump melted away.

"I should go, Dad," Chris said. Bennie let him out of the car and hugged him hard. As always, Chris went still in his embrace, but whether he was savoring it or enduring it Bennie could never tell.

He drew back and looked at his son. The baby he and Stephanie had nuzzled and kissed—now this painful, mysterious presence. Bennie was tempted to say, *Don't tell your mother about the medicine,* craving an instant of connection with Chris before he went inside. But he hesitated, employing a mental calculation Dr. Beet had taught him: Did he really think the kid would tell Stephanie about the gold? No. And that was his alert: Betrayal Bonding. Bennie said nothing.

He got back in the car, but didn't turn the key. He was watching Chris scale the undulating lawn toward his former house. The grass was fluorescently bright. His son seemed to buckle under his enormous backpack. What the hell was in it? Bennie had seen professional photographers carry less. As Chris neared the house he blurred a little, or maybe it was Bennie's eyes watering. He found it excruciating, watching his son's long journey to the front door. He worried Sasha would speak—say something like *He's a great kid,* or *That was fun*—something that would require Bennie to turn and look at her. But Sasha knew better; she knew everything. She sat with Bennie in silence, watching Chris climb the fat, bright grass to the front door, then open it without turning and go inside.

They didn't speak again until they'd passed from the Henry Hudson Parkway onto the West Side Highway, heading into Lower Manhattan. Bennie played some early Who, the Stooges, bands he'd listened to before he was even old enough to go to a concert. Then he got into Flipper, the Mutants, Eye Protection—seventies Bay Area groups he and his gang had slam-danced to at the Mabuhay Gardens when they weren't practicing with their own unlistenable band, the Flaming Dildos. He sensed Sasha paying attention and toyed with the idea that he was confessing to her his disillusionment—his *hatred* for the industry he'd given his life to. He began weighing each musical choice, drawing out his argument through the songs themselves—Patti Smith's ragged poetry (but why did she quit?), the jock hardcore of Black Flag and the Circle Jerks giving way to alternative, that great compromise, down, down, down to the singles he'd just today been petitioning radio stations to add, husks of music, lifeless and cold as the squares of office neon cutting the blue twilight.

"It's incredible," Sasha said, "how there's just nothing there."

Astounded, Bennie turned to her. Was it possible that she'd followed his musical rant to its grim conclusion? Sasha was looking downtown, and he followed her eyes to the empty space where the Twin Towers had been. "There should be *something*, you know?" she said, not looking at Bennie. "Like an echo. Or an outline."

Bennie sighed. "They'll put something up," he said. "When they're finally done squabbling."

"I know." But she kept looking south, as if it were a problem her mind couldn't solve. Bennie was relieved she hadn't understood. He remembered his mentor, Lou Kline, telling him in the nineties that rock and roll had peaked at Monterey Pop. They'd been in Lou's house in LA with its waterfalls, the pretty girls Lou always had, his car collection out front, and Bennie had looked into his idol's famous face and thought, *You're finished.* Nostalgia was the end—everyone knew that. Lou had died three months ago, after being paralyzed from a stroke.

At a stoplight, Bennie remembered his list. He took out the parking ticket and finished it off.

"What do you keep scribbling on that ticket?" Sasha asked. Bennie handed it to her, his reluctance to have the list seen by human eyes overwhelming him a half second late. To his horror, she began reading it aloud:

"Kissing Mother Superior, incompetent, hairball, poppy seeds, on the can."

Bennie listened in agony, as if the words themselves might provoke a catastrophe. But they were neutralized the instant Sasha spoke them in her scratchy voice.

"Not bad," she said. "They're titles, right?"

"Sure," Bennie said. "Can you read them one more time?" She did, and now they sounded like titles to him, too. He felt peaceful, cleansed.

"'Kissing Mother Superior' is my favorite," Sasha said. "We've gotta find a way to use that one."

They'd pulled up outside her building on Forsyth. The street felt desolate and underlit. Bennie wished she could live in a better place. Sasha gathered up her ubiquitous black bag, a shapeless wishing well from which she'd managed to wrest whatever file or number or slip of paper he'd needed for the past twelve years. Bennie seized her thin white hand. "Listen," he said. "Listen, Sasha."

She looked up. Bennie felt no lust at all—he wasn't even hard. What he felt for Sasha was love, a safety and closeness like what he'd had with Stephanie before he'd let her down so many times that she couldn't stop being mad. "I'm crazy for you, Sasha," he said. "Crazy."

"Come on, Bennie," Sasha chided lightly. "None of that."

He held her hand between both of his. Sasha's fingers were trembly and cold. Her other hand was on the door.

"Wait," Bennie said. "Please."

She turned to him, somber now. "There's no way, Bennie," she said. "We need each other."

They looked at one another in the failing light. The delicate bones of Sasha's face were lightly freckled—it was a girl's face, but she'd stopped being a girl when he wasn't watching.

Sasha leaned over and kissed Bennie's cheek: a chaste kiss, a kiss between brother and sister, mother and son, but Bennie felt the softness of her skin, the warm movement of her breath. Then she was out of the car. She waved to him through the window and said something he didn't catch. Bennie lunged across the empty seat, his face near the glass, staring fixedly as she said it again. Still, he missed it. As he struggled to open the door, Sasha said it once more, mouthing the words extra slowly:

"See. You. Tomorrow."

3

Ask Me If I Care

Late at night, when there's nowhere left to go, we go to Alice's house. Scotty drives his pickup, two of us squeezed in front with him, blasting bootleg tapes of the Stranglers, the Nuns, Negative Trend, the other two stuck in back where you freeze all year long, getting tossed in the actual air when Scotty tops the hills. Still, if it's Bennie and me I hope for the back, so I can push against his shoulder in the cold, and hold him for a second when we hit a bump.

The first time we went to Sea Cliff, where Alice lives, she pointed up a hill at fog sneaking through the eucalyptus trees and said her old school was up there: an all-girls school where her little sisters go now. K through six you wear a green plaid jumper and brown shoes, after that a blue skirt and white sailor top, and you can pick your own shoes. Scotty goes, Can we see them? and Alice goes, My uniforms? but Scotty goes, No, your alleged sisters.

She leads the way upstairs, Scotty and Bennie right behind her. They're both fascinated by Alice, but it's Bennie who entirely loves her. And Alice loves Scotty, of course.

Bennie's shoes are off, and I watch his brown heels sink into the white cotton-candy carpet, so thick it muffles every trace of us. Jocelyn and I come last. She leans close to me, and inside her whisper I smell cherry gum covering up the five hundred cigarettes we've smoked. I can't smell the gin we drank from my dad's hidden supply at the beginning of the night, pouring it into Coke cans so we can drink it on the street.

Jocelyn goes, Watch, Rhea. They'll be blond, her sisters.

I go, According to?

Rich children are always blond, Jocelyn goes. It has to do with vitamins.

Believe me, I don't mistake that for information. I know everyone Jocelyn knows.

The room is dark except for a pink night-light. I stop in the doorway and Bennie hangs back too, but the other three go crowding into the space between the beds. Alice's little sisters are sleeping on their sides, covers tucked around their shoulders. One looks like Alice, with pale wavy hair, the other is dark, like Jocelyn. I'm afraid they'll wake up and be scared of us in our dog collars and safety pins and shredded T-shirts. I think: We shouldn't be here, Scotty shouldn't have asked to come in, Alice shouldn't have said yes, except she says yes to everything Scotty asks. I think: I want to lie down in one of those beds and go to sleep.

Ahem, I whisper to Jocelyn as we're leaving the room.
Dark hair.

She whispers back, Black sheep.

Nineteen eighty is almost here, thank God. The hippies are
getting old, they blew their brains on acid and now they're
begging on street corners all over San Francisco. Their hair
is tangled and their bare feet are thick and gray as shoes.
We're sick of them.

At school, we spend every free minute in the Pit. It's not
a pit in the strictly speaking sense; it's a strip of pavement
above the playing fields. We inherited it from last year's Pitters who graduated, but still we get nervous walking in if
other Pitters are already there: Tatum, who wears a different
color Danskin every day, or Wayne, who grows sinsemilla
in his actual closet, or Boomer, who's always hugging everyone since his family did EST. I'm nervous walking in
unless Jocelyn is already there, or (for her) me. We stand in
for each other.

On warm days, Scotty plays his guitar. Not the electric he
uses for Flaming Dildos gigs, but a lap steel guitar that you
hold a different way. Scotty actually built this instrument:
bent the wood, glued it, painted on the shellac. Everyone
gathers around, there's no way not to when Scotty plays. One
time the entire J.V. soccer team climbed up from the athletic field to listen, looking around in their jerseys and long
red socks like they didn't know how they got there. Scotty is
magnetic. And I say this as someone who does not love him.

The Flaming Dildos have had a lot of names: the Crabs,

the Croks, the Crimps, the Crunch, the Scrunch, the Gawks, the Gobs, the Flaming Spiders, the Black Widows. Every time Scotty and Bennie change the name, Scotty sprays black over his guitar case and Bennie's bass case, and then he makes a stencil of the new name and sprays it on. We don't know how they decide if they should keep a name, because Bennie and Scotty don't actually talk. But they agree on everything, maybe through ESP. Jocelyn and I write all the lyrics and work out the tunes with Bennie and Scotty. We sing with them in rehearsal, but we don't like being onstage. Alice doesn't either—the only thing we have in common with her.

Bennie transferred last year from a high school in Daly City. We don't know where he lives, but some days we visit him after school at Revolver Records, on Clement, where he works. If Alice comes with us, Bennie will take his break and share a pork bun in the Chinese bakery next door, while the fog gallops past the windows. Bennie has light brown skin and excellent eyes, and he irons his hair in a Mohawk as shiny black as a virgin record. He's usually looking at Alice, so I can watch him as much as I want.

Down the path from the Pit is where the cholos hang out, with their black leather coats and clicky shoes and dark hair in almost invisible nets. Sometimes they talk to Bennie in Spanish, and he smiles at them but never answers. Why do they keep speaking Spanish to him? I go to Jocelyn, and she looks at me and goes, Rhea, Bennie's a cholo. Isn't that obvious?

That's factually crazy, I go, and my face is getting hot. He has a Mohawk. And he's not even friends with them.

Jocelyn goes, Not all cholos are friends. Then she says, The good news is, rich girls won't go with cholos. So he'll never get Alice, period-the-end.

Jocelyn knows I'm waiting for Bennie. But Bennie is waiting for Alice, who's waiting for Scotty, who's waiting for Jocelyn, who's known Scotty the longest and makes him feel safe, I think, because even though Scotty is magnetic, with bleached hair and a studly chest that he likes to uncover when it's sunny out, his mother died three years ago from sleeping pills. Scotty's been quieter since then, and in cold weather he shivers like someone is shaking him.

Jocelyn loves Scotty back, but she isn't *in love* with him. Jocelyn is waiting for Lou, an adult man who picked her up hitchhiking. Lou lives in LA, but he said he would call the next time he comes to San Francisco. That was weeks ago.

No one is waiting for me. In this story, I'm the girl no one is waiting for. Usually the girl is fat, but my problem is more rare, which is freckles: I look like someone threw handfuls of mud at my face. When I was little, my mom told me they were special. Thank God I'll be able to remove them, when I'm old enough and can pay for it myself. Until that time I have my dog collar and green rinse, because how can anyone call me "the girl with freckles" when my hair is green?

Jocelyn has chopped black hair that looks permanently wet, and twelve ear piercings that I gave her with a pointed earring, not using ice. She has a beautiful half-Chinese face. It makes a difference.

Jocelyn and I have done everything together since fourth grade: hopscotch, jump rope, charm bracelets, buried treasure, Harriet the Spying, blood sisters, crank calls, pot, coke, quaaludes. She's seen my dad puking into the hedge outside our building, and I was with her on Polk Street the night she recognized one of the leather boys hugging outside the White Swallow and it was her dad, who was on a "business trip," before he moved away. So I still can't believe I missed the day she met the man, Lou. She was hitchhiking home from downtown and he pulled up in a red Mercedes and drove her to an apartment he uses on his trips to San Francisco. He unscrewed the bottom of a can of Right Guard, and a Baggie of cocaine dropped out. Lou did some lines off Jocelyn's bare butt and they went all the way twice, not including when she went down on him. I made Jocelyn repeat each detail of this story until I knew everything she knew, so we could be equal again.

Lou is a music producer who knows Bill Graham personally. There were gold and silver record albums on his walls and a thousand electric guitars.

The Flaming Dildos rehearsal is on Saturday, in Scotty's garage. When Jocelyn and I get there, Alice is setting up the new tape recorder her stepfather bought her, with a real microphone. She's one of those girls that like machines— another reason for Bennie to love her. Joel, the Dildos' steady drummer, comes next, driven by his dad, who waits outside in his station wagon for the whole practice, reading World War II books. Joel is AP everything and he's applied to Harvard, so I guess his dad isn't taking any chances.

Where we live, in the Sunset, the ocean is always just over your shoulder and the houses have Easter-egg colors.

But the second Scotty lets the garage door slam down, we're suddenly enraged, all of us. Bennie's bass snickers to life, and pretty soon we're screaming out the songs, which have titles like "Pet Rock," and "Do the Math," and "Pass Me the Kool-Aid," but when we holler them aloud in Scotty's garage the lyrics might as well be: *fuck fuck fuck fuck fuck fuck*. Every once in a while a kid from Band and Orchestra pounds on the garage door to try out (invited by Bennie), and every time Scotty ropes up the door we glare out at the bright day shaking its head at us.

Today we try a sax, a tuba, and a banjo, but sax and banjo keep hogging the stage, and tuba covers her ears as soon as we start to play. Practice is almost over when there's another banging on the garage door and Scotty pulls it up. An enormous pimpled kid in an AC/DC T-shirt is standing there, holding a violin case. He goes, I'm looking for Bennie Salazar?

Jocelyn and Alice and I stare at one another in shock, which feels for a second like we're all three friends, like Alice is part of us.

"Hey guy," Bennie says. "Good timing. Everybody, this is Marty."

Even smiling, there's no hope for Marty's face. But I'm worried he might think the same of me, so I don't smile back.

Marty plugs in his violin and we launch into our best song, "What the Fuck?":

> *You said you were a fairy princess*
> *You said you were a shooting star*
> *You said we'd go to Bora Bora*
> *Now look at where the fuck we are . . .*

Bora Bora was Alice's idea—we'd never heard of it. While everyone howls out the chorus (*What the fuck? / What the fuck? / What the fuck?*), I watch Bennie listen, eyes closed, his Mohawk like a million antennas pricking up from his head. When the song ends, he opens his eyes and grins. "I hope you got that, Al," he goes, and Alice rewinds the tape to make sure.

Alice takes all our tapes and turns them into one top tape, and Bennie and Scotty drive from club to club, trying to get people to book the Flaming Dildos for a gig. Our big hope is the Mab, of course: the Mabuhay Gardens, on Broadway, where all the punk bands play. Scotty waits in the truck while Bennie deals with the rude assholes inside the clubs. We have to be careful with Scotty. In fifth grade, the first time his mom went away, he sat all day on the patch of grass outside his house and stared at the sun. He refused to go to school or come in. His dad sat with him trying to cover his eyes, and after school, Jocelyn came and sat there, too. Now there are permanent gray smudges in Scotty's vision. He says he likes them—actually, what he says is: "I consider them a visual enhancement." We think they remind him of his mom.

We go to the Mab every Saturday night, after practice. We've heard Crime, the Avengers, the Germs, and a trillion other bands. The bar is too expensive, so we drink from my dad's supply ahead of time. Jocelyn needs to drink more than me to get buzzed, and when she feels the booze hit she takes a long breath, like finally she's herself again.

In the Mab's graffiti-splattered bathroom we eavesdrop: Ricky Sleeper fell off the stage at a gig, Joe Rees of Target

Video is making an entire movie of punk rock, two sisters we always see at the club have started turning tricks to pay for heroin. Knowing all this makes us one step closer to being real, but not completely. When does a fake Mohawk become a real Mohawk? Who decides? How do you know if it's happened?

During the shows we slam-dance in front of the stage. We tussle and push and get knocked down and pulled back up until our sweat is mixed up with real punks' sweat and our skin has touched their skin. Bennie does less of this. I think he actually listens to the music.

One thing I've noticed: no punk rockers have freckles. They don't exist.

One night, Jocelyn answers her phone and it's Lou going, Hello beautiful. He's been calling for days and days, he goes, but the phone just rings. Why not try calling at *night*? I ask when Jocelyn repeats this.

That Saturday, after rehearsal, she goes out with Lou instead of us. We go to the Mab, then back to Alice's house. By now we treat the place like we own it: we eat the yogurts her mom makes in glass cups on a warming machine, we lie on the living room couch with our sock feet on the armrests. One night her mom made us hot chocolate and brought it into the living room on a gold tray. She had big tired eyes and tendons moving in her neck. Jocelyn whispered in my ear, Rich people like to hostess, so they can show off their nice stuff.

Tonight, without Jocelyn here, I ask Alice if she still has

those school uniforms she mentioned long ago. She looks surprised. Yeah, she goes. I do.

I follow her up the fluffy stairs to her actual room, which I've never seen. It's smaller than her sisters' room, with blue shag carpeting and crisscross wallpaper in blue and white. Her bed is under a mountain of stuffed animals, which all turn out to be frogs: bright green, light green, Day-Glo green, some with stuffed flies attached to their tongues. Her bedside lamp is shaped like a frog, plus her pillow.

I go, I didn't know you were into frogs, and Alice goes, How would you?

I haven't really been alone with Alice before. She seems not as nice as when Jocelyn is around.

She opens her closet, stands on a chair, and pulls down a box with some uniforms inside: a green plaid one-piece from when she was little, a sailor suit two-piece from later on. I go, Which did you like better?

Neither, she goes. Who wants to wear a uniform?

I go, I would.

Is that a joke?

What kind of joke would it be?

The kind where you and Jocelyn laugh about how you made a joke and I didn't get it.

My throat turns very dry. I go, I won't. Laugh with Jocelyn.

Alice shrugs. Ask me if I care, she goes.

We sit on her rug, the uniforms across our knees. Alice wears ripped jeans and drippy black eye makeup, but her hair is long and gold. She isn't a real punk, either.

After a while I go, Why do your parents let us come here?

They're not my parents. They're my mother and stepfather.

Okay.

They want to keep an eye on you, I guess.

The foghorns are extra loud in Sea Cliff, like we're alone on a ship sailing through the thickest fog. I hug my knees, wishing so much that Jocelyn was with us.

Are they right now? I go, softly. Keeping an eye?

Alice takes a huge breath and lets it back out. No, she goes. They're asleep.

Marty the violinist isn't even in high school—he's a sophomore at SF State, where Jocelyn and I and Scotty (if he passes Algebra II) are headed next year. Jocelyn goes to Bennie, The shit will hit the fan if you put that dork onstage.

I guess we'll find out, Bennie goes, and he looks at his watch like he's thinking. In two weeks and four days and six hours and I'm-not-sure-how-many-minutes.

We stare at him, not comprehending. Then he tells us: Dirk Dirksen from the Mab gave him a call. Jocelyn and I shriek and hug onto Bennie, which for me is like touching something electric, his actual body in my arms. I remember every hug I've given him. I learn one thing each time: how warm his skin is, how he has muscles like Scotty even though he never takes his shirt off. This time I find his heartbeat, which pushes my hand through his back.

Jocelyn goes, Who else knows?

Scotty, of course. Alice, too, but it's only later that this bothers us.

. . .

I have cousins in Los Angeles, so Jocelyn calls Lou from our apartment, where the charge won't stand out on the phone bill. I'm two inches away on my parents' flowered bedspread while she dials the phone with a long black fingernail. I hear a man's voice answer, and it shocks me that he's real, Jocelyn didn't make him up, even though I never supposed such a thing. He doesn't go, *Hey beautiful*, though. He goes, I told you to let me call you.

Jocelyn goes, Sorry, in an empty little voice. I grab the phone and go, What kind of hello is that? Lou goes, Who the Christ am I talking to? and I tell him Rhea. Then he goes in a calmer voice, Nice to meet you, Rhea. Now, would you hand the phone back to Jocelyn?

This time she pulls the cord away. Lou seems to be doing most of the talking. After a minute or two, Jocelyn hisses at me, You have to leave. Go!

I walk out of my parents' bedroom into our kitchen. There's a fern hanging from the ceiling by a chain, dropping little brown leaves in the sink. The curtains have a pineapple pattern. My two brothers are on the balcony, grafting bean plants for my little brother's science project. I go outside with them, the sun poking into my eyes. I try to force myself to look straight at it, like Scotty did.

After a while, Jocelyn comes out. Happiness is floating up from her hair and skin. Ask me if I care, I think.

Later she tells me Lou said yes: he'll come to the Dildos gig at the Mab, and maybe he'll give us a record contract. It's not a promise, he warned her, but we'll have a good time anyway, right, beautiful? Don't we always?

. . .

The night of the concert, I come with Jocelyn to meet Lou for dinner at Vanessi's, a restaurant on Broadway next door to Enrico's, where tourists and rich people sit outside drinking Irish coffees and gawking at us when we walk by. We could have invited Alice, but Jocelyn goes, Her parents probably take her to Vanessi's all the time. I go, You mean her mother and stepfather.

A man is sitting in a round corner booth, smiling teeth at us, and that man is Lou. He looks as old as my dad, meaning forty-three. He has shaggy blond hair, and his face is handsome, I guess, the way dads can sometimes be.

C'mere, beautiful, Lou actually does say, and he lifts an arm to Jocelyn. He's wearing a light blue denim shirt and some kind of copper bracelet. She slides around the side of the table and fits right under his arm. Rhea, Lou goes, and lifts up his other arm for me, so instead of sliding in next to Jocelyn, like I was just about to do, I end up on Lou's other side. His arm comes down around my shoulder. And like that, we're Lou's girls.

A week ago, I looked at the menu outside Vanessi's and saw linguine with clams. All week long I've been planning to order that dish. Jocelyn picks the same, and after we order, Lou hands her something under the table. We both slide out of the booth and go to the ladies' room. It's a tiny brown bottle full of cocaine. There's a miniature spoon attached to a chain, and Jocelyn heaps up the spoon two times for each nostril. She sniffs and makes a little sound and shuts

her eyes. Then she fills the spoon again and holds it for me.
By the time I walk back to the table I've got eyes blinking all
over my head, seeing everything in the restaurant at once.
Maybe the coke we did before wasn't really coke. We sit
down and tell Lou about a new band we've heard of called
Flipper, and Lou tells us about being on a train in Africa that
didn't completely stop at the stations—it just slowed down
so people could jump off or on. I go, I want to see Africa!
and Lou goes, Maybe we'll go together, the three of us, and
it seems like this really might happen. He goes, The soil in
the hills is so fertile it's red, and I go, My brothers are grafting bean plants, but the soil is just regular brown soil, and
Jocelyn goes, What about the mosquitoes? and Lou goes,
I've never seen a blacker sky or a brighter moon, and I realize
that I'm beginning my adult life right now, on this night.

When the waiter brings my linguine and clams I can't
take one bite. Only Lou eats: an almost-raw steak, a Caesar
salad, red wine. He's one of those people who never stops
moving. Three times strangers come to our table to say hello
to Lou, but he doesn't introduce us. We talk and talk while
our food gets cold, and when Lou finishes eating, we leave
Vanessi's.

On Broadway he keeps an arm around each of us. We pass
the usual things: the scuzzy guy in a fez trying to lure people
inside the Casbah, the strippers lounging in doorways of the
Condor and Big Al's. Punk rockers rove in laughing, shoving
packs. Traffic pushes along Broadway, people honking and
waving from their cars like we're all at one gigantic party.
With my thousand eyes it looks different, like I'm a differ-

ent person seeing it. I think, After my freckles are gone, my whole life will be like this.

The door guy at the Mab recognizes Lou and whisks us past the snaking line of people waiting for the Cramps and the Mutants, who are playing later on. Inside, Bennie and Scotty and Joel are onstage setting up with Alice. Jocelyn and I put on our dog collars and safety pins in the bathroom. When we come back out, Lou's already introducing himself to the band. Bennie shakes Lou's hand and goes, It's an honor, sir.

After the usual sarcastic introduction from Dirk Dirksen, the Flaming Dildos open with "Snake in the Grass." No one is dancing or even really listening; they're still coming into the club or killing time until the bands they came for start playing. Normally Jocelyn and I would be directly in front of the stage, but tonight we stand in back, leaning against a wall with Lou. He's bought us both gin and tonics. I can't tell if the Dildos sound good or bad, I can barely hear them, my heart is beating too hard and my thousand eyes are peering all over the room. According to the muscles on the side of Lou's face, he's grinding his teeth.

Marty comes on for the next number, but he spazzes out and drops his violin. The barely interested crowd gets just interested enough to yell some insults when he crouches to replug it with his plumber's crack displaying. I can't even look at Bennie, it matters so much.

When they start playing "Do the Math," Lou yells in my ear, Whose idea was the violin?

I go, Bennie's.

Kid on bass?

I nod, and Lou watches Bennie for a minute and I watch him too. Lou goes, Not much of a player.

But he's—, I try to explain. The whole thing is his—

Something gets tossed at the stage that looks like glass, but when it hits Scotty's face thank God it's only ice from a drink. Scotty flinches but keeps on playing, and then a Budweiser can flies up and clips Marty right in the forehead. Jocelyn and I look at each other panicked, but when we try to move, Lou anchors us. The Dildos start playing "What the Fuck?" but now garbage is spewing at the stage, chucked by four guys with safety-pin chains connecting their nostrils to their earlobes. Every few seconds another drink strikes Scotty's face. Finally he just plays with his eyes shut, and I wonder if he's seeing the scar spots. Alice is trying to tackle the garbage throwers now, and suddenly people are slam-dancing *hard*, the kind of dancing that's basically fighting. Joel clobbers his drums as Scotty tears off his dripping T-shirt and snaps it at one of the garbage throwers, right in the guy's face with a twangy crack, and then at another one— *snrack*—like my brothers snapping bath towels, but sharper. The Scotty magnet is starting to work—people watch his bare muscles shining with sweat and beer. Then one of the garbage throwers tries to storm the stage, but Scotty kicks him in the chest with the flat of his boot—there's a kind of gasp from the crowd as the guy flies back. Scotty's smiling now, grinning like I almost never see him grin, wolf teeth flashing, and I realize that, out of all of us, Scotty is the truly angry one.

I turn to Jocelyn, but she's gone. Maybe my thousand eyes

are what tell me to look down. I see Lou's fingers spread out over her black hair. She's kneeling in front of him, giving him head, like the music is a disguise and no one can see them. Maybe no one does. Lou's other arm is around me, which I guess is why I don't run, although I could, that's the thing. But I stand there while Lou mashes Jocelyn's head against himself again and again so I don't know how she can breathe, until it starts to seem like she's not even Jocelyn, but some kind of animal or machine that can't be broken. I force myself to look at the band, Scotty snapping the wet shirt at people's eyes and knocking them with his boot, Lou grasping my shoulder, squeezing it harder, turning his head to my neck and letting out a hot, stuttering groan I can hear even through the music. He's that close. A sob cracks open in me. Tears leak out from my eyes, but only the two in my face. The other thousand eyes are closed.

The walls of Lou's apartment are covered with electric guitars and gold and silver record albums, just like Jocelyn said. But she never mentioned that it was on the thirty-fifth floor, six blocks away from the Mab, or the green marble slabs in the elevator. I think that was a lot to leave out.

In the kitchen, Jocelyn pours Fritos into a dish and takes a glass bowl of green apples out of the refrigerator. She's already passed around quaaludes, offering one to every person except me. I think she's afraid to look at me. *Who's the hostess now?* I want to ask.

In the living room, Alice is sitting with Scotty, who wears a Pendleton shirt from Lou's closet and looks white and shaky, maybe from having stuff thrown at him, maybe because he understands for real that Jocelyn has a boyfriend and it isn't him, and never will be. Marty is there, too; he's got a cut on his cheek and an almost-black eye and he keeps going, That was intense, to no one in particular. Joel got driven straight home, of course. Everyone agrees the gig went well.

When Lou leads Bennie up a curling staircase to his recording studio, I tag along. He calls Bennie "kiddo" and explains each machine in the room, which is small and warm with black foam points all over the walls. Lou's legs move restlessly and he eats a green apple with loud cracks, like he's gnawing rock. Bennie glances out the door toward the rail overlooking the living room, trying to get a glimpse of Alice. I keep being about to cry. I'm worried that what happened in the club counts as having sex with Lou—that I was part of it.

Finally I go back downstairs. Off the living room I notice a door partly open, a big bed just beyond it. I go in and lie facedown on a velvet bedspread. A peppery incense smell trickles up around me. The room is cool and dim, with pictures in frames on both sides of the bed. My whole body hurts. After a few minutes someone comes in and lies down next to me, and I know it's Jocelyn. We don't say anything, we just lie there side by side in the dark. Finally I go, You should've told me.

Told you what? she goes, but I don't even know. Then she goes, There's too much, and I feel like something is ending, right at that minute.

After a while, Jocelyn turns on a lamp by the bed. Look, she goes. She's holding a framed picture of Lou in a swimming pool surrounded by kids, the two littlest ones almost babies. I count six. Jocelyn goes, They're his *children*. That blond girl, everyone calls her Charlie, she's twenty. Rolph, that one, he's our age. They went to Africa with him.

I lean close to the picture. Lou looks so happy, surrounded by his kids like any normal dad, that I can't believe this Lou with us is the very same Lou. Then I notice his son Rolph. He has blue eyes and black hair and a bright, sweet smile. I get a crawling feeling in my stomach. I go, Rolph is decent, and Jocelyn laughs and goes, Really. Then she goes, Don't tell Lou I said that.

He comes into the bedroom a minute later, rock-crunching another apple. I realize the apples are completely for Lou, he eats them nonstop. I slide off the bed without looking at him, and he shuts the door behind me.

It takes me a second to get what's going on in the living room. Scotty is sitting cross-legged, picking at a gold guitar in the shape of a flame. Alice is behind him with her arms around his neck, her face next to his, her hair falling into his lap. Her eyes are closed with joy. I forget who I actually am for a second—all I can think is how Bennie will feel when he sees this. I look around for him, but there's just Marty peering at the albums on the wall, trying to be inconspicuous. And then I notice the music flooding out of every part of the apartment at once—the couch, the walls, even the floor— and I know Bennie's alone in Lou's studio, pouring music around us. A minute ago it was "Don't Let Me Down." Then it was Blondie's "Heart of Glass." Now it's Iggy Pop's "The Passenger":

I am the passenger
And I ride and I ride
I ride through the city's backside
I see the stars come out of the sky

Listening, I think, You will never know how much I understand you.

I notice Marty looking over at me kind of hesitant, and I see how this is supposed to work: I'm the dog, so I get Marty. I slide open a glass door and go onto Lou's balcony. I've never seen San Francisco from so high up: it's a soft blue-black, with colored lights and fog like gray smoke. Long piers reach out into the flat dark bay. There's a mean wind, so I run in for my jacket and then come back out and curl up tightly on a white plastic chair. I stare at that view until I start to get calm. I think, The world is actually huge. That's the part no one can really explain.

After a while the door slides open. I don't look up, thinking it's Marty, but it turns out to be Lou. He's barefoot, wearing shorts. His legs are tan even in the dark. I go, Where's Jocelyn?

Asleep, Lou goes. He's standing at the railing, looking out. It's the first time I've seen him be still.

I go, Do you even remember being our age?

Lou grins at me in my chair, but it's a copy of the grin he had at dinner. I *am* your age, he goes.

Ahem, I go. You have six kids.

So I do, he goes. He turns his back, waiting for me to disappear. I think, I didn't have sex with this man. I don't even know him. Then he goes, I'll never get old.

You're already old, I tell him.

He swivels around and peers at me huddled in my chair. You're scary, he goes. You know that?

It's the freckles, I go.

It's not the freckles, it's *you*. He keeps looking at me, and then something shifts in his face and he goes, I like it.

Do not.

I do. You're gonna keep me honest, Rhea.

I'm surprised he remembers my name. I go, It's too late for that, Lou.

Now he laughs, really laughs, and I understand that we're friends, Lou and I. Even if I hate him, which I do. I get out of my chair and come to the railing, where he is.

People will try to change you, Rhea, Lou goes. Don't let 'em.

But I want to change.

No, he goes, serious. You're beautiful. Stay like this.

But the freckles, I go, and my throat gets that ache.

The freckles are the best part, Lou says. Some guy is going to go apeshit for those freckles. He's going to kiss them one by one.

I start to cry, I don't even hide it.

Hey, Lou goes. He leans down so our faces are together, and stares straight into my eyes. He looks tired, like someone walked on his skin and left footprints. He goes, The world is full of shitheads, Rhea. Don't listen to them—listen to me.

And I know that Lou is one of those shitheads. But I listen.

. . .

Two weeks after that night, Jocelyn runs away. I find out with everyone else.

Her mother comes straight to our apartment. She and my parents and older brother sit me down: What do I know? Who is this new boyfriend? I tell them Lou. He lives in LA and has six children. He knows Bill Graham personally. I think Bennie might know who Lou actually is, so Jocelyn's mom comes to our school to talk with Bennie Salazar. But he's hard to find. Now that Alice and Scotty are together, Bennie has stopped coming to the Pit. He and Scotty still don't talk, but before they were like one person. Now it's like they've never met.

I can't stop wondering: If I'd pulled away from Lou and fought the garbage throwers, would Bennie have settled for me like Scotty settled for Alice? Could that one thing have made all the difference?

They track down Lou in a matter of days. He tells Jocelyn's mom that she hitchhiked all the way to his house without even warning him. He says she's safe, he's taking care of her, it's better than having her on the street. Lou promises to bring her back when he comes to the city next week. Why not *this* week? I wonder.

While I'm waiting for Jocelyn, Alice invites me over. We take the bus from school, a long ride to Sea Cliff. Her house looks smaller in daylight. In the kitchen, we mix honey with her mother's homemade yogurts and eat two each. We go up to her room, where all the frogs are, and sit on her built-in window seat. Alice tells me she's planning to get real frogs and keep them in a terrarium. She's calm and happy now that Scotty loves her. I can't tell if she's actually real, or if she's stopped caring if she's real or not. Or is not caring what *makes* a person real?

I wonder if Lou's house is near the ocean. Does Jocelyn look at the waves? Do they ever leave Lou's bedroom? Is Rolph there? I keep getting lost in these questions. Then I hear giggling, pounding from somewhere. I go, Who's that?

My sisters, Alice goes. They're playing tetherball.

We head downstairs and outside into Alice's backyard, where I've only been in the dark. It's sunny now, with flowers in patterns and a tree with lemons on it. At the edge of the yard, two little girls are slapping a bright yellow ball around a silver pole. They turn to us, laughing in their green uniforms.

4

Safari

I. Grass

"Remember, Charlie? In Hawaii? When we went to the beach at night and it started to rain?"

Rolph is talking to his older sister, Charlene, who despises her real name. But because they're crouched around a bonfire with the other people on the safari, and because Rolph doesn't speak up all that often, and because their father, Lou, sitting behind them on a camp chair (as they draw in the dust with little sticks), is a record producer whose personal life is of general interest, those near enough to hear are listening closely.

"Remember? How Mom and Dad stayed at the table for one more drink—"

"Impossible," their father interjects, with a wink at the bird-watching ladies to his left. Both women wear binoculars even in the dark, as if hoping to spot birds in the firelit tree overhead.

"Remember, Charlie? How the beach was still warm, and that crazy wind was blowing?"

But Charlie is focused on her father's legs, which have intertwined behind her with those of his girlfriend, Mindy. Soon they will bid the group good night and retreat to their tent, where they'll make love on one of the narrow rickety cots inside it, or possibly on the ground. From the adjacent tent she and Rolph share, Charlie can hear them—not sounds, exactly, but movement. Rolph is too young to notice.

Charlie throws back her head, startling her father. Lou is in his late thirties, square-jawed surfer's face gone a little draggy under the eyes. "You were married to Mom on that trip," she informs him, her voice distorted by the arching of her neck, which is encircled by a puka-shell choker.

"Yes, Charlie," Lou says. "I'm aware of that."

The elderly bird-watching ladies trade a sad smile. Lou is one of those men whose restless charm has generated a contrail of personal upheaval that is practically visible behind him: two failed marriages and two more kids back home in LA, who were too young to bring on this three-week safari. The safari is a new business venture of Lou's old army buddy, Ramsey, with whom he drank and misbehaved, having barely avoided Korea almost twenty years ago.

Rolph pulls at his sister's shoulder. He wants her to remember, to feel it all again: the wind, the endless black ocean, the two of them peering into the dark as if awaiting a signal from their distant, grown-up lives. "Remember, Charlie?"

"Yeah," Charlie says, narrowing her eyes. "I do remember that."

The Samburu warriors have arrived—four of them, two holding drums, a child in the shadows minding a yellow longhorn cow. They came yesterday, too, after the morning game run, when Lou and Mindy were "napping." That's when Charlie exchanged shy glances with the most beautiful warrior, who has scar tissue designs coiled like railroad tracks over the rigorous architecture of his chest and shoulders and back.

Charlie stands up and moves closer to the warriors: a skinny girl in shorts and a raw cotton shirt with small round buttons made of wood. Her teeth are slightly crooked. When the drummers pat their drums, Charlie's warrior and the other one begin to sing: guttural noises pried from their abdomens. She sways in front of them. During her ten days in Africa, she has begun to act like a different sort of girl—the sort that intimidates her back home. In a cinder-block town they visited a few days ago, she drank a muddy-looking concoction in a bar and wound up giving away her silver butterfly earrings (a birthday gift from her father) in a hut belonging to a very young woman whose breasts were leaking milk. She was late returning to the jeeps; Albert, who works for Ramsey, had to go and find her. "Prepare yourself," he warned. "Your dad is having kittens." Charlie didn't care and doesn't now; there's a charge for her in simply commanding the fickle beam of her father's attention, feeling his disquiet as she dances, alone, by the fire.

Lou lets go of Mindy's hand and sits up straight. He wants to grab his daughter's skinny arm and yank her away from these black men, but does no such thing, of course. That would be letting her win.

The warrior smiles at Charlie. He's nineteen, only five years older than she is, and has lived away from his village since he was ten. But he's sung for enough American tourists to recognize that in her world, Charlie is a child. Thirty-five years from now, in 2008, this warrior will be caught in the tribal violence between the Kikuyu and the Luo and will die in a fire. He'll have had four wives and sixty-three grandchildren by then, one of whom, a boy named Joe, will inherit his *lalema*: the iron hunting dagger in a leather scabbard now hanging at his side. Joe will go to college at Columbia and study engineering, becoming an expert in visual robotic technology that detects the slightest hint of irregular movement (the legacy of a childhood spent scanning the grass for lions). He'll marry an American named Lulu and remain in New York, where he'll invent a scanning device that becomes standard issue for crowd security. He and Lulu will buy a loft in Tribeca, where his grandfather's hunting dagger will be displayed inside a cube of Plexiglas, directly under a skylight.

"Son," Lou says, into Rolph's ear. "Let's take a walk."

The boy rises from the dust and walks with his father away from the fire. Twelve tents, each sleeping two safari guests, make a circle around it, along with three outhouses and a shower stall, where water warmed on the fire is released from a sack with a rope pull. Out of view, near the kitchen, are some smaller tents for the staff, and then the black, muttering expanse of the bush, where they've been cautioned never to go.

"Your sister's acting nuts," Lou says, striding into the dark.

"Why?" Rolph asks. He hasn't noticed anything nutty in Charlie's behavior. But his father hears the question differently.

"Women are crazy," he says. "You could spend a goddamn lifetime trying to figure out why."

"Mom's not."

"True," Lou reflects, calmer now. "In fact, your mother's not crazy *enough*."

The singing and drumbeats fall suddenly away, leaving Lou and Rolph alone under a sharp moon.

"What about Mindy?" Rolph asks. "Is she crazy?"

"Good question," Lou says. "What do you think?"

"She likes to read. She brought a lot of books."

"Did she."

"I like her," Rolph says. "But I don't know if she's crazy. Or what the right amount is."

Lou puts his arm around Rolph. If he were an introspective man, he would have understood years ago that his son is the one person in the world with the power to soothe him. And that, while he expects Rolph to be like him, what he most enjoys in his son are the many ways he is different: quiet, reflective, attuned to the natural world and the pain of others.

"Who cares," Lou says. "Right?"

"Right," Rolph agrees, and the women fall away like those drumbeats, leaving him and his father together, an invincible unit. At eleven years old, Rolph knows two clear things about himself: He belongs to his father. And his father belongs to him.

They stand still, surrounded by the whispering bush. The sky is crammed with stars. Rolph closes his eyes and opens them again. He thinks, I'll remember this night for the rest of my life. And he's right.

When they finally return to camp, the warriors have gone. Only a few die-hards from the Phoenix Faction (as Lou calls the safari members who hail from that dubious place) still sit by the fire, comparing the day's animal sightings. Rolph creeps into his tent, pulls off his pants, and climbs onto his cot in a T-shirt and underwear. He assumes that Charlie is asleep. When she speaks, he can hear in her voice that she's been crying.

"Where did you go?" she says.

II. Hills

"What on earth have you got in that backpack?"

It's Cora, Lou's travel agent. She hates Mindy, but Mindy doesn't take it personally—it's Structural Hatred, a term she coined herself and is finding highly useful on this trip. A single woman in her forties who wears high-collared shirts to conceal the thready sinews of her neck will structurally despise the twenty-three-year-old girlfriend of a powerful male who not only employs said middle-aged female but is paying her way on this trip.

"Anthropology books," she tells Cora. "I'm in the Ph.D. program at Berkeley."

"Why don't you read them?"

"Carsick," Mindy says, which is plausible, God knows,

in the shuddering jeeps, though untrue. She isn't sure why she hasn't cracked her Boas or Malinowski or John Murra, but assumes she must be learning in other ways that will prove equally fruitful. In bold moments, fueled by the boiled black coffee they serve each morning in the meal tent, Mindy has even wondered if her insights on the link between social structure and emotional response could amount to more than a rehash of Lévi-Strauss—a refinement; a contemporary application. She's only in her second year of coursework.

Their jeep is last in a line of five, nosing along a dirt road through grassland whose apparent brown masks a wide internal spectrum of color: purples, greens, reds. Albert, the surly Englishman who is Ramsey's second in command, is driving. Mindy has managed to avoid Albert's jeep for several days, but he's developed a reputation for discovering the best animals, so although there's no game run today—they're relocating to the hills, where they'll spend the night in a hotel for the first time this trip—the children begged to ride with him. And keeping Lou's children happy, or as close to happy as is structurally possible, is part of Mindy's job.

Structural Resentment: The adolescent daughter of a twice-divorced male will be unable to tolerate the presence of his new girlfriend, and will do everything in her limited power to distract him from said girlfriend's presence, her own nascent sexuality being her chief weapon.

Structural Affection: A twice-divorced male's preadolescent son (and favorite child) will embrace and accept his father's new girlfriend because he hasn't yet learned to separate his father's loves and desires from his own. In a sense, he, too, will love and desire her, and she will feel maternal toward him, though she isn't old enough to be his mother.

Lou opens the large aluminum case where his new camera is partitioned in its foam padding like a dismantled rifle. He uses the camera to stave off the boredom that afflicts him when he can't physically move around. He's rigged a tiny cassette player with a small set of foam earphones to listen to demo tapes and rough mixes. Occasionally he'll hand the device to Mindy, wanting her opinion, and each time, the experience of music pouring directly against her eardrums—hers alone—is a shock that makes her eyes well up; the privacy of it, the way it transforms her surroundings into a golden montage, as if she were looking back on this lark in Africa with Lou from some distant future.

Structural Incompatibility: A powerful twice-divorced male will be unable to acknowledge, much less sanction, the ambitions of a much younger female mate. By definition, their relationship will be temporary.

Structural Desire: The much younger temporary female mate of a powerful male will be inexorably drawn to the single male within range who disdains her mate's power.

Albert drives with one elbow out the window. He's been a largely silent presence on this safari, eating quickly in the meal tent, providing terse answers to people's questions. ("Where do you live?" "Mombasa." "How long have you been in Africa?" "Eight years." "What brought you here?" "This and that.") He rarely joins the group around the fire after dinner. On a trip to the outhouse one night Mindy glimpsed Albert at the other fire near the staff tents, drinking a beer and laughing with the Kikuyu drivers. With the tour group, he rarely smiles. Whenever his eyes happen to graze Mindy's, she senses shame on her behalf: because of her prettiness; because she sleeps with Lou; because she keeps telling herself this trip constitutes anthropological research into group dynamics and ethnographic enclaves, when really what she's after is luxury, adventure, and a break from her four insomniac roommates.

Next to Albert, in the shotgun seat, Chronos is ranting about animals. He's the bassist for the Mad Hatters, one of Lou's bands, and has come on the trip as Lou's guest along with the Hatters' guitarist and a girlfriend each. These four are locked in a visceral animal-sighting competition (*Structural Fixation:* A collective, contextually induced obsession that becomes a temporary locus of greed, competition, and envy). They challenge one another nightly over who saw more and at what range, invoking witnesses from their respective jeeps and promising definitive proof when they develop their film back home.

Behind Albert sits Cora, the travel agent, and beside her, gazing from his window, is Dean, a blond actor whose genius for stating the obvious—"It's hot," or "The sun is setting," or "There aren't many trees"—is a staple source of amusement for Mindy. Dean is starring in a movie whose sound track Lou is helping to create; the presumption seems to be that its release will bring Dean immediate and stratospheric fame. In the seat behind him, Rolph and Charlie are showing their *Mad* magazine to Mildred, one of the bird-watching ladies. She or her companion, Fiona, can usually be found near Lou, who flirts with them tirelessly and needles them to take him bird-watching. His indulgence of these women in their seventies (strangers to him before this trip) intrigues Mindy; she can find no structural reason for it.

In the last row, beside Mindy, Lou thrusts his torso from the open roof and takes pictures, ignoring the rule to stay seated while the jeep is moving. Albert swerves suddenly, and Lou is knocked back into his seat, camera smacking his forehead. He swears at Albert, but the words are lost in the jeep's wobbly jostle through tall grass. They've left the road. Chronos leans out his open window, and Mindy realizes that Albert must be taking this detour for him, giving Chronos a chance to advance against his rivals. Or was the temptation to knock Lou down too sweet to resist?

After a minute or two of chaotic driving, the jeep emerges a few feet from a pride of lions. Everyone gawks in startled silence—it's the closest they've been to any animal on this trip. The motor is still running, Albert's hand tentatively on the wheel, but the lions appear so relaxed, so indifferent, that he kills the engine. In the ticking-motor silence they can hear the lions breathe: two females, one male, three cubs. The cubs and one of the females are gorging on a bloody zebra carcass. The others are dozing.

"They're eating," says Dean.

Chronos's hands shake as he spools film into his camera. "Fuck," he keeps muttering. "Fuck."

Albert lights a cigarette—forbidden in the brush—and waits, as indifferent to the scene as if he'd paused outside a restroom.

"Can we stand?" the children ask. "Is it safe?"

"I'm sure as hell going to," Lou says.

Lou, Charlie, Rolph, Chronos, and Dean all climb on top

of their seats and jam their upper halves through the open roof. Mindy is now effectively alone inside the jeep with Albert, Cora, and Mildred, who peers at the lions through her bird-watching binoculars.

"How did you know?" Mindy asks, after a silence.

Albert swivels around to look at her down the length of the jeep. He has unruly hair and a soft brown mustache. There is a suggestion of humor in his face. "Just a guess."

"From half a mile away?"

"He probably has a sixth sense," Cora says, "after so many years here."

Albert turns back around and blows smoke through his open window.

"Did you see something?" Mindy persists.

She expects Albert not to turn again, but he does, leaning over the back of his seat, his eyes meeting hers between the children's bare legs. Mindy feels a jolt of attraction roughly akin to having someone seize her intestines and twist. She understands now that it's mutual; she sees this in Albert's face.

"Broken bushes," he says, resting his eyes on her. "Like something got chased. It could have been nothing."

Cora, sensing her exclusion, sighs wearily. "Can someone come down so I can look too?" she calls to those above the roof.

"Coming," Lou says, but Chronos is faster, ducking back into the front seat and then leaning out his window. Cora rises in her big print skirt. Mindy's face pounds with blood. Her own window, like Albert's, is on the jeep's left side, facing away from the lions. Mindy watches him wet his fingers and snuff out his cigarette. They sit in silence, hands dangling separately from their windows, a warm breeze stirring the hair on their arms, ignoring the most spectacular animal sighting of the safari.

"You're driving me crazy," Albert says, very softly. The sound seems to travel out his window and back in through Mindy's, like one of those whispering tubes. "You must know that."

"I didn't," she murmurs back.

"Well, you are."

"My hands are tied."

"Forever?"

She smiles. "Please. An interlude."

"Then?"

"Grad school. Berkeley."

Albert chuckles. Mindy isn't sure what that chuckle means—is it funny that she's in graduate school, or that Berkeley and Mombasa, where he lives, are irreconcilable locations?

"Chronos, you crazy fuck, get back in here."

It's Lou's voice, from overhead. But Mindy feels sluggish, almost drugged, and reacts only when she hears the change in Albert's voice. "No," he hisses. "*No!* Back in the jeep."

Mindy swivels toward the window on her other side. Chronos is skulking among the lions, holding his camera close to the faces of the sleeping male and female, taking pictures.

"Walk backward," Albert says, with hushed urgency. "Backward, Chronos, gently."

Movement comes from a direction no one is expecting:

the female gnawing at the zebra. She vaults at Chronos in an agile, gravity-defying spring that anyone with a house cat would recognize. She lands on his head, flattening him instantly. There are screams, a gunshot, and those overhead tumble back into their seats so violently that at first Mindy thinks *they've* been shot. But it's the lioness; Albert has killed her with a rifle he'd secreted somewhere, maybe under his seat. The other lions have run away; all that's left is the zebra carcass and the body of the lioness, Chronos's legs splayed beneath her.

Albert, Lou, Dean, and Cora bolt from the jeep. Mindy starts to follow, but Lou pushes her back, and she realizes that he wants her to stay with his children. She leans over the back of their seat and puts an arm around each of them. As they stare through the open windows, a wave of nausea rolls through Mindy; she feels in danger of passing out. Mildred is still in her spot beside the children, and it occurs to Mindy, vaguely, that the elderly bird-watcher was inside the jeep the whole time that she and Albert were talking.

"Is Chronos dead?" Rolph asks flatly.

"I'm sure he's not," Mindy says.

"Why isn't he moving?"

"The lion is on top of him. See, they're trying to pull her off. He's probably fine under there."

"There's blood on the lion's mouth," Charlie says.

"That's from the zebra. Remember, she was eating a zebra?" It takes enormous effort to keep her teeth from chattering, but Mindy knows that she must hide her terror from the children—her belief that whatever turns out to have happened is her fault.

They wait in pulsing isolation, surrounded by the hot, blank day. Mildred rests a knobby hand on Mindy's shoulder, and Mindy feels her eyes fill with tears.

"He'll be fine," the old woman says gently. "You watch."

By the time the group throngs the bar of the mountain hotel after dinner, everyone seems to have gained something. Chronos has gained a blistering victory over his bandmate and both girlfriends, at the cost of thirty-two stitches on his left cheek that you could argue are also a gain (he's a rock star, after all) and several huge antibiotic pills administered by an English surgeon with hooded eyes and beery breath— an old friend of Albert's whom he unearthed in a cinder-block town about an hour away from the lions.

Albert has gained the status of a hero, but you wouldn't know it to look at him. He gulps a bourbon and mutters his responses to the giddy queries of the Phoenix Faction. No one has yet confronted him on the damning basics: *Why were you in the bush? How did you get so close to the lions? Why didn't you stop Chronos from getting out of the jeep?* But Albert knows that Ramsey, his boss, will ask these questions, and that they will likely lead to his being fired: the latest in a series of failures brought on by what his mother, back in Minehead, calls his "self-destructive tendencies."

The members of Ramsey's safari have gained a story they'll tell for the rest of their lives. It will prompt some of them, years from now, to search for each other on Google and Facebook, unable to resist the wish-fulfillment fantasy these portals offer: *What ever happened to . . . ?* In a few cases, they'll meet again to reminisce and marvel at one another's physical transformations, which will seem to melt away with the minutes. Dean, whose success will elude him until middle age, when he'll land the role of a paunchy, outspoken plumber in a popular sitcom, will meet for an espresso with Louise (now a chubby twelve-year-old from the Phoenix Faction), who will Google him after her divorce. Postcoffee, they'll repair to a Days Inn off San Vicente for some unexpectedly moving sex, then to Palm Springs for a golf weekend, and finally to the altar, accompanied by Dean's four adult children and Louise's three teenagers. But this outcome will be the stark exception—mostly, the reunions will lead to a mutual discovery that having been on safari thirty-five years before doesn't qualify as having much in common, and they'll part ways wondering what, exactly, they'd hoped for.

The passengers in Albert's jeep have gained the status of witnesses, to be questioned endlessly about what they saw and heard and felt. A gang of children, including Rolph, Charlie, a set of eight-year-old twin boys from Phoenix, and Louise, the chubby twelve-year-old, stampede along a slatted path to a blind beside a watering hole: a wooden hut full of long benches with a slot they can peek through, invisible to the animals. It's dark inside. They rush to the slot, but no animals are drinking at the moment.

"Did you actually see the lion?" Louise asks, with wonder.

"Lio*ness*," Rolph says. "There were two, plus a lion. And three cubs."

"She means the one that got shot," Charlie says, impatient. "Obviously we saw it. We were inches away!"

"Feet," Rolph corrects her.

"Feet are *made* out of inches," Charlie says. "We saw everything."

Rolph has already started to hate these conversations—the panting excitement behind them, the way Charlie seems to revel in it. A thought has been troubling him. "I wonder what will happen to the cubs," he says. "The lioness who got shot must have been their mom—she was eating with them."

"Not necessarily," Charlie says.

"But if she was . . ."

"Maybe the dad will take care of them," Charlie says, doubtfully. The other children are quiet, considering the question.

"Lions tend to raise their cubs communally"—a voice comes from the far end of the blind. Mildred and Fiona were already there or have just slipped in; being old and female, they're easily missed. "The pride will likely take care of them," Fiona says, "even if the one killed was their mother."

"Which it might not have been," Charlie adds.

"Which it might not have been," Mildred agrees.

It doesn't occur to the children to ask Mildred, who was also in the jeep, what she saw.

"I'm going back," Rolph tells his sister.

He follows the path back up to the hotel. His father and Mindy are still in the smoky bar; the strange, celebratory feeling unnerves Rolph. His mind bends again and again to the jeep, but his memories are a muddle: the lioness springing; a jerk of impact from the gun; Chronos moaning during the drive to the doctor, blood collecting in an actual puddle under his head on the floor of the jeep, like in a comic book.

All of it is suffused with the feel of Mindy holding him from behind, her cheek against his head, her smell: not bready, like his mom's, but salty, bitter almost—a smell that seems akin to the lions themselves.

He stands by his father, who pauses in the middle of an army story he's telling with Ramsey. "You tired, Son?"

"Want me to walk you upstairs?" Mindy asks, and Rolph nods: he does want that.

The blue, mosquitoey night pushes in from the hotel windows. Outside the bar, Rolph is suddenly less tired. Mindy collects her key from the front desk, then says, "Let's go out on the porch."

They step outside. Dark as it is, the silhouettes of mountains against the sky are even darker. Rolph can dimly hear the voices of the other children, down in the blind. He's relieved to have escaped them. He stands with Mindy at the edge of the porch and looks at the mountains. Her salty, tangy smell surrounds him. Rolph senses her waiting for something and he waits, too, his heart stamping.

There is a cough farther down the porch. Rolph sees the orange tip of a cigarette move in the dark, and Albert comes toward them with a creak of boots. "Hello there," he says to Rolph. He doesn't speak to Mindy, and Rolph decides the one hello must be for both of them.

"Hello," he greets Albert.

"What are you up to?" Albert asks.

Rolph turns to Mindy. "What are we up to?"

"Enjoying the night," she says, still facing the mountains, but her voice is tense. "We should go up," she tells Rolph, and walks abruptly back inside the hotel. Rolph is troubled by her rudeness. "Are you coming?" he asks Albert.

"Why not?"

The three of them ascend the stairs, sounds of merriment jingling up from the bar. Rolph feels an odd pressure to make conversation. "Is your room up here, too?" he asks.

"Down the hall," Albert says. "Number three."

Mindy unlocks the door to Rolph's room and steps inside, leaving Albert in the hall. Rolph is suddenly angry with her.

"Want to see my room?" he asks Albert. "Mine and Charlie's?"

Mindy emits a single syllable of laughter—the way his mother laughs when things have annoyed her to a point of absurdity. Albert steps into his room. It's plain, with wood furniture and dusty flowered curtains, but after ten nights in tents it feels lavish.

"Very nice," Albert says. With his longish brown hair and mustache, he looks like a real explorer, Rolph thinks. Mindy crosses her arms and stares out the window. There is a feeling in the room that Rolph can't identify. He's angry with Mindy and thinks that Albert must be too. *Women are crazy.* Mindy's body is slender and elastic; she could slip through a keyhole, or under a door. Her thin purple sweater rises and falls quickly as she breathes. Rolph is surprised by how angry he is.

Albert taps a cigarette from his pack, but doesn't light it. It is unfiltered, tobacco emerging at both ends. "Well," he says, "good night, you two."

Rolph had imagined Mindy tucking him into bed, her

arm around him again as it was in the jeep. Now this seems out of the question. He can't change into his pajamas with Mindy there; he doesn't even want her to *see* his pajamas, which have small blue elves all over them. "I'm fine," he tells her, hearing the coldness in his voice. "You can go back."

"Okay," she says. She turns down his bed, plumps the pillow, adjusts the open window. Rolph senses her finding reasons not to leave the room.

"Your dad and I will be just next door," Mindy says. "You know that, right?"

"Duh," he mutters. Then, chastened, he says, "I know."

III. Sand

Five days later, they take a long, very old train overnight to Mombasa. Every few minutes, it slows down just enough for people to leap from the doors, bundles clutched to their chests, and for others to scramble on. Lou's group and the Phoenix Faction install themselves in the cramped bar car, which they share with African men in suits and bowler hats. Charlie is allowed to drink one beer, but she sneaks two more with the help of handsome Dean, who stands beside her narrow bar stool. "You're sunburned," he says, pressing a finger to Charlie's cheek. "The African sun is strong."

"True," Charlie says, grinning as she swigs her beer. Now that Mindy has pointed out Dean's platitudes, Charlie finds him hilarious.

"You have to wear sunscreen," he says.

"I know—I did."

"Once isn't enough. You have to reapply."

Charlie catches Mindy's eye and succumbs to giggles. Her father moves close. "What's so funny?"

"Life," Charlie says, leaning against him.

"*Life!*" Lou snorts. "How old are you?"

He hugs her to him. When Charlie was little he did this all the time, but as she grows older it happens less. Her father is warm, almost hot, his heartbeat like someone banging on a heavy door.

"Ow," Lou says. "Your quill is stabbing me." It's a black-and-white porcupine quill—she found it in the hills and uses it to pin up her long hair. Her father slides it out, and the golden, tangled mass of Charlie's hair collapses onto her shoulders like a shattered window. She's aware of Dean watching.

"I like this," Lou says, squinting at the quill's translucent point. "It's a dangerous weapon."

"Weapons are necessary," Dean says.

By the next afternoon, the safarigoers have settled into a hotel a half hour up the coast from Mombasa. On a white beach traversed by knobby-chested men selling beads and gourds, Mildred and Fiona gamely appear in floral-print swimsuits, binoculars still at their necks. The livid Medusa tattoo on Chronos's chest is less startling than his small potbelly—a disillusioning trait he shares with a number of the men, the fathers especially. Not Lou; he's lean, a little ropy, tanned from occasional surfing. He walks toward the cream-colored sea with his arm around Mindy, who looks even better than expected (and expectations were high) in her sparkling blue bikini.

Charlie and Rolph lie together under a palm tree. Charlie disdains the red Danskin one-piece she chose with her mother for this trip and decides she will borrow a pair of sharp scissors from the front desk and cut it into a bikini.

"I never want to go home," she says sleepily.

"I miss Mom," Rolph says. His father and Mindy are swimming. He can see the glitter of her swimsuit through the pale water.

"But if Mom could come."

"Dad doesn't love her anymore," Rolph says. "She's not crazy enough."

"What's that supposed to mean?"

Rolph shrugs. "You think he loves Mindy?"

"No way. He's tired of Mindy."

"What if Mindy loves him?"

"Who cares?" Charlie says. "They all love him."

After his swim, Lou goes in search of spears and snorkeling gear, resisting the temptation to follow Mindy back to their room, though clearly she'd like him to. She's gone bananas in the sack since they left the tents (women can be funny about tents)—hungry for it now, pawing off Lou's clothes at odd moments, ready to start again when he's barely finished. He feels tenderly toward Mindy, now that the trip is winding down. She's studying something at Berkeley, and Lou has never traveled for a woman. It's doubtful that he'll lay eyes on her again.

Rolph is reading in the sand when Lou arrives with the snorkeling equipment, but he puts aside *The Hobbit* without protest and stands. Charlie ignores them, and Lou wonders fleetingly if he should have included her. He and Rolph walk to the edge of the sea and pull on their masks and flippers, hanging their spears from belts at their sides. Rolph looks thin; he needs more exercise. He's timid in the water. His mother is a reader and a gardener, and Lou is constantly having to fight her influence. He wishes that Rolph could live with him, but the lawyers just shake their heads whenever he mentions it.

The fish are gaudy, easy targets, nibbling at coral. Lou has speared seven by the time he realizes Rolph hasn't killed a single one.

"What's the problem, Son?" he asks, when they surface.

"I just like watching them," Rolph says.

They've drifted toward a spit of rocks extending into the sea. Carefully they climb from the water. Tide pools throng with starfish and urchins and sea cucumbers; Rolph crouches, poring over them. Lou's fish hang from a netted bag at his waist. From the beach, Mindy is watching them through Fiona's binoculars. She waves, and Lou and Rolph wave back.

"Dad," Rolph asks, lifting a tiny green crab from a tide pool, "what do you think about Mindy?"

"Mindy's great. Why?"

The crab splays its little claws; Lou notes with approval that his son knows how to hold it safely. Rolph squints up at him. "You know. Is she the right amount of crazy."

Lou gives a hoot of laughter. He'd forgotten the earlier conversation, but Rolph forgets nothing—a quality that delights his father. "She's crazy enough. But crazy isn't everything."

"I think she's rude," Rolph says.

"Rude to *you*?"

"No. To Albert."

Lou turns to his son, cocking his head. "Albert?"

Rolph releases the crab and begins to tell the story. He remembers each thing—the porch, the stairs, "Number three"—realizing as he speaks how much he's wanted to tell his father this, as punishment to Mindy. His father listens keenly, without interrupting. But as Rolph goes on he senses the story landing heavily, in a way he doesn't understand.

When he finishes talking, his father takes a long breath and lets it out. He looks back at the beach. It's nearly sunset, and people are shaking fine white sand from their towels and packing up for the day. The hotel has a disco, and the group plans to go dancing there after dinner.

"When exactly did this happen?" Lou asks.

"The same day as the lions—that night." Rolph waits a moment, then asks, "Why do you think she was rude like that?"

"Women are cunts," his father says. "That's why."

Rolph gapes at him. His father is angry, a muscle jumping in his jaw, and without warning Rolph is angry too: assailed by a deep, sickening rage that stirs in him very occasionally—when he and Charlie come back from a riotous weekend around their father's pool, rock stars jamming on the roof, guacamole and big pots of chili, to find their mother alone in her bungalow, drinking peppermint tea. Rage at this man who casts everyone aside.

"They are not—" He can't make himself repeat the word.

"They are," Lou says tightly. "Pretty soon you'll know it for sure."

Rolph turns away from his father. There is nowhere to go, so he jumps into the sea and begins slowly paddling back toward shore. The sun is low, the water choppy and full of shadows. Rolph imagines sharks just under his feet, but he doesn't turn or look back. He keeps swimming toward that white sand, knowing instinctively that his struggle to stay afloat is the most exquisite torture he can concoct for his father—also that, if he sinks, Lou will jump in instantly and save him.

That night, Rolph and Charlie are allowed to have wine at dinner. Rolph dislikes the sour taste, but enjoys the swimmy blur it makes of his surroundings: the giant beaklike flowers all over the dining room; his father's speared fish cooked by the chef with olives and tomatoes; Mindy in a shimmery green dress. His father's arm is around her. He isn't angry anymore, so neither is Rolph.

Lou has spent the past hour in bed, fucking Mindy senseless. Now he keeps one hand on her slim thigh, reaching under her hem, waiting for that cloudy look she gets. Lou is a man who cannot tolerate defeat—can't *perceive* it as anything but a spur to his own inevitable victory. He has to win. He doesn't give a shit about Albert—Albert is invisible, Albert is nothing (in fact, Albert has left the group and returned to his Mombasa apartment). What matters now is that *Mindy* understand this.

He refills Mildred's and Fiona's wineglasses until their cheeks are patchy and flushed. "You still haven't taken me bird-watching," he chides them. "I keep asking, but it never happens."

"We could go tomorrow," Mildred says. "There are some coastal birds we're hoping to see."

"Is that a promise?"

"A solemn promise."

"Come on," Charlie whispers to Rolph. "Let's go outside."

They slip from the crowded dining room and skitter onto the silvery beach. The palm trees make a slapping, rainy sound, but the air is dry.

"It's like Hawaii," Rolph says, wanting it to be true. The ingredients are there: the dark, the beach, his sister. But it doesn't feel the same.

"Without the rain," Charlie says.

"Without Mom," Rolph says.

"I think he's going to marry Mindy," Charlie says.

"No way! You said he didn't love her."

"So? He can still marry her."

They sink onto the sand, still faintly warm, radiating a lunar glow. The ghost sea tumbles against it.

"She's not so bad," Charlie says.

"I don't like her. And why are you the world's expert?"

Charlie shrugs. "I know Dad."

Charlie doesn't know herself. Four years from now, at eighteen, she'll join a cult across the Mexican border whose charismatic leader promotes a diet of raw eggs; she'll nearly die from salmonella poisoning before Lou rescues her. A cocaine habit will require partial reconstruction of her nose, changing her appearance, and a series of feckless, domineering men will leave her solitary in her late twenties, trying to broker peace between Rolph and Lou, who will have stopped speaking.

But Charlie *does* know her father. He'll marry Mindy because that's what winning means, and because Mindy's eagerness to conclude this odd episode and return to her studies will last until precisely the moment she opens the door to her Berkeley apartment and walks into the smell of simmering lentils: one of the cheap stews she and her roommates survive on. She'll collapse on a swaybacked couch they found on the sidewalk and unpack her many books, realizing that in weeks of lugging them through Africa, she's read virtually nothing. And when the phone rings her heart will flip.

Structural Dissatisfaction: Returning to circumstances that once pleased you, having experienced a more thrilling or opulent way of life, and finding that you can no longer tolerate them.

But we're getting off the subject.

Rolph and Charlie are galloping up the beach, drawn by the pulse of light and music from the open-air disco. They run barefoot into the crowd, trailing powdery sand onto a translucent dance floor overlaid on lozenges of flashing color. The shuddering bass line seems to interfere with Rolph's heartbeat.

"C'mon," Charlie says. "Let's dance."

She begins to undulate in front of him—the way the new Charlie is planning to dance when she gets home. But Rolph is embarrassed; he can't dance that way. The rest of the group surrounds them; chubby Louise, one year older than he, is dancing with Dean, the actor. Ramsey flings his arms around one of the Phoenix Faction moms. Lou and Mindy dance close together, their whole bodies touching, but Mindy is thinking of Albert, as she will periodically after marrying Lou and having two daughters, his fifth and sixth children, in quick succession, as if sprinting against the inevitable drift of his attention. On paper he'll be penniless, and Mindy will end up working as a travel agent to support her little girls. For a time her life will be joyless; the girls will seem to cry too much, and she'll think longingly of this trip to Africa as the last happy moment of her life, when she still had a choice, when she was free and unencumbered. She'll dream senselessly, futilely, of Albert, wondering what he might be doing at particular times, how her life would have turned out if she'd run away with him as he'd suggested, half joking, when she visited him in room number three. Later, of course, she'll recognize "Albert" as nothing more than a focus of regret for her own immaturity and disastrous choices. When both her children are in high school, she'll finally resume her studies, complete her Ph.D. at UCLA, and begin an academic career at forty-five, spending long periods of the next thirty years doing social structures fieldwork in the Brazilian rain forest. Her youngest daughter will go to work for Lou, become his protégée, and inherit his business.

"Look," Charlie tells Rolph, over the music. "The birdwatchers are watching us."

Mildred and Fiona are sitting on chairs beside the dance floor, waving at Rolph and Charlie in their long print dresses. It's the first time the children have seen them without binoculars.

"I guess they're too old to dance," Rolph says.

"Or maybe we remind them of birds," Charlie says.

"Or maybe when there are no birds, they watch people," Rolph says.

"Come on, Rolphus," Charlie says. "Dance with me."

She takes hold of his hands. As they move together, Rolph feels his self-consciousness miraculously fade, as if he is growing up right there on the dance floor, becoming a boy who dances with girls like his sister. Charlie feels it, too. In fact, this particular memory is one she'll return to again and again, for the rest of her life, long after Rolph has shot himself in the head in their father's house at twenty-eight: her brother as a boy, hair slicked flat, eyes sparkling, shyly learning to dance. But the woman who remembers won't be Charlie; after Rolph dies, she'll revert to her real name—Charlene—unlatching herself forever from the girl who danced with her brother in Africa. Charlene will cut her hair short and go to law school. When she gives birth to a son she'll want to name him Rolph, but her parents will still be too shattered. So she'll call him that privately, just in her mind, and years later, she'll stand with her mother among a crowd of cheering parents beside a field, watching him play, a dreamy look on his face as he glances at the sky.

"Charlie!" Rolph says. "Guess what I just figured out."

Charlie leans toward her brother, who is grinning with his news. He cups both hands into her hair to be heard above the thudding beat. His warm, sweet breath fills her ear.

"I don't think those ladies were ever watching birds," Rolph says.

5

You (Plural)

It's all still there: the pool with its blue and yellow tiles from
Portugal, water laughing softly down a black stone wall. The
house is the same, except quiet. The quiet makes no sense.
Nerve gas? Overdoses? Mass arrests? I wonder as we follow a
maid through a curve of carpeted rooms, the pool blinking
at us past every window. What else could have stopped the
unstoppable parties?

But it's nothing like that. Twenty years have passed.

He's in the bedroom, in a hospital bed, tubes up his nose.
The second stroke really knocked him out—the first one
wasn't so bad, just one of his legs was a little shaky. That's
what Bennie told me on the phone. Bennie from high
school, our old friend. Lou's protégé. He tracked me down
at my mother's, even though she left San Francisco years ago

and followed me to LA. Bennie the organizer, rounding up people from the old days to say good-bye to Lou. It seems you can find almost anyone on a computer. He found Rhea all the way in Seattle, with a different last name.

Of our old gang, only Scotty has disappeared. No computer can find him.

Rhea and I stand by Lou's bed, unsure what to do. We know him from a time when there was no such thing as normal people dying.

There were clues, hints about some bad alternative to being alive (we remembered them together over coffee, Rhea and I, before coming to see him—staring at each other's new faces across the plastic table, our familiar features rinsed in weird adulthood). There was Scotty's mom, of course, who died from pills when we were still in high school, but she wasn't normal. My father, from AIDS, but I hardly saw him by then. Anyway, those were catastrophes. Not like this: prescriptions by the bed, a leaden smell of medicine and vacuumed carpet. It reminds me of being in the hospital. Not the smell, exactly (the hospital doesn't have carpets), but the dead air, the feeling of being far away from everything.

We stand there, quiet. My questions all seem wrong: How did you get so old? Was it all at once, in a day, or did you peter out bit by bit? When did you stop having parties? Did everyone else get old too, or was it just you? Are other people still here, hiding in the palm trees or holding their breath underwater? When did you last swim your laps? Do your bones hurt? Did you know this was coming and hide that you knew, or did it ambush you from behind?

Instead I say, "Hi Lou," and at the very same time, Rhea says, "Wow, everything is just the same!" and we both laugh.

Lou smiles, and the shape of that smile, even with the yellow shocked teeth inside it, is familiar, a warm finger poking at my gut. His smile, coming open in this strange place.

"You girls. Still look gorgeous," he gasps.

He's lying. I'm forty-three and so is Rhea, married with three children in Seattle. I can't get over that: three. I'm back at my mother's again, trying to finish my B.A. at UCLA Extension after some long, confusing detours. "Your desultory twenties," my mother calls my lost time, trying to make it sound reasonable and fun, but it started before I was twenty and lasted much longer. I'm praying it's over. Some mornings, the sun looks wrong outside my window. I sit at the kitchen table shaking salt into the hairs on my arm, and a feeling shoves up in me: It's finished. Everything went past, without me. Those days I know not to close my eyes for too long, or the fun will really start.

"Oh Lou, we're two old bags—admit it," Rhea says, swatting at his frail shoulder.

She shows him the pictures of her kids, holding them close to his face.

"She's cute," he says about the oldest, Nadine, who is sixteen. I think he winks, or maybe it's his eye twitching.

"Cut it out, you," Rhea says.

I don't say anything. I feel it—the finger—again. In my stomach.

"What about your kids?" Rhea asks Lou. "You see them much?"

"Some," he says, in his strangled new voice.

He had six, from three marriages he bored through and then kicked away. Rolph, the second oldest, was his favorite. Rolph lived here, in this house, a gentle boy with blue eyes that broke a little whenever he stared down his father. Rolph and I were the same age, exactly. Same birthday, same year. I used to imagine us, tiny babies in different hospitals, crying at the same time. We stood naked once, side by side in a full-length mirror, trying to see if being born the same day had left a clue on us. Some mark we could find.

By the end, Rolph wouldn't speak to me, would walk out of a room when I came in it.

Lou's big bed with the crushed purple spread is gone—thank God. The TV is new, flat and long, and its basketball game has a nervous sharpness that makes the room and even us look smudged. A guy comes in dressed in black, a diamond in his ear, and he fiddles with Lou's tubes and takes his blood pressure. From under the covers, tubes twirl from other parts of Lou into clear plastic bags I try not to look at.

A dog barks. Lou's eyes are shut, and he snores. The stylish nurse-butler checks his wristwatch and leaves.

So this is it—what cost me all that time. A man who turned out to be old, a house that turned out to be empty. I can't help it, I start to cry. Rhea puts her arms around me. Even after all the years, she doesn't hesitate. Her skin hangs loose—freckled skin ages prematurely, Lou told me once, and Rhea is *all* freckles. "Our friend Rhea," he said, "she's doomed."

"You have three children," I sob into her hair.

"Shhh."

"What do I have?"

Kids I remember from high school are making movies, making computers. Making movies *on* computers. A revolution, I keep hearing people say. I'm trying to learn Spanish. At night, my mother tests me with flash cards.

Three children. The oldest, Nadine, is almost my age when I met Lou. Seventeen, hitchhiking. He was driving a red Mercedes. In 1979, that could be the beginning of an exciting story, a story where anything might happen. Now it's a punch line. "It was all for no reason," I say.

"That's never true," Rhea says. "You just haven't found the reason yet."

The whole time, Rhea knew what she was doing. Even dancing, even sobbing. Even with a needle in her vein, she was half pretending. Not me.

"I got lost," I say.

It's turning out to be a bad day, a day when the sun feels like teeth. Tonight, when my mother comes home from work and sees me, she'll say, "Forget the Spanish," and fix us Virgin Marys with little umbrellas. With Dave Brubeck on the stereo, we'll play dominoes or gin rummy. When I look at my mother she gives me a smile, each time. But exhaustion has carved up her face.

The silence takes on a kind of intelligence, and we see Lou watching us. His eyes are so vacant, I think he might be dead. "Haven't been. Outside. In weeks," he says, coughing a little. "Haven't wanted to."

Rhea pushes the bed. I come a step behind, pulling the IV drip on its wheels. As we move him through the house, I feel dread, as if the combination of sunlight and hospital bed could cause an explosion. I'm afraid the real Lou will be outside by the pool where he lived with a red phone on a long cord and a bowl of green apples, and the real Lou and this old Lou will have a fight. *How dare you? I've never had an old person in my house and I'm not going to start now.* Age, ugliness—they had no place. They would never get in from outside.

"There," he says, meaning by the pool, like always.

There's still a phone: a black remote on a small glass table, a fruit shake next to it. The nurse-butler or some other employee, spreading his wings on the empty grounds.

Or Rolph? Could Rolph still be here, taking care of his dad? Rolph in the house? And I feel him, then, exactly like before, when I could tell if he'd walked in a room without having to look. Just by how the air moved. Once, we hid behind the pool house after a concert, Lou yelling for me, "Jocelyn! Joc-elyn!" Rolph and I giggling while the generator droned in our chests. Later I thought: My first kiss. Which was crazy. Everything I would ever do, I'd done by then.

In the mirror, Rolph's chest was smooth. There was no mark. The mark was everywhere. The mark was youth.

And when it happened, in Rolph's tiny bedroom, sun sneaking through the shades in stripes, I pretended it was new. He looked inside my eyes, and I felt how normal I could still be. We were smooth, both of us.

"Where's that. Thing," Lou asks, meaning the button pad to tilt the bed. He wants to sit up and look out like he used to, in his red bathing suit, tanned legs smelling of chlorine. The phone in his hand and me between his legs, his palm on my head. The birds must have chirped then, too, but we didn't hear them over the music. Or are there more birds now?

The bed whines as it hoists him up. He looks out, eyes reaching. "I got old," he says.

The dog is barking again. The water sways in the pool, as if someone has just gotten in, or out.

"What about Rolph?" I ask, my first words since "Hi."

"Rolph," Lou says, and blinks.

"Your son? Rolph?"

Rhea shakes her head at me—my voice is too loud. I feel a kind of anger that fills up my head sometimes and rubs out my thoughts like chalk. Who is this old man dying in front of me? I want the other one, the selfish, devouring man, the one who turned me around between his legs out here in the wide open, pushing the back of my head with his free hand while he laughed into the phone. Not caring that every room in the house faced this pool—his son's, for example. I have a thing or two to say to that one.

Lou is trying to speak. We lean close, listening. Habit, I guess.

"Rolph didn't make it," he says.

"What are you talking about?" I say.

Now the old man is crying. Tears leak down his face.

"What's the point, Jocelyn?" Rhea asks me, and in that second, different parts of my brain find each other, and I realize that I already knew about Rolph. And Rhea knew—everyone knew. An old tragedy.

"He was. Twenty-eight," Lou says.

I shut my eyes.

"Long time ago," he says, the words splitting in his wheezy chest. "But."

Yes, it was. Twenty-eight was a long time ago. The sun hurts my eyes, so I keep them shut.

"Losing a child," Rhea murmurs. "I can't imagine it."

The anger squeezes, it mashes me from inside. My arms ache. I reach underneath Lou's hospital bed, I heave it up and over so he slides into the turquoise pool and the IV needle tears out of his arm, blood spinning after it, feathering in the water and turning a kind of yellow. I'm that strong, even after so much. I jump in after him, Rhea shrieking now, I jump in and I hold him down, lock his head between my kneecaps and hold him there until everything goes soft and we're just waiting, Lou and I are waiting, and then he shakes, flailing between my legs, jerking as the life goes out of him. When he's absolutely still, I let him float to the top.

I open my eyes. No one has moved. Lou is still crying, searching the pool with his blank eyes. Through the sheet, Rhea is touching his chest.

It's a bad day. The sun hurts my head.

"I should kill you," I say, looking at him straight. "You deserve to die."

"Enough," Rhea says, with her sharp mother's voice.

Suddenly, Lou looks in my eyes. It feels like the first time all day. Finally I can see him, that man who said, *You're the best thing that ever happened to me,* and *We'll see the whole goddamn world,* and *How come I need you so much?* And *Looking for a ride, kiddo?* Grinning in the hard sun, puddles of it on his bright red car. *Just tell me where.*

He looks scared, but he smiles. The old smile, back again. "Too late," he says.

Too late. I tilt my head at the roof. Rolph and I sat up there a whole night once, spying down on a party Lou was having for one of his bands. Even after the noise stopped, we stayed, our backs on the cool tiles. We were waiting for the sun. It came up fast, small and bright and round. "Like a baby," Rolph said, and I started to cry. This fragile new sun in our arms.

Every night, my mother ticks off another day I've been clean. It's more than a year, my longest yet. "Jocelyn, you've got so much life in front of you," she says. And when I believe her, for a minute, there's a lifting over my eyes. Like walking out of a dark room.

Lou is speaking again. Trying to speak. "Stand on each side. Of me. Would you, girls?"

Rhea holds his hand, and I take the other one. It's not the same hand as before, it is bulbous and dry and heavy. Rhea and I look at each other across him. We're there, the three of us, like before. We're back to the beginning.

He's stopped crying. He's looking at his world. The pool, the tiles. We never did get to Africa, or anywhere. We barely left this house.

"Nice to be. With you girls," he says, fighting to breathe.

Clutching our hands, as if we might flee. But we don't. We look at the pool and we listen to the birds.

"Another minute," he says. "Thank you, girls. One more. Like this."

6

X's and O's

Here's how it started: I was sitting on a bench in Tompkins Square Park reading a copy of *Spin* I'd swiped from Hudson News, observing East Village females crossing the park on their way home from work and wondering (as I often did) how my ex-wife had managed to populate New York with thousands of women who looked nothing like her but still brought her to mind, when I made a discovery: my old friend Bennie Salazar was a record producer! It was right in *Spin* magazine, a whole article about Bennie and how he'd made his name on a group called the Conduits that went mul- tiplatinum three or four years ago. There was a picture of Bennie receiving some kind of award, looking out of breath and a little cross-eyed—one of those frozen, hectic instants you just know has a whole happy life attached. I looked at

the picture for less than a second; then I closed the magazine. I decided not to think about Bennie. There's a fine line
between thinking about somebody and thinking about *not*
thinking about somebody, but I have the patience and the
self-control to walk that line for hours—days, if I have to.

After one week of not thinking about Bennie—thinking
so much about not thinking about Bennie that there was
barely room left in my brain for thoughts of any other kind—
I decided to write him a letter. I addressed it to his record
label, which turned out to be inside a green glass building
on Park Avenue and Fifty-second Street. I took the subway
up there and stood outside the building with my head back,
looking up, up, wondering how high Bennie's office might
possibly be. I kept my eyes on the building as I dropped the
letter into the mailbox directly in front of it. *Hey Benjo,* I'd
written (that was what I used to call him). *Long time no see. I
hear you're the man, now. Congrats. Couldn't have happened
to a luckier guy. Best wishes, Scotty Hausmann.*

He wrote back! His letter arrived in my dented East Sixth
Street mailbox about five days later, typed, which I guess
meant a secretary had done it, but I could tell it was Bennie
all right:

*Scotty baby—Hey thanks for the note. Where have you
been hiding yourself? I still think of the Dildo days sometimes.
Hope you're playing that slide guitar. Yours, Bennie,* with his
little wiggly signature above the typed name.

Bennie's letter had quite an effect on me. Things had gotten—what's the word? Dry. Things had gotten sort of dry for
me. I was working for the city as a janitor in a neighborhood
elementary school and, in summers, collecting litter in the

park alongside the East River near the Williamsburg Bridge. I felt no shame whatsoever in these activities, because I understood what almost no one else seemed to grasp: that there was only an infinitesimal difference, a difference so small that it barely existed except as a figment of the human imagination, between working in a tall green glass building on Park Avenue and collecting litter in a park. In fact, there may have been no difference at all.

I happened to have the next day off—the day after Bennie's letter came—so I went to the East River early that morning and fished. I did this all the time, and I ate the fish, too. Pollution was present, yes, but the beauty of it was that you knew all about that pollution, unlike the many poisons you consumed each day in ignorance. I fished, and God must've been on my side, or maybe it was Bennie's good luck rubbing off on me, because I pulled from the river my best catch of all time: an enormous striped bass! My fishing pals, Sammy and Dave, were shocked to see me catch this superb fish. I stunned it, wrapped it in newspaper, bagged it, and carried it home under my arm. I put on the closest thing I had to a suit: khaki pants and a jacket that I dry-cleaned a *lot*. The week before, I'd taken it to the cleaners still in its dry-cleaning bag, which caused a breakdown in the gal behind the counter—"Why you clean? You already clean, bag not open, you waste your money." I know I'm getting off the subject here, but let me just say that I whipped my jacket out of its plastic bag with such force that she went quiet, and I laid it carefully on the dry-cleaning counter. *"Merci por vous consideración, madame,"* I said, and she accepted the garment without another word. Suffice it to say that the jacket

I put on that morning to visit Bennie Salazar was one clean jacket.

Bennie's building looked like a place where they could implement tough security checks if they needed to, but that day I guess they didn't need to. More of Bennie's good luck flowing down on me like honey. Not that my luck was generally so bad—I would have called it neutral, occasionally edging toward bad. For example, I caught fewer fish than Sammy, though I fished more often and had the better rod. But if it was Bennie's good luck I was getting that day, did that mean my good luck was also his good luck? That my visiting him unexpectedly was good luck for *him*? Or had I somehow managed to divert his luck and siphon it away for a time, leaving him without any luck that day? And, if I *had* managed to do the latter, how had I done it, and (most important) how could I do it forever?

I checked the directory, saw that Sow's Ear Records was on forty-five, took the elevator up there, and breezed through a pair of beige glass doors into a waiting room, which was very swank. The decor reminded me of a seventies bachelor pad: black leather couches, thick shag rug, heavy glass-and-chrome tables covered with *Vibe* and *Rolling Stone* and the like. Carefully dim lighting. This last was a must, I knew, so musicians could wait there without putting their bloodshot eyes and track marks on display.

I slapped my fish on the marble reception desk. It made a good hard wet *thwack*—I swear to God, it sounded like nothing so much as a fish. *She* (reddish hair, green eyes, flower petal mouth, the sort of chick who makes you want to lean over and say to her oh so sweetly, *You must be* really *intelli-*

gent; how else would you have gotten this job?) looked up and said, "Hi there."

"I'm here to see Bennie," I said. "Bennie Salazar."

"Is he expecting you?"

"Not at this moment."

"Your name?"

"Scotty."

She wore a headset that I realized, when she spoke into a tiny extension over her mouth, was actually a telephone. After she said my name, I caught a curl to her lips, like she was hiding a smile. "He's in a meeting," she told me. "But I can take a mess—"

"I'll wait."

I deposited my fish on the glass coffee table next to the magazines and settled into a black leather couch. Its cushions sighed out the most delicious smell of leather. A deep comfort seeped through me. I began to feel sleepy. I wanted to stay there forever, abandon my East Sixth Street apartment and live out the remainder of my life in Bennie's waiting room.

True: it had been a while since I'd spent much time in public. But was such a fact even relevant in our "information age," when you could scour planet Earth and the universe without ever leaving the green velvet couch you'd pulled from a garbage dump and made the focal point of your East Sixth Street apartment? I began each night by ordering Hunan string beans and washing them down with Jägermeister. It was amazing how many string beans I could eat: four orders, five orders, more sometimes. I could tell by the number of plastic packets of soy sauce and chopsticks included with my delivery that Fong Yu believed I was serving string beans to a party of eight or nine vegetarians. Does the chemical composition of Jägermeister cause a craving for string beans? Is there some property of string beans that becomes addictive on those rare occasions when they're consumed with Jägermeister? I asked myself these questions as I shoveled string beans into my mouth, huge crunchy forkfuls, and watched TV—weird cable shows, most of which I couldn't identify and didn't watch much of. You might say I created my own show out of all those other shows, which I suspected was actually better than the shows themselves. In fact, I was sure of it.

Here was the bottom line: if we human beings are *information processing machines*, reading X's and O's and translating that information into what people oh so breathlessly call "experience," and if I had access to all that same information via cable TV and any number of magazines that I browsed through at Hudson News for four- and five-hour stretches on my free days (my record was eight hours, including the half hour I spent manning the register during the lunch break of one of the younger employees, who thought I worked there)—if I had not only the information but the artistry to *shape* that information using the computer inside my brain (real computers scared me; if you can find Them, then They can find you, and I didn't want to be found), then, technically speaking, was I not having all the same experiences those other people were having?

I tested my theory by standing outside the public library at Fifth Avenue and Forty-second Street during a gala benefit for heart disease. I made this choice randomly: at closing time, as I was leaving the Periodicals Room, I noticed well-dressed individuals tossing white cloths over tables and carrying large orchid bouquets into the library's grand entrance hall, and when I asked a blond gal with a notepad what was going on, she told me about the gala benefit for heart disease. I went home and ate my string beans, but instead of turning on the TV that night, I took the subway back to the library, where the heart disease gala was now in full swing. I heard "Satin Doll" playing inside, I heard giggles and yelps and big scoops of laughter, I saw approximately one hundred long black limousines and shorter black town cars idling alongside the curb, and I considered the fact that nothing more than a series of atoms and molecules combined in a particular way to form something known as a *stone wall* stood between me and those people inside the public library, dancing to a horn section that was awfully weak in the tenor sax department. But a strange thing happened as I listened: I felt pain. Not in my head, not in my arm, not in my leg; everywhere at once. I told myself there was no difference between being "inside" and being "outside," that it all came down to X's and O's that could be acquired in any number of different ways, but the pain increased to a point where I thought I might collapse, and I limped away.

Like all failed experiments, that one taught me something I didn't expect: one key ingredient of so-called experience is the delusional faith that it is unique and special, that those included in it are privileged and those excluded from it are missing out. And I, like a scientist unwittingly inhaling toxic fumes from the beaker I was boiling in my lab, had, through *sheer physical proximity*, been infected by that same delusion and in my drugged state had come to believe I was Excluded: condemned to stand shivering outside the public library at Fifth Avenue and Forty-second Street forever and always, imagining the splendors within.

I went to the russet-haired receptionist's desk, balancing my fish on two hands. Juice was starting to leak through the paper. "This is a fish," I told her.

She cocked her head, a look on her face like all of a sudden she'd recognized me. "Ah," she said.

"Tell Bennie pretty soon it's gonna stink."

I sat back down. My "neighbors" in the waiting room were a male and a female, both of the corporate persuasion. I sensed them edging away from me. "I'm a musician," I said, by way of introduction. "Slide guitar."

They did not reply.

Finally Bennie came out. He looked trim. He looked fit. He wore black trousers and a white shirt buttoned at the neck but no tie. I understood something for the very first time when I looked at that shirt: I understood that expensive shirts looked better than cheap shirts. The fabric wasn't shiny, no—shiny would be cheap. But it glowed, like there was light coming through from the inside. It was a fucking beautiful shirt, is what I'm saying.

"Scotty, man, how goes it?" Bennie said, patting me warmly on the back as we shook hands. "Sorry to keep you waiting. Hope Sasha took good care of you." He gestured at the girl I'd been dealing with, whose carefree smile could be roughly translated as: *He's officially not my problem anymore.* I gave her a wink whose exact translation was: *Don't be so sure, darling.*

"Here, c'mon back to my office," Bennie said. He had his arm around my shoulders and was steering me toward a hallway.

"Hey wait—I forgot!" I cried, and ran back to get the fish. As I slung the bag from the coffee table into my hands a little fish juice flew from one corner, and the corporate types both jumped to their feet as if it were nuclear runoff. I looked over at "Sasha," expecting to find her cowering, but she was watching it all with a look I would have to call amused.

Bennie waited for me by the hall. I noticed, with satisfaction, that his skin had gotten more brown since high school. I'd read about this: your skin gradually darkens from all those cumulative years of sunlight, and Bennie's had done so to a point where calling him Caucasian was a stretch.

"Shopping?" he asked, eyeing my bundle.

"Fishing," I told him.

Bennie's office was awesome, and I don't mean that in the male teenage skateboarding sense—I mean it in the old-fashioned literal sense. The desk was a giant jet black oval with a wet-looking surface like the most expensive pianos have. It reminded me of a black ice-skating rink. Behind the desk was nothing but view—the whole city flung out in front of us the way street vendors fling out their towels packed with cheap, glittery watches and belts. That's how New York looked: like a gorgeous, easy thing to have, even for me. I stood just inside the door, holding my fish. Bennie went around to the other side of the wet black oval of his desk. It looked frictionless, like you could slide a coin over the surface and it would float to the edge and drop to the floor. "Have a seat, Scotty," he said.

"Wait," I said. "This is for you." I came forward and gently set the fish on his desk. I felt like I was leaving an offering at a Shinto shrine on top of the tallest mountain in Japan. The view was tripping me out.

"You're giving me a fish?" Bennie said. "That's a fish?"

"Striped bass. I caught it in the East River this morning."

Bennie looked at me like he was waiting for a cue to laugh.

"It's not as polluted as people think," I said, sitting down on a small black chair, one of two facing Bennie's desk.

He stood, picked up the fish, came around his desk, and handed it back to me. "Thanks, Scotty," he said. "I appreciate the thought, I really do. But a fish is bound to go to waste, here at my office."

"Take it home and eat it!" I said.

Bennie smiled his peaceful smile, but he made no move to retrieve the fish. Fine, I thought, I'll eat it myself.

My black chair had looked uncomfortable—I'd thought, lowering myself onto it, This is going to be one of those hellish chairs that makes your ass ache and then go numb. But it was without question the most comfortable chair I had ever sat in, even more comfortable than the leather couch in the waiting room. The couch had put me to sleep—this chair was making me levitate.

"Talk to me, Scotty," Bennie said. "You have a demo tape you want me to hear? You've got an album, a band? Songs you're looking to have produced? What's on your mind."

He was leaning against the front of the black lozenge, ankles crossed—one of those poses that appears to be very relaxed but is actually very tense. As I looked up at him, I experienced several realizations, all in a sort of cascade: (1) Bennie and I weren't friends anymore, and we never would be. (2) He was looking to get rid of me as quickly as possible with the least amount of hassle. (3) I already knew that would happen. I'd known it before I arrived. (4) It was the reason I had come to see him.

"Scotty? You still there?"

"So," I said. "You're a big shot now, and everyone wants something from you."

Bennie went back around to his desk chair and sat there facing me with arms folded in a pose that looked less relaxed than the first one, but was actually more so. "Come on, Scotty," he said. "You write me a letter out of nowhere, now you show up at my office—I'm guessing you didn't come here just to bring me a fish."

"No, that was a gift," I said. "I came for this reason: I want to know what happened between A and B."

Bennie seemed to be waiting for more.

"A is when we were both in the band, chasing the same girl. B is now."

I knew instantly that it had been the right move to bring up Alice. I'd said something literally, yes, but underneath that I'd said something else: we were both a couple of asswipes, and now only I'm an asswipe; why? And underneath that, something else: once an asswipe, always an asswipe. And deepest of all: You were the one chasing. But she picked me.

"I've busted my balls," Bennie said. "That's what happened."

"Ditto."

We looked at each other across the black desk, the seat of Bennie's power. There was a long, strange pause, and in that pause I felt myself pulling Bennie back—or maybe it was him pulling me—back to San Francisco, where we were two out of four Flaming Dildos, Bennie one of the lousier bass players you were likely to hear, a kid with brownish skin and hair on his hands, and my best friend. I felt a kick of anger so violent it made me dizzy. I closed my eyes and imagined coming at Bennie across that desk and ripping off his head, yanking it from the neck of that beautiful white shirt like a knobby weed with long tangled roots. I pictured carrying it into his swank waiting room by his bushy hair and dropping it on Sasha's desk.

I rose from my chair, but at that same moment, Bennie got up, too—sprang up, I should say, because when I looked at him, he was already standing.

"Mind if I look out your window?" I asked.

"Not at all." He didn't sound afraid, but I smelled that he was. Vinegar: that's what fear smells like.

I went to the window. I pretended to look at the view, but my eyes were closed.

After a while, I sensed that Bennie had moved closer to me. "You still doing any music, Scotty?" he asked gently.

"I try," I said. "Mostly by myself, just to keep loose." I was able to open my eyes, but not to look at him.

"You were amazing on that guitar," he said. Then he asked, "Are you married?"

"Divorced. From Alice."

"I know," he said. "I meant remarried."

"It lasted four years."

"I'm sorry, buddy."

"All for the best," I said. Then I turned to look at Bennie. He was standing with his back to the window, and I wondered if he ever bothered to look out, if having so much beauty at close range meant anything at all to him. "What about you?" I asked.

"Married. Three-month-old son." He smiled, then—a waffly, embarrassed smile at the thought of his baby boy, like he knew he didn't deserve that much. And behind Bennie's smile the fear was still there: that I'd tracked him down to snatch away these gifts life had shoveled upon him, wipe them out in a few emphatic seconds. This made me want to scream with laughter: *Hey "buddy," don't you get it? There's nothing you have that I don't have! It's all just X's and O's, and you can come by those a million different ways.* But two thoughts distracted me as I stood there, smelling Bennie's fear: (1) I didn't have what Bennie had. (2) He was right.

Instead, I thought of Alice. This was something I almost never let myself do—just think of her, as opposed to think about *not* thinking about her, which I did almost constantly. The thought of Alice broke open in me, and I let it fan out until I saw her hair in the sun—gold, her hair was gold—and I smelled those oils she used to dab on her wrists with a dropper. Patchouli? Musk? I couldn't remember the names. I saw her face with all the love still in it, no anger, no fear—none of the sorry things I learned to make her feel. *Come inside,* her face said, and I did. For a minute, I came inside.

I looked down at the city. Its extravagance felt wasteful, like gushing oil or some other precious thing Bennie was hoarding for himself, using it up so no one else could get any. I thought: If I had a view like this to look down on every day, I would have the energy and inspiration to conquer the world. The trouble is, when you most need such a view, no one gives it to you.

I took a long inhale and turned to Bennie. "Health and happiness to you, brother," I said, and I smiled at him for the first and only time: I let my lips open and stretch back, something I very rarely do because I'm missing most of my teeth on both sides. The teeth I have are big and white, so those black gaps come as a real surprise. I saw the shock in Bennie's face when he saw. And all at once I felt strong, as if some balance had tipped in the room and all of Bennie's power—the desk, the view, the levitating chair—suddenly belonged to me. Bennie felt it too. Power is like that; everyone feels it at once.

I turned and walked toward the door, still grinning. I felt light, as if I were wearing Bennie's white shirt and light was pouring out from inside it.

"Hey, Scotty, hold on," Bennie said, sounding shaken. He veered back toward his desk, but I kept walking, my grin leading the way into the hall and back toward the reception area where Sasha sat, my shoes whispering on the carpet with each slow, dignified step. Bennie caught up with me and handed me a business card: sumptuous paper with embossed print. It felt precious. I held it very carefully. "President," I read.

"Don't be a stranger, Scotty," Bennie said. He sounded bewildered, as if he'd forgotten how I had come to be there; as if he'd invited me himself and I were leaving prematurely. "You ever have any music you want me to hear, send it on."

I couldn't resist one last look at Sasha. Her eyes were serious, almost sad, but she was still flying the flag of her pretty smile. "Take care, Scotty," she said.

Outside the building, I walked directly to the box where I had mailed my letter to Bennie a few days earlier. I bent my neck and squinted up at the tower of green glass, trying to count the floors to forty-five. And only then did I notice that my hands were empty—I'd left my fish in Bennie's office! This struck me as hilarious, and I laughed out loud, imagining the corporate types seating themselves in the levitating chairs in front of Bennie's desk, one of them lifting the wet, heavy bag from the floor and then recognizing it—*Oh, Christ, it's that guy's fish*—dropping it, revolted. And what would Bennie do? I wondered, as I walked slowly toward the subway. Would he dispose of the fish forever then and there, or would he put it in the office refrigerator and take it home that night to his wife and baby son, and tell them about my visit? And if he got that far, was it possible that he might open up the bag and take a look, just for the hell of it?

I hoped so. I knew he'd be amazed. It was a shiny, beautiful fish.

I wasn't good for much the rest of that day. I get a lot of headaches from eye damage I had as a kid, and the pain is so intense that it throws off bright, excruciating pictures. That afternoon, I lay on my bed and closed my eyes and saw a burning heart suspended in darkness, shooting off light in every direction. It wasn't a dream, because nothing happened. The heart just hung there.

· · ·

Having gone to bed in the late afternoon, I was up and out of my apartment and under the Williamsburg Bridge with my line in the East River well before sunrise. Sammy and Dave showed up soon after. Dave didn't actually care about fish—he was there to watch the East Village females on their early morning jogs, before they went to school at NYU or to work at a boutique or whatever East Village girls do with their days. Dave complained about their jog bras, which didn't allow enough bounce for his satisfaction. Sammy and I barely listened.

That morning when Dave started up, I felt an inclination to speak. "You know, Dave," I said, "I think that's the point."

"What's the point?"

"That their breasts *don't* bounce," I said. "It hurts them. That's why they wear jog bras in the first place."

He gave me a wary look. "Since when are you the expert?"

"My wife used to jog," I said.

"Used to? You mean she quit?"

"She quit being my wife. She probably still jogs."

It was a quiet morning. I heard the slow *pop, pop* of tennis balls on the courts behind the Williamsburg Bridge. Aside from the joggers and tennis players, there were usually a few junkies out by the river in the early mornings. I always looked for one particular couple, a male and female in thigh-length leather jackets, with skinny legs and ruined faces. They had to be musicians. I'd been out of the game a long time, but I could spot a musician anywhere.

The sun rose, big and shiny and round, like an angel lifting her head. I'd never seen it so brilliant out there. Silver poured over the water. I wanted to jump in and swim. Pollution? I thought. Give me some more. And then I noticed the girl. I spotted her peripherally because she was small and ran with a high, leaping gait that was different from the others. She had light brown hair, and when the sunlight touched it, something happened that you couldn't miss. Rumpelstiltskin, I thought. Dave was gaping at her, and even Sammy turned to look, but I kept my eyes on the river, watching my line for a tug. I saw the girl without having to look.

"Hey Scotty," Dave said, "I think your wife just ran by."

"I'm divorced," I said.

"Well, that was her."

"No," I said. "She lives in San Francisco."

"Maybe she's your next wife," Sammy suggested.

"She's *my* next wife," Dave said. "And you know the first thing I'm gonna teach her? Don't clamp them down. Let them *bounce*."

I looked at my line flicking in the sun. My luck was gone; I knew I wouldn't catch anything. Soon I had to be at work. I reeled in my line and began walking north along the river. The girl was already a long way ahead, her hair shaking with every step. I followed her, but at such a distance that I wasn't following her, really. I was just walking in the same direction. My eyes held her so tightly that I didn't even notice the junkie couple in my path until they'd almost passed me. They were huddled up against each other, looking haggard and sexy the way young people can for a little while, until they just look haggard. "Hey," I said, stepping in their way.

We must've seen each other twenty times on that river,

but the guy aimed his sunglasses at me like he'd never seen me before, and the girl didn't look at me at all. "Are you musicians?" I asked.

The guy turned away, shaking me off. But the girl looked up. Her eyes seemed raw, peeled away, and I wondered if the sun hurt them, and why her boyfriend or husband or whatever he was didn't give her his glasses. "He's awesome," she said, using the word in the male teenage skateboarding sense. Or maybe not, I thought. Maybe she meant it literally.

"I believe you," I said. "I believe he's an awesome musician."

I reached into my shirt pocket and took out Bennie's card. I'd used a piece of Kleenex to remove it from yesterday's jacket and place it in today's shirt, making sure not to bend or fold or smudge it. Its embossed letters reminded me of a Roman coin. "Call this man," I said. "He runs a record label. Tell him Scotty sent you."

They both looked at the card, squinting in the angled sunlight.

"Call him," I said. "He's my buddy."

"Sure," the guy said, without conviction.

"I really hope you will," I said, but I felt helpless. I could do this only once; I would never have that card again.

While the guy studied the card, the girl looked at me. "He'll call," she said, and then she smiled: small orderly teeth, the kind you only get from wearing braces. "I'll make him."

I nodded and turned, leaving the junkies behind. I walked north, forcing my eyes to see as far as they could see. But the jogger had vanished while I looked away.

"Hey," I heard behind me, two ragged voices. When I turned, they called out, "Thanks," both at the same time.

It had been a long time since anyone had thanked me for something. "Thanks," I said, to myself. I said it again and again, wanting to hold in my mind the exact sound of their voices, to feel again the kick of surprise in my chest.

Is there some quality of warm spring air that causes birds to sing more loudly? I asked myself that question as I took the overpass across the FDR onto East Sixth Street. Flowers were just coming open in the trees. I trotted underneath them, smelling their powdery pollen as I hurried toward my apartment. I wanted to drop off my jacket at the dry cleaner on my way to work—I'd been looking forward to it since yesterday. I'd left the jacket crumpled on the floor beside my bed, and I would bring it in like that, all used up. I'd toss it on the counter oh so casually, daring the gal to challenge me. But how could she?

I've been somewhere, and I need my jacket cleaned, I would say, like anyone else. And she would make it new again.

B

7

A to B

I

Stephanie and Bennie had lived in Crandale a year before they were invited to a party. It wasn't a place that warmed easily to strangers. They'd known that going in and hadn't cared—they had their own friends. But it wore on Stephanie more than she'd expected, dropping off Chris for kindergarten, waving or smiling at some blond mother releasing blond progeny from her SUV or Hummer, and getting back a pinched, quizzical smile whose translation seemed to be: *Who are you again?* How could they not know, after months of daily mutual sightings? They were snobs or idiots or both, Stephanie told herself, yet she was inexplicably crushed by their coldness.

During that first winter in town, the sister of one of Bennie's artists sponsored them for membership to the Crandale

Country Club. After a process only slightly more arduous than applying for citizenship, they were admitted in late June. They arrived at the club on their first day carrying bathing suits and towels, not realizing that the CCC (as it was known) provided its own monochromatic towels to reduce the cacophony of poolside color. In the ladies' locker room, Stephanie passed one of the blondes whose children went to Chris's school, and for the first time she got an actual "Hello," her own appearance in two separate locations having apparently fulfilled some triangulation Kathy required as proof of personhood. That was her name: Kathy. Stephanie had known it from the beginning.

Kathy was carrying a tennis racket. She wore a tiny white dress beneath which white tennis shorts, hardly more than underpants, were just visible. Her prodigious childbearing had left no mark on her narrow waist and well-tanned biceps. Her shining hair was in a tight ponytail, stray wisps secured with gold bobby pins.

Stephanie changed into her bathing suit and met Bennie and Chris near the snack bar. As they stood there uncertainly, holding their colorful towels, Stephanie recognized a distant *thop, thop* of tennis balls. The sound induced a swoon of nostalgia. Like Bennie, she came from nowhere, but a different type of nowhere—his was the urban nowhere of Daly City, California, where his parents had worked to a point of total absence while a weary grandmother raised Bennie and his four sisters. But Stephanie hailed from suburban, midwestern nowhere, and there had been a club whose snack bar served thin, greasy burgers rather than *salade niçoise* with fresh seared tuna, like this one, but where tennis had been played on sun-cracked courts, and where Stephanie had achieved a certain greatness at around age thirteen. She hadn't played since.

At the end of that first day, dopey from sun, they'd showered, changed back into their clothes, and sat on a flagstone terrace where a pianist rolled out harmless melodies on a shining upright. The sun was beginning to set. Chris tumbled on some nearby grass with two girls from his kindergarten class. Bennie and Stephanie sipped gin and tonics and watched the fireflies. "So this is what it's like," Bennie said.

A number of possible replies occurred to Stephanie: allusions to the fact that they still didn't know anyone; her suspicion that there wasn't anyone worth knowing. But she let them pass. It was Bennie who had chosen Crandale, and in some deep way Stephanie understood why: they'd flown in private jets to islands owned by rock stars, but this country club was the farthest distance Bennie had traveled from the dark-eyed grandmother in Daly City. He'd sold his record label last year; how better to mark success than by going to a place where you didn't belong?

Stephanie took Bennie's hand and kissed a knuckle. "Maybe I'll buy a tennis racket," she said.

The party invitation came three weeks later. The host, a hedge-fund manager known as Duck, had invited them after learning that Bennie had discovered the Conduits, Duck's favorite rock group, and released their albums. Stephanie had found the two deep in conversation by the pool when she returned from her first tennis lesson. "I wish they'd get back together," Duck mused. "What ever happened to that spastic guitarist?"

"Bosco? He's still recording," Bennie said tactfully. "His new album will be out in a couple of months: *A to B*. His solo work is more interior." He left out the part about Bosco being obese, alcoholic, and cancer-ridden. He was their oldest friend.

Stephanie had perched on the edge of Bennie's deck chair, flushed because she'd hit well, her topspin still intact, her serve slicingly clear. She'd noticed one or two blond heads pausing by the court to watch and had been proud of how different she looked from these women: her cropped dark hair and tattoo of a Minoan octopus encompassing one calf, her several chunky rings. Although it was also true that she'd bought a tennis dress for the occasion, slim and white, tiny white shorts underneath: the first white garment Stephanie had owned in her adult life.

At the cocktail party, she spotted Kathy—who else?— across a crowded expanse of terrace. As Stephanie was wondering whether she would again merit an actual hello or be downgraded to a crabbed *Who are you?* smile, Kathy caught her eye and began moving toward her. Introductions were made. Kathy's husband, Clay, wore seersucker shorts and a pink oxford shirt, an ensemble that might have seemed ironic on a different sort of person. Kathy wore classic navy, setting off the bright blue of her eyes. Stephanie sensed Bennie's gaze lingering on Kathy and felt herself go tense—a residual spasm of unease that passed as quickly as his attention (he was now talking to Clay). Kathy's blond hair hung loose, still bobby-pinned at the sides. Stephanie wondered idly how many bobby pins the woman went through in a week.

"I've seen you on the court," Kathy said.

"It's been a while," Stephanie said. "I'm just getting back into it."

"We should rally sometime."

"Sure," Stephanie said casually, but she felt her heartbeat in her cheeks, and when Clay and Kathy moved on she was beset by a giddiness that shamed her. It was the silliest victory of her life.

II

Within a few months, anyone would have said that Stephanie and Kathy were friends. They had a standing tennis date two mornings a week, and they'd become successful doubles partners in an interclub league, playing other blond women in small tennis dresses from nearby towns. There was an easy symmetry to their lives right down to their names—Kath and Steph, Steph and Kath—and their sons, who were in the same first-grade class. Chris and Colin, Colin and Chris; how was it that of all the names Stephanie and Bennie had considered when she was pregnant—Xanadou, Peek-a-boo, Renaldo, Cricket—they'd ended up choosing the single one that melded flawlessly with the innocuous Crandale namescape?

Kathy's elevated status in the pecking order of local blondes gave Stephanie an easy and neutral entrée, a protected status that absorbed even her short dark hair and tattoos; she was different but okay, exempt from the feral scratching that went on among some others. Stephanie would never have said that she *liked* Kathy; Kathy was a Republican, one of those people who used the unforgivable phrase "meant to be"—usually when describing her own good fortune or the disasters that had befallen other people. She knew little about Stephanie's life—would surely have been dumbstruck to learn, for example, that the celebrity reporter who had made headlines a few years back by assaulting Kitty Jackson, the young movie star, while interviewing her for *Details* magazine, was Stephanie's older brother, Jules. Occasionally Stephanie wondered whether her friend might understand more than she gave her credit for; *I know you hate us,* she imagined Kathy thinking, *and we hate you too, and now that we've resolved that, let's go rub out those bitches from Scarsdale.* Stephanie loved the tennis with a ravenous aggression that half embarrassed her; she dreamed about line calls and backhands. Kathy was still the better player, but the margin was shrinking, a fact that seemed to pique and amuse them equally. As partners and opponents, mothers and neighbors, Steph and Kath were seamlessly matched. The only problem was Bennie.

Stephanie hadn't believed him at first when he'd told her, the summer after the invasion—their second in Crandale—that he felt people giving him odd looks by the pool. She'd assumed he meant women who were admiring the clutch of brown muscles above his swim trunks, his wide dark eyes, and she'd snipped, "Since when do you have a problem with being looked at?"

But Bennie hadn't meant that, and soon Stephanie felt it too: some hesitation or question around her husband. It didn't seem to bother Bennie deeply; he'd been asked, "What kind of name is Salazar?" enough times in his life to be fairly immune to skepticism about his origins and race, and he'd perfected an arsenal of charms to obliterate that skepticism, especially in women.

Around the middle of that second summer, at another hedge-fund-fueled cocktail party, Bennie and Stephanie found themselves chatting, along with Kathy and Clay (or Cardboard, as they secretly called him) and some others, with Bill Duff, a local congressman who had come from a meeting with the Council on Foreign Relations. The topic was the presence of Al Qaeda in the New York area. Operatives were present, Bill confided, especially in the outer boroughs, possibly in communication with one another (Stephanie noticed Clay's pale eyebrows suddenly lift, and his head gave a single odd jerk, as if he had water in one ear), but the question was: how strong a link did they have to the mother ship—here Bill laughed—because any kook with a grudge could call himself Al Qaeda, but if he lacked money, training, backup (Clay gave another quick head shake, then flicked his eyes at Bennie, to his right), it made no sense to allocate resources . . .

Bill paused midsentence, clearly baffled. Another couple broke in, and Bennie took Stephanie's arm and moved away. His eyes looked placid, almost sleepy, but his grip hurt her wrist.

They left the party soon after. Bennie paid the babysitter, a sixteen-year-old nicknamed Scooter, and drove her home. He was back before Stephanie had even glanced at the clock and reflected on Scooter's prettiness. She heard him setting the burglar alarm; then he thundered upstairs in a way that made Sylph, the cat, dive under the bed in terror. Stephanie ran from the bedroom and met Bennie at the top of the stairs. "What the fuck am I doing here?" he cried.

"Shh. You'll wake up Chris."

"It's a horror show!"

"That was ugly," she said, "although Clay's an extr—"

"You're *defending* them?"

"Of course not. But he's one guy."

"You think everyone in that group didn't know what was going on?"

Stephanie was afraid that it might be true—had they all known? She wanted Bennie not to think so. "That's totally paranoid. Even Kathy says—"

"Again! Look at you!"

He stood at the top of the stairs with fists clenched. Stephanie went to him and took him in her arms, and Bennie relaxed against her, almost knocking her over. They held each other until his breathing slowed. Stephanie said softly, "Let's move."

Bennie pulled back, startled.

"I mean it," she said. "I don't give a shit about these people. It was an experiment, right? Moving to a place like this."

Bennie didn't answer. He looked around them at the floors, whose rose parquet designs he'd sanded himself on hands and knees, not trusting whomever they might pay for such intricate work; at the windows in their bedroom door that he'd spent weeks excavating with a razor from under layers of paint; at the stairwell nooks he'd ruminated over, placing one *objet* after another inside and adjusting the lights. His father had been an electrician; Bennie could light anything.

"Let *them* move," he said. "This is my fucking house."

"Fine. But if it comes to that, I'm saying we can go. To-morrow. In a month. In a year."

"I want to die here," Bennie said.

"Jesus," Stephanie said, at which point they were stung by sudden, itchy laughter that soon became hysterics, both of them doubled over on the parquet, shushing each other.

So they'd stayed. After that, when Bennie noticed Steph-anie putting on her tennis whites in the morning, he'd say, "Going to play with the fascists?" Stephanie knew he wanted her to quit, renounce her partnership with Kathy to protest Cardboard's bigotry and idiocy. But Stephanie had no inten-tion of quitting. If they were going to live in a place whose so-cial life revolved around a country club, she sure as hell was going to stay on good terms with the woman who guaranteed her easy assimilation. She had no wish to be an outcast like Noreen, their neighbor to the right, who had clanging man-nerisms and wore oversize sunglasses, whose hands shook violently—from medication, Stephanie presumed. Noreen had three lovely, anxious children, but none of the women talked to her. She was a ghost. No thank you, Stephanie thought.

In the fall, when the weather cooled, she began arranging her tennis games for later in the day, when Bennie wouldn't be home to see her change clothes. Now that she was work-ing freelance for La Doll's PR firm, scheduling Manhattan meetings as she wished, this was easy. It was slightly decep-tive, of course, but only through omission—to protect Ben-nie from knowledge that distressed him. Stephanie never denied having played if he asked. And besides, hadn't he engaged in his share of deceptions over the years? Didn't he owe her a few of her own?

III

The following spring, Stephanie's older brother, Jules, was paroled from Attica Correctional Facility and came to live with them. He'd been gone five years, the first on Rikers Island awaiting trial for the attempted rape of Kitty Jackson, another four after the rape charge was dropped (at Kitty Jackson's request) and he was convicted of kidnapping and aggravated assault—outrageous, given that the starlet had walked into Central Park with Jules of her own free will and sustained not a single injury. In fact, she'd ended up testifying for the *defense*. But the DA had persuaded the jury that Kitty's support for Jules was a version of Stockholm syndrome. "The fact that she insists on protecting this man is further evidence of how deeply he has hurt her. . . ." Stephanie recalled him intoning at her brother's trial, which she'd watched over ten agonizing days, trying to look upbeat.

In prison, Jules had seemed to regain the composure he'd lost so spectacularly in the months before the assault. He went on medication for his bipolar disorder and made peace with the end of his marriage engagement. He edited a weekly prison newspaper, and his coverage of the impact of 9/11 on the lives of inmates won him a special citation from the PEN Prison Writing Program. Jules had been allowed to come to New York and receive the award, and Bennie, Stephanie, and her parents had all wept through his halting acceptance speech. He'd taken up basketball, shed his gut, and miraculously overcome his eczema. He seemed ready, finally, to resume the serious journalism career he'd come to New York more than twenty years before to pursue. When the parole board granted his early release, Stephanie and Bennie had joyfully offered to house him while he got back on his feet.

But now, two months after Jules's arrival, an ominous stasis had set in. He'd had a few interviews early on that he'd approached in a state of sweaty terror, but nothing had come of them. Jules doted on Chris, spending hours while Chris was at school assembling vast cities out of microscopic Lego pieces to surprise him when he returned. But with Stephanie, her brother maintained a sardonic distance, seeming to regard her futile scurrying (this morning, for example, as the three of them rushed toward school and work) with wry bemusement. His hair was straggly and his face looked deflated, sapped in a way that pained Stephanie.

"You driving into the city?" Bennie asked, as she hustled breakfast plates into the sink.

She wasn't driving in—yet. As the weather warmed, she'd resumed her morning tennis games with Kathy. But she'd found a clever new way to edit these games out of Bennie's view; she kept her tennis whites at the club, dressed for work in the morning, kissed him good-bye, then proceeded to the club to change and play. Stephanie minimized the deception by making the lie purely chronological; if Bennie asked where she was going, she always cited an actual meeting that would take place later on that day, so if he inquired in the evening how it had gone, she could answer honestly.

"I'm meeting Bosco at ten," she said. Bosco was the only rocker whose PR she still handled. The meeting was actually at three.

"Bosco, before noon?" Bennie asked. "Was that his idea?"

Stephanie instantly saw her mistake; Bosco spent his nights in an alcoholic fog; the chances of his being conscious at 10:00 a.m. were nil. "I think so," she said, the act of lying to her husband's face bringing on a tingly vertigo. "You're right, though. It's weird."

"It's scary," Bennie said. He kissed Stephanie good-bye and headed for the door with Chris. "Will you call me after you see him?"

In that moment, Stephanie knew she would cancel her game with Kathy—stand Kathy up, in essence—and drive to Manhattan to meet Bosco at ten. There was no other way.

When they'd gone, Stephanie felt the tension that always seemed to arise when she was alone with Jules, her own unspoken questions about his plans and timetable clashing silently with his armature against them. Beyond Lego assembly, it was hard to know what Jules did all day. Twice Stephanie had come home to find the TV in her bedroom tuned to a porn channel, and this had so disturbed her that she'd asked Bennie to bring the extra set to the guest room, where Jules was staying.

She went upstairs and left a voice mail on Kathy's cell phone canceling their game. When she returned to the kitchen, Jules was peering out the window of the breakfast nook. "What's the deal with your neighbor?" he asked.

"Noreen?" Stephanie said. "We think she's nuts."

"She's doing something near your fence."

Stephanie went to the window. It was true; she glimpsed Noreen's overbleached ponytail—like a caricature of everyone else's subtly natural highlights—moving up and down beside the fence. Her giant black sunglasses gave her the cartoonish look of a fly, or a space alien. Stephanie shrugged, impatient with Jules for even having the time to fixate on Noreen. "I've got to run," she said.

"Can I hitch a ride to the city?"

Stephanie felt a little pop in her chest. "Of course," she said. "You have a meeting?"

"Not really. I just feel like getting out."

As they walked to the car, Jules glanced behind them and said, "I think she's watching us. Noreen. Through the fence."

"Wouldn't surprise me."

"You just let that go on?"

"What can we do? She's not hurting us. She's not even on our property."

"She could be dangerous."

"Takes one to know one, eh?"

"Not nice," Jules said.

In the Volvo, Stephanie slipped an advance copy of Bosco's new album, *A to B*, into the CD player out of some sense that in doing so she was strengthening her alibi. Bosco's recent albums consisted of gnarled little ditties accompanied by a ukulele. It was only out of friendship that Bennie still released them.

"Can I please turn this off?" Jules asked after two songs, then did so before Stephanie had answered. "This is who we're going to see?"

"*We?* I thought you were hitching a ride."

"Can I come with you?" Jules asked. "Please?"

He sounded humble and plaintive: a man with nowhere to go and nothing to do. Stephanie wanted to scream; was this some kind of punishment for lying to Bennie? In the past thirty minutes she'd been forced to cancel a tennis game she was dying to play, piss Kathy off, embark on an invented errand to visit a person who was sure to be unconscious, and now bring her rudderless, hypercritical brother along to witness the demise of her alibi. "I'm not sure how much fun it'll be," she said.

"That's okay," Jules said. "I'm used to not-fun."

He watched nervously as Stephanie maneuvered from the Hutch onto the Cross Bronx Expressway; being in the car seemed to worry him. When they had fully entered the flow of traffic, he asked, "Are you having an affair?"

Stephanie stared at him. "You're out of your mind."

"Watch the road!"

"Why are you asking me that?"

"You seem jumpy. You and Bennie both. Not like I remember you guys."

Stephanie was stricken. "Bennie seems jumpy?" The old fear rose in her so quickly, like a hand at her throat, despite Bennie's promise two years ago, when he turned forty, and the fact that she had no reason to doubt him.

"You seem, I don't know. Polite."

"Compared to people in prison?"

Jules smiled. "Okay," he said. "Maybe it's just the place. Crandale, New York," he said, elongating the words. "I'll bet it's crawling with Republicans."

"About half and half."

Jules turned to her, incredulous. "Do you *socialize* with Republicans?"

"It happens, Jules."

"You and Bennie? Hanging out with *Republicans*?"

"Are you aware that you're shouting?"

"Watch the road!" Jules bellowed.

Stephanie did, her hands shaking on the wheel. She felt like turning around and taking her brother back home, but that would involve missing her nonexistent meeting.

"I go away for a few years and the whole fucking world is upside down," Jules said angrily. "Buildings are missing. You get strip-searched every time you go to someone's office. Everybody sounds stoned, because they're e-mailing people the whole time they're talking to you. Tom and Nicole are with different people. . . . And now my rock-and-roll sister and her husband are hanging around with *Republicans*. What the fuck!"

Stephanie took a long, calming breath. "What are your plans, Jules?"

"I told you. I want to come with you and meet this—"

"I mean what are you going to *do*."

There was a long pause. Finally Jules said, "I have no idea."

Stephanie glanced at him. They'd turned onto the Henry Hudson Parkway, and Jules was looking at the river, his face devoid of energy or hope. She felt a contraction of fear around her heart. "When you first came to New York," she said, "all those years ago, you were full of ideas."

Jules snorted. "Who isn't, at twenty-four?"

"I mean you had a direction."

He'd graduated from the University of Michigan a couple of years before. One of Stephanie's freshman suitemates at NYU had left school for treatment of anorexia, and Jules had occupied the girl's room for three months, wandering the city with a notebook, crashing parties at the *Paris Review.* By the time the anorexic returned, he'd gotten himself a job at *Harper's,* an apartment on Eighty-first and York, and three roommates—two of whom now edited magazines. The third had won a Pulitzer.

"I don't get it, Jules," Stephanie said. "I don't get what happened to you."

Jules stared at the glittering skyline of Lower Manhattan without recognition. "I'm like America," he said.

Stephanie swung around to look at him, unnerved. "What are you talking about?" she said. "Are you off your meds?"

"Our hands are dirty," Jules said.

IV

Stephanie parked in a lot on Sixth Avenue, and she and Jules picked their way into Soho through crowds of shoppers holding room-sized bags from Crate and Barrel. "So. Who the hell is this Bosco person?" Jules asked.

"Remember the Conduits? He was the guitarist."

Jules stopped walking. *"That's* who we're going to see? Bosco from the Conduits? The skinny redhead?"

"Yeah, well. He's changed a little."

They turned south on Wooster, heading for Canal. Sunlight skipped off the cobblestones, releasing in Stephanie's mind a pale balloon of memory: shooting the Conduits' first album cover on this very street, laughing, jittery, Bosco powdering his freckles while the photographer fiddled. The memory mooned her as she rang Bosco's bell and waited, praying silently: *Please don't be home please don't answer please*. Then at least the charade part of the day would be over.

No voice on the intercom, just a buzz. Stephanie pushed open the door with a disoriented sense that maybe she *had* arranged to meet Bosco at ten. Or had she pressed the wrong bell?

They went in and called for the elevator. It took a long time to descend, grinding inside its tube. "Is that thing healthy?" Jules asked.

"You're welcome to wait down here."

"Quit trying to get rid of me."

Bosco was unrecognizable as the scrawny, stovepipe-panted practitioner of a late-eighties sound somewhere between punk and ska, a hive of redheaded mania who had made Iggy Pop look indolent onstage. More than once, club owners had called 911 during Conduits shows, convinced that Bosco was having a seizure.

Nowadays he was huge—from medications, he claimed, both postcancer and antidepressant—but a glance into his trash can nearly always revealed an empty gallon box of Dreyer's Rocky Road ice cream. His red hair had devolved into a stringy gray ponytail. An unsuccessful hip replacement had left him with the lurching, belly-hoisting walk of a refrigerator on a hand truck. Still, he was awake, dressed— even shaven. The blinds of his loft were up and a tinge of shower humidity hung in the air, pleasantly cut by the smell of brewing coffee.

"I was expecting you at three," Bosco said.

"I thought we said ten," Stephanie said, looking inside her purse to avoid his gaze. "Did I get the time wrong?"

Bosco was no fool; he knew she was lying. But he was curious, and his curiosity fell naturally on Jules. Stephanie introduced them.

"It's an honor," Jules said gravely.

Bosco scrutinized him for signs of irony before shaking his hand.

Stephanie perched on a folding chair near the black leather recliner where Bosco spent the bulk of his time. It was positioned by a dusty window through which the Hudson River and even a bit of Hoboken were visible. Bosco brought Stephanie coffee and then began a juddering immersion into his chair, which suctioned around him in a gelatinous grip. They were meeting to discuss PR for *A to B*. Now that Bennie had corporate bosses to answer to, he couldn't spend a dime on Bosco beyond the cost of producing and shipping his CD. So Bosco paid Stephanie by the hour to act as his publicist and booking agent. These were mostly symbolic titles; he'd been too sick to do much of anything for the last two albums, and his lassitude had been roughly matched by the world's indifference toward him.

"Whole different story this time," Bosco began. "I'm going to make you *work*, Stephi-babe. This album is going to be my comeback."

Stephanie assumed he was joking. But he met her gaze evenly from within the folds of black leather.

"Comeback?" she asked.

Jules had been wandering the loft, eyeing the framed gold and platinum Conduit albums paving the walls, the few guitars Bosco hadn't sold off, and his collection of pre-Columbian artifacts, which he hoarded in pristine glass cases and refused to sell. At the word "comeback," Stephanie felt her brother's attention suddenly engage.

"The album's called *A to B*, right?" Bosco said. "And that's the question I want to hit straight on: how did I go from being a rock star to being a fat fuck no one cares about? Let's not pretend it didn't happen."

Stephanie was too startled to respond.

"I want interviews, features, you name it," Bosco went on. "Fill up my life with that shit. Let's document every fucking humiliation. This is reality, right? You don't look good anymore twenty years later, especially when you've had half your guts removed. Time's a goon, right? Isn't that the expression?"

Jules had drifted over from across the room. "I've never heard that," he said. "'Time is a goon'?"

"Would you disagree?" Bosco said, a little challengingly.

There was a pause. "No," Jules said.

"Look," Stephanie said, "I love your honesty, Bosco—"

"Don't give me 'I love your honesty, Bosco,'" he said. "Don't get all PR-y on me."

"I'm your publicist," Stephanie reminded him.

"Yeah, but don't start believing that shit," Bosco said. "You're too old."

"I was trying to be tactful," Stephanie said. "The bottom line is, no one cares that your life has gone to hell, Bosco. It's a joke that you think this is interesting. If you were still a rock star, it might be, but you aren't a rock star—you're a relic."

"That is *harsh*," Jules said.

Bosco laughed. "She's pissed that I called her old."

"True," Stephanie admitted.

Jules looked from one to the other, uneasy. Any sort of conflict seemed to rattle him.

"Look," Stephanie said, "I can tell you this is a great, innovative idea and let it die on its own, or I can level with you: It's a ridiculous idea. Nobody cares."

"You haven't heard the idea yet," Bosco said.

Jules carried over a folding chair and sat down. "I want to tour," Bosco said. "Like I used to, doing all the same stuff on-stage. I'm going to move like I moved before, only more so."

Stephanie put down her cup. She wished Bennie were here; only Bennie could appreciate the depth of self-delusion she was witnessing. "Let me get this straight," she said. "You want to do a lot of interviews and press around the fact that you're an ailing and decrepit shadow of your former self. And then you want to do a tour—"

"A national tour."

"A national tour, performing as if you *were* that former self."

"Bingo."

Stephanie took a deep breath. "I see a few problems, Bosco."

"I thought you might," he said, winking at Jules. "Shoot."

"Well, number one, getting a writer interested in this is going to be tough."

"I'm interested," Jules said, "and I'm a writer."

God help me, Stephanie almost said, but restrained herself. She hadn't heard her brother call himself a writer in many years.

"Okay, so you've got one writer interested—"

"He gets everything," Bosco said. He turned to Jules. "You get everything. Total access. You can watch me take a shit if you want to."

Jules swallowed. "I'll think about it."

"I'm just saying, there are no limits."

"Okay," Stephanie began again, "so you've—"

"You can film me, too," Bosco told Jules. "You can make a documentary, if you're interested."

Jules was starting to look afraid.

"Can I finish a fucking sentence, here?" Stephanie asked. "You've got a writer for this story that will be of no interest to anyone—"

"Can you believe this is my *publicist*?" Bosco asked Jules. "Should I fire her?"

"Good luck finding someone else," Stephanie said. "Now, about the tour."

Bosco was grinning, sealed inside his glutinous chair that for anyone else would have qualified as a couch. She felt sudden pity for him. "Getting bookings isn't going to be easy," she said gently. "I mean, you haven't toured in a while, you're not . . . You say you want to perform like before, but . . ." Bosco was laughing in her face, but Stephanie soldiered on. "Physically, you aren't—I mean, your health . . ." She was dancing around the fact that Bosco wasn't remotely capable of performing in his old manner, and that trying to do so would kill him—probably sooner rather than later.

"Don't you get it, Steph?" Bosco finally exploded. "That's the *whole point*. We know the outcome, but we don't know when, or where, or who will be there when it finally happens. It's a Suicide Tour."

Stephanie started to laugh. The idea struck her as inexplicably funny. But Bosco was abruptly serious. "I'm done," he said. "I'm old, I'm sad—that's on a good day. I want out of this mess. But I don't want to fade away, I want to *flame* away—I want my death to be an attraction, a spectacle, a mystery. A work of art. Now, Lady PR," he said, gathering up his drooping flesh and leaning toward her, eyes glittering in his overblown head, "you try to tell me no one's going to be interested in that. Reality TV, hell—it doesn't get any realer than this. Suicide is a weapon; that we all know. But what about an art?"

He watched Stephanie anxiously: a big, ailing man with one bold idea left, ablaze with hope that she would like it. There was a long pause while Stephanie tried to assemble her thoughts.

Jules spoke first: "It's genius."

Bosco eyed him tenderly, moved by his own speech and moved to find that Jules was also moved.

"Look, guys," Stephanie said. She was aware of a perverse flicker of thought in herself: If this idea did, somehow, have legs (which it almost certainly did not—it was crazy, maybe illegal, unsavory to the point of grotesqueness), then she'd want to get a *real* writer on it.

"Uh nuh nuh nuh," Bosco told her, wagging a finger as if she'd spoken this rogue qualm aloud. With sighs and groans and refusals of their offers of help, he heaved himself from his chair, which made small whimpering noises of release, and staggered across the room. He reached a cluttered desk and leaned against it, panting audibly. Then he rummaged for paper and pen.

"What's your name again?" he called.

"Jules. Jules Jones."

Bosco wrote for several minutes.

"Okay," he said, then made his laborious return and handed the paper to Jules. Jules read it aloud: "I, Bosco, of sound mind and body, hereby grant to you, Jules Jones, sole and exclusive media rights to cover the story of my decline and Suicide Tour."

Bosco's exertions had left him spent. He sagged against his chair, reeling in breath, his eyes closed. Bosco the demented scarecrow performer appeared spectrally, naughtily in Stephanie's mind, disowning the morose behemoth before them. A wave of sadness felled her.

Bosco opened his eyes and looked at Jules. "There," he said. "It's yours."

At lunch in MoMA's sculpture garden, Jules was a man reborn: jazzed, juiced, riffing his thoughts on the newly renovated museum. He'd gone straight to the gift shop and bought a datebook and pen (both covered with Magritte clouds) to record his appointment with Bosco at ten the next morning.

Stephanie ate her turkey wrap and gazed at Picasso's *She-Goat*, wishing she could share her brother's elation. It felt impossible, as if Jules's excitement were being siphoned from

inside her, leaving Stephanie drained to the exact degree
that he was invigorated. She found herself wishing, inanely,
that she hadn't missed her tennis game.

"What's the matter?" Jules finally asked, chugging his
third cranberry and soda. "You seem down."

"I don't know," Stephanie said.

He leaned toward her, her big brother, and Stephanie had
a flash of how they'd been as kids, an almost-physical sense
of Jules as her protector, her watchdog, coming to her tennis
matches and massaging her calves when they cramped. That
feeling had been buried under Jules's chaotic intervening
years, but now it pushed back up, warm and vital, sending
tears into Stephanie's eyes.

Her brother looked stunned. "Steph," he said, taking her
hand, "what's wrong?"

"I feel like everything is ending," she said.

She was thinking of the old days, as she and Bennie now
called them—not just pre-Crandale but premarriage, pre-
parenthood, premoney, pre–hard drug renunciation, prere-
sponsibility of any kind, when they were still kicking around
the Lower East Side with Bosco, going to bed after sunrise,
turning up at strangers' apartments, having sex in quasi
public, engaging in daring acts that had more than once included (for her) shooting heroin, because none of it was serious. They were young and lucky and strong—what did they
have to worry about? If they didn't like the result, they could
go back and start again. And now Bosco was sick, hardly able
to move, feverishly planning his death. Was this outcome a
freak aberration from natural laws, or was it normal—a thing

they should have seen coming? Had they somehow brought it on?

Jules put his arm around her. "If you'd asked me this morning, I would have said we were finished," he said. "All of us, the whole country—the fucking world. But now I feel the opposite."

Stephanie knew. She could practically hear the hope sluicing through her brother. "So what's the answer?" she asked.

"Sure, everything is ending," Jules said, "but not yet."

V

Stephanie got through her next meeting, with a designer of small patent-leather purses; then ignored a warning instinct and stopped by the office. Her boss, La Doll, was on the phone, as always, but she muted the call and yelled from her office, "What's wrong?"

"Nothing," Stephanie said, startled. She was still in the hall.

"All good with Purse-Man?" La Doll kept effortless track of her employees' schedules, even freelancers like Stephanie.

"Just fine."

La Doll finished her call, shot some espresso from the Krups machine on her desk into her bottomless thimble-sized cup, and called, "Come, Steph."

Stephanie entered her boss's soaring corner office. La Doll was one of those people who seem, even to those who know them well, digitally enhanced: the bright blond bob cut; the predatory lipstick; the roving, algorithmic eyes. "Next time," she said, tweezing Stephanie briefly with her gaze, "cancel the meeting."

"I'm sorry?"

"I could feel your gloom from the hall," La Doll said. "It's like having the flu. Don't expose the clients."

Stephanie laughed. She had known her boss forever— long enough to know that she was absolutely serious. "God, you're a bitch," she said.

La Doll chuckled, already dialing again. "It's a burden," she said.

Stephanie drove back to Crandale (Jules had taken the train) to pick up Chris at soccer practice. At seven, her son was still willing to throw his arms around Stephanie after a day apart. She hugged him, breathing the wheaty smell of his hair. "Is Uncle Jules home?" Chris asked. "Was he building anything?"

"Actually, Uncle Jules worked today," she said, feeling a prick of pride as she spoke the words. "He was working in the city."

The day's vicissitudes had resolved into a single droning wish to talk to Bennie. Stephanie had spoken with Sasha, his assistant, whom she'd long distrusted as the gatekeeper of Bennie's misbehavior but grown fond of in the years since his reform. Bennie had called on his way home, stuck in traffic, but by then Stephanie wanted to explain it in person. She pictured laughing with Bennie about Bosco and feeling her strange unhappiness lift. One thing she knew: she was finished with lying about the tennis.

Bennie still wasn't home when she and Chris got back. Jules appeared with a basketball and challenged Chris to a game of horse, and they repaired to the driveway, the garage door shuddering from their blows. The sun was beginning to set.

Bennie finally returned and went straight upstairs to shower. Stephanie put some frozen chicken thighs in warm water to thaw, then followed him up. Steam drifted from the open bathroom door into their bedroom, twirling in the last rays of sun. Stephanie felt like showering, too—they had a double shower with handmade fixtures whose exorbitant price they'd argued over. But Bennie had been adamant.

She kicked off her shoes and unbuttoned her blouse, tossing it on the bed with Bennie's clothes. The contents of his pockets were scattered on the small antique table where he always left them. Stephanie glanced at what was there, an old habit left over from the days when she'd lived in suspicion. Coins, gum wrappers, a parking garage ticket. As she moved away, something stuck to the bottom of her bare foot. She plucked it off—a bobby pin—and headed for the wastebasket. Before dropping it in, she glanced at the pin: generic light gold, identical to bobby pins you'd find in the corners of nearly any Crandale woman's house. Except her own.

Stephanie paused, holding the pin. There were a thousand reasons it could be here—a party they'd had, friends who might have come up to use the bathroom, the cleaning woman—but Stephanie knew whose it was as if she had already known, as if she weren't discovering the fact but remembering it. She sank onto the bed in her skirt and bra, hot and shivery, blinking from shock. Of course. It took no imagination at all to see how everything had converged: pain; revenge; power; desire. He'd slept with Kathy. Of course.

Stephanie pulled her shirt back on and buttoned it carefully, still holding the bobby pin. She went into the bathroom, searching out Bennie's lean brown shape through the steam and running water. He hadn't seen her. And then she stopped, halted by a sense of dreadful familiarity, of knowing everything they would say: the jagged trek from denial to self-lacerating apology for Bennie; from rage to bruised acceptance for herself. She had thought they would never make that trek again. Had truly believed it.

She left the bathroom and tossed the pin in the trash. She slipped noiselessly down the front stairs in her bare feet. Jules and Chris were in the kitchen, glugging water from the Brita. Her only thought was of getting away, as if she were carrying a live grenade from inside the house, so that when it exploded, it would destroy just herself.

The sky was electric blue above the trees, but the yard felt dark. Stephanie went to the edge of the lawn and sat, her forehead on her knees. The grass and soil were still warm from the day. She wanted to cry but she couldn't. The feeling was too deep.

She lay down, curled on her side in the grass, as if she were shielding the damaged part of herself, or trying to contain the pain that issued from it. Every turn of her thoughts increased her sense of horror, her belief that she couldn't recover, had no more resources to draw on. Why was this worse than the other times? But it was.

She heard Bennie's voice from the kitchen: "Steph?"

She got up and staggered into a flowerbed. She and Bennie had planted it together: gladioli, hosta, black-eyed Susans. She heard stems crunching under her feet, but she didn't look down. She went all the way to the fence and knelt in the dirt.

"Mom?" Chris's voice, from upstairs. Stephanie covered her ears.

Then came another voice, so close to Stephanie that she heard it even through her hands. It spoke in a whisper: "Hello there."

It took her a moment to separate this new, nearby voice from the ones inside the house. She felt no fear, only a kind of numb curiosity. "Who's that?"

"It's me."

Stephanie realized her eyes were shut. She opened them now and looked through the slats of fence. Amid the shadows she made out Noreen's white face peeking through from the other side. She'd taken off her sunglasses; Stephanie vaguely noted a pair of skittish eyes. "Hi Noreen," she said.

"I like to sit in this spot," Noreen said.

"I know."

Stephanie wanted to move away, but she couldn't seem to move. She closed her eyes again. Noreen didn't speak, and as the minutes passed she seemed to fade into the rummaging breeze and chatter of insects, as if the night itself were alive. Stephanie hunched in the dirt for a long time, or what felt like a long time—maybe it was only a minute. She knelt until the calling started up again—Jules too, his panicked voice careening through the dark. At last she tottered to her feet. In unfolding herself, she felt the painful thing settle inside her. Her knees shook from its new, awkward weight.

"Good night, Noreen," she said as she began picking her way back through the flowers and bushes toward the house.

"Good night," she faintly heard.

8

Selling the General

Dolly's first big idea was the hat. She picked teal blue, fuzzy, with flaps that came down over the general's large dried-apricot ears. The ears were unsightly, Dolly thought, and best covered up.

When she saw the general's picture in the *Times* a few days later, she almost choked on her poached egg: he looked like a baby, a big sick baby with a giant mustache and a double chin. The headline couldn't have been worse:

GENERAL B.'s ODD HEADGEAR SPURS CANCER RUMORS
LOCAL UNREST GROWS

Dolly bolted to her feet in her dingy kitchen and turned in a frantic circle, spilling tea on her bathrobe. She looked wildly at the general's picture. And then she realized: the ties. They hadn't cut off the ties under the hat as she'd instructed, and a big fuzzy bow under the general's double chin was disastrous. Dolly ran barefoot into her office/bedroom and began plowing through fax pages, trying to unearth the most recent sequence of numbers she was supposed to call to reach Arc, the general's human relations captain. The general moved a lot to avoid assassination, but Arc was meticulous about faxing Dolly their updated contact information. These faxes usually came at around 3:00 a.m., waking Dolly and sometimes her daughter, Lulu. Dolly never mentioned the disruption; the general and his team were under the impression that she was the top publicist in New York, a woman whose fax machine would be in a corner office with a panoramic view of New York City (as indeed it had been for many years), not ten inches away from the foldout sofa where she slept. Dolly could only attribute their misapprehension to some dated article that had drifted their way from *Vanity Fair* or *InStyle* or *People,* where Dolly had been written about and profiled under her then moniker: La Doll.

The first call from the general's camp had come just in time; Dolly had hocked her last piece of jewelry. She was copyediting textbooks until 2:00 a.m., sleeping until five, and then providing polite phone chitchat to aspiring English speakers in Tokyo until it was time to wake Lulu and fix her breakfast. And all of that wasn't nearly enough to keep Lulu in Miss Rutgers's School for Girls. Often Dolly's three allotted hours of sleep were spent in spasms of worry at the thought of the next monstrous tuition bill.

And then Arc had called. The general wanted an exclusive retainer. He wanted rehabilitation, American sympathy, an end to the CIA's assassination attempts. If Qaddafi could do it, why not he? Dolly wondered seriously if overwork and lack of sleep were making her hallucinate, but she named a price. Arc began taking down her banking information. "The general presumed your fee would be higher," he said, and if Dolly had been able to speak at that moment she would have said, *That's my weekly retainer, hombre, not my monthly*, or *Hey, I haven't given you the formula that lets you calculate the actual* price, or *That's just for the two-week trial period when I decide whether I want to work with you*. But Dolly couldn't speak. She was weeping.

When the first installment appeared in her bank account, Dolly's relief was so immense that it almost obliterated the tiny anxious muttering voice inside her: *Your client is a genocidal dictator*. Dolly had worked with shitheads before, God knew; if she didn't take this job someone else would snap it up; being a publicist is about not judging your clients—these excuses were lined up in formation, ready for deployment should that small dissident voice pluck up its courage to speak with any volume. But lately, Dolly couldn't even hear it.

Now, as she scuttled over her frayed Persian rug looking for the general's most recent numbers, the phone rang. It was 6:00 a.m. Dolly lunged, praying Lulu's sleep wouldn't be disturbed.

"Hello?" But she knew who it was.

"We are not happy," said Arc.

"Me either," Dolly said. "You didn't cut off the—"

"The general is not happy."

"Arc, listen to me. You need to cut off the—"

"The general is not happy, Miss Peale."

"Listen to me, Arc."

"He is not happy."

"That's because—look, take a scissors—"

"He is not happy, Miss Peale."

Dolly went quiet. There were times, listening to Arc's silken monotone, when she'd been sure she'd heard a curl of irony around the words he'd been ordered to say, like he was speaking to her in code. Now there was a prolonged pause. Dolly spoke very softly. "Arc, take a scissors and cut the ties off the hat. There shouldn't be a goddamned bow under the general's chin."

"He will no longer wear this hat."

"He *has* to wear the hat."

"He will not wear it. He refuses."

"Cut off the ties, Arc."

"Rumors have reached us, Miss Peale."

Her stomach lurched. "Rumors?"

"That you are not 'on top' as you once were. And now the hat is unsuccessful."

Dolly felt the negative forces pulling in around her. Standing there with the traffic of Eighth Avenue grinding past beneath her window, fingering her frizzy hair that she'd stopped coloring and allowed to grow in long and gray, she felt a jab of some deep urgency.

"I have enemies, Arc," she said. "Just like the general."

He was silent.

"If you listen to my enemies, I can't do my job. Now take out that fancy pen I can see in your pocket every time you get your picture in the paper and write this down: *Cut the strings off the hat. Lose the bow. Push the hat farther back on the general's head so some of his hair fluffs out in front.* Do that, Arc, and let's see what happens."

Lulu had come into the room and was rubbing her eyes in her pink pajamas. Dolly looked at her watch, saw that her daughter had lost a half hour of sleep, and experienced a small inner collapse at the thought of Lulu feeling tired at school. She put her arms around her daughter's shoulders. Lulu received this embrace with the regal bearing that was her trademark.

Dolly had forgotten Arc, but now he spoke from the phone at her neck: "I will do this, Miss Peale."

It was several weeks before the general's picture appeared again. Now the hat was pushed back and the ties were gone. The headline read:

EXTENT OF B'S WAR CRIMES MAY BE EXAGGERATED, NEW EVIDENCE SHOWS

It was the hat. He looked sweet in the hat. How could a man in a fuzzy blue hat have used human bones to pave his roads?

La Doll had met with ruin on New Year's Eve two years ago, at a wildly anticipated party that was projected, by the cultural history–minded pundits she'd considered worth inviting, to rival Truman Capote's Black and White Ball. The Party, it was called, or the List. As in: *Is he on the list?* A party to celebrate—what? In retrospect, Dolly wasn't sure; the fact that Americans had never been richer, despite the turmoil roiling the world? The Party had nominal hosts, all famous, but the real hostess, as everyone knew, was La Doll, who had more connections and access and juju than all of these people combined. And La Doll had made a very human mistake—or so she tried to soothe herself at night when memories of her demise plowed through her like a hot poker, causing her to writhe in her sofa bed and swill brandy from the bottle—she'd thought that because she could do something very, very well (namely, get the best people into one room at one time), she could do other things well, too. Like design. And La Doll had had a vision: broad, translucent trays of oil and water suspended beneath small brightly colored spotlights whose heat would make the opposing liquids twist and bubble and swirl. She'd imagined people craning their necks to look up, spellbound by the shifting liquid shapes. And they did look up. They marveled at the lit trays; La Doll saw them do it from a small booth she'd had constructed high up and to one side so she could view the panorama of her achievement. From there, she was the first to notice, as midnight approached, that something was awry with the translucent trays that held the water and oil: they were sagging a little—were they? They were slumping like sacks from their chains and *melting*, in other words. And then they began to collapse, flop and drape and fall away, sending scalding oil onto the heads of every glamorous person in the country and some other countries, too. They were

burned, scarred, maimed in the sense that tear-shaped drop-
lets of scar tissue on the forehead of a movie star or small bald
patches on the head of an art dealer or a model or generally
fabulous person constitute maiming. But something shut
down in La Doll as she stood there, away from the burning
oil: she didn't call 911. She gaped in frozen disbelief as her
guests shrieked and staggered and covered their heads, tore
hot, soaked garments from their flesh and crawled over the
floor like people in medieval altar paintings whose earthly
luxuries have consigned them to hell.

The accusations later—that she'd done it on purpose, was
a sadist who'd stood there delighting as people suffered—
were actually more terrible, for La Doll, than watching
the oil pour mercilessly onto the heads of her five hundred
guests. Then she'd been protected by a cocoon of shock. But
what followed she had to witness in a lucid state: They hated
her. They were dying to get rid of her. It was as if she weren't
human, but a rat or a bug. And they succeeded. Even before
she'd served her six months for criminal negligence, before
the class-action suit that resulted in her entire net worth
(never nearly as large as it had seemed) being distributed
in small parcels to her victims, La Doll was gone. Wiped
out. She emerged from jail thirty pounds heavier and fifty
years older, with wild gray hair. No one recognized her,
and the world where she'd thrived had shortly proceeded to
vaporize—now even the rich believed they were poor. After
a few gleeful headlines and photos of her new, ruined state,
they forgot about her.

Dolly was left alone to ponder her miscalculations—and
not just the obvious ones involving the melting tempera-

ture of plastic and the proper distribution of weight-bearing chains. Her deeper error had preceded all that: she'd overlooked a seismic shift—had conceived of an event crystallizing an era that had already passed. For a publicist, there could be no greater failure. She deserved her oblivion. Now and then, Dolly found herself wondering what sort of event or convergence *would* define the new world in which she found herself, as Capote's party had, or Woodstock, or Malcolm Forbes's seventieth birthday, or the party for *Talk* magazine. She had no idea. She had lost her power to judge; it would be up to Lulu and her generation to decide.

When the headlines relating to General B. had definitively softened, when several witnesses against him were shown to have received money from the opposition, Arc called again. "The general pays you each month a sum," he said. "That is not for one idea only."

"It was a good idea, Arc. You have to admit."

"The general is impatient, Miss Peale," he said, and Dolly imagined him smiling. "The hat is no longer new."

That night, the general came to Dolly in a dream. The hat was gone, and he was meeting a pretty blonde outside a revolving door. The blonde took his arm, and they spun back inside, pressed together. Then Dolly was aware of herself in the dream, sitting in a chair watching the general and his lover, thinking what a good job they were doing playing their roles. She jolted awake as if someone had shaken her. The dream nearly escaped, but Dolly caught it, pressed it to her chest. She understood: the general should be linked to a movie star.

Dolly scrambled off the sofa bed, waxy legs flashing in the street light that leaked in through a broken blind. A movie star. Someone recognizable, appealing—what better way to humanize a man who seemed inhuman? *If he's good enough for her . . .* that was one line of thinking. And also: *The general and I have similar tastes: her.* Or else: *She must find that triangular head of his sexy.* Or even: *I wonder how the general dances?* And if Dolly could get people to ask that question, the general's image problems would be solved. It didn't matter how many thousands he'd slaughtered—if the collective vision of him could include a dance floor, all that would be behind him.

There were scores of washed-up female stars who might work, but Dolly had a particular one in mind: Kitty Jackson, who ten years ago had debuted as a scrappy, gymnastic crime stopper in *Oh, Baby, Oh.* Kitty's real fame had come a year later, when Jules Jones, the older brother of one of Dolly's protégés, had attacked her during an interview for *Details* magazine. The assault and trial had enshrined Kitty in a glowing mist of martyrdom. So people were all the more spooked, when the mist burned off, to find the actress sharply altered: gone was the guileless ingénue she had been, and in her place was one of those people who "couldn't take the bullshit." Kitty's ensuing bad behavior and fall from grace were relentlessly cataloged in the tabloids: on set for a Western, she'd emptied a bag of horseshit onto an iconic actor's head; she'd set free several thousand lemurs on a Disney film. When an überpowerful producer tried to maneuver her into bed, she'd called his wife. No one would hire Kitty anymore, but the public would remember her—that was what mattered to Dolly. And she was still only twenty-eight.

Kitty wasn't hard to find; no one was putting much energy into hiding her. By noon, Dolly had reached her: sleepy sounding, smoking audibly. Kitty heard Dolly out, asked her to repeat the generous fee she'd quoted, then paused. In that pause, Dolly detected a mix of desperation and squeamishness that she recognized too well. She felt a queasy jab of pity for the actress, whose choices had boiled down to this one. Then Kitty said yes.

Singing to herself, wired on espresso made on her old Krups machine, Dolly called Arc and laid out her plan.

"The general does not enjoy American movies," came Arc's response.

"Who cares? *Americans* know who she is."

"The general has very particular tastes," Arc said. "He is not flexible."

"He doesn't have to touch her, Arc. He doesn't have to speak to her. All he has to do is stand near her and get his picture taken. And he has to smile."

". . . Smile?"

"He has to look happy."

"The general rarely smiles, Miss Peale."

"He wore the hat, didn't he?"

There was a long pause. Finally Arc said, "You must accompany this actress. Then we will see."

"Accompany her where?"

"Here. To us."

"Oh, Arc."

"It is required," he said.

Entering Lulu's bedroom, Dolly felt like Dorothy waking up in Oz: everything was in color. A pink shade encircled the overhead lamp. Pink gauzy fabric hung from the ceiling. Pink winged princesses were stenciled onto the walls: Dolly had learned how to make the stencils in a jailhouse art class and had spent days decorating the room while Lulu was at school. Long strings of pink beads hung from the ceiling. When she was home, Lulu emerged from her room only to eat.

She was part of a weave of girls at Miss Rutgers's School, a mesh so fine and scarily intimate that even her mother's flameout and jail sentence (during which Lulu's grandmother had come from Minnesota to care for her) couldn't dissolve it. It wasn't thread holding these girls together; it was steel wire. And Lulu was the rod around which the wires were wrapped. Overhearing her daughter on the phone with her friends, Dolly was awed by her authority: she was stern when she needed to be, but also soft. Kind. Lulu was nine.

She sat in a pink beanbag chair, doing homework on her laptop and IMing her friends (since the general, Dolly had been paying for wireless). "Hi Dolly," Lulu said, having stopped calling Dolly "Mom" when she got out of jail. She narrowed her eyes at her mother as if she had difficulty making her out. And Dolly did feel like a black-and-white incursion into this bower of color, a refugee from the dinginess surrounding it.

"I have to take a business trip," she told Lulu. "To visit a client. I thought you might want to stay with one of your friends so you won't miss school."

School was where Lulu's life took place. She'd been adamant about not allowing her mother, who once had been a fixture at Miss Rutgers's, to jeopardize Lulu's status with her new disgrace. Nowadays, Dolly dropped Lulu off around the corner, peering past dank Upper East Side stone to make sure she got safely in the door. At pickup time, Dolly waited in the same spot while Lulu dawdled with her friends outside school, toeing the manicured bushes and (in spring) tulip beds, completing whatever transactions were required to affirm and sustain her power. When Lulu had a play date, Dolly came no farther than the lobby to retrieve her. Lulu would emerge from an elevator flushed, smelling of perfume or freshly baked brownies, take her mother's hand, and walk with her past the doorman into the night. Not in apology—Lulu had nothing to apologize for—but in sympathy that things had to be so hard for both of them.

Lulu cocked her head, curious. "A business trip. That's good, right?"

"It is good, absolutely," Dolly said a little nervously. She'd kept the general a secret from Lulu.

"How long will you be gone?"

"A few days. Four, maybe."

There was a long pause. Finally Lulu said, "Can I come?"

"With me?" Dolly was taken aback. "But you'd have to miss school."

Another pause. Lulu was performing some mental calculation that might have involved measuring the peer impact of missing school versus being a guest in someone's home, or the question of whether you could manage an extended stay at someone's home without that someone's parents having contact with your mother. Dolly couldn't tell. Maybe Lulu didn't know herself.

"Where?" Lulu asked.

Dolly was flustered; she'd never been much good at saying no to Lulu. But the thought of her daughter and the general in one location made her throat clamp. "I—I can't tell you that."

Lulu didn't protest. "But Dolly?"

"Yes, sweetheart?"

"Can your hair be blond again?"

They waited for Kitty Jackson in a lounge by a private runway at Kennedy Airport. When the actress finally arrived, dressed in jeans and a faded yellow sweatshirt, Dolly was smitten with regrets—she should have met Kitty first! The girl looked too far gone; people might not even recognize her! Her hair was still blond (defiantly uncombed and also, it appeared, unwashed), her eyes still wide and blue. But a sardonic expression had taken up residence in her face, as if those blue eyes were rolling heavenward even as they gazed right at you. That look, more than the first spidery lines under Kitty's eyes and alongside her mouth, made her seem no longer young, or even close. She wasn't Kitty Jackson anymore.

While Lulu used the bathroom, Dolly hastily laid things out for the actress: look as glamorous as possible (Dolly cast a worried glance at Kitty's small suitcase); cozy up to the general with some serious PDA while Dolly took pictures with a hidden camera. She had a real camera, too, but that was a prop. Kitty nodded, the shadow of a smirk tweaking the corners of her mouth.

"You brought your daughter?" was her sole response. "To meet the general?"

"She's not going to meet the general," Dolly hissed, checking to make sure Lulu hadn't emerged from the bathroom. "She doesn't know anything *about* the general! Please don't mention his name in front of her."

Kitty regarded Dolly skeptically. "Lucky girl," she said.

They boarded the general's plane at dusk. After takeoff, Kitty ordered a martini from the general's airline hostess, sucked it down, reclined her seat to a horizontal position, pulled a sleep mask (the only thing on her that looked new) over her eyes, and commenced to snore. Lulu leaned over her, studying the actress's face, which looked young, untouched in repose.

"Is she sick?"

"No." Dolly sighed. "Maybe. I don't know."

"I think she needs a vacation," Lulu said.

Twenty checkpoints presaged their arrival at the general's compound. At each, two soldiers with submachine guns peered into the black Mercedes, where Dolly and Lulu and Kitty sat in the backseat. Four times, they were forced outside into the scouring sunshine and patted down at gunpoint. Each time, Dolly scrutinized her daughter's studied calm for signs of trauma. In the car Lulu sat very straight, pink Kate Spade bookbag nestled in her lap. She met the eyes of the machine-gun holders with the same even look she must have used to stare down the many girls who had tried in vain, over the years, to unseat her.

High white walls enclosed the road. They were lined with hundreds of plump shiny black birds whose long purple beaks curved like scythes. Dolly had never seen birds like these. They looked like birds that would screech, but each time a car window slid down to accommodate another squinting gunslinger, Dolly was unsettled by the silence.

Eventually a section of wall swung open and the car veered off the road and pulled to a stop in front of a massive compound: lush green gardens, a sparkle of water, a white mansion whose end was nowhere in sight. The birds squatted along its roof, looking down.

Their driver opened the car doors, and Dolly and Lulu and Kitty stepped out into the sun. Dolly felt it on her neck, newly exposed by a discount version of her trademark blond chin-length cut. The heat forced Kitty out of her sweatshirt; mercifully, she wore a clean white T-shirt underneath. Her arms had a lovely tan, although a scatter of raw pink patches marred the skin above one wrist. Scars. Dolly stared at them. "Kitty, are those . . ." She faltered. "On your arms, are they . . . ?"

"Burns," Kitty said. And she gave Dolly a look that made her stomach twist until she remembered very dimly, like something that had happened in a fog or when she was a small child, someone asking her—begging her—to put Kitty Jackson on the list, and telling them no. Absolutely not, it was out of the question—Kitty's stock was too low.

"I made them myself," Kitty said.

Dolly stared at her, uncomprehending. Kitty grinned, and for a second she looked sweetly mischievous, like the star of *Oh, Baby, Oh.* "Lots of people have," she said. "You didn't know?"

Dolly wondered if this might be a joke. She didn't want to fall for it in front of Lulu.

"You can't find a person who wasn't at that party," Kitty said. "And they've got proof. We've all got proof—who's going to say we're lying?"

"I know who was there," Dolly said. "I've still got the list in my head."

"But . . . who are you?" Kitty said, still smiling.

Dolly was quiet. She felt Lulu's gray eyes on her.

Then Kitty did something unexpected: she reached through the sunlight and took Dolly's hand. Her grip was warm and firm, and Dolly felt a prickling in her eyes.

"To hell with them, right?" Kitty said tenderly.

A trim, compact man in a beautifully cut suit emerged from the compound to greet them. Arc.

"Miss Peale. We meet at last," he said with a smile. "And Miss Jackson"—he turned to Kitty—"it is a great honor as well as a pleasure." He kissed Kitty's hand with a slightly teasing look, Dolly thought. "I have seen your movies. The general and I watched them together."

Dolly steeled herself for what Kitty might say, but her answer arrived in a ringing voice like a child's, except for the slight curve of flirtation. "Oh, I'm sure you've seen better movies."

"The general was impressed."

"Well, I'm honored. I'm honored that the general found them worth watching."

With trepidation, Dolly glanced at the actress, wishing only that the mockery she took for granted not be too scaldingly manifest. To her amazement, it wasn't there at all—not a trace. Kitty looked humble, absolutely sincere, as if ten years had dropped away and she were a grateful, eager starlet once more.

"Alas, I have unfortunate news," Arc said. "The general has had to make a sudden trip." They stared at him. "It is very regrettable," he went on. "The general sends his sincere apologies."

"But we . . . can we go to where he is?" Dolly asked.

"Perhaps," Arc said. "You will not mind some additional travels?"

"Well," Dolly said, glancing at Lulu. "It depends how—"

"Absolutely not," Kitty interrupted. "We'll go wherever the general wants us to go. We'll do what it takes. Right, kiddo?"

Lulu was slow to connect the diminutive "kiddo" to herself. It was the first time Kitty had spoken to her directly. Lulu glanced at the actress, then smiled. "Right," she said.

They would leave for a new location the following morning. That evening, Arc offered to drive them into the city, but Kitty demurred. "I'll pass on the grand tour," she said as they settled into their two-bedroom suite, which opened onto a private swimming pool. "I'd rather enjoy these digs. They used to put me up in places like this." She gave a bitter laugh.

"Don't overdo it," Dolly said, noticing Kitty headed for the wet bar.

Kitty turned, narrowing her eyes. "Hey. How was I out there? Any complaints so far?"

"You were perfect," Dolly said. Then, lowering her voice so Lulu wouldn't hear, she added, "Just don't forget who we're dealing with."

"But I want to forget," Kitty said, pouring herself a gin and tonic. "I'm actively trying to forget. I want to be like Lulu—innocent." She raised her glass to Dolly and took a sip.

Dolly and Lulu rode with Arc in his charcoal gray Jaguar, a driver peeling downhill along tiny streets, sending pedestrians lunging against walls and darting into doorways to avoid being crushed. The city shimmered below: millions of white slanted buildings steeping in a smoky haze. Soon they were surrounded by it. The city's chief source of color seemed to be the laundry flapping on every balcony.

The driver pulled over beside an outdoor market: heaps of sweating fruit and fragrant nuts and fake-leather purses. Dolly eyed the produce critically as she and Lulu followed Arc among the stalls. The oranges and bananas were the largest she'd seen, but the meat looked dangerous. Dolly could see from the careful nonchalance of vendors and customers alike that they knew who Arc was.

"Is there anything you would like?" Arc asked Lulu.

"Yes, please," Lulu said, "one of those." It was a star fruit; Dolly had seen them at Dean & DeLuca. Here they lay in obscene heaps, studded with flies. Arc took one, nodding curtly at the vendor, an older man with a skeletal chest and a kind, anxious face. The man smiled, nodding eagerly at Dolly and Lulu, but his eyes looked frightened.

Lulu took the dusty, unwashed fruit, wiped it carefully on her short-sleeved polo shirt, and sank her teeth into its bright green rind. Juice sprayed her collar. She laughed and wiped her mouth on her hand. "Mom, you have to try this," she said, and Dolly took a bite. She and Lulu shared the star fruit, licking their fingers under Arc's watchful eyes. Dolly felt oddly buoyant. Then she realized why: *Mom*. It was the first time Lulu had spoken the word in nearly a year.

Arc led the way inside a crowded tea shop. A group of men scattered from a corner table to give them a place to sit, and a forced approximation of the shop's former happy bustle resumed. A waiter poured sweet mint tea into their cups with a shaking hand. Dolly tried to give him a reassuring look, but his eyes fled hers.

"Do you do this often?" she asked Arc. "Walk around the city?"

"The general makes a habit of moving among the people," Arc said. "He wants them to feel his humanity, to witness it. Of course, he must do this very carefully."

"Because of his enemies."

Arc nodded. "The general unfortunately has many enemies. Today, for example, there were threats to his home, and it was necessary to relocate. He does this often, as you know."

Dolly nodded. *Threats to his home?*

Arc smiled. "His enemies believe he is here, but he is far away."

Dolly glanced at Lulu. The star fruit had left a shiny ring around her mouth. "But . . . *we're* here," she said.

"Yes," Arc said. "Only us."

Dolly lay awake most of that night, listening to coos and rustles and squawks that mimicked sounds of assassins prowling the grounds in search of the general and his cohort: herself, in other words. She had become the helpmate and fellow target of General B., a source of terror and anxiety to those he ruled.

How had it come to this? As usual, Dolly found herself revisiting the moment when the plastic trays first buckled and the life she had relished for so many years poured away. But tonight, unlike countless other nights when Dolly tipped down that memory chute, Lulu lay across from her in the king-sized bed, asleep in a frilly nightie, her doe's knees tucked under her. Dolly felt the warmth of her daughter's body, this child of her middle age, of an accidental pregnancy resulting from a fling with a movie-star client. Lulu believed her father was dead; Dolly had shown her pictures of an old boyfriend.

She slid across the bed and kissed Lulu's warm cheek. It had made no sense at all to have a child—Dolly was pro-choice, riveted to her career. Her decision had been clear, yet she'd hesitated to make the appointment—hesitated through morning sickness, mood swings, exhaustion. Hesitated until she knew, with a shock of relief and petrified joy, that it was too late.

Lulu stirred and Dolly moved closer, gathering her daughter in her arms. Unlike when she was awake, Lulu relaxed into her mother's touch. Dolly felt a swell of irrational gratitude toward the general for providing this one bed—it was such a rare luxury to hold her daughter, to feel the faint patter of her heartbeat.

"I'll always protect you, sweetheart," Dolly whispered into Lulu's ear. "Nothing bad will ever happen to us—you know that, right?"

Lulu slept on.

The next day they piled into two black armored cars that resembled jeeps, only heavier. Arc and some soldiers went in the first car, Dolly and Lulu and Kitty in the second. Sitting in the backseat, Dolly thought she could feel the weight of the car shoving them into the earth. She was exhausted, full of dread.

Kitty had undergone a staggering metamorphosis. She'd washed her hair, applied makeup, and slipped into a sleeveless sage-colored dress made of crushed velvet. It brought out flecks of green in her blue eyes and made them look turquoise. Kitty's shoulders were athletically golden, her lips pinkly glossed, her nose lightly freckled. The effect was beyond anything Dolly could have hoped for. She found Kitty almost painful to look at, and tried to avoid it.

They breezed through the checkpoints and soon were on the open road, circling the pale city from above. Dolly noticed vendors by the road. Often they were children, who held up handfuls of fruit or cardboard signs as the jeeps approached. When the vehicles flew past, the children fell back against the embankment, perhaps from the speed. Dolly let out a cry the first time she saw this and leaned forward, wanting to say something to the driver. But what exactly? She hesitated, then sat back and tried not to look at the windows. Lulu watched the children, her math book open in her lap.

It was a relief when they left the city behind and began driving through empty land that looked like desert, antelopes and cows nibbling the stingy plant life. Without asking permission, Kitty began to smoke, exhaling through a slice of open window. Dolly fought the impulse to scold her for affronting Lulu's lungs with secondhand smoke.

"So," Kitty said, turning to Lulu. "What big plans are you hatching?"

Lulu seemed to turn the question over. "You mean . . . for my life?"

"Why not."

"I haven't decided yet," Lulu said, thoughtful. "I'm only nine."

"Well, that's sensible."

"Lulu is very sensible," Dolly said.

"I mean what do you *imagine*," Kitty said. She was restless, fidgeting her dry, manicured fingers as if she wanted another cigarette but was making herself wait. "Or do kids not do that anymore."

Lulu, in her wisdom, seemed to divine that what Kitty really wanted was to talk. "What did you imagine," she asked, "when you were nine?"

Kitty considered this, then laughed and lit up. "I wanted to be a jockey," she said. "Or a movie star."

"You got one of your wishes."

"I did," Kitty said, closing her eyes as she exhaled smoke through the window. "I did get my wish."

Lulu turned to her gravely. "Was it not as fun as you thought?"

Kitty opened her eyes. "The acting?" she said. "Oh, I loved that, I still do—I miss it. But the people were monsters."

"What kind?"

"Liars," Kitty said. "They seemed nice at first, but that was all an act. The outright horrible ones, the ones who basically wanted to kill you—at least they were being honest."

Lulu nodded, as if this were a problem she'd dealt with herself. "Did you try lying too?"

"I did. I tried it a lot. But I couldn't forget I was lying, and when I told the truth I got punished. It's like finding out there's no Santa Claus—you wish you could go back and believe in all that again, but it's too late."

She turned suddenly to Lulu, stricken. "I mean—I hope I—"

Lulu laughed. "I never believed in Santa Claus," she said.

They drove and drove. Lulu did math. Then social studies. She wrote an essay on owls. After what felt like hundreds of miles of desert, punctuated by bathroom stops at outposts patrolled by soldiers, they tilted up into the hills. The foliage grew dense, filtering out the sunlight.

Without warning, the cars swung off the road and stopped. Dozens of soldiers in camouflage seemed to materialize from the trees. Dolly and Lulu and Kitty stepped out of the car into a jungle crazed with birdcalls.

Arc came over, stepping carefully in his fine leather shoes. "The general is waiting," he said. "He is eager to greet you."

Everyone moved as a group through the jungle. The earth under their feet was bright red and soft. Monkeys romped in the trees. Eventually they reached a set of crude concrete steps built into the side of a hill. More soldiers appeared, and there was a creak and grind of boots as all of them climbed. Dolly kept her hands on Lulu's shoulders. She heard Kitty humming behind her: not a tune, just the same two notes, over and over.

The hidden camera was ready in Dolly's purse. As they climbed the steps, she took out the activator and nestled it in her palm.

At the top of the stairs the jungle had been cleared away to accommodate a slab of concrete that might have been a landing pad. Sunlight pushed down through the humid jungle air, making wisps of steam at their feet. The general stood in the middle of the concrete, flanked by soldiers. He looked short, but that was always true of famous people. He wasn't wearing the blue hat, or any hat, and his thick hair stood up oddly around his grim triangular face. He wore his usual military regalia, but something about it all seemed slightly askew, or in need of cleaning. The general looked tired— there were pouches under his eyes. He looked grumpy. He looked like someone had just hustled him out of bed and said, *They're here*, and he'd had to be reminded of who the hell they were talking about.

There was a pause when no one seemed to know what to do.

Then Kitty reached the top of the stairs. Dolly heard the humming behind her, but she didn't turn to look; instead, she watched the general recognize Kitty, watched the power of that recognition move across his face in a look of appetite and uncertainty. Kitty came toward him slowly—poured toward him, really, that was how smoothly she moved in her sage green dress, as if the jerking awkwardness of walking were something she'd never experienced. She poured toward the general and took his hand as if to shake it, smiling, circling him a little, seeming embarrassed to the point of laughter, like they knew each other too well to shake hands. Dolly was so taken by the strangeness of it all that at first she didn't even think to shoot; she missed the handshake completely. It was only when Kitty pressed her narrow green body to the general's uniformed chest and closed her eyes for a moment that Dolly came to—*click*—and the general seemed disconcerted, unsure what to do, patting Kitty's back out of politeness—*click*—at which point Kitty took both his hands (heavy and warped, the hands of a bigger man) into her own slender hands and leaned back, smiling into his face—*click*—laughing a little, shyly, her head back like it was all so silly, so self-conscious-making for them both. And then the general smiled. It happened without warning: his lips pulled away to reveal two rows of small yellow teeth—*click*—that made him appear vulnerable, eager to please. *Click, click, click*—Dolly was shooting as fast as she could without moving her hand, because that smile was *it*, the thing no one had seen, the hidden human side of the general that would dumbfound the world.

All this happened in the span of a minute. Not a word had been spoken. Kitty and the general stood hand in hand, both a little flushed, and it was all Dolly could do not to scream, because they were done! She had what she needed, without a word having been said. She felt a mix of awe and love for Kitty—this miracle, this genius who had not merely posed with the general, but tamed him. That was how it felt to Dolly—like there was a one-way door between the general's world and Kitty's, and the actress had eased him across it without his even noticing. He couldn't go back! And Dolly had made this happen—for the first time in her life, she had done a helpful thing. And Lulu had seen it.

Kitty's face still held the winsome smile she'd been wearing for the general. Dolly watched the actress scan the crowd, taking in the dozens of soldiers with their automatic weapons, Arc and Lulu and Dolly with her ecstatic shining face, her brimming eyes. And Kitty must have known then that she'd pulled it off, engineered her own salvation, clawed her way back from oblivion and cleared the way to resume the work she adored. All with a little help from the despot to her left.

"So," Kitty said, "is this where you bury the bodies?"

The general glanced at her, not understanding. Arc stepped quickly forward, as did Dolly. Lulu came too.

"Do you bury them here, in pits," Kitty asked the general in the most friendly, conversational voice, "or do you burn them first?"

"Miss Jackson," Arc said, with a tense, meaningful look. "The general cannot understand you."

The general wasn't smiling anymore. He was a man who couldn't abide not knowing what was going on. He'd let go of Kitty's hand and was speaking sternly to Arc.

Lulu tugged Dolly's hand. "Mom," she hissed, "make her stop!"

Her daughter's voice startled Dolly out of a momentary paralysis. "Knock it off, Kitty," she said.

"Do you eat them?" Kitty asked the general. "Or do you leave them out so the vultures can do it?"

"Shut up, Kitty," Dolly said, more loudly. "Stop playing games."

The general spoke harshly to Arc, who turned to Dolly. His smooth forehead was visibly moist. "The general is becoming angry, Miss Peale," he said. And there was the code; Dolly read it clearly. She went to Kitty and seized her tanned arm. She leaned close to Kitty's face.

"If you keep this up," Dolly said softly, "we will all die."

But one glance into Kitty's fervid, self-annihilating eyes told her it was hopeless; Kitty couldn't stop. "Oops!" she said loudly, in mock surprise. "Was I not supposed to bring up the genocide?"

Here was a word the general knew. He flung himself away from Kitty as if she were on fire, commanding his soldiers in a strangled voice. They shoved Dolly away, knocking her to the ground. When she looked back at Kitty, the soldiers had contracted around her, and the actress was obscured from view.

Lulu was shouting, trying to drag Dolly onto her feet. "Mommy, do something, do something! Make them stop!"

"Arc," Dolly called, but Arc was lost to her now. He'd taken his place beside the general, who was screaming with rage. The soldiers were carrying Kitty; Dolly had an impression of kicking from within their midst. She could still hear Kitty's high, reaching voice:

"Do you drink their blood, or just use it to mop your floors?

"Do you wear their teeth on a string?"

There was the sound of a blow, then a scream. Dolly jumped to her feet. But Kitty was gone; the soldiers carried her inside a structure hidden in the trees beside the landing pad. The general and Arc followed them in and shut the door. The jungle was eerily silent: just parrot calls and Lulu's sobs.

While the general raged, Arc had whispered orders to two soldiers, and as soon as the general was out of sight, they hustled Dolly and Lulu down the hill through the jungle and back to the cars. The drivers were waiting, smoking cigarettes. During the ride Lulu lay with her head in Dolly's lap, crying as they sped back through the jungle and then the desert. Dolly rubbed her daughter's soft hair, wondering numbly if they were being taken to prison. But eventually, as the sun leaked toward the horizon, they found themselves at the airport. The general's plane was waiting. By then, Lulu had sat up and moved across the seat.

Lulu slept hard during the flight, clutching her Kate Spade bookbag. Dolly didn't sleep. She stared straight ahead at Kitty's empty seat.

In the dark of early morning, they took a taxi from Kennedy to Hell's Kitchen. Neither of them spoke. Dolly was amazed to find their building intact, the apartment still at the top of the stairs, the keys in her purse.

Lulu went straight to her room and shut the door. Dolly sat in her office, addled from lack of sleep, and tried to organize her thoughts. Should she start with the embassy? Congress? How long would it take to get someone on the phone who could actually help her? And what exactly would she say?

Lulu emerged from her room in her school uniform, hair brushed. Dolly hadn't even noticed it was light out. Lulu looked askance at her mother, still in yesterday's clothes, and said, "It's time to go."

"You're going to school?"

"Of course I'm going to school. What else would I do?"

They took the subway. The silence between them had become inviolable; Dolly feared it would never end. Watching Lulu's wan, pinched face, she felt a cold wave of conviction: if Kitty Jackson died, her daughter would be lost to her.

At their corner, Lulu turned without saying good-bye.

Shopkeepers were lifting metal gates on Lexington Avenue. Dolly bought a cup of coffee and drank it. She wanted to be near Lulu. She decided to wait on that corner until her daughter's school day had ended: five and a half more hours. Meanwhile, she would make calls on her cell phone. But Dolly was distracted by thoughts of Kitty in the green dress, oil burns winking on her arms, then her own obscene pride, thinking she'd tamed the general and made the world a better place.

The phone was idle in her hand. These were not the sorts of calls she knew how to make.

When the gate behind her shuddered up, Dolly saw that it was a photo print shop. The hidden camera was still inside her purse. It was something to do; she went in, handed it over, and asked for prints and a CD of everything they could download.

She was still standing outside the shop an hour later when the guy came out with her pictures. By then she'd made a few calls about Kitty, but no one seemed to take her seriously. Who could blame them? Dolly thought.

"These shots . . . did you use Photoshop, or what?" the guy asked. "They look, like, totally real."

"They are real," she said. "I took them myself."

The guy laughed. "Come on," he said, and Dolly felt a shudder deep in her brain. As Lulu had said this morning: *What else would I do?*

She rushed back home and called her old contacts at the *Enquirer* and the *Star*, a few of whom were still there. Let the news trickle up. This had worked for Dolly before.

Minutes later, she was e-mailing images. Within a couple of hours, pictures of General B. nuzzling Kitty Jackson were being posted and traded on the Web. By nightfall, reporters from the major papers around the world had started calling. They called the general, too, whose human relations captain emphatically denied the rumors.

That night, while Lulu did homework in her room, Dolly

ate cold sesame noodles and set out to reach Arc. It took fourteen tries.

"We can no longer speak, Miss Peale," he said.

"Arc."

"We cannot speak. The general is angry."

"Listen to me."

"The general is angry, Miss Peale."

"Is she alive, Arc? That's all I need to know."

"She is alive."

"Thank you." Tears filled Dolly's eyes. "Is she—are they—treating her okay?"

"She is unharmed, Miss Peale," Arc said. "We will not speak again."

They were silent, listening to the hum of the overseas connection. "It is a pity," Arc said, and hung up.

But Dolly and Arc did speak again. Months later—a year, almost—when the general came to New York to speak at the UN about his country's transition to democracy. Dolly and Lulu had moved away from the city by then, but one evening they drove into Manhattan to meet Arc at a restaurant. He wore a black suit and a wine-colored tie that matched the excellent cabernet he poured for himself and Dolly. He seemed to savor telling the story, as if he'd memorized its details especially for her: how three or four days after she and Lulu had left the general's redoubt, the photographers began showing up, first one or two whom the soldiers ferreted out of the jungle and imprisoned, then more, too many to capture or even count—they were superb hiders, crouching like monkeys in the trees, burying themselves in shallow pits, camouflaging inside bunches of leaves. Assassins had never managed to locate the general with any precision, but the photographers made it look easy: scores of them surging across the borders without visas, curled in baskets and wine casks, rolled up in rugs, juddering over unpaved roads in the backs of trucks and eventually surrounding the general's enclave, which he didn't dare leave.

It took ten days to persuade the general he had no choice but to face his inquisitors. He donned his military coat with the medals and epaulets, pulled the blue hat over his head, took Kitty's arm, and walked with her into the phalanx of cameras awaiting him. Dolly remembered how perplexed the general had looked in those pictures, newly born in his soft blue hat, unsure how to proceed. Beside him Kitty was smiling, wearing a black close-fitting dress that Arc must have gone to some trouble to procure, so apt was it: casual and intimate, plain yet revealing, the sort of dress a woman wears in private, with her lover. Her eyes were hard to read, but each time Dolly looked at them, rubbing her gaze obsessively over the newsprint, she'd heard Kitty's laugh in her ears.

"Have you seen Miss Jackson's new movie?" Arc asked. "I thought it was her finest yet."

Dolly had seen it: a romantic comedy in which Kitty played a jockey, appearing effortless on horseback. Dolly had gone with Lulu at the local theater in the small upstate town where they'd moved shortly after the other generals began to call: first G., then A., then L. and P. and Y. Word had gotten out, and Dolly was deluged with offers of work from mass murderers hungry for a fresh start. "I'm out of the game," she'd told them, and directed them to her former competitors.

Lulu had opposed the move at first, but Dolly was firm. And Lulu had settled in quickly at the local public school, where she took up soccer and found a new coterie of girls who seemed to follow her everywhere. No one in town had ever heard of La Doll, so Lulu had nothing to hide.

Dolly received a generous lump sum from the general shortly after his rendezvous with the photographers. "A gift to express our immense gratitude for your invaluable guidance, Miss Peale," Arc had said over the telephone, but Dolly had heard his smile and understood: hush money. She used it to open a small gourmet shop on Main Street, where she sold fine produce and unusual cheeses, artfully displayed and lit by a system of small spotlights Dolly designed herself. "This feels like Paris" was a comment she often heard from New Yorkers who came on weekends to their country houses.

Now and then Dolly would get a shipment of star fruit, and she always made sure to put a few aside to eat with Lulu. She would bring them back to the small house they shared at the end of a quiet street. After supper, the radio on, windows open to the yawning night, she and Lulu would feast on the sweet, strange flesh.

9

Forty-Minute Lunch:
Kitty Jackson Opens Up About
Love, Fame, and Nixon!

JULES JONES reports

Movie stars always look small the first time you
see them, and Kitty Jackson is no exception, exceptional though she may be in every other way.

Actually, small isn't the word; she's minute—
a human bonsai in a white sleeveless dress, seated
at a back table of a Madison Avenue restaurant,
talking on a cell phone. She smiles at me as I take
my seat and rolls her eyes at the phone. Her hair
is that blond you see everywhere, "highlighted,"
my ex-fiancée calls it, though on Kitty Jackson

this tousled commingling of blond and brown appears both more natural and more costly than it did on Janet Green. Her face (Kitty's) is one you can imagine looking merely pretty among the other faces in, say, a high school classroom: upturned nose, full mouth, big blue eyes. Yet on Kitty Jackson, for reasons I can't pinpoint exactly—the same reasons, I suppose, that her highlighted hair looks superior to ordinary (Janet Green's) highlighted hair—this unexceptional face registers as extraordinary.

She's still on the phone, and five minutes have passed.

Finally she signs off, folds her phone into a disk the size of an after-dinner mint and stows it in a small white patent-leather purse. Then she starts to apologize. It is instantly clear that Kitty belongs in the category of nice stars (Matt Damon) rather than of difficult stars (Ralph Fiennes). Stars in the nice category act as if they're just like you (i.e., me) so that you will like them and write flattering things about them, a strategy that is almost universally successful despite every writer's belief that he's far too jaded to fantasize that the *Vanity Fair* cover is incidental to Brad Pitt's desire to give him a tour of his house. Kitty is sorry for the twelve flaming hoops I've had to jump through and the several miles of piping hot coals I've sprinted across for the privilege of spending forty minutes in her company. She's sorry for having just spent the first six of those minutes talking to somebody else. Her welter of apologies reminds me of why I prefer difficult stars, the ones who barricade themselves inside their stardom and spit through the cracks. There is something out of control about a star who cannot be nice, and the erosion of a subject's self-control is the sine qua non of celebrity reporting.

The waiter takes our order. And since the ten minutes of badinage I proceed to exchange with Kitty are simply not worth relating, I'll mention instead (in the footnote-ish fashion that injects a whiff of cracked leather bindings into pop-cultural observation) that when you're a young movie star with blondish hair and a highly recognizable face from that recent movie whose grosses can only be explained by the conjecture that every person in America saw it at least twice, people treat you in a manner that is somewhat different—in fact is entirely different—from the way they treat, say, a balding, stoop-shouldered, slightly eczematous guy approaching middle age. On the surface it's the same—"May I take your order?" etc.—but throbbing just beneath that surface is the waiter's hysterical recognition of my subject's fame. And with a simultaneity that can only be explained using principles of quantum mechanics, specifically, the properties of so-called entangled particles, that same pulse of

recognition reaches every part of the restaurant
at once, even tables so distant from ours that there
is simply no way they can see us.[1] Everywhere,

1. I've engaged in a bit of sophistry, here, suggesting that entangled particles can explain anything when, to date, they themselves
have not been satisfactorily explained. Entangled particles are sub-
atomic "twins": photons created by splitting a single photon in half
with a crystal, which still react identically to stimuli applied to only
one of them, even when separated from each other by many miles.

How, puzzled physicists ask, can one particle possibly "know"
what is happening to the other? How, when the people occupying
tables nearest to Kitty Jackson inevitably recognize her, do people
outside the line of vision of Kitty Jackson, who could not conceiv-
ably have had the experience of seeing Kitty Jackson, recognize her
simultaneously?

Theoretical explanations:

(1) The particles are communicating.

Impossible, because they would have to do so at a speed
faster than the speed of light, thus violating relativity theory.
In other words, in order for an awareness of Kitty's presence to
sweep the restaurant simultaneously, the diners at tables nearest to her would have to convey, through words or gestures,
the fact of her presence to diners farther away who cannot see
her—all at a speed faster than the speed of light. And that is
impossible.

(2) The two photons are responding to "local" factors en-
gendered by their former status as a single photon. (This was
Einstein's explanation for the phenomenon of entangled particles, which he termed "spooky action at a distance.")

Nope. Because we've already established that they're *not*
responding to each other; they're all responding simultaneously to Kitty Jackson, whom only a small fraction of them
can actually see!

(3) It's one of those quantum mechanical mysteries.

Apparently so. All that can be said for sure is that in the
presence of Kitty Jackson, the rest of us become entangled by our
sheer awareness that we ourselves are *not* Kitty Jackson, a fact so
brusquely unifying that it temporarily wipes out all distinctions between us—our tendency to cry inexplicably during parades, or the

people are swiveling, craning, straining and con-
torting, levitating inadvertently from chairs as
they grapple with the urge to lunge at Kitty and
pluck off tufts of her hair and clothing.

I ask Kitty how it feels to always be the center
of attention.

"Weird," she says. "It's so all of a sudden. You
feel like there's no way you deserve it."

See? Nice.

"Oh, come now," I say, and lob her a compli-
ment on her performance as the homeless junkie
turned FBI gunslinger/acrobat in *Oh, Baby,
Oh*—the sort of shameless bit of fawning that
makes me wonder whether I might prefer death
by lethal injection to my present vocation as a
celebrity reporter. Wasn't she proud?

"I *was* proud," she says. "But in a way, I didn't
even know what I was doing yet. With my new
movie, I feel more—"

"Hold that thought!" I cry, though the waiter
has not yet reached our table, and the tray he
bears aloft is probably not even ours. Because I
don't want to hear about Kitty's new movie; I
couldn't care less and neither could you, I know;

---

fact that we never learned French, or have a fear of insects that we do
our best to conceal from women, or liked to eat construction paper
as a child—in the presence of Kitty Jackson, we no longer are in
possession of these traits; indeed, so indistinguishable are we from
every other non–Kitty Jackson in our vicinity that when one of us
sees her, the rest simultaneously react.

her prattle about the challenging role and the trusting relationship she had with her director and what an honor it was to work opposite such a seasoned star as Tom Cruise is the bitter pill we both must swallow in exchange for the privilege of spending some collective time in Kitty's company. But let's put it off as long as possible!

Luckily, it *is* our tray (food arrives faster if you're dining with a star): a Cobb salad for Kitty; a cheeseburger, fries and Caesar salad for me.

A bit of theory as we settle down to lunch: the waiter's treatment of Kitty is actually a kind of sandwich, with the bottom bread being the bored and slightly effete way he normally acts with customers, the middle being the crazed and abnormal way he feels around this famous nine-teen-year-old girl, and the top bread being his attempt to contain and conceal this alien middle layer with some mode of behavior that at least approximates the bottom layer of boredom and effeteness that is his norm. In the same way, Kitty Jackson has some sort of bottom bread that is, presumably, "her," or the way Kitty Jackson once behaved in suburban Des Moines where she grew up, rode a bike, attended proms, earned decent grades and, most intriguingly, jumped horses, thereby winning a substantial number of ribbons and trophies and, at least briefly, entertaining thoughts of becoming a jockey. On top of that is her extraordinary and possibly slightly psychotic reaction to her newfound fame—the middle of the sandwich—and on top of that is her own attempt to approximate layer number one with a simulation of her normal, or former, self.

Sixteen minutes have passed.

"Rumor has it," I say, my mouth full of half-masticated hamburger in a calculated effort to disgust my subject, thus puncturing her prophylactic shield of niceness and commencing the painstaking attrition of her self-control, "that you've become involved with your costar."

That gets her attention. I've rather sprung this on her, having learned the hard way that sidling up to the personal questions gives difficult subjects too much time to get their hackles up, and nice ones too much time to gently and blushingly sidestep.

"That's absolutely not true!" Kitty cries. "Tom and I have a wonderful friendship. I love Nicole. She's been a role model for me. I've even babysat their children."

I unsheathe my Big Fat Grin, a meaningless tactic intended purely to unnerve and fluster my subject. If my methods seem unnecessarily harsh, I invite you to recall that I have been allotted forty minutes, nearly twenty of which have now elapsed, and let me add, on a personal note, that if the piece stinks—i.e., if it fails to unveil some aspect of Kitty that you haven't seen before (as have, I'm told, my pieces on hunting elk with Leonardo DiCaprio, reading Homer with Sharon Stone and digging for clams with Jeremy Irons)—it might very well be killed, thus further reducing my stock in New York and Los Angeles and prolonging the "bizarre string of failures you've been having, buddy" (—Atticus Levi, my friend and editor, over lunch last month).

"Why are you smiling like that?" Kitty asks, with hostility.

See? No more nice.

"Was I smiling?"

She turns her attention to her Cobb salad. And so do I. Because I have so little to go on, so few ports of entry to the inner sanctum of Kitty Jackson, that I'm reduced to observing and now relaying the fact that over the course of lunch, she eats all of her lettuce, approximately 2½ bites of chicken and several tomato wedges. She ignores: olives, blue cheese, boiled eggs, bacon and avocado—in other words, all of the parts of the Cobb salad that, technically speaking, *make it a Cobb salad*. As for the dressing, which she has requested "on the side," she doesn't touch it except to dip in the end of her index finger, once, and suck the dressing off.[2]

---

2. Occasionally, life affords you the time, the repose, the *dolce far niente* to ask the sorts of questions that go largely unexamined in the brisk course of ordinary life: How well do you recall the mechanics of photosynthesis? Have you ever managed to use the word "ontology" in a conversational sentence? At what precise moment did you tip just

"I'll tell you what I'm thinking," I finally say, relieving the vibrato of tension that has been building at our table. "I'm thinking, nineteen years old. Mega-grossing movie behind her, half

---

slightly out of alignment with the relatively normal life you had been enjoying theretofore, cant infinitesimally to the left or the right and thus embark upon the trajectory that ultimately delivered you to your present whereabouts—in my case, Rikers Island Correctional Facility?

After several months of subjecting each filament and nanosecond of my lunch with Kitty Jackson to a level of analysis that would make Talmudic scholars look hasty in their appraisal of the Sabbath, I have concluded that my own subtle yet decisive realignment occurred at precisely the moment when Kitty Jackson dipped her finger into the bowl of salad dressing "on the side" and sucked the dressing off.

Here, carefully teased apart and restored to chronological order, is a reconstruction of the brew of thoughts and impulses that I now believe coursed through my mind at that time:

Thought 1 (at the sight of Kitty dipping her finger and sucking it): Can it possibly be that this ravishing young girl is *coming on to me*?

Thought 2: No, that's out of the question.

Thought 3: But *why* is it out of the question?

Thought 4: Because she's a famous nineteen-year-old movie star and you're "heavier all of a sudden—or am I just noticing it more?" (—Janet Green, during our last, failed sexual encounter) and have a skin problem and no worldly clout.

Thought 5: But she just dipped her finger into a bowl of salad dressing and sucked it off in my presence! What else can that possibly mean?

Thought 6: It means you're so far outside the field of Kitty's sexual consideration that her internal sensors, which normally stifle behavior that might be construed as overly encouraging, or possibly incendiary, such as dipping a finger into salad dressing and sucking it off in the company of a man who might interpret it as a sign of sexual interest, are not operative.

Thought 7: Why not?

Thought 8: Because you do not register as a "man" to Kitty Jackson, and so being around you makes her no more self-conscious than would the presence of a dachshund.

the world doing a rain dance at her window, and where can she possibly go next? What can she possibly do?"

In Kitty's face I see a number of things: relief that I haven't said something worse, something about Tom Cruise, and mingled with that relief (and partly because of it) a fleeting desire to see me as more than yet another crank with a tape recorder—to see me as someone who understands the incredible strangeness of her world. How I wish it were true! I would like nothing more than to understand the strangeness of Kitty's world—to burrow inside that strangeness never to emerge. But the best I can hope for is to conceal from Kitty Jackson the bald impossibility of any real communion between us, and the fact that I've managed to do so for twenty-one minutes is a triumph.

Why do I keep mentioning—"inserting," as it may seem—myself into this story? Because I'm trying to wrest readable material from a nineteen-year-old girl who is very, very nice; I'm trying to build a story that not only unlocks the velveteen secrets of her teenager's heart, but also contains action, development, along with—God help me—some intimation of meaning. But my problem is this: Kitty's a snooze. The most interesting thing about her is the effect she has upon others, and since the "other" whose inner life is most readily available for our collective inspection happens to be myself, it is only natural—indeed, it is *required* ("I'm begging you; please make this work so I don't look like an asshole for assigning it to you"—Atticus Levi, during a recent phone conversation in which I expressed to him my despair of writing further celebrity profiles)—that the alleged story of my lunch with Kitty Jackson actually be the story of the myriad effects Kitty Jackson has upon me during the course of said lunch. And for those effects to be remotely comprehensible, you must bear in mind that Janet Green, my girlfriend of three years and my fiancée for one month and thirteen days, dumped me two weeks ago for a male memoirist whose recent book details his adolescent penchant for masturbating into the family fish tank ("At least he's working on himself!"—Janet Green, during a recent phone conversation in which I tried to point out what a colossal error she'd made).

"I wonder that all the time—what will happen next," Kitty says. "Sometimes I imagine myself looking back on right now, and I think, like, where will I be standing when I look back? Will right now look like the beginning of a great life or . . . or what?"

And how exactly is "a great life" defined in Kitty Jackson's lexicon?

"Oh, you know." Giggle. Blush. We're back to

nice, but a different nice than before. We've had a tiff, and now we're making up.

"Fame and fortune?" I prod.

"Somewhat. But also just—happiness. I want to find true love, I don't care how corny that sounds. I want children. That's why, in this new movie, I bond so strongly with my surrogate mother . . ."

But my Pavlovian efforts to suppress the PR component of our lunch have succeeded, and Kitty falls silent. No sooner have I congratulated myself on this triumph, however, than I catch Kitty glancing, sidelong, at her watch (Hermès). How does this gesture affect me? Well, I feel slopping within me a volatile stew of anger, fear, and lust: anger because this naïf has, for reasons that are patently unjustifiable, far more power in the world than I will ever have, and once my forty minutes are up, nothing short of criminal stalking could force the intersection of my subterranean path with her lofty one; fear because, having glanced at my own watch (Timex), I've discovered that thirty of those forty minutes have elapsed, and I have, as yet, no "event" to form the centerpiece of my profile; lust because her neck is very long, with a thin, nearly translucent gold necklace around it. Her shoulders, exposed by the white halter top of her sundress, are small and tan and very delicate, like two little

squabs. But that makes them sound unappeal-
ing, and they were phenomenally appealing! By
"squabs" I mean that they looked so good (her
shoulders) that I could briefly imagine pulling
apart all those little bones and sucking the meat
off them one by one.[3]

I ask Kitty how it feels to be a sex goddess.

"It doesn't feel like anything," she says, bored
and annoyed. "That's something other people
feel."

"Men, you mean."

---

3. For those who will inevitably interpret this caprice as further evidence that I am, indeed, a "numb nuts," a "creepazoid," or a
"sick puppy" (—excerpts from correspondence received from strangers while in jail), I can offer only the following: On a spring day almost four years ago, I noticed a girl with short thick legs and a long
narrow torso, wearing a pink tie-dyed T-shirt, picking up dog poop
with a Duane Reade bag. She was one of those muscley girls who
turn out to have been a swimmer or a diver in high school (though
I later learned she'd been neither), and her dog was a mangy, wet-
looking little terrier of the sort that would seem, even by the most
neutral and objective standards, unlovable. But she loved it. "Here,
Whiskers," she cooed. "Come on, girl." Watching her, I saw it all:
the small, overheated apartment strewn with running shoes and leo-
tards, the biweekly dinners at her parents', the soft dark fuzz on her
upper lip that she bleached each week with a tart-smelling white
cream. And the feeling I had was not of wanting her so much as
being surrounded by her, blundering inside her life without having
moved.

"May I help you with that?" I asked, stepping into the sunlight where she and Whiskers stood and slipping the Duane Reade
bag full of poop from her hand.

Janet grinned. It was like someone waving a flag. "Are you
insane?" she said.

"I guess," she says, and a new expression flickers over her comely face and alights there, a look that I would have to designate as abrupt weariness.

I feel it too: abruptly weary. In fact, generally weary. "Christ, it's all such a farce," I say, in an unguarded moment of self-expression that has no strategic purpose and which, therefore, I'll doubtless regret within seconds. "Why do we bother to participate?"

Kitty tilts her head at me. I sense that she can detect my general weariness, possibly even guess at some of its causes. She is regarding me, in other words, with pity. I am now perilously close to succumbing to the single greatest hazard of celebrity reporting: permitting my subject to reverse the beam of scrutiny, at which point I will no longer be able to see her. With a sudden pressure heralded by pricks of sweat along my drastically receding hairline, I swab the bottom of my salad plate with a vast hunk of bread and jam it into my mouth like a dentist packing a tooth. And just then—ah yes—I feel the niggling onset of a sneeze; here it comes, Hail Mary, bread or no bread, nothing can halt the shouting simultaneous eruption of every cavity in my head. Kitty looks terrified; she shrinks from me while I sort out the mess.

Disaster averted. Or at least forestalled.

"You know," I say, when finally I've managed to swallow my bread and blow my nose at the cost of nearly three minutes, "I'd love to take a walk. What do you say?"

Kitty springs from her chair at the prospect of escaping into the open air. It's a perfect day, after all, sunlight leaping through the restaurant windows. But her excitement is immediately tempered by an equal and opposite degree of caution. "What about Jake?" she asks, referring to her publicist, who will appear when our forty minutes are up and wave his wand to turn me back into a pumpkin.

"Can't he just call and meet up with us?" I ask.

"Okay," she says, doing her best to simulate the first wave of genuine enthusiasm she felt, despite the middle layer of wariness that has intruded. "Sure, let's go."

I hastily pay the bill. Now, I've orchestrated our debouchment for several reasons: One, I want to filch a few extra minutes off Kitty in an attempt to salvage this assignment and, in a larger sense, my once-promising, now-dwindling literary reputation ("I think she was maybe disappointed that you didn't try writing another novel after the first one didn't sell . . ."—Beatrice Green, over hot tea, after I threw myself sobbing upon her Scarsdale doorstep, pleading for insights into her daughter's defection). Two, I want

to see Kitty Jackson erect and in motion. To this
end, I follow behind as she leads the way out of
the restaurant, weaving among tables with her
head down in the manner of both exceptionally
attractive women and also famous people (not to
mention those like Kitty, who are both). Here's a
translation of her posture and gait into English:
*I know I'm famous and irresistible—a combination
whose properties closely resemble radioactivity—and
I know that you in this room are helpless against me.
It's embarrassing for both of us to look at each other
and see our mutual knowledge of my radioactivity
and your helplessness, so I'll keep my head down and
let you watch me in peace.* While all this is happening, I'm taking in Kitty's legs, which are
long, considering her modest height, as well as
brown, and not that orangey brown of tanning
salons, but a rich, tawny chestnut that makes me
think of—well, of horses.

Central Park is one block away. The time
elapsed is forty-one minutes and counting. We
enter the park. It is green and splashy with light
and shadow, giving the impression that we've
dived together into a deep, still pond. "I forget when we started," Kitty says, looking at her
watch. "How much more time do we have?"

"Oh, we're okay," I mumble. I'm feeling kind
of dreamy. I'm looking at Kitty's legs as we walk
(as much as I can without crawling beside her
on the ground—a thought that crosses my mind)

and discovering that above the knee they are flecked with hairs of finest gold. Because Kitty is so young and well nourished, so sheltered from the gratuitous cruelty of others, so unaware as yet that she will reach middle age and eventually die (possibly alone), because she has not yet disappointed herself, merely startled herself and the world with her own premature accomplishments, Kitty's skin—that smooth, plump, sweetly fragrant sac upon which life scrawls the record of our failures and exhaustion—is perfect. And by "perfect" I mean that nothing hangs or sags or snaps or wrinkles or ripples or bunches— I mean that her skin is like the skin of a leaf, except it's not green. I can't imagine such skin having an unpleasant odor or texture or taste— ever being, for example (it is frankly inconceivable), even mildly eczematous.

We sit together on a grassy slope. Kitty has resumed talking dutifully about her new movie, the specter of her returning publicist doubtless having reminded her that the promotion of said movie is the sole reason she is in my company.

"Oh, Kitty," I say. "Forget the movie. We're out here in the park, it's a gorgeous day. Let's leave those other two people behind us. Let's talk about . . . about horses."

What a look! What a gaze! Every cheesy metaphor you can fathom comes to mind: sun breaking through clouds, flowers yawning into bloom, the sudden and mystical appearance of a rainbow. It's done. I've reached behind or around or within—I've touched the real Kitty. And for reasons I cannot understand, reasons that surely must rank among the most mysterious of quantum mechanical mysteries, I experience this contact as revelatory, urgent, as if, in bridging the crevasse between myself and this young actress, I am being lifted above an encroaching darkness.

Kitty opens her small white purse and takes out a picture. A picture of a horse! With a white starburst on its nose. His name is Nixon. "Like the president?" I ask, but Kitty looks disturbingly blank at this reference. "I just liked the sound of that name," she says, and describes the sensation of feeding Nixon an apple—how he takes it between his horsey jaws and smashes it all at once with a cascade of milky, steaming juice. "I hardly ever get to see him," she says, with genuine sadness. "I have to hire someone else to ride him because I'm never home."

"He must be lonely without you," I say.

Kitty turns to me. I believe she's forgotten who I am. I have an urge to push her backward onto the grass, and I do.

"Hey!" my subject cries, her voice muffled and startled but not yet frightened, exactly.

"Pretend you're riding Nixon," I say.

"HEY!" she yells, and I cover her mouth with my hand. Kitty is writhing beneath me, but her writhing is stymied by my height—six foot three—and my weight, two hundred sixty pounds, approximately one-third of which is concentrated in my "spare tire of a" (—Janet Green, during our last, failed sexual encounter) gut, which pinions her like a sandbag. I hold her mouth with one hand and worm the other hand between our two flailing bodies until finally— yes!—I manage to seize hold of my zipper. How is all this affecting me? Well, we're lying on a hill in Central Park, a somewhat secluded spot that is still, technically speaking, in plain sight. So I feel anxious, dully aware that I'm placing my career and reputation at some risk with this caper. But more than that, I feel this crazy— what?—rage, it must be; what else could account for my longing to slit Kitty open like a fish and let her guts slip out, or my separate, corollary desire to break her in half and plunge my arms into whatever pure, perfumed liquid swirls within her. I want to rub it onto my raw, "scrofulous" (ibid.), parched skin in hopes that it will finally be healed. I want to fuck her (obviously) and then kill her, or possibly kill her in the act of fucking her ("fuck her to death" and "fuck her brains out" being acceptable variations on this basic goal). What I have no interest in doing is killing her and *then* fucking her, because it's her life—the inner life of Kitty Jackson—that I so desperately long to reach.

As it turns out, I do neither.

Let us return to the moment: one hand covering Kitty's mouth and doing its best to anchor her rather spirited head, the other fumbling with my zipper, which I'm having some trouble depressing, possibly because of the writhing motions of my subject beneath me. What I have no control over, unfortunately, are Kitty's hands, one of which has found its way into her white purse, where a number of items are sequestered: a picture of a horse, a potato chip–sized cell phone, which has been ringing nonstop for the past several minutes, and a canister of something that I'd have to surmise is Mace, or perhaps some form of tear gas, judging by its impact when sprayed directly into my face: a hot, blinding sensation in my eye area accompanied by gushing tears, a strangling sensation in my throat, spastic choking and severe nausea, all of which prompt me to leap to my feet and double over in a swoon of agony (still pinning Kitty to the ground with one foot), at which point she avails herself of yet another item in said purse: a set of keys with a small Swiss Army knife attached, whose diminutive and rather dull blade she nevertheless manages to sink through my khakis and into my calf.

By now I'm bellowing and honking like a be-

sieged buffalo, and Kitty is running away, her
tawny limbs no doubt dappled with light falling through the trees, though I'm too distressed
even to look.

I think I'd have to call that the end of our
lunch. I got twenty extra minutes, easy.

The end of lunch, yes, but the beginning of so
much else: a presentation before the grand jury
followed by my indictment for attempted rape,
kidnapping and aggravated assault; my present
incarceration (despite the heroic efforts of Atticus Levi to raise my $500,000 bail) and impend-
ing trial, which is to begin this month—on the
very day, as luck would have it, that Kitty's new
movie, *Whip-poor-will Falls*, opens nationally.

Kitty sent me a letter in jail. "I apologize for
whatever part I played in your emotional breakdown," she wrote, "and also for stabing [*sic*] you."
There was a circle over each *i* and a smiley face
at the end.

What did I tell you? *Nice.*

Of course, our little contretemps has been
enormously helpful to Kitty. Front-page headlines, followed by a flurry of hand-wringing
follow-up articles, editorials and op-ed pieces
addressing an array of related topics: the "in-
creasing vulnerability of celebrities" (*The New
York Times*); the "violent inability of some men to
cope with feelings of rejection" (*USA Today*); the

imperative that magazine editors vet their freelance writers more thoroughly (*The New Republic*), and the lack of adequate daytime security in
Central Park.[4] Kitty, the martyrish figurehead

4. To the Editor:

In the earnest spirit of your recent editorial ("Vulnerability
in Our Public Spaces," Aug. 9), and as the embodiment, if you will,
of the "mentally unstable or otherwise threatening people" you so
yearn to eradicate from the public domain in the wake of my "brutal
attack" on that "too trusting young star," allow me to make a suggestion that is sure to appeal to Mayor Giuliani, at the very least:
why not simply erect checkpoints at the entrances to Central Park
and demand identification from those who wish to enter?

Then you will be able to call up their records and evaluate the
relative success or failure of their lives—marriage or lack thereof,
children or lack thereof, professional success or lack thereof, healthy
bank account or lack thereof, contact with childhood friends or lack
thereof, ability to sleep peacefully at night or lack thereof, fulfill-
ment of sprawling, loopy youthful ambitions or lack thereof, ability
to fight off bouts of terror and despair or lack thereof—and using
these facts, you can assign each person a ranking based on the likeli-
hood that their "personal failures will occasion jealous explosions
directed at those more accomplished."

The rest is easy: simply encode each person's ranking into an
electronic bracelet and affix it to their wrist as they enter the park,
and then monitor those encoded points of light on a radar screen,
with personnel at the ready to intervene, should the perambula-
tions of low-ranking nonfamous people begin to encroach upon the
"safety and peace of mind that celebrities deserve, as much as anyone
else."

I ask only this: that in keeping with our hallowed cultural
tradition, you rank infamy equally with fame, so that when my
public excoriation is complete—when the *Vanity Fair* reporter I
entertained in prison two days ago (following her interviews with
my chiropractor and building superintendent) has done her worst,
along with the TV "news" magazines; when my trial and sentence
are concluded and I'm allowed at last to return to the world, to stand

of this juggernaut, is already being touted as the
Marilyn Monroe of her generation, and she isn't
even dead.

Her new movie looks to be a hit, whatever it's
about.

---

beneath a public tree and touch its scraggly bark—then I, like Kitty,
will be afforded some protection.

Who knows? I might even glimpse her one day as we both
promenade in Central Park. I doubt we would actually speak. I'd
prefer to stand at a distance next time, and wave.

Respectfully,
Jules Jones

10

Out of Body

Your friends are pretending to be all kinds of stuff, and your special job is to call them on it. Drew says he's going straight to law school. After practicing awhile, he'll run for state senator. Then U.S. senator. Eventually, president. He lays all this out the way you'd say, *After Modern Chinese Painting I'll go the gym, then work in Bobst until dinner,* if you even made plans anymore, which you don't—if you were even in school anymore, which you aren't, although that's supposedly temporary.

You look at Drew through layers of hash smoke floating in the sun. He's leaning back on the futon couch, his arm around Sasha. He's got a big, hey-come-on-in face and a head of dark hair, and he's built—not with weight-room muscle like yours, but in a basic animal way that must come from all that swimming he does.

"Just don't try and say you didn't inhale," you tell him.

Everyone laughs except Bix, who's at his computer, and you feel like a funny guy for maybe half a second, until it occurs to you that they probably only laughed because they could see you were *trying* to be funny, and they're afraid you'll jump out the window onto East Seventh Street if you fail, even at something so small.

Drew takes a long hit. You hear the smoke creak in his chest. He hands the pipe to Sasha, who passes it to Lizzie without smoking any.

"I promise, Rob," Drew croaks at you, holding in smoke, "if anyone asks, I'll tell them the hash I smoked with Robert Freeman Jr. was excellent."

Was that "Jr." mocking? The hash is not working out as planned: you're just as paranoid as with pot. You decide, no, Drew doesn't mock. Drew is a believer—last fall, he was one of the diehards passing out leaflets in Washington Square and registering students to vote. After he and Sasha got together, you started helping him—mostly with the jocks because you know how to talk to them. Coach Freeman, aka your pop, calls Drew's type "woodsy." They're loners, Pop says—skiers, woodchoppers—not team players. But you know all about teams; you can talk to people on teams (only Sasha knows you picked NYU because it hasn't had a football team in thirty years). On your best day you registered twelve team-playing Democrats, prompting Drew to exclaim, when you gave him the paperwork, "You've got the *touch*, Rob." But you never registered yourself, that was the thing, and the longer you waited, the more ashamed of this you got. Then it was too late. Even Sasha, who knows all your secrets, has no idea that you never cast a vote for Bill Clinton.

Drew leans over and gives Sasha a wet kiss, and you can tell the hash is getting him horny because you feel it too—it makes your teeth ache in a way that will only let up if you hit someone or get hit. In high school you'd get in fights when you felt like this, but no one will fight with you now—the fact that you hacked open your wrists with a box cutter three months ago and nearly bled to death seems to be a deterrent. It functions like a force field, paralyzing everyone in range with an encouraging smile on their lips. You want to hold up a mirror and ask: *How exactly are those smiles supposed to help me?*

"No one smokes hash and becomes president, Drew," you say. "It'll never happen."

"This is my period of youthful experimentation," he says, with an earnestness that would be laughable in a person who wasn't from Wisconsin. "Besides," he says, "who's going to tell them?"

"I am," you say.

"I love you too, Rob," Drew says, laughing.

Who said I loved you? you almost ask.

Drew lifts Sasha's hair and twists it into a rope. He kisses the skin under her jaw. You stand up, seething. Bix and Lizzie's apartment is tiny, like a dollhouse, full of plants and the smell of plants (wet and planty), because Lizzie loves plants. The walls are covered with Bix's collection of Last Judgment posters—naked babyish humans getting separated into good and bad, the good ones rising into green fields and golden light, the bad ones vanishing into mouths of monsters. The window is wide open, and you climb out onto the fire escape. The March cold crackles your sinuses.

Sasha joins you on the fire escape a second later. "What are you doing?" she asks.

"Don't know," you say. "Fresh air." You wonder how long you can go on speaking in two-word sentences. "Nice day."

Across East Seventh Street, two old ladies have folded bath towels on their windowsills and are resting their elbows on them while they peer down at the street below. "Look there," you say, pointing. "Two spies."

"It makes me nervous, Bobby," Sasha says. "You out here." She's the only one who gets to call you that; you were "Bobby" until you were ten, but according to your pop it's a girl's name after that.

"How come?" you say. "Third floor. Broken arm. Or leg. Worst case."

"Please come in."

"Relax, Sash." You park yourself on the grille steps leading up to the fourth-floor windows.

"Party migrate out here?" Drew origamis himself through the living room window onto the fire escape and leans over the railing to look down at the street. From inside, you hear Lizzie answer the phone—"Hi, Mom!"—trying to fluff the hash out of her voice. Her parents are visiting from Texas, which means that Bix, who's black, is spending his nights in the electrical engineering lab where he's doing his Ph.D. research. Lizzie's parents aren't even staying with her—they're at a hotel! But if Lizzie is sleeping with a black man in the same city where her parents are, they will just *know*.

Lizzie pokes her torso out the window. She's wearing a tiny blue skirt and tan patent-leather boots that go up higher than her knees. To herself, she's already a costume designer.

"How's the bigot?" you ask, realizing with chagrin that the sentence has three words.

Lizzie turns to you, flushed. "Are you referring to my mother?"

"Not me."

"You can't talk that way in my apartment, Rob," she says, using the Calm Voice they've all been using since you got back from Florida, a voice that leaves you no choice but to test how hard you have to push before it cracks.

"I'm not." You indicate the fire escape.

"Or on my fire escape."

"Not yours," you correct her. "Bix's, too. Actually, no. The city's."

"Fuck you, Rob," Lizzie says.

"You too," you say, grinning with satisfaction at the sight of real anger on a human face. It's been a while.

"Calm down," Sasha tells Lizzie.

"Excuse me? I should calm down?" Lizzie says. "He's being a total asshole. Ever since he got back."

"It's only been two weeks," Sasha says.

"I love how they talk about me like I'm not here," you observe to Drew. "Do they think I'm dead?"

"They think you're stoned."

"They're correct."

"Me too." Drew climbs the fire escape until he's a few stairs above you and perches there. He takes a long breath, savoring it, and you take one too. In Wisconsin, Drew has shot an elk with a bow and arrow, skinned it, cut off the meat into sections, and carried it home in a backpack, wearing snowshoes. Or maybe he was kidding. He and his brothers built a log cabin with their bare hands. He grew up next to a lake, and every morning, even in winter, Drew swam there. Now he swims in the NYU pool, but the chlorine hurts his eyes and it's not the same, he says, with a ceiling over you. Still, he swims there a lot, especially when he's bummed or tense or in a fight with Sasha. "You must've grown up swimming," he said when he first heard you were from Florida, and you said, Of course. But the truth is you've never liked the water—something only Sasha knows about you.

You lurch from the steps to the other end of the fire escape platform, where a window looks into the little alcove where Bix's computer lives. Bix is in front of it, dreadlocks thick as cigars, typing messages to other graduate students that they'll read on their computers, and reading messages they send back. According to Bix, this computer-message-sending is going to be *huge*—way beyond the telephone. He's big on predicting the future, and you haven't really challenged him—maybe because he's older, maybe because he's black.

Bix jumps at the sight of you looming outside his window in your baggy jeans and football jersey, which you've taken to wearing again, for some reason. "Shit, Rob," he says, "what are you doing out there?"

"Watching you."

"You've got Lizzie all stressed-out."

"I'm sorry."

"So come in here and tell her that."

You climb in through Bix's window. There's a Last Judgment poster hanging right over his desk, from the Albi Cathedral. You remember it from your Intro to Art History class last year, a class you loved so much you added art history to your business major. You wonder if Bix is religious.

In the living room Sasha and Lizzie are sitting on the futon couch, looking grim. Drew is still out on the fire escape.

"I'm sorry," you tell Lizzie.

"It's okay," she says, and you know you should leave it there—it's fine, leave it alone, but some crazy engine inside you won't let you stop: "I'm sorry your mom is a bigot. I'm sorry Bix has to have a girlfriend from Texas. I'm sorry I'm an asshole. I'm sorry I make you nervous because I tried to kill myself. I'm sorry to get in the way of your nice afternoon. . . ." Your throat tightens up and your eyes get wet as you watch their faces go from stony to sad, and it's all kind of moving and sweet except that you're not completely there—a part of you is a few feet away, or above, thinking, Good, they'll forgive you, they won't desert you, and the question is, which one is really "you," the one saying and doing whatever it is, or the one watching?

You leave Bix and Lizzie's with Sasha and Drew and head west, toward Washington Square. The cold spasms in the scars on your wrists. Sasha and Drew are a braid of elbows and shoulders and pockets, which presumably keeps them warmer than you. When you were back in Tampa, recovering, they took a Greyhound to Washington, D.C., for the inauguration and stayed up all night and watched the sun

rise over the Mall, at which point (they both say) they felt
the world start to change right under their feet. You snick-
ered when Sasha told you this, but ever since, you find yourself watching strangers' faces on the street and wondering if
they feel it, too: a change having to do with Bill Clinton or
something even bigger that's everywhere—in the air, underground—obvious to everyone but you.

At Washington Square you and Sasha say good-bye to
Drew, who peels off to take a swim and wash the hash from
his head. Sasha's wearing her backpack, heading for the library.

"Thank God," you say. "He's gone." You can't seem to
stop talking in two-word sentences now, even though you'd
like to.

"Nice," Sasha remarks.

"I'm kidding. He's great."

"I know."

Your high is wearing off, leaving a box of lint where your
head should be. Getting high is new for you—your *not* getting high was the whole reason Sasha picked you out the
first day of Freshman Orientation last year, in Washington
Square. Blocking your sun with her henna-red hair, her quick
eyes looking at you from the side rather than head-on. "I'm in
need of a fake boyfriend," she said. "Are you up for it?"

"How about your real one?" you said.

She sat down beside you and laid things out: in high
school, back in LA, she'd run away with the drummer for
a band you'd never heard of, left the country, and traveled
alone in Europe and Asia—never even graduated. Now, a
freshman, she was almost twenty-one. Her stepfather had

pulled every string to get her in here. Last week, he'd told her he was hiring a detective to make sure she "toed the line" on her own in New York. "Someone could be watching me right now," she said, looking across the square crowded with kids who all seemed to know one another. "I feel like someone is."

"Should I put my arm around you?"

"Please."

You've heard somewhere that the act of smiling makes people feel happier; putting your arm around Sasha made you want to protect her. "Why me?" you asked. "Out of curiosity."

"You're cute," she said. "Plus, you don't look druggy."

"I'm a football player," you said. "Was."

You and Sasha had books to buy; you bought them together. You visited her dorm, where you caught Lizzie, her roommate, miming approval when your back was turned. At five-thirty, you were both loading up your cafeteria trays, you going heavy on the spinach because everyone says football muscle turns to Jell-O when you stop playing. You both got your library cards, went back to your dorms, then met at the Apple for drinks at eight. It was packed with students. Sasha kept glancing around, and you figured she was thinking about the detective, so you put your arm around her and kissed the side of her face and her hair, which had a burned smell, the not-realness of it all relaxing you in a way you'd never managed to be with girls at home. At which point Sasha explained step 2: each of you had to tell the other something that would make it impossible for you ever to really go out.

"Have you done this before?" you asked, incredulous.

She'd drunk two white wines (which you'd matched two-to-one with beers) and was starting on her third. "Of course not."

"So . . . I tell you I used to torture kitty cats, and that stops you from wanting to jump my bones?"

"Did you?"

"Fuck, no."

"I'll go first," Sasha said.

She'd started shoplifting at thirteen with her girlfriends, hiding beaded combs and sparkly earrings inside their sleeves, seeing who could get away with more, but it was different for Sasha—it made her whole body glow. Later, at school, she'd replay each step of an escapade, counting the days until they could do it again. The other girls were nervous, competitive, and Sasha struggled to show only that much.

In Naples, when she ran out of money, she stole things from stores and sold them to Lars, the Swede, waiting her turn on his kitchen floor with other hungry kids holding tourists' wallets, costume jewelry, American passports. They grumbled about Lars, who never gave them what they deserved. He'd played the flute in concerts back in Sweden, supposedly, but the source of that rumor might have been Lars himself. They weren't allowed beyond his kitchen, but someone had glimpsed a piano through a closing door, and Sasha often heard a baby crying. Her first time, Lars made Sasha wait longer than anyone, holding a pair of spangly platform shoes she'd swiped from a boutique. And when everyone else was paid and gone, he had squatted beside her on the kitchen floor and unbuttoned his pants.

For months she'd done business with Lars, arriving sometimes without having managed to take anything, just needing money. "I thought he was my boyfriend," she said. "But I think I wasn't thinking anymore." She was better now, hadn't stolen anything in two years. "That wasn't me, in Naples," she told you, looking out at the crowded bar. "I don't know who it was. I feel sorry for her."

And maybe from a sense that she'd dared you, or that anything at all could be said in the chamber of truth where you and Sasha now found yourselves, or that she'd blown out a vacuum some law of physics required you to fill, you told her about James, your teammate: how one night, the two of you took out two girls in your pop's car, and after you'd brought them home (early—it was a game night), you and James drove to a secluded place and spent maybe an hour alone in the car. It happened just that one time, without discussion or agreement; the two of you had barely spoken after that. At times you'd wondered if you'd made it up.

"I'm not a fag," you told Sasha.

It wasn't you in the car with James. You were somewhere else, looking down, thinking, That fag is fooling around with another guy. How can he do that? How can he want it? How can he live with himself?

In the library, Sasha spends two hours typing a paper on Mozart's early life and sneaking sips of a Diet Coke. Being older, she feels behind—she's taking six courses a semester plus summer school so she can graduate in three years. She's a business/arts double major, like you, but in music. You rest your head in your arms on the table and sleep until she's done. Then you walk together through the dark to your dorm, on Third Avenue. You smell popcorn from the elevator—sure enough, all three suitemates are home, along with Pilar, a girl you quasi-dated last fall to distract yourself after Sasha paired off with Drew. The minute you walk in, the Nirvana volume drops and the windows fly open. You now seem to be in the same category as a professor or a cop: you make people instantly nervous. There's got to be a way to enjoy this.

You follow Sasha into her room. Most students' rooms are like hamster burrows padded with scraps and tufts of home—pillows and stuffed doggies and plug-in pots and furry slippers—but Sasha's room is practically empty; she showed up last year with nothing but a suitcase. In one corner is a rented harp she's learning to play. You lie faceup on her bed while she gathers her shower bag and green kimono and goes out. She comes back quickly (not wanting to leave you alone, you have a feeling), wearing the kimono, her head in a towel. You watch from the bed as she shakes out her long hair and uses a wide-tooth comb to get the snarls out. Then she slips out of the kimono and starts getting dressed: lacy black bra and panties, torn jeans, a faded black T-shirt, Doc Martens. Last year, after Bix and Lizzie got together, you started spending nights in Sasha's room, sleeping in Lizzie's empty bed, three feet away from Sasha's. You know the scar on her left ankle from a break that had to be operated on when it didn't heal right; you know the Big Dipper of reddish moles around her belly button and her mothball breath when she first wakes up. Everyone assumed you were a couple—it was that deep between you and Sasha. She would cry in her sleep, and you'd climb into her bed and hold her until her breathing got regular and slow. She felt so light in your arms. You'd fall asleep holding Sasha and wake up with a hard-on and just lie there, feeling this body you knew so well, its skin and smells, alongside your own need to fuck someone, waiting for the two to merge into one impulse. *Come on, pull this all together and act like someone normal for a change,* but you were scared to put your lust to the test, not wanting to ruin it with Sasha if things went wrong. It was the biggest mistake of your life, not fucking Sasha—you saw this with brutal clarity when she fell in love with Drew, and it clobbered you with remorse so extreme that you thought at first you couldn't survive it. You might have held on to Sasha and become normal at the same time, but you didn't even try—you gave up the one chance God threw your way, and now it's too late.

Out in the world, Sasha would grab your hand or throw her arms around you and kiss you—that was for the detective. He could be anywhere, watching you toss snowballs in Washington Square, Sasha jumping onto your back, her fluffy mittens leaving fibers on your tongue. He was the invisible companion you saluted over bowls of steamed vegetables at Dojo ("I want him to see me eating healthy food," she said). Occasionally you raised practical questions about the detective—Had her stepfather mentioned him again? Did she know for certain it was a man? How long did she think the surveillance would last?—but this line of thinking seemed to irritate Sasha, so you let it go. "I want him to know I'm happy," she said. "I want him to see me well again— how I'm still normal, even after everything." And you wanted that too.

When she met Drew, Sasha forgot about the detective. Drew is detectiveproof. Even her stepfather likes him.

It's after ten by the time you and Sasha meet up with Drew on Third Avenue and Saint Marks. His eyes are bloodshot from swimming; his hair is wet. He kisses Sasha like they've been apart for a week. "My older woman," he calls her some- times, and loves the fact that she's been on her own in the wider world. Of course, Drew knows nothing about how bad things were for Sasha in Naples, and lately you have the feel- ing she's starting to forget, begin over again as the person she is to Drew. This makes you sick with envy; why couldn't you do that for Sasha? Who's going to do it for you?

On East Seventh you pass Bix and Lizzie's, but the lights are off—Lizzie is out with her parents. The streets are full of people, most of whom seem to be laughing, and you won- der again about that change Sasha felt when the sun rose in Washington, D.C.—whether these people feel it, too, and their laughter comes from that.

On Avenue A, the three of you stand outside the Pyramid Club, listening. "Still the second band," Sasha says, so you walk up the street for egg creams at the Russian newsstand and drink them on a bench in Tompkins Square Park, which just reopened last summer.

"Look," you say, opening your hand. Three yellow pills. Sasha sighs; she's running out of patience.

"What are they?" Drew asks.

"E."

He has an optimist's attraction to everything new—a faith that it will enrich him, not hurt him. Lately you've found yourself using this quality in Drew, scattering bread crumbs for him one by one. "I want to do it with *you*," he tells Sasha, but she shakes her head. "I missed your druggy moment," he says wistfully.

"Thank God," Sasha says.

You pop one of the pills and put the other two back in your pocket. You start to feel the E as soon as you enter the club. The Pyramid is jammed. The Conduits have been big on college campuses for years, but Sasha is convinced their new album is pure genius and will go multiplatinum. She likes to get right up against the stage, the band in her face, but you need more distance. Drew stays close to Sasha, but when the Conduits' nutcase of a lead guitarist, Bosco, starts flinging himself around like a berserk scarecrow, you notice him edging back.

You've entered a state of tingling, stomachy happiness that feels the way you hoped adulthood would be as a kid: a blur of lost bearings, release from the drone of meals and homework and church and *That's not a nice way to talk to your sister, Robert Jr.* You wanted a brother. You want Drew to be your brother. Then you could have built the log cabin together and slept inside it, snow piling up outside the windows. You could have slaughtered the elk and, afterward, slick with blood and fur, peeled off your clothes together beside a bonfire. If you could see Drew naked, even just once, it would ease a deep, awful pressure inside you.

Bosco is getting tossed over your head, his shirt gone, skinny torso slimed with beer and sweat. Your hands slip over the flinty muscles of his back. He's still playing his guitar, hollering without a microphone. Drew spots you and moves closer, shaking his head. He'd never been to a concert before he met Sasha. You shimmy one of the remaining yellow pills from your pocket and push it into his hand.

Something was funny a while ago, but you can't remember what. Drew doesn't seem to know, either, although you're both convulsed with helpless hysterics.

Sasha thought you would wait for her inside after the show, so it takes her a while to find the two of you out on the pavement. Her eyes move between you in the acid street-light. "Ah," she says. "I get it."

"Don't be mad," Drew says. He's trying not to look at you—if you look at each other, you're gone. But you can't stop looking at Drew.

"I'm not mad," Sasha says. "I'm bored." She got introduced to the Conduits' producer, Bennie Salazar, and he's invited her to a party. "I thought we could all go," she tells Drew, "but you're too high."

"He doesn't want to go with you," you bellow, your nose running with laughter and snot. "He wants to come with me."

"That's true," Drew says.

"Fine," Sasha says angrily. "Then everyone's happy."

The two of you reel away from her. Hilarity keeps you busy for several blocks, but there's a sickness to it, like an itch that if you keep on scratching, will grind straight through skin and muscle and bone, shredding your heart. At one point you both have to stop walking and sit on a stoop, leaning against each other, almost sobbing. You buy a half gallon of orange juice and guzzle it on a corner, juice gushing over both your chins and soaking your puffy jackets. You hold the carton upside down above your mouth, catching the last drops in the back of your throat. When you toss it away, the city rises darkly around you. You're on Second Street and Avenue B. People are exchanging little vials in their hand-shakes. But Drew stretches out his arms, feeling the E in his fingertips. You've never seen him afraid; only curious.

"I feel bad," you say, "about Sasha."

"Don't worry," Drew says. "She'll forgive us."

After your wrists had been stitched and bandaged and someone else's blood had been pumped inside you and your parents were waiting at the Tampa Airport for the first flight out, Sasha pushed aside the IV coils and climbed into your bed at St. Vincent's. Even through the painkillers, there was a thudding ache around your wrists.

"Bobby?" she whispered. Her face was almost touching yours. She was breathing your breath, and you were breathing hers, malty from fear and lack of sleep. It was Sasha who found you. Ten more minutes, they said.

"Bobby, listen to me."

Sasha's green eyes were right up against yours, the lashes interlocking. "In Naples," she said, "there were kids who

were just lost. You knew they were never going to get back to
what they'd been, or have a normal life. And then there were
other ones who you thought, maybe they will."

You tried to ask which kind Lars, the Swede, was, but it
came out a mush.

"Listen," she said. "Bobby. In a minute, they're going to
kick me out."

You opened your eyes, which you hadn't realized were shut
again. "What I'm saying is, *We're the survivors*," Sasha said.

She spoke in a way that briefly cleared your head of the
cloudy things they were pumping inside you: like she'd
opened an envelope and read a result that you urgently
needed to know. Like you'd been caught offsides and had to
be straightened out.

"Not everyone is. But we are. Okay?"

"Okay."

She lay alongside you, every part of you touching, like
you'd done so many nights before she met Drew. You felt
Sasha's strength seeping into your skin. You tried to hold
her, but your hands were stuffed-animal stumps, and you
couldn't move them.

"Which means you can't do that again," she said. "Ever.
Ever. Ever. Ever. Do you promise me, Bobby?"

"I promise." And you meant it. You wouldn't break a
promise to Sasha.

"Bix!" Drew shouts. He charges up Avenue B, boots clobber-
ing the pavement. Bix is alone, hands in the pockets of his
green army jacket.

"Whoa," he says, laughing when he sees from Drew's eyes how high he is. Your own high is just beginning to waver. You'd been planning to take that last pill, but you offer it to Bix instead.

"I don't really do this anymore," Bix says, "but rules are for bending, right?" A custodian made him leave the lab; he's been walking around for two hours.

"And Lizzie's asleep," you say, "in your apartment."

Bix gives you a cold look that empties your good mood. "Let's not get started on that," he says.

You walk together, waiting for Bix to come onto the E. It's after 2:00 a.m., the hour when (it turns out) regular people go home to bed, and drunk, crazy, fucked-up people stay out. You don't want to be with those people. You want to go back to your suite and knock on Sasha's door, which she leaves unlocked when Drew isn't spending the night.

"Earth to Rob," Bix says. His face is soft and his eyes are shiny and bewitched.

"I was thinking I might go home," you say.

"You can't!" Bix cries. Love for his fellow creatures radiates from within him like an aura; you can feel its glow on your skin. "You're central to the action."

"Right," you mutter.

Drew slings his arm around you. He smells like Wisconsin—woods, fires, ponds—although you've never been near it. "Truth, Rob," he says, serious. "You're our aching, pounding heart."

You wind up at an after-hours club Bix knows about on Ludlow, crowded with people too high to go home. You all dance together, subdividing the space between now and tomorrow until time seems to move backward. You share a strong joint with a girl whose bangs are very short, leaving her bright forehead exposed. She dances near you, her arms around your neck, and Drew shouts in your ear over the music, "She wants to go home with you, Rob." But eventually the girl gives up, or forgets—or you forget—and she disappears.

The sky is just getting light when the three of you leave the club. You walk north together to Leshko's, on Avenue A, for scrambled eggs and piles of fried potatoes, then stagger, stuffed, back onto the groggy street. Bix is between you and Drew, one arm around each of you. Fire escapes dangle off the sides of buildings. A croupy church bell starts up and you remember: it's Sunday.

Someone seems to be leading the way toward the Sixth Street overpass to the East River, but really you're all moving in tandem, like on a Ouija board. The sun blazes into view, spinning bright and metallic against your eyeballs, ionizing the water's surface so you can't see a bit of pollution or crud underneath. It looks mystical, biblical. It raises a lump in your throat.

Bix squeezes your shoulder. "Gentlemen," he says, "good morning."

You stand together at the river's edge, looking out, the last patches of old snow piled at your feet. "Look at that water," Drew says. "I wish I could swim in it." After a minute he says, "Let's remember this day, even when we don't know each other anymore."

You look over at Drew, squinting in the sun, and for a second the future tunnels out and away, some version of "you"

at the end of it, looking back. And right then you feel it—
what you've seen in people's faces on the street—a swell of
movement, like an undertow, rushing you toward something
you can't quite see.

"Oh, we'll know each other forever," Bix says. "The days
of losing touch are almost gone."

"What does that mean?" Drew asks.

"We're going to meet again in a different place," Bix says.
"Everyone we've lost, we'll find. Or they'll find us."

"Where? How?" Drew asks.

Bix hesitates, like he's held this secret so long he's afraid of
what will happen when he releases it into the air. "I picture
it like Judgment Day," he says finally, his eyes on the water.
"We'll rise up out of our bodies and find each other again in
spirit form. We'll meet in that new place, all of us together,
and first it'll seem strange, and pretty soon it'll seem strange
that you could ever lose someone, or get lost."

Bix knows, you think—he's always known, in front of that
computer, and now he's passing the knowledge on. But what
you say is: "Will you finally get to meet Lizzie's parents?"

The surprise lands cleanly in Bix's face, and he laughs, a
big, billowing noise. "I don't know, Rob," he says, shaking his
head. "Maybe not—maybe that part will never change. But I
like to think so." He rubs his eyes, which look suddenly tired,
and says, "Speaking of which. Time to head back home."

He walks away, hands in the pockets of his army jacket,
but it's a while before it feels like he's really gone. You pull
your last joint from your wallet and smoke it with Drew,
walking south. The river is quiet, no boats in sight, a couple
of toothless geezers fishing under the Williamsburg Bridge.

"Drew," you say.

He's looking at the water with that stoned distraction that makes anything seem worth studying. You laugh, nervous, and he turns. "What?"

"I wish we could live in that cabin. You and me."

"What cabin?"

"The one you built. In Wisconsin." You see confusion in Drew's face, and you add, "If there is a cabin."

"Of course there's a cabin."

Your high granulates the air, then Drew's face, which reconstitutes with a new wariness in it that frightens you. "I would miss Sasha," he says slowly. "Wouldn't you?"

"You don't really know her," you say, breathless, a little desperate. "You don't know who you'd be missing."

A massive storage hangar has intervened between the path and the river, and you walk alongside it. "What don't I know about Sasha?" Drew asks in his usual friendly tone, but it's different—you sense him already turning away, and you start to panic.

"She was a hooker," you say. "A hooker and a thief—that's how she survived in Naples."

As you speak these words, a howling starts up in your ears. Drew stops walking. You're sure he's going to hit you, and you wait for it.

"That's insane," he says. "And fuck you for saying it."

"Ask her," you shout, to be heard above the howling. "Ask about Lars the Swede who used to play the flute."

Drew starts walking again, his head down. You walk beside him, your steps narrating your panic: *What have you done? What have you done? What have you done? What have you done?* The FDR is over your heads, tires roaring, gasoline in your lungs.

Drew stops again. He looks at you through the dim, oily air like he's never seen you before. "Wow, Rob," he says. "You are really and truly an asshole."

"You're the last to know."

"Not me. Sasha."

He turns and walks quickly away, leaving you alone. You charge after him, seized by a wild conviction that containing Drew will seal off the damage you've done. She doesn't know, you tell yourself, she still doesn't know. As long as Drew is in sight, she doesn't know.

You stalk him along the river's edge, maybe twenty feet between you, half running to keep up. He turns once: "Go away! I don't want to be near you!" But you sense his confusion about where to go, what to do, and it reassures you. *Nothing has happened yet.*

Between the Manhattan and Brooklyn Bridges, Drew stops beside what might be called a beach. It's made entirely out of garbage: old tires, trash, splintered wood, and glass and filthy paper and old plastic bags tapering gradually into the East River. Drew stands on this rubble, looking out, and you wait a few feet behind him. Then he begins to undress. You don't believe it's happening at first; off comes his jacket, his sweater, his two T-shirts and undershirt. And there is Drew's bare torso, strong and tight as you'd imagined, though thinner, the dark hair on his chest in the shape of a spade.

In jeans and boots, Drew picks his way to where garbage and water meet. An angular ṣlab of concrete juts out, the failed foundation of something long forgotten, and he scrambles on top of it. He unlaces his boots and removes them, then kicks off his jeans and boxers. Even through your dread, you feel a faint appreciation for the beauty and inelegance of a man undressing.

He glances back at you, and you glimpse his naked front, the dark pubic hair and strong legs. "I've always wanted to do this," he says in a flat voice, and takes a long, leaping, shallow dive, slamming the East River's surface and letting out something between a scream and a gasp. He surfaces, and you hear him trying to catch his breath. It can't be more than forty-five degrees out.

You climb the slab of concrete and start taking off clothes, sodden with dread but moved by a wavering sense that if you can master this dread it will mean something, prove something about you. Your scars twang in the cold. Your dick has shriveled to the size of a walnut and your football bulk is starting to slide, but Drew isn't even watching you. He's swimming: strong clear swimmer's strokes.

You make a clumsy leap, your body crashing onto the water, your knee hitting something hard under the surface. The cold locks in around you, knocking out your breath. You swim crazily to get away from the garbage, which you picture underneath, rusty hooks and claws reaching up to slash your genitals and feet. Your knee aches from whatever it hit.

You lift up your head and see Drew floating on his back. "We can get back out of here, right?" you yell.

"Yes, Rob," he answers in that new, flat voice. "Same way we got in."

You don't say anything else. It takes all your strength to tread water and yank in breath. Eventually the cold begins to feel almost tropically warm against your skin. The shrieking in your ears subsides, and you can breathe again. You look around, startled by the mythic beauty of what surrounds you: water encircling an island. A distant tugboat jutting out its rubbery lip. The Statue of Liberty. A thunder of wheels on the Brooklyn Bridge, which looks like the inside of a harp. Church bells, meandering and off-key, like the chimes your mother hangs on the porch. You're moving fast, and when you look for Drew you can't find him. The shore is far away. A person is swimming near it, but at such a distance that when the swimmer pauses, waving frantic arms, you can't see who it is. You hear a faint shout—*"Rob!"*—and realize you've been hearing that voice for a while. Panic scissors through you, bringing crystalline engagement with physical facts: you're caught in a current—there are currents in this river—you knew that—heard it somewhere and forgot—you shout, but feel the smallness of your voice, the seismic indifference of the water around you—all this in an instant.

"Help! Drew!"

As you flail, knowing you're not supposed to panic—panicking will drain your strength—your mind pulls away as it does so easily, so often, without your even noticing sometimes, leaving Robert Freeman Jr. to manage the current alone while you withdraw to the broader landscape, the water and buildings and streets, the avenues like endless hallways, your dorm full of sleeping students, the air thick with their communal breath. You slip through Sasha's open window, floating over the sill lined with artifacts from her travels: a white seashell, a small gold pagoda, a pair of red dice. Her harp in one corner with its small wood stool. She's asleep in her narrow bed, her burned red hair dark against the sheets. You kneel beside her, breathing the familiar smell of Sasha's sleep, whispering into her ear some mix of *I'm sorry* and *I believe in you* and *I'll always be near you, protecting you,* and *I will never leave you, I'll be curled around your heart for the rest of your life,* until the water pressing my shoulders and chest crushes me awake and I hear Sasha screaming into my face: *Fight! Fight! Fight!*

11

Good-bye, My Love

When Ted Hollander first agreed to travel to Naples in search of his missing niece, he drew up for his brother-in-law, who was footing the bill, a plan for finding her that involved cruising the places where aimless, strung-out youths tended to congregate—the train station, for example—and asking if they knew her. "Sasha. American. *Capelli rossi*"—red hair—he'd planned to say, had even practiced his pronunciation until he could roll the *r* in front of *rossi* to perfection. But since arriving in Naples a week ago, he hadn't said it once.

Today, he ignored his resolve to begin looking for Sasha and visited the ruins of Pompeii, observing early Roman wall paintings and small, prone bodies scattered like Easter eggs among the columned courtyards. He ate a can of tuna under an olive tree and listened to the crazy, empty silence.

In the early evening he returned to his hotel room, heaved his aching body onto the king-sized bed, and phoned his sister, Beth, Sasha's mother, to report that another day's efforts had been unsuccessful.

"Okay," Beth sighed from Los Angeles, as she did at the end of each day. The energy of her disappointment endowed it with something like consciousness; Ted experienced it as a third presence on the phone.

"I'm sorry," he said. A drop of poison filled his heart. He would look for Sasha tomorrow. Yet even as he made this vow, he was reaffirming a contradictory plan to visit the Museo Nazionale, home of an Orpheus and Eurydice he'd admired for years: a Roman marble relief copied from a Greek original. He had always wanted to see it.

Mercifully, Hammer, Beth's second husband, who normally had a volley of questions for Ted that boiled down to one very simple question, *Am I getting my money's worth?* (thus filling Ted with truant anxiety), either wasn't around or chose not to weigh in. After hanging up, Ted went to the minibar and dumped a vodka over ice. He brought drink and phone to the balcony and sat in a white plastic chair, looking down at the Via Partenope and the Bay of Naples. The shore was craggy, the water of questionable purity (though arrestingly blue), and those game Neapolitans, most of whom seemed to be fat, were disrobing on the rocks and leaping into the bay in full view of pedestrians, tourist hotels, and traffic. He dialed his wife.

"Oh, hi hon!" Susan was startled to hear from him so early in the day—usually he called before he went to bed, which was closer to dinnertime on the East Coast. "Is everything okay?"

"Everything's fine."

Already, her brisk, merry tone had disheartened him. Susan was often on Ted's mind in Naples, but a slightly different version of Susan: a thoughtful, knowing woman with whom he could speak without speaking. It was this slightly different version of Susan who had listened with him to the quiet of Pompeii, alert to lingering reverberations of screams, of sliding ash. How could so much devastation have been silenced? This was the sort of question that had come to preoccupy Ted in his week of solitude, a week that felt like both a month and a minute.

"I've got a nibble on the Suskind house," Susan said, apparently hoping to cheer him with this dispatch from the realm of real estate.

Yet each disappointment Ted felt in his wife, each incremental deflation, was accompanied by a seizure of guilt; many years ago, he had taken the passion he felt for Susan and folded it in half, so he no longer had a drowning, helpless feeling when he glimpsed her beside him in bed: her ropy arms and soft, generous ass. Then he'd folded it in half again, so when he felt desire for Susan, it no longer brought with it an edgy terror of never being satisfied. Then in half again, so that feeling desire entailed no immediate need to act. Then in half again, so he hardly felt it. His desire was so small in the end that Ted could slip it inside his desk or a pocket and forget about it, and this gave him a feeling of safety and accomplishment, of having dismantled a perilous apparatus that might have crushed them both. Susan was baffled at first, then distraught; she'd hit him twice across the face; she'd run from the house in a thunderstorm and slept at a motel; she'd wrestled Ted to the bedroom floor in a pair of black crotchless underpants. But eventually a sort of amnesia had overtaken Susan; her rebellion and hurt had melted away, deliquesced into a sweet, eternal sunniness that was terrible in the way that life would be terrible, Ted supposed, without death to give it gravitas and shape. He'd presumed at first that her relentless cheer was mocking, another phase in her rebellion, until it came to him that Susan had forgotten how things were between them before Ted began to fold up his desire; she'd forgotten and was happy—had never not been happy—and while all of this bolstered his awe at the gymnastic adaptability of the human mind, it also made him feel that his wife had been brainwashed. By him.

"Hon," Susan said. "Alfred wants to talk to you."

Ted braced himself for his moody, unpredictable son. "Hiya, Alf!"

"Dad, don't use that voice."

"What voice?"

"That fake 'Dad' voice."

"What do you want from me, Alfred? Can we have a conversation?"

"We lost."

"So you're what, five and eight?"

"Four and nine."

"Well. There's time."

"There's no time," said Alfred. "Time is running out."

"Is your mother still there?" Ted asked, a bit desperately. "Can you put her back on?"

"Miles wants to talk to you."

Ted spoke with his other two sons, who had further scores to report. He felt like a bookie. They played every sport imaginable and some that (to Ted) were not: soccer, hockey, baseball, lacrosse, basketball, football, fencing, wrestling, tennis, skateboarding (not a sport!), golf, Ping-Pong, Video Voodoo (absolutely not a sport, and Ted refused to sanction it), rock climbing, Rollerblading, bungee jumping (Miles, his oldest, in whom Ted sensed a joyous will to self-destruct), backgammon (not a sport!), volleyball, Wiffle ball, rugby, cricket (what country was this?), squash, water polo, ballet (Alfred, of course), and, most recently, Tae Kwon Do. At times it seemed to Ted that his sons took up sports merely to ensure his presence beside the greatest possible array of playing surfaces, and he duly appeared, hollering away his voice among piles of dead leaves and the tang of wood smoke in fall, among iridescent clover in spring, and through the soggy, mosquito-flecked summers of upstate New York.

After speaking to his wife and boys, Ted felt drunk, anxious to get out of the hotel. He seldom drank; booze flung a curtain of exhaustion over his head, robbing him of the two precious hours he had each night—two, maybe three, after dinner with Susan and the boys—in which to think and write about art. Ideally, he should have been thinking and writing about art at all times, but a confluence of factors made such thinking and writing both unnecessary (he was tenured at a third-rate college with little pressure to publish) and impossible (he taught three art history courses a semester and had taken on vast administrative duties—he needed money). The site of his thinking and writing was a small office wedged in one corner of his shaggy house, on whose door he'd installed a lock to keep his sons out. They gathered wistfully outside it, his boys, with their chipped, heartbreaking faces. They were not permitted to so much as knock upon the door to the room in which he thought and wrote about art, but Ted hadn't found a way to keep them from prowling outside it, ghostly feral creatures drinking from a pond in moonlight, their bare feet digging at the carpet, their fingers sweating on the walls, leaving spoors of grease that Ted would point out each week to Elsa, the cleaning woman. He would sit in his office, listening to the movements of his boys, imagining that he felt their hot, curious breath. I will not let them in, he would tell himself. I will sit and think about art. But he found, to his despair, that often he couldn't think about art. He thought about nothing at all.

At dusk, Ted strolled up the Via Partenope to the Piazza Vittoria. It was teeming with families, kids punting the ubiquitous soccer balls, exchanging salvos of earsplitting Italian. But there was another presence, too, in the fading light: the aimless, unclean, vaguely threatening youths who trolled this city where unemployment was at 33 percent, members of a disenfranchised generation who slunk around the decrepit palazzi where their fifteenth-century forebears had lived in splendor, who shot dope on the steps of churches in whose crypts those same forebears now lay, their diminu-

tive coffins stacked like cordwood. Ted shrank from these
youths, though he was six foot four and weighed in at two
hundred thirty, with a face that looked innocuous enough
in the bathroom mirror but often prompted colleagues to
ask him what was the matter. He was afraid Sasha would be
among these kids—that it was she, eyeing him through the
jaundiced street light that permeated Naples after dark. He'd
emptied his wallet of all but one credit card and minimal
cash. He left the piazza quickly in search of a restaurant.

Sasha had disappeared two years ago, at seventeen. Disappeared like her father, Andy Grady, a berserk financier
with violet eyes who'd walked away from a bad business
deal a year after his divorce from Beth and hadn't been
heard from again. Sasha had resurfaced periodically, re-
questing money wires in several far-flung locales, and twice
Beth and Hammer had flown wherever it was and tried in
vain to intercept her. Sasha had fled an adolescence whose
catalog of woes had included drug use, countless arrests
for shoplifting, a fondness for keeping company with rock
musicians (Beth had reported, helplessly), four shrinks,
family therapy, group therapy, and three suicide attempts,
all of which Ted had witnessed from afar with a horror
that gradually affixed to Sasha herself. As a little girl, she'd
been lovely—bewitching, even—he remembered this from
a summer he'd spent with Beth and Andy in their house
on Lake Michigan. But she'd become a glowering presence at the occasional Christmas or Thanksgiving when
Ted saw her, and he'd steered his boys away, afraid her self-
immolation would somehow taint them. He wanted nothing to do with Sasha. She was lost.

.   .   .

Ted rose early the next morning and took a taxi to the Museo Nazionale, cool, echoey, empty of tourists despite the fact that it was spring. He drifted among dusty busts of Hadrian and the various Caesars, experiencing a physical quickening in the presence of so much marble that verged on the erotic. He sensed the proximity of the Orpheus and Eurydice before he saw it, felt its cool weight across the room but prolonged the time before he faced it, reminding himself of the events leading up to the moment it described: Orpheus and Eurydice in love and newly married; Eurydice dying of a snakebite while fleeing the advances of a shepherd; Orpheus descending to the underworld, filling its dank corridors with music from his lyre as he sang of his longing for his wife; Pluto granting Eurydice's release from death on the sole condition that Orpheus not look back at her during their ascent. And then the hapless instant when, out of fear for his bride as she stumbled in the passage, Orpheus forgot himself and turned.

Ted stepped toward the relief. He felt as if he'd walked inside it, so completely did it enclose and affect him. It was the moment before Eurydice must descend to the underworld a second time, when she and Orpheus are saying goodbye. What moved Ted, mashed some delicate glassware in his chest, was the quiet of their interaction, the absence of drama or tears as they gazed at each other, touching gently. He sensed between them an understanding too deep to articulate: the unspeakable knowledge that everything is lost.

Ted stared at the relief, transfixed, for thirty minutes. He walked away and returned. He left the room and came back. Each time, the sensation awaited him: a fibrillating excitement such as he hadn't felt for years in response to a work of art, compounded by further excitement that such excitement was still possible.

He spent the rest of the day upstairs among the Pompeian mosaics, but his mind never left the Orpheus and Eurydice. He visited it again before leaving the museum.

By now it was afternoon. Ted began to walk, still dazed, until he found himself among a skein of backstreets so narrow they felt dark. He passed churches blistered with grime, moldering palazzi whose squalid interiors leaked sounds of wailing cats and children. Soiled, forgotten coats of arms were carved above their massive doorways, and these unsettled Ted: such universal, defining symbols made meaningless by nothing more than time. He imagined the slightly different version of Susan beside him, sharing his wonderment.

As the Orpheus and Eurydice relaxed its hold, Ted became aware of a subterranean patter around him, an interplay of glances, whistles, and signals that seemed to include nearly everyone, from the crone draped in black outside the church to the kid in the green T-shirt who kept buzzing past Ted on his Vespa, grazingly close. Everyone but himself. From a window, an old woman was using a rope to lower a basket full of Marlboro packs to the street. Black market, Ted thought, watching uneasily as a girl with tangled hair and sunburned arms removed a packet of cigarettes and placed some coins in the basket. As it swung upward again, toward the window, Ted recognized the cigarette buyer as his niece.

So acutely had he been dreading this encounter that he felt no real surprise at the staggering coincidence of its actually taking place. Sasha lit one of the Marlboros, brow creased, and Ted slowed his pace, pretending to admire the greasy wall of a palazzo. When she began walking again, he followed. She wore faded black jeans and a dishwater gray T-shirt. She walked erratically and with a slight limp, slowly, then briskly, so that Ted had to concentrate in order not to overtake her or fall behind.

He was sliding into the city's knotty entrails, a poor, un-touristed area where the sound of flapping laundry mingled with the bristly chatter of pigeons' wings. Without warning, Sasha pivoted around to face him. She stared, bewildered, into his face. "Is that?" she stammered. "Uncle—"

"My God! Sasha!" Ted cried, wildly mugging surprise. He was a lousy fake.

"You scared me," Sasha said, still disbelieving. "I felt someone—"

"You scared me, too," Ted rejoined, and they laughed, nervous. He should have hugged her right away. Now it felt too late.

To fend off the obvious question (*What was he doing in Naples?*), Ted kept talking: Where was she going?

"To—to visit friends," Sasha said. "What about you?"

"Just . . . walking!" he said, too loudly. They had fallen into step. "Is that a limp?"

"I broke my ankle in Tangiers," she said. "I fell down a long flight of steps."

"I hope you saw a doctor."

Sasha gave him a pitying look. "I wore a cast for three and a half months."

"Then why the limp?"

"I'm not sure."

She had grown up. And so uncompromising was this adulthood, so unstinting its inventory of breasts and hips and gently indented waist, the expert flicking away of her cigarette, that Ted experienced the change as instantaneous. A miracle. Her hair was not nearly as red as it had been. Her face was fragile and mischievous, pale enough to absorb hues from the world around her—purple, green, pink—like a face painted by Lucian Freud. She looked like a girl who a century ago would not have lived long, would have died in childbirth. A girl whose feathery bones did not quite heal.

"You live here?" he asked. "Naples?"

"A nicer part," Sasha said, with a tinge of snobbery. "What about you, Uncle Teddy? Do you still live in Mount Gray, New York?"

"I do," he said, startled by her recall.

"Is your house very big? Are there lots of trees? Do you have a tire swing?"

"Trees galore. A hammock no one uses."

Sasha paused, closing her eyes as if to imagine it. "You have three sons," she said. "Miles, Ames, and Alfred."

She was right; even the order was right. "I'm amazed you remember," Ted said.

"I remember everything," Sasha said.

She had stopped before one of the seedy palazzi, its coat of arms painted over with a yellow smiley face that Ted found macabre. "This is where my friends live," she said. "Good-bye, Uncle Teddy. It was so nice running into you." She shook his hand with damp, spidery fingers.

Ted, unprepared for this abrupt parting, stammered a little. "Wait, but—can't I take you to dinner?"

Sasha tilted her head, searching his eyes. "I'm awfully busy," she said, with apology. And then, as if softened by some deep, unfailing will to politeness, "But yes. I'm free tonight."

It was only as Ted pushed open the door to his hotel room, the medley of 1950s beige tones greeting him after each day he'd spent not looking for Sasha, that he was rocked by the sheer outlandishness of what had just happened. It was time to make his daily call to Beth, and he imagined his sister's dumbstruck jubilation at the landslide of good news since yesterday: not only had he located her daughter, but Sasha had seemed clean, reasonably healthy, mentally coherent, and in possession of friends; in short, better than they'd had any right to expect. And yet Ted felt no such joy. Why? he wondered, lying flat on the bed with arms crossed, shutting his eyes. Why this longing for yesterday, even this morning— for the relative peace of knowing he should look for Sasha but failing to do so? He didn't know. He didn't know.

Beth and Andy's marriage had died spectacularly the summer Ted lived with them on Lake Michigan while managing a construction site two miles farther up the lake. Apart from the marriage itself, the casualties by summer's end included the majolica plate Ted had given Beth for her birthday; sundry items of damaged furniture; Beth's left shoulder, which Andy dislocated twice; and her collarbone, which he broke. When they fought, Ted would take Sasha outside, through the razor-edged grass, to the beach. She had long red hair and blue-white skin that Beth was always trying to keep from burning. Ted took his sister's worries seriously and always brought the sunscreen with him when they went out to the sand—sand that was too hot in the late afternoons for Sasha to walk on without screaming. He would carry her in his arms, light as a cat in her red-and-white two-piece, set her on a towel, and rub cream onto her shoulders and back and face, her tiny nose—she must have been five—and wonder what would become of her, growing up amid so much violence. He insisted she wear her white sailor hat in the sun, though she didn't want to. He was a graduate student in art history, working as a contractor to pay his tuition.

"A con-trac-tor," Sasha repeated, fastidiously. "What's that?"

"Well, he organizes different workmen to build a house."

"Are there floor sanders?"

"Sure. You know any floor sanders?"

"One," she said. "He sanded floors in our house. His name is Mark Avery."

Ted was instantly suspicious of this Mark Avery.

"He gave me a fish," Sasha offered.

"A goldfish?"

"No," she said, laughing, swatting his arm. "A bathtub fish."

"Does it squeak?"

"Yes, but I don't like the sound."

These conversations went on for hours. Ted had the uneasy sense that the child was spinning them out as a way of filling the time, distracting them both from whatever was going on inside that house. And this made her seem much older than she really was, a tiny little woman, knowing, world-weary, too accepting of life's burdens even to mention them. She never once alluded to her parents, or to what it was she and Ted were hiding from out on that beach.

"Will you take me swimming?"

"Of course," he always said.

Only then would he allow her to doff her protective cap. Her hair was long and silken; it blew in his face when he carried her (as she always wished) into Lake Michigan. She would gird him with her thin legs and arms, warm from the sun, and rest her head on his shoulder. Ted sensed her mounting dread as they approached the water, but she refused to let him turn back. "No. It's okay. Go," she would mutter grimly into his neck, as if her submersion in Lake Michigan were an ordeal she was required to endure for some greater good. Ted tried different ways of making it easier for her—going in little by little, or plunging straight in—but always Sasha would gasp in pain and tighten the grip of her legs and arms around him. When it was over, when she was in, she was herself again, dog-paddling despite his efforts to teach her the crawl. ("I know how to swim!" she would say, impatiently. "I just don't like to.") Splashing him, teeth chattering gamely. But the entire process unsettled Ted, as if he were hurting her, forcing this immersion upon his niece when what he longed to do—fantasized about doing—was rescue her: wrap her in a blanket and secrete her from the house before dawn; paddle away in an old rowboat he'd found; carry her down the beach and not turn around. He was twenty-five. He trusted no one else. But he could do nothing, really, to protect his niece, and as the weeks eked away, he began to anticipate summer's end as a black, ominous presence. Yet when the time came it was strangely easy. Sasha clung to her mother, barely glancing at Ted as he loaded up his car and said good-bye, and he set off feeling angry at her, wounded in a way he knew was childish but couldn't seem to help, and when that feeling passed it left him exhausted, too tired even to drive. He parked outside a Dairy Queen and slept.

"How do I know you know how to swim, if you won't show me?" he asked Sasha once, as they sat on the sand.

"I took lessons with Rachel Costanza."

"You're not answering my question."

She smiled at him a little helplessly, as if she longed to hide behind her childishness but sensed that, somehow, it was already too late for that. "She has a Siamese cat named Feather."

"Why won't you swim?"

"Oh, Uncle Teddy," she said, in one of her eerie imita-tions of her mother. "You wear me out."

Sasha arrived at his hotel at eight o'clock wearing a short red dress, black patent-leather boots, and a regalia of cosmetics that sharpened her face into a small, shrill mask. Her narrow eyes curved like hooks. Ted glimpsed her across the lobby and felt reluctance verging on paralysis. He had hoped, cru-elly, that she wouldn't show up.

Still, he made himself cross the lobby and take her arm. "There's a good restaurant up the street," he said, "unless you have other ideas."

She did. Blowing smoke from the window of a taxi, Sasha harangued the driver in halting Italian as the car shrieked down alleys and the wrong way up one-way streets to the Vomero, an affluent neighborhood Ted had not seen. It was high on a hill. Reeling, he paid the driver and stood with Sasha in a gap between two buildings. The flat, sparkling city arrayed itself before them, lazily toeing the sea. Hockney, Ted thought. Diebenkorn. John Moore. In the distance, Mount Vesuvius reposed benignly. Ted pictured the slightly different version of Susan standing near him, taking it in.

"This is the best view in Naples," Sasha said challengingly, but Ted sensed her waiting, gauging his approval.

"It's a wonderful view," he assured her, and added, as they ambled among the leafy residential streets, "This is the prettiest neighborhood I've seen in Naples."

"I live here," Sasha said. "A few streets over."

Ted was skeptical. "I should've met you up here, then. Saved you the trip."

"I doubt you would have found it," Sasha said. "Foreigners are helpless in Naples. Most of them get robbed."

"Aren't you a foreigner?"

"Technically," Sasha said. "But I know my way around."

They reached an intersection thronged with what had to be college students (strange how they looked the same everywhere): boys and girls in black leather jackets riding on Vespas, lounging on Vespas, perching and even standing on Vespas. The density of Vespas made the whole square seem to vibrate, and the fumes of their exhaust worked on Ted like a mild narcotic. In the dusk, a chorus line of palm trees vamped against a Bellini sky. Sasha threaded her way among the students with brittle self-consciousness, eyes locked ahead.

In a restaurant on the square, she asked for a window table and ordered their meal: fried zucchini flowers followed by pizza. Again and again she peeked outside at the youths on their Vespas. It was poignantly clear that she longed to be among them. "Do you know any of those kids?" Ted asked.

"They're students," she said dismissively, as if the word were a synonym for "nothing."

"They look about your age."

Sasha shrugged. "Most of them still live at home," she said. "I want to hear about you, Uncle Teddy. Are you still an art history professor? By now you must be an expert."

Jarred once again by her memory, Ted felt the pressure that arose in him when he tried to talk about his work—a confusion about what had originally driven him to disappoint his parents and rack up mountainous debt so he could write a dissertation claiming (in breathless tones that embarrassed him now) that Cézanne's distinctive brushstrokes were an effort to represent *sound*—namely, in his summer landscapes, the hypnotic chant of locusts.

"I'm writing about the impact of Greek sculpture on the French Impressionists," he said, attempting liveliness, but it landed like a brick.

"Your wife, Susan," Sasha said. "Her hair is blond, right?"

"Yes, Susan is blond. . . ."

"My hair used to be red."

"It's still red," he said. "Reddish."

"But not like it was." She watched him, awaiting confirmation.

"No."

There was a pause. "Do you love her? Susan?"

This cool inquiry landed somewhere near Ted's solar plexus. "*Aunt* Susan," he corrected her.

Sasha looked chastened. "Aunt."

"Of course I love her," Ted said quietly.

Dinner arrived: pizza draped in buffalo mozzarella, buttery and warm in Ted's throat. After a second glass of red wine, Sasha began to talk. She had run away from home with Wade, the drummer for the Pinheads (a band that seemed to require no introduction), who were playing in Tokyo. "We stayed at the Okura Hotel, meaning *fancy*," she said. "It was April, that's cherry blossom season in Japan, and every tree was covered with all these pink flowers, and businessmen sang and danced underneath them in paper hats!" Ted, who had never been to the Far East or even the Near East, felt a twist of envy.

After Tokyo, the band had gone to Hong Kong. "We stayed in a white high-rise on a hill, with the most incredible view," she said. "Islands and water and boats and planes . . ."

"So, is Wade with you now? In Naples?"

She blinked. "Wade? No."

He'd left her there, in Hong Kong, in the tall white building; she'd lingered in the apartment until its owner had asked her to leave. Then she'd moved to a youth hostel inside a building full of sweatshops, people asleep under their sewing machines on piles of fabric scraps. Sasha relayed these details lightheartedly, as if it had all been a romp. "Then I made some friends," she said, "and we crossed into China."

"Are those the friends you were meeting yesterday?"

Sasha laughed. "I meet new people everywhere I go," she said. "That's how it is when you travel, Uncle Teddy."

She was flushed—from the wine or maybe the pleasure of remembering. Ted waved for the bill and paid it. He felt leaden, depressed.

The teenagers had dispersed into the chilly night. Sasha didn't have a coat. "Please wear my jacket," Ted said, removing the worn, heavy tweed, but she wouldn't hear of it. He sensed that she wanted to remain fully visible in her red dress. The tall boots exaggerated her limp.

After a walk of many blocks, they reached a generic-looking nightclub whose doorman waved them listlessly inside. By now it was midnight. "Friends of mine own this place," Sasha said, leading the way into a tumult of bodies, fluorescent purple light, and a beat with all the variety of a jackhammer. Even Ted, no connoisseur of nightclubs, felt the tired familiarity of the scene, yet Sasha seemed enthralled. "Buy me a drink, Uncle Teddy, would you?" she said, pointing at a ghastly concoction at a nearby table. "Like that, with a little umbrella."

Ted shoved his way toward the bar. Being away from his niece felt like opening a window, loosening an airless oppression. But what was the problem, exactly? Sasha had been having a ball, seeing the world; hell, she'd done more in two years than Ted had done in twenty. So why was he so eager to escape her?

Sasha had commandeered two seats at a low table, a

setup that made Ted feel like an ape, knees jammed under his chin. As she hoisted the umbrella drink to her lips, the purple light leached into slivers of pale scar tissue on the inside of her wrist. When she set down the drink, Ted took her arm in his hands and turned it over; Sasha allowed this until she saw what he was looking at, then yanked her arm away. "That's from before," she said. "In Los Angeles."

"Let me see."

She wouldn't. And to his own surprise, Ted reached across the table and grasped her wrists in his hands, taking a certain angry pleasure in hurting his niece as he wrested them over by force. He noticed that her nails were red; she'd painted them this afternoon. Sasha relented, averting her eyes as he studied her forearms in the cold, weird light. They were scarred and scuffed like furniture.

"A lot are by accident," Sasha said. "My balance was really off."

"You've had a bad time." He wanted her to admit it.

There was a silence. Finally Sasha said, "I kept thinking I saw my father. Isn't that crazy?"

"I don't know."

"In China, Morocco. I'd look across a room—bam—I saw his hair. Or his legs, I still remember the exact shape of his legs. Or how he threw back his head when he laughed—remember, Uncle Teddy? How his laugh was kind of a yell?"

"I do, now that you say it."

"I thought he might be following me," Sasha said, "making sure I was okay. And then, when it seemed like he wasn't, I got really scared."

Ted let go of her arms, and she folded them in her lap. "I

thought he could keep track of me because of my hair. But now it isn't even red."

"I recognized you."

"True." She leaned toward him, her pale face close to Ted's, sharp with expectation. "Uncle Teddy," she said, "what are you doing here?"

It was the question he'd been dreading, yet the answer slid from Ted like meat falling off a bone. "I'm here to look at art," he said. "To look at art and think about art."

There: a sudden, lifting sensation of peace. Relief. He hadn't come for Sasha, it was true.

"Art?"

"That's what I like to do," he said, and smiled, remembering the Orpheus and Eurydice this afternoon. "That's what I'm always trying to do. That's what I care about."

In Sasha's face there was a slackening, as if some weight she'd been bracing herself against had been removed. "I thought you came to look for me," she said.

Ted watched her from a distance. A peaceful distance.

Sasha lit one of her Marlboros. After two drags, she squashed it out. "Let's dance," she said, a heaviness about her as she rose from her seat. "Come on, Uncle Teddy," taking his hand, herding him toward the dance floor, a liquid mass of bodies that provoked in Ted a frightened sensation of shyness. He hesitated, resisting, but Sasha hauled him in among the other dancers and instantly he felt buoyed, suspended. How long had it been since he'd danced in a nightclub? Fifteen years? More? Hesitantly, Ted began to move, feeling hulking, bearish in his professor's tweed, moving his feet in some approximation of dance steps until he noticed

that Sasha wasn't moving at all. She stood still, watching
him. And then she reached for him, encircled Ted with her
long arms and clung to him so that he felt her modest bulk,
the height and weight of this new Sasha, his grown-up niece
who had once been so small, and the irrevocability of that
transformation released in Ted a ragged sorrow, so his throat
seized up and a painful tingling fizzed in his nostrils. He
cleaved to Sasha. But she was gone, that little girl. Gone with
the passionate boy who had loved her.

Finally she pulled away. "Wait here," she said, not meeting his eyes. "I'll be right back." Disoriented, Ted hovered
among the dancing Italians until a mounting sense of awkwardness drove him from the floor. He lingered near it.
Eventually, he circled the club. She'd mentioned having
friends there—could she be talking to them somewhere?
Had she gone outside? Anxious, foggy from his own drink,
Ted ordered a San Pellegrino at the bar. And only then, as he
reached for his wallet and found it gone, did he realize that
she'd robbed him.

Sunlight pried open his sticky eyelids, forcing him awake.
He'd forgotten to close the blinds. It had been five o'clock
by the time he'd finally gone to bed, after hours of helpless
wandering and a series of lousy directions to the police station; after locating it finally and relaying his sad tale (minus
the pickpocket's identity) to an officer with oiled hair and an
attitude of pristine indifference; after the offer of a ride to his
hotel (which was all he'd really been after) from an elderly

couple he'd met at the station, whose passports had been stolen on the Amalfi ferryboat.

Now Ted rose from bed with a throbbing head and rampaging heart. Phone messages littered the table: five from Beth, three from Susan, and two from Alfred (*I lose*, read one, in the broken English of the hotel clerk). Ted left them where he'd thrown them. He showered, dressed without shaving, drained a vodka at the minibar, and removed cash and another credit card from his room safe. He had to find Sasha now—today—and this imperative, which had seized him at no specific moment, assumed an immediacy that was the perfect inverse of his prior shirking. There were other things he needed to do—call Beth, call Susan, eat—but doing them now was out of the question. He had to find her.

But where? Ted deliberated this question while downing three espressos in the hotel lobby, letting the caffeine and vodka greet in his brain like fighting fish. Where to look for Sasha in this sprawling, malodorous city? He reviewed the strategies he'd already failed to execute: approaching dissolute kids at the train station and youth hostels, but no, no. He'd waited too long for any of that.

Without a clear plan, he took a taxi to the Museo Nazionale and set off in what seemed the direction he'd walked yesterday, after viewing the Orpheus and Eurydice. Nothing looked the same, but surely his state of mind could account for the difference, the tiny metronome of panic now ticking within him. Nothing looked the same, yet everything looked familiar: the stained churches and slanting crusty walls, the hangnail-shaped bars. After following a narrow street to its wriggling conclusion, he emerged onto a thoroughfare lined with a gauntlet of weary palazzi, their bottom floors gouged open to accommodate cheap clothing and shoe stores. A breeze of recognition fluttered over Ted. He followed the avenue slowly, looking right and left, until he caught sight of the yellow smiley face overlaying a palimpsest of swords and crosses.

He pushed open the small rectangular door cut into a broad, curved entrance originally built to receive horse-drawn coaches, then followed a passageway into a cobbled courtyard still warm from recent sunlight. It smelled of rotting melons. A bandy-legged old woman wearing blue kneesocks under her dress bobbled toward him, her hair in a scarf.

"Sasha," Ted said into her faded wet eyes. "American. *Capelli rossi.*" He tripped on the *r* and tried again. "*Rossi,*" he said, rolling it this time. "*Capelli rossi.*" Realizing as he spoke that the description was no longer quite accurate.

"No, no," the woman muttered. As she began to lurch away, Ted followed, slipped a twenty-dollar bill into her soft hand and inquired again, rolling the *r* this time without a hitch. The woman made a clicking noise, jerked her chin, and then, looking almost sad, gestured for Ted to follow her. He did, filled with disdain at how easily she'd been bought, how little her protection was worth. To one side of the front door was a broad flight of stairs, splotches of rich, Neapolitan marble still winking up through the grime. The woman began climbing slowly, clutching the rail. Ted followed.

The second floor, as he'd been lecturing his undergraduates for years, was the *piano nobile*, where palace owners brandished their wealth before guests. Even now, lousy with molting pigeons and stuccoed with piles of their refuse, its vaulted arches overlooking the courtyard were splendid. Seeing him notice, the woman said, *"Bellissima, eh? Ecco, guardate!"* and with a pride Ted found touching, she threw open the door to a big dim room whose walls were stained with what looked like patches of mold. The woman pulled a switch, and a lightbulb dangling from a wire transfigured the moldy shapes into painted murals in the style of Titian and Giorgione: robust naked women clutching fruit; clumps of dark leaves. A whisper of silvery birds. This must have been the ballroom.

On the third floor Ted noticed two boys sharing a ciga-rette in a doorway. Another lay asleep under a straggling assortment of laundry: wet socks and underwear pinned carefully to a wire. Ted smelled dope and stale olive oil, heard a mutter of invisible activity, and realized that this palazzo had become a rooming house. The irony of finding himself smack in the midst of the demimonde he'd tried to avoid amused Ted. So here we are, he thought. At last.

On the fifth and top floor, where servants once had lived, the doors were smaller, set along a narrow hallway. Ted's elderly guide stopped to rest against a wall. His contempt for her yielded to gratitude: what effort that twenty dollars had cost her! How badly she must need it. "I'm sorry," he said, "I'm sorry you had to walk so far." But the woman shook her head, not understanding. She tottered partway down the hall and rapped sharply on one of the narrow doors. It opened and Ted saw Sasha, half asleep, dressed in a pair of men's pajamas. At the sight of Ted her eyes widened, but her face remained impassive. "Hi, Uncle Teddy," she said mildly.

"Sasha," he said, realizing only then that he, too, was breathless from the climb. "I wanted to . . . talk to you."

The woman's gaze jumped between them; then she turned and walked away. The moment she rounded a corner, Sasha shut the door in his face. "Go away," she said. "I'm busy."

Ted moved nearer the door, flattening his palm against the splintery wood. Across it, he felt the spooked, angry presence of his niece. "So this is where you live," he said.

"I'm moving someplace better."

"When you've picked enough pockets?"

There was a pause. "That wasn't me," she said. "That was a friend of mine."

"You've got friends all over the place, but I never actually see them."

"Go! Leave, Uncle Teddy."

"I'd like to," Ted said. "Believe me."

But he couldn't bring himself to leave, or even really move. He stood until his legs began to ache, then bent his knees and slid to the floor. It was already afternoon, and an aureole of musty light issued from a window at one end of the hall. Ted rubbed his eyes, feeling as if he might sleep.

"Are you still there?" Sasha barked through the door.

"Still here."

The door opened a crack, and Ted's wallet bounced on his head and dropped to the floor.

"Go to hell," Sasha said, and shut the door again.

Ted opened the wallet, found its contents untouched, and replaced it in his pocket. Then he sat. For a long time—hours, it seemed (he'd forgotten his watch)—there was silence. Occasionally Ted heard other, disembodied tenants moving inside their rooms. He imagined he was an element of the palace itself, a sensate molding or step whose fate it was to witness the ebb and flow of generations, to feel the place relax its medieval bulk more deeply into the earth. Another year, another fifty. Twice he stood up to let tenants pass, girls with jumpy hands and cracked leather purses. They hardly glanced at him.

"Are you still there?" Sasha asked, from behind the door.

"Still here."

She emerged from the room and locked the door quickly behind her. She wore blue jeans, a T-shirt, and plastic flip-flops, and carried a faded pink towel and a small bag. "Where are you going?" he asked, but she stalked down the hall without comment. Twenty minutes later she was back, hair hanging wet, trailing a floral smell of soap. She opened her door with the key, then hesitated. "I mop the halls to pay for this room, okay? I sweep the fucking courtyard. Does that make you happy?"

"Does it make *you* happy?" he countered.

The door shook on its hinges.

As Ted sat, feeling the evolution of the afternoon, he found himself thinking of Susan. Not the slightly different version of Susan, but Susan herself—his wife—on a day many years ago, before Ted had begun folding up his desire into the tiny shape it had become. On a trip to New York, riding the Staten Island Ferry for fun, because neither one of them had ever done it, Susan turned to him suddenly and said, "Let's make sure it's always like this." And so entwined were their thoughts at that point that Ted knew exactly why she'd said it: not because they'd made love that morning or drunk a bottle of Pouilly-Fuissé at lunch—because she'd felt the passage of time. And then Ted felt it, too, in the leaping brown water, the scudding boats and wind—motion, chaos everywhere—and he'd held Susan's hand and said, "Always. It will always be like this."

Recently, he'd mentioned that trip in some other context, and Susan had looked him full in the face and chimed, in her sunny new voice, "Are you sure that was me? I don't remember a thing about it!" and administered a springy little kiss to the top of Ted's head. Amnesia, he'd thought. Brainwashing. But it came to him now that Susan had simply been lying. He'd let her go, conserving himself for—what? It frightened Ted that he had no idea. But he'd let her go, and she was gone.

"Are you there?" Sasha called, but he didn't answer.

She threw open the door and peered out. "You are," she said, with relief. Ted looked up at her from the floor and said nothing. "You can come inside, I guess," she said.

He hauled himself to his feet and stepped into her room. It was tiny: a narow bed, a desk, a sprig of mint in a plastic cup filling the room with its scent. The red dress, hanging from a hook. The sun was just beginning to set, skidding over rooftops and church steeples and landing in the room through a single window by the bed. Its sill was crowded with what appeared to be souvenirs of Sasha's travels: a tiny gold pagoda, a guitar pick, a long white seashell. In the middle of the window, dangling from a string, hung a crude circle made from a bent coat hanger. Sasha sat on her bed, watching Ted take in her meager possessions. He recognized, with merciless clarity, what he'd somehow failed to grasp yesterday: how alone his niece was in this foreign place. How empty-handed.

As if sensing the movement of his thoughts, Sasha said, "I get to know a lot of people. But it never really lasts."

On the desk lay a small stack of books in English: *The History of the World in 24 Lessons. The Sumptuous Treasures of Naples.* At the top, a worn volume entitled *Learning to Type.*

Ted sat on the bed beside his niece and put his arm around her shoulders. They felt like birds' nests under his coat. The prickling sensation ached in his nostrils.

"Listen to me, Sasha," he said. "You can do it alone. But it's going to be so much harder."

She didn't answer. She was looking at the sun. Ted looked, too, staring through the window at the riot of dusty color. Turner, he thought. O'Keeffe. Paul Klee.

On another day more than twenty years after this one, after Sasha had gone to college and settled in New York; after she'd reconnected on Facebook with her college boyfriend and married late (when Beth had nearly given up hope) and had two children, one of whom was slightly autistic; when she was like anyone, with a life that worried and electrified and overwhelmed her, Ted, long divorced—a grandfather—would visit Sasha at home in the California desert. He would step through a living room strewn with the flotsam of her young kids and watch the western sun blaze through a sliding glass door. And for an instant he would remember Naples: sitting with Sasha in her tiny room; the jolt of surprise and delight he'd felt when the sun finally dropped into the center of her window and was captured inside her circle of wire.

Now he turned to her, grinning. Her hair and face were aflame with orange light.

"See," Sasha muttered, eyeing the sun. "It's mine."

12

Great Rock and Roll Pauses

By Alison Blake

May 14th & 15th, 202-

1. After Lincoln's Game

2. In My Room

3. One Night Later

4. The Desert

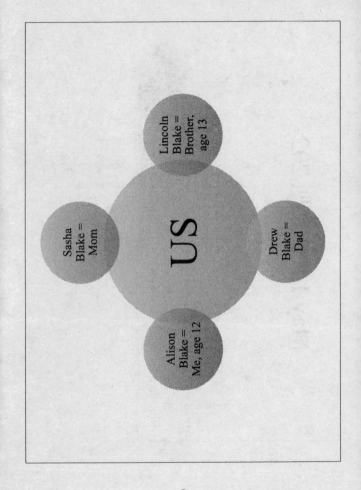

After Lincoln's Game

1

Walking to the Car

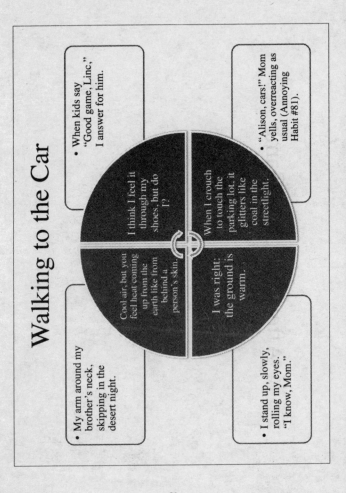

- My arm around my brother's neck, skipping in the desert night.

- When kids say "Good game, Linc," I answer for him.

Cool air, but you feel heat coming up from the earth like from behind a person's skin.

I think I feel it through my shoes, but do I?

When I crouch to touch the parking lot, it glitters like coal in the streetlight.

I was right: the ground is warm.

- I stand up, slowly, rolling my eyes. "I know, Mom."

- "Alison, cars!" Mom yells, overreacting as usual (Annoying Habit #81).

Annoying Habit #48

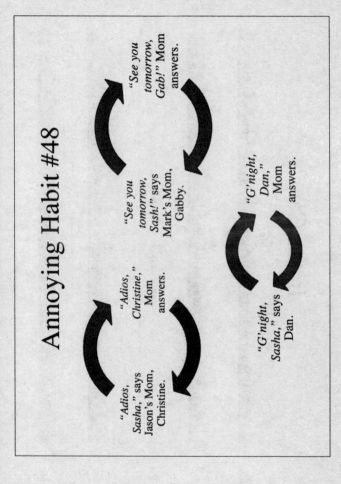

"Adios, Sasha," says Jason's Mom, Christine.

"Adios, Christine," Mom answers.

"See you tomorrow, Sash!" says Mark's Mom, Gabby.

"See you tomorrow, Gab!" Mom answers.

"G'night, Sasha," says Dan.

"G'night, Dan," Mom answers.

In the Car

Me:
"Why do you have to repeat people's *exact words* when you say good-bye to them?"

Mom:
"What are you talking about?"

I tell her precisely what I'm talking about.

Mom:
"Any chance of easing up on the scrutiny, Ally?"

Me:
"Not possible."

Dad Is Working

Desert Landscape

When I was little, there were lawns.

Now, you need a lot of credits for a lawn or else a turbine, which is expensive.

Our house is next to the desert. Two months ago, a lizard laid eggs in the sand by our deck.

Mom and Lincoln and I sit at our picnic table, looking up at the stars.

Mom makes sculptures in the desert out of trash and our old toys.

Eventually her sculptures fall apart, which is "part of the process."

Lincoln

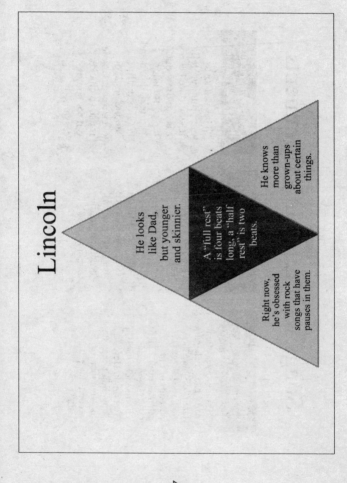

He looks like Dad, but younger and skinnier.

A "full rest" is four beats long, a "half rest" is two beats.

Right now, he's obsessed with rock songs that have pauses in them.

He knows more than grown-ups about certain things.

Songs with Lincoln's Comments

"Bernadette," by the Four Tops

- "This is an excellent early pause. The voice tapers off, and then you've still got 1.5 seconds of total silence, from 2:38 to 2:395, before the chorus kicks back in. You think, Hey, the song didn't end after all—but then, 26.5 seconds later, it does end."

"Foxey Lady," by Jimi Hendrix

- "Another great early pause: 2 seconds long, coming 2:23 seconds into a 3:19-minute-long song. But this one isn't total silence; we can hear Jimi breathing in the background."

"Young Americans," by David Bowie

- "This is a lost opportunity. Hell, it would've been so easy to draw out the pause after '...break down and cry...,' to a full second, or 2, or even 3, but Bowie must've chickened out for some reason."

278

Dad vs. Mom

Dad Would Say (if he were here):

"Wow, you've really analyzed those songs, Linc."

"I admire you for digging into the minutiae."

"You spend time with any other kids today?"

Mom Says:

"I like 'Bernadette' the best of those three."

"I don't think of Bowie as a chicken, so there must be some reason he opted not to pause there."

"Please don't say 'hell.'"

Now Just the Pauses...

Lincoln loops the pause in each song so it lasts for minutes.

If my friends are around, I ignore Lincoln's music.

When it's just us, the pauses are my favorite.

They sound like this:

Mom Says:

"There's a smokiness to the 'Bernadette' pause, probably because it's recorded on 8-track."

"It's a little eerie to hear Hendrix snickering continuously—I'm not sure that qualifies as a true pause."

"God, it's a beautiful night. I wish your Dad were here."

Why Dad Isn't Here

Doctor
- Today he operated on the heart of a girl younger than me.
- Her parents are illegal.

"Good Man"
- That's what everyone says about Dad.
- Because of his clinic.

Boss
- At work, people follow Dad around with questions.
- In his office, he'll shut the door with a giant sigh and say, "Allycat, tell me what you did today."

Weak Point
- He can't understand Lincoln.
- For example:

Lincoln Wants to Say/Ends Up Saying:

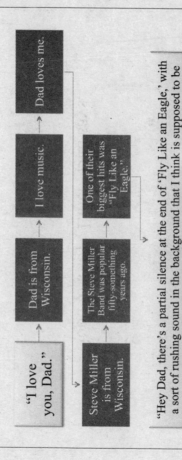

"I love you, Dad." → Dad is from Wisconsin. → I love music. → Dad loves me.

Steve Miller is from Wisconsin. → The Steve Miller Band was popular fifty-something years ago. → One of their biggest hits was "Fly Like an Eagle."

"Hey Dad, there's a partial silence at the end of 'Fly Like an Eagle,' with a sort of rushing sound in the background that I think is supposed to be the wind, or maybe time rushing past!"

"Good to know, Linc," Dad says.

What I Notice During the Looped Pauses

A whisper of orange on the horizon.

A thousand black turbines.

Miles of solar panels like a black ocean I've never seen close up.

You can't get used to the stars, no matter how long you live here.

There was desert in Pakistan, but I don't remember it.

All I remember is this.

In My Room

2

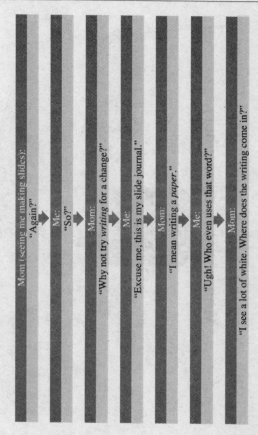

Annoying Habit #92

Mom (seeing me making slides):
"Again?"

Me:
"So?"

Mom:
"Why not try *writing* for a change?"

Me:
"Excuse me, this is my slide journal."

Mom:
"I mean writing a *paper*."

Me:
"Ugh! Who even uses that word?"

Mom:
"I see a lot of white. Where does the writing come in?"

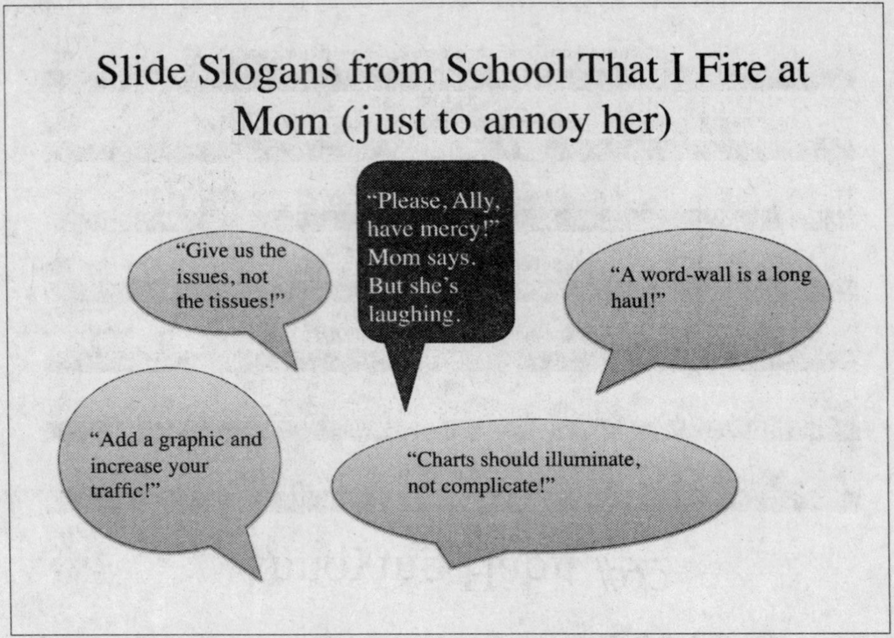
Slide Slogans from School That I Fire at Mom (just to annoy her)
"Give us the issues, not the tissues!"
"Please, Ally, have mercy!" Mom says. But she's laughing.
"A word-wall is a long haul!"
"Add a graphic and increase your traffic!"
"Charts should illuminate, not complicate!"

Mom Spots the Toy Horse

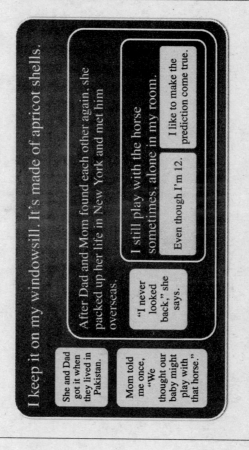

I keep it on my windowsill. It's made of apricot shells.

She and Dad got it when they lived in Pakistan.

Mom told me once, "We thought our baby might play with that horse."

After Dad and Mom found each other again, she packed up her life in New York and met him overseas.

"I never looked back," she says.

I still play with the horse sometimes alone in my room.

Even though I'm 12.

I like to make the prediction come true.

"Oh Ally, I love seeing that horse," Mom says.

"What about this?" I Ask, and Open the Book.

Conduit: A Rock-and-Roll Suicide, by Jules Jones

Mom bought the book, but she never mentions it.

It's about a fat rock star who wants to die onstage, but ends up recovering and owning a dairy farm.

There's a picture of Mom on page 128.

Sasha in the Picture

The caption is: "Outside the Pyramid Club, early 1990s."

She's on the street with some people including the rock star (before he got fat).

Her hair is bright red and tangled.

Mom's mouth is smiling, but her eyes are sad.

She looks like someone I want to know, or maybe even be.

Her face is sharp and pretty, like a fox.

292

Mom's Reasons for Not Talking About That Time

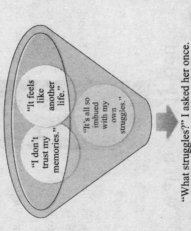

"What struggles?" I asked her once.

"Nothing you need to think about," Mom said.

Lincoln's Bed Is on the Other Side of the Wall from My Bed

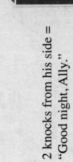

- 2 knocks from his side = "Good night, Ally."
- Mom will go to his room next.
- Lincoln gets her longest.

- 2 knocks from my side = "Good night, Linc."
- I can hear them talking through the wall.
- I get her first.

Mom Sits on the Edge of My Bed

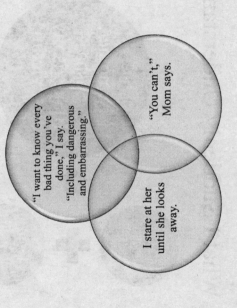

"I want to know every bad thing you've done," I say. "Including dangerous and embarrassing."

"You can't," Mom says.

I stare at her until she looks away.

What I Suddenly Understand

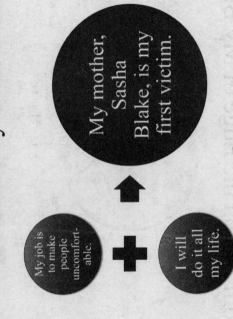

My job is to make people uncomfortable.

+

I will do it all my life.

→

My mother, Sasha Blake, is my first victim.

Lincoln Appears When I'm Half Asleep

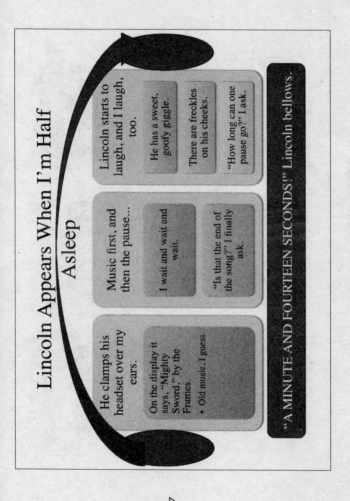

He clamps his headset over my ears.

On the display it says, "Mighty Sword," by the Frames.

• Old music, I guess.

Music first, and then the pause...

I wait and wait and wait.

"Is that the end of the song?" I finally ask.

Lincoln starts to laugh, and I laugh, too.

He has a sweet, goofy giggle.

There are freckles on his cheeks.

"How long can one pause go?" I ask.

"A MINUTE AND FOURTEEN SECONDS!" Lincoln bellows.

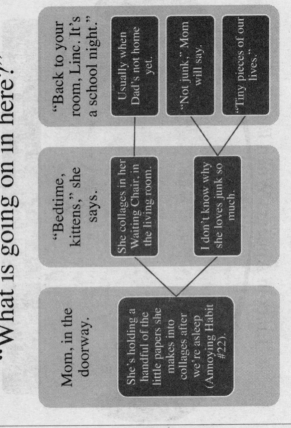

"What is going on in here?"

Mom, in the doorway.

She's holding a handful of the little papers she makes into collages after we're asleep (Annoying Habit #22).

"Bedtime, kittens," she says.

She collages in her Waiting Chair, in the living room.

I don't know why she loves junk so much.

"Back to your room, Linc. It's a school night."

Usually when Dad's not home yet.

"Not junk," Mom will say.

"Tiny pieces of our lives."

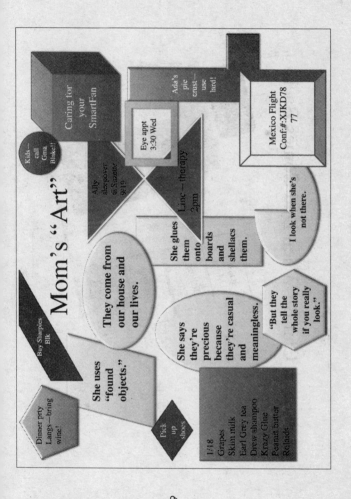

Mom's "Art"

They come from our house and our lives.

She uses "found objects."

She says they're precious because they're casual and meaningless.

"But they tell the whole story if you really look."

She glues them onto boards and shellacs them.

I look when she's not there.

Buy Sharpies Blk

Dinner prty Langs—bring wine!

Pick up shoes

1/18
Grapes
Skim milk
Earl Grey tea
Drew shampoo
Krazy Glue
Peanut butter
Refuds

Kids—call Gma Blake!

Caring for your SmartFan

Ally sleepover @ Suzane 9/19

Linc—therapy 2pm

Eye appt 3:30 Wed

Ada's pie crust—use lard!

Mexico Flight Conf.#:XJKD78 77

299

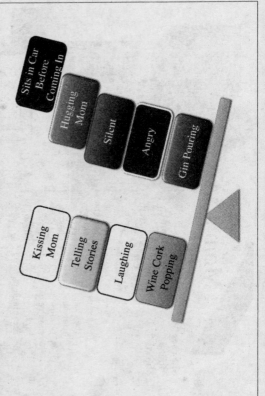

Ways It Can Be When Dad Comes Back

Sits in Car Before Coming In
Hugging Mom
Silent
Angry
Gin Pouring

Kissing Mom
Telling Stories
Laughing
Wine Cork Popping

Dad Comes Home Late

I hear the brushing door through my sleep.

I peek through my door slit.

Mom has her arms around Dad.

His face is in her hair.

They don't say anything.

There's a blanket on Mom's Waiting Chair where she fell asleep.

One Night Later

3

Dad Barbecues Chicken on the Deck

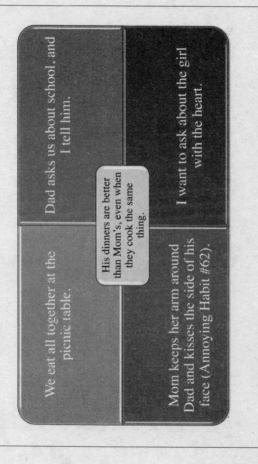

Facts About Dad

Right after he shaves, his skin will squeak if you push your finger across it.

His hair is thick and wavy, unlike a lot of dads.

He can still lift me onto his shoulders.

When he chews I hear his teeth smash together.
• They should be in pieces, but they're strong and white.

When he can't sleep, he walks into the desert.

It's a mystery why he loves Mom so much.

304

Dad's Laugh

It's hard to make Dad laugh.

When he does, it's a big sound like a bark or a roar.

Maybe the bark or roar is his surprise at laughing.

Mom says Dad used to laugh more.

"Everyone laughs more as a kid," she says (including college).

True Story

When Dad was in college, he went swimming with a guy named Rob, and Rob drowned.

That was when Dad decided to become a doctor.

"Why not become a lifeguard?" I'll sometimes ask. "Or a swim instructor."

"Good point," Dad says. "Think I still can?"

Before that, Dad wanted to be president.

"Who doesn't, at 18?" he'll say.

Dad will tell anyone this stuff.

"Keeping secrets can kill you" is one of his favorite sayings.

Rob Was Mom's Best Friend.

She keeps his picture in her wallet.

He's primordially cute, with reddish face stubble and nice eyes, like a mountain climber.

Still, Dad is more handsome.

If you look carefully, you can tell that Rob will die young.

He has that look of someone who's only in old pictures.

"Did you love him?" I asked Mom.

"Yes. As a friend."

"What was he like?"

"He was sweet and confused, like a lot of kids."

"Why did he drown?"

"He wasn't a strong swimmer, and he got caught in a current."

"Why couldn't Dad rescue him?"

"He tried."

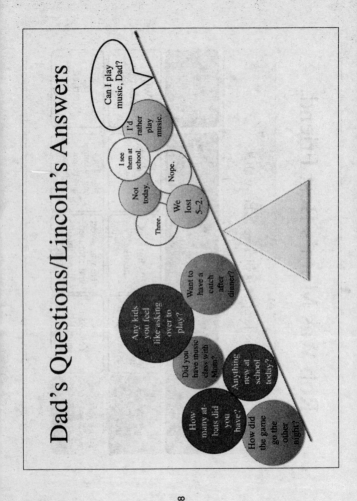

Signs That Dad Isn't Happy

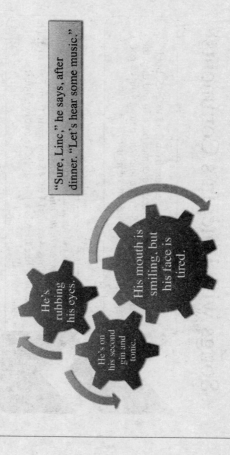

309

Songs with Lincoln's Comments

"Long Train Runnin'" by the Doobie Brothers

- "The pause is only 2 seconds, from 2:43 to 2:45, but it's basically perfect: the refrain comes back in and then the song goes until 3:28 — even after the pause, you've got almost another full minute of music."

"Supervixen" by Garbage

- "This one is unique, because the pauses happen when there's *no rest in the music.* They're just second-long interruptions — from :14 to :15 and again from 3:08 to 3:09. It sounds like there's a gap in the recording, but it's intentional!"

Dad, to Mom, Whispering Under the Music
(but I can hear him)

"Should we be encouraging this?"
"Of course we should."

"How is this helping him connect to other kids?"
"It connects him to the world."

"Why not try to divert him onto something else?"
"This is what he cares about right now."

"But what *is* it, Sasha? What is *this*?"
"Drew," Mom says, "it's music."

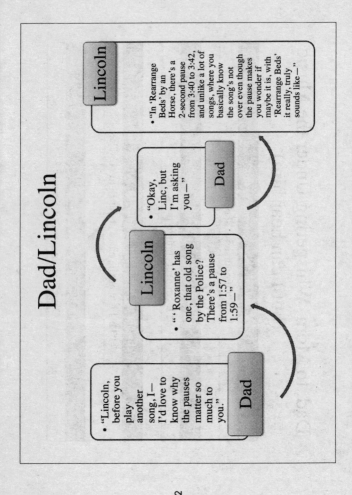

Dad/Lincoln

Dad: "Lincoln, before you play another song, I—I'd love to know why the pauses matter so much to you."

Lincoln: "'Roxanne' has one, that old song by the Police? There's a pause from 1:57 to 1:59—"

Dad: "Okay, Linc, but I'm asking you—"

Lincoln: "In 'Rearrange Beds' by an Horse, there's a 2-second pause from 3:40 to 3:42, and unlike a lot of songs, where you basically know the song's not over even though the pause makes you wonder if maybe it is, with 'Rearrange Beds' it really, truly sounds like—"

312

"Stop!" Dad shouts. "Stop. Please. Forget I asked."

Lincoln Starts to Cry

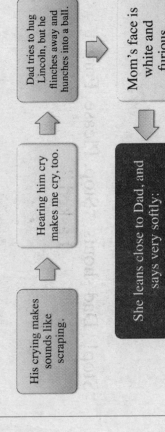

His crying makes sounds like scraping.

Hearing him cry makes me cry, too.

Dad tries to hug Lincoln, but he flinches away and hunches into a ball.

Mom's face is white and furious.

She leans close to Dad, and says very softly:

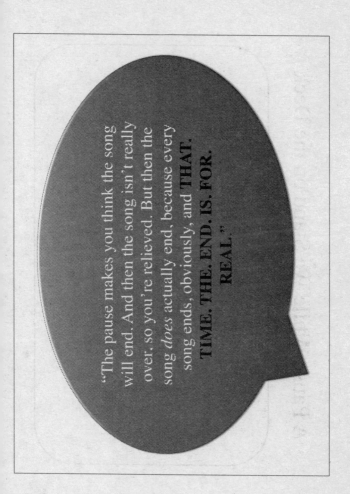

"The pause makes you think the song will end. And then the song isn't really over, so you're relieved. But then the song *does* actually end, because every song ends, obviously, and THAT. TIME. THE. END. IS. FOR. REAL."

A Pause While We Stand on the Deck

Then Dad Gathers Lincoln into His Arms

Lincoln fights him, but Dad is stronger. "Okay," Dad says softly. "Okay, Linc. I'm sorry."

Even when Lincoln stops struggling, his jab keeps blades shut, shoulder his thoughts.

They look so much alike, it's like watching Dad hug his skinny, long-ago self.

Lincoln Runs Inside and Slams His Bedroom Door

```
                    ┌──────────────────┐
                    │ I stay on the    │
┌──────────────┐    │ porch with Dad.  │
│ Mom follows  │    └──────────────────┘
│ him.         │             │
└──────────────┘    ┌──────────────────┐
                    │ The sunset is a  │
                    │ bonfire over our │
                    │ heads.           │
                    └──────────────────┘
                         │         │
        ┌────────────────┘         └────────────────┐
┌──────────────────┐              ┌──────────────────┐
│ Dad drains his gin│             │ "Feel like a     │
│ and tonic and     │             │ walk, Ally?" he  │
│ shakes the bare   │             │ asks.            │
│ ice.              │             └──────────────────┘
└──────────────────┘
```

The Desert

4

It Starts Where Our Lawn Used to Be

Three steps down from our deck, the desert surrounds us:

- Mountains like cutout paper shapes.
- Big-top sky full of stars.
- Mom's sculptures made of train tracks and doll heads fading into the dust.

"Careful of snakes," Dad says.

- "It's too cold," I say. "They're sleeping."
- "Let's keep it that way," Dad says.

Sounds

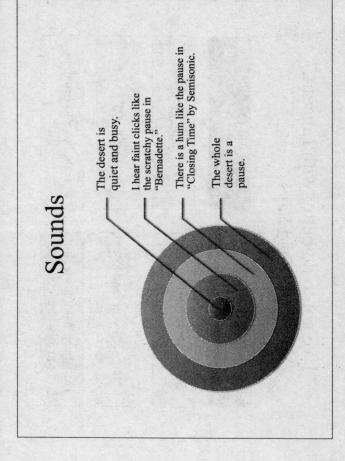

The desert is quiet and busy.

I hear faint clicks like the scratchy pause in "Bernadette."

There is a hum like the pause in "Closing Time" by Semisonic.

The whole desert is a pause.

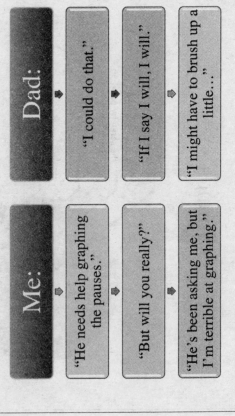

"I've got to do better with Lincoln," Dad Says.

Me:
- "He needs help graphing the pauses."
- "But will you really?"
- "He's been asking me, but I'm terrible at graphing."

Dad:
- "I could do that."
- "If I say I will, I will."
- "I might have to brush up a little…"

The Old Golf Course

There are lots of grayish swells and dips, like the moon.

The clubhouse is still there, roped off and collapsing.

"I remember this trap," he says.

"You used to play here, right?" I ask.

"Sure. All doctors play golf".

Dad stands in a shallow hole and grins at me.

I remember riding the cart between purple flower beds.

Dad doesn't like most doctors. "They're arrogant," he says.

Dad doesn't have time for friends.

"You're the only friends I need," he'll say. Meaning us.

A Long, Empty Stretch of Walking

"Is Mom mad?" I ask.

- "I believe she is."

"Will she forgive you?"

- "Of course."

"How do you know?"

- "Your mother is the forgiving type. Thank God."

"Did she forgive you when Rob drowned?"

- Dad stops walking and turns to me. The moon has just come up. "What made you think of him?"

"Sometimes I just do."

- "Me too," Dad says.

After a Long Time, We Reach the Solar Panels

I've never walked this far.	The panels go on for miles.	It's like finding a city or another planet.
They look evil.	Like angled oily black things.	But they're actually mending the Earth.
There were protests when they were built, years ago.	Their shade made a lot of desert creatures homeless.	But at least they can live where all the lawns and golf courses used to be.

"But it wasn't your fault, right?"

"It was no one's fault," Dad says.

"She died this morning," Dad says.

"The girl from yesterday," I say. "With the sick heart."

Suddenly, There's a Whirring Noise Around Us

Thousands of solar panels lift and tilt at the same time, in the same way.

I clutch at Dad's arm: "Why are they doing that?"

"They're collecting moonlight," Dad says, and I remember: it's weaker, but we use it.

The panels shift and move.

"Is this where you come when you walk in the night?" I ask.

We Stand a Long Time, Watching the Solar Panels Move

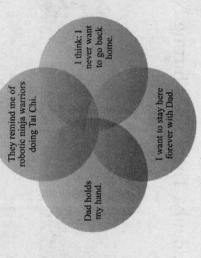

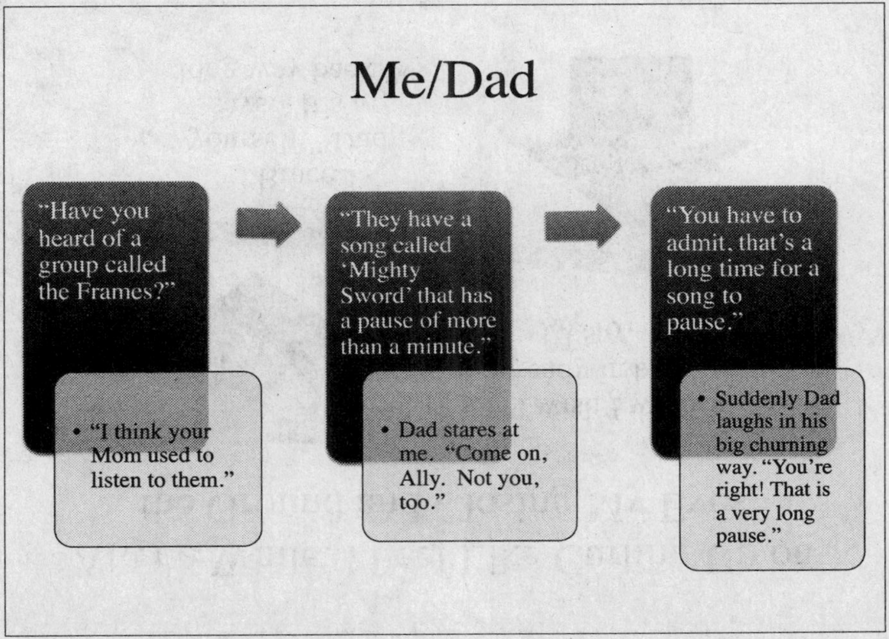
Me/Dad
"Have you heard of a group called the Frames?"
"I think your Mom used to listen to them."
"They have a song called 'Mighty Sword' that has a pause of more than a minute."
Dad stares at me. "Come on, Ally. Not you, too."
"You have to admit, that's a long time for a song to pause."
Suddenly Dad laughs in his big churning way. "You're right! That is a very long pause."

After a While, I Feel Like Curling Up on the Ground and Closing My Eyes

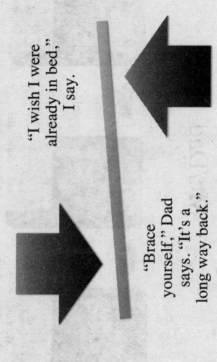

"I wish I were already in bed," I say.

"Brace yourself," Dad says. "It's a long way back."

We Walk for Several Years

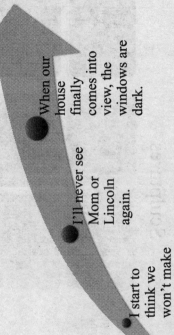

I start to think we won't make it.

I'll never see Mom or Lincoln again.

When our house finally comes into view, the windows are dark.

331

Dad Points to a Snake on one of Mom's Sculptures

It's coiled like a silver rope on my old puppet theater.

Dad lifts me onto his shoulders.

He's the strongest man in the world.

He carries me toward our house.

It looks abandoned, like the clubhouse at the golf course.

"Do you think they're inside?" I ask.

Dad doesn't answer.

Suddenly I'm scared.

What I'm Afraid Of

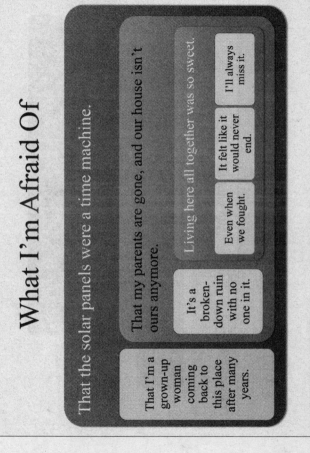

That the solar panels were a time machine.

That my parents are gone, and our house isn't ours anymore.

That I'm a grown-up woman coming back to this place after many years.

It's a broken-down ruin with no one in it.

Living here all together was so sweet.

Even when we fought.

It felt like it would never end.

I'll always miss it.

Dad Sets Me Down on Our Porch

I run to the sliding glass door and yank it open.

Inside there's a light.

Familiar things fall back over me like the softest, oldest blanket.

I start to cry.

What I Hear as I'm Falling Asleep

"Okay. I know."

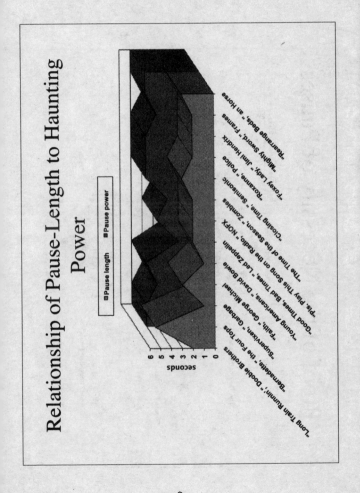

Relationship of Pause-Length to Haunting Power

Pause length   Pause power

seconds

"Long Train Runnin'", Doobie Brothers
"Bernadette", the Four Tops
"Superfixin", George Michael
"Faith", George Michael
"Young Americans", David Bowie
"Good Times, Bad Times", Led Zeppelin
"...ple, Play This Song on the radio.", NOFX
"The Time of the Season", Zombies
"Closing Time", Semisonic
"Roxanne", Police
"Foxy Lady", Jimi Hendrix
"Mighty Sword", Frames
"Rearrange Beds", an Horse

Proof of the Necessity of Pauses

Legend: Pause power ▓ Song excellence

Axes: "Supervixen", "Faith", "Young Americans", "Good Times, Bad Times", "Please Play This...", "The Time of the Season", "Long Train Runnin'", "Bernadette"

Scale: 0 1 2 3 4 5

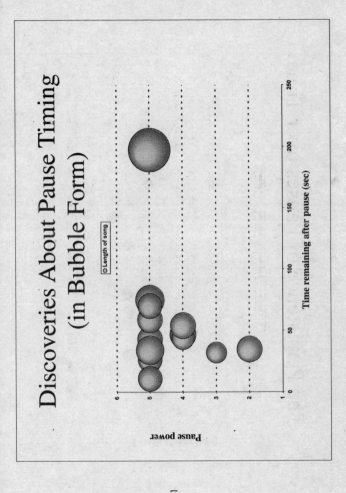

341

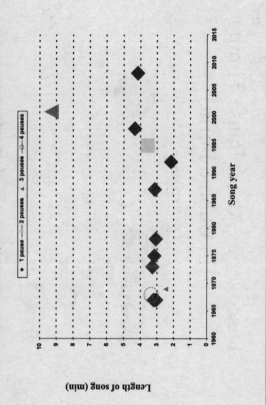

The Persistence of Pauses over Time

The End

13

Pure Language

"You don't want to do this," Bennie murmured. "Am I right?"

"Absolutely," Alex said.

"You think it's selling out. Compromising the ideals that make you, 'you.'"

Alex laughed. "I know that's what it is."

"See, you're a purist," Bennie said. "That's why you're perfect for this."

Alex felt the flattery working on him like the first sweet tokes of a joint you know will destroy you if you smoke it all. The long awaited brunch with Bennie Salazar was winding down, and Alex's hyper-rehearsed pitch to be hired as a mixer had already flopped. But now, as they eyed each other from lean perpendicular couches doused in winter sun that poured from a skylight in Bennie's Tribeca loft, Alex felt the sudden, riveting engagement of the older man's curiosity. Their wives were in the kitchen; their baby daughters were between them on a red Persian carpet, warily sharing a kitchen set.

"If I won't do it," Alex said, "then I can't really be perfect."

"I think you will."

Alex was annoyed, intrigued. "How come?"

"A feeling," Bennie said, rousing himself slightly from his deep recline. "That we have some history together that hasn't happened yet."

Alex had first heard Bennie Salazar's name from a girl he'd dated once, when he was new to New York and Bennie was still famous. The girl had worked for him—Alex remembered this clearly—but it was practically all he could remember; her name, what she'd looked like, what exactly they'd done together—those details had been erased. The only impressions Alex retained of their date involved winter, darkness, and something about a *wallet,* of all things, but had it been lost? Found? Stolen? The girl's wallet, or his own? The answers were maddeningly absent—it was like trying to remember a song that you knew made you feel a certain way, without a title, artist, or even a few bars to bring it back. The girl hovered just beyond reach, having left the wallet in Alex's brain as a kind of calling card, to tease him. In the days leading up to this brunch with Bennie, Alex had found himself oddly fixated on her.

"Das mine!" protested Ava, Bennie's daughter, affirming Alex's recent theory that language acquisition involved a phase of speaking German. She snatched a plastic skillet away from his own daughter, Cara-Ann, who lurched after it, roaring, "Mine pot! Mine pot!" Alex jumped to his feet, then noticed that Bennie hadn't stirred. He forced himself to sit back down.

"I know you'd rather mix," Bennie said, somehow audible over the caterwauling without seeming to raise his voice. "You love music. You want to work with sound. You think I don't know what that feels like?"

The girls fell on each other in a gladiatorial frenzy of yowling, scratching, and yanking wisps of fledgling hair. "Everything okay in there?" Alex's wife, Rebecca, called from the kitchen.

"We're good," Alex called back. He marveled at Bennie's calm; was this how it was when you started the kid thing all over again after a second marriage?

"The problem is," Bennie went on, "it's not about sound anymore. It's not about *music*. It's about reach. That's the bitter fucking pill I had to swallow."

"I know."

Meaning: he knew (as did everyone in the industry) how Bennie had gotten canned from his own label, Sow's Ear Records, many years ago, after serving his corporate controllers a boardroom lunch of cow pies ("and we're talking *in the steam trays*," wrote a secretary who'd narrated the melee in real time on Gawker). "You're asking me to feed the people shit?" Bennie had allegedly roared at the appalled executives. "Try eating some yourselves and see how it tastes!" After that, Bennie had returned to producing music with a raspy, analog sound, none of which had really sold. Now, pushing sixty, he was seen as irrelevant; Alex usually heard him referred to in the past tense.

When Cara-Ann sank her freshly minted incisors into Ava's shoulder, it was Rebecca who rushed in from the kitchen and pried her off, casting a mystified look at Alex, now suspended in Zen-like serenity upon the couch. Lupa came with her: the dark-eyed mother Alex had avoided in playgroup at first because she was beautiful, until he'd learned she was married to Bennie Salazar.

When wounds had been bandaged and order restored, Lupa kissed Bennie's head (his trademark bushy hair now silver), and said, "I keep waiting for you to play Scotty."

Bennie smiled up at his much younger wife. "I've been saving him," he said. Then he worked his handset, untapping from the staggering sound system (which seemed to route the music straight through Alex's pores) a baleful male vocalist accompanied by torqued, boinging slide guitar. "We released this a couple of months ago," Bennie said. "You've heard of him, Scotty Hausmann? He's doing well with the pointers."

Alex glanced over at Rebecca, who scorned the term "pointer" and would politely but firmly correct anyone who used it to describe Cara-Ann. Luckily, his wife hadn't heard. Now that Starfish, or kiddie handsets, were ubiquitous, any child who could point was able to download music—the youngest buyer on record being a three-month-old in Atlanta, who'd purchased a song by Nine Inch Nails called "Ga-ga." Fifteen years of war had ended with a baby boom, and these babies had not only revived a dead industry but become the arbiters of musical success. Bands had no choice but to reinvent themselves for the preverbal; even Biggie had released yet another posthumous album whose title song was a remix of a Biggie standard, "Fuck You, Bitch," to sound like "You're Big, Chief!" with an accompanying picture of Biggie dandling a toddler in Native American headdress. Starfish had other features—finger drawing, GPS systems for babies just learning to walk, PicMail—but Cara-Ann had never touched one, and Rebecca and Alex had agreed that she would not until age five. They used their own handsets sparingly in front of her.

"Listen to this guy," Bennie said. "Just listen."

The mournful vibrato; the jangly quaver of slide guitar—to Alex it sounded dire. But this was Bennie Salazar, who'd discovered the Conduits all those years ago. "What do *you* hear?" Alex asked him.

Bennie shut his eyes, every part of him alive with the palpable act of listening. "He's absolutely pure," he said. "Untouched."

Alex closed his own eyes. Immediately sounds thickened in his ears: choppers, church bells, a distant drill. The usual confetti of horns and sirens. The tingle of track lighting overhead, a dishwasher slop. Cara-Ann's sleepy "No . . ." as Rebecca pulled on her sweater. They were about to go. Alex felt a spasm of dread, or something like it, at the thought of leaving this brunch with Bennie Salazar empty-handed.

He opened his eyes. Bennie's were already open, his brown, tranquil gaze fixed on Alex's face. "I think you hear what I hear, Alex," he said. "Am I right?"

That night, when Rebecca and Cara-Ann were firmly asleep, Alex extracted himself from the porridgy warmth of their shared bed in its foam of mosquito netting and went to the living room/playroom/guest room/office. When he stood close to the middle window and looked straight up, he could see the top of the Empire State Building, lit tonight in red and gold. This wedge of view had been a selling point back when Rebecca's parents had bought her the Garment District one-bedroom many years ago, right after the crash. Alex and Rebecca had planned to sell the apartment when she got pregnant, then learned that the squat building their own overlooked had been bought by a developer who planned to raze it and build a skyscraper that would seal off their air and light. The apartment became impossible to sell. And now, two years later, the skyscraper had at last begun to rise, a fact that filled Alex with dread and doom but also a vertiginous sweetness—every instant of warm sunlight through their three east-facing windows felt delicious, and this sliver of sparkling night, which for years he'd watched from a cushion propped against the sill, often while smoking a joint, now appeared agonizingly beautiful, a mirage.

Alex loved the dead of night. Without the rant of construction and omnipresent choppers, hidden portals of sound opened themselves to his ears: the teakettle whistle and sock-footed thump of Sandra, the single mother who lived in the apartment overhead; a hummingbird thrum that Alex presumed was her teenage son masturbating to his handset in the adjacent room. From the street, a single cough, errant conversational strands: ". . . you're asking me to be a different person . . ." and "Believe it or not, drinking keeps me clean."

Alex leaned against his cushion and lit up a joint. He'd

spent the afternoon trying—and failing—to tell Rebecca what he'd agreed to do for Bennie Salazar. Bennie had never used the word "parrot"; since the Bloggescandals, the term had become an obscenity. Even the financial disclosure statements that political bloggers were required to post hadn't stemmed the suspicion that people's opinions weren't really their own. "Who's paying you?" was a retort that might follow any bout of enthusiasm, along with laughter—who would let themselves be bought? But Alex had promised Bennie fifty parrots to create "authentic" word of mouth for Scotty Hausmann's first live concert, to be held in Lower Manhattan next month.

Using his handset, he began devising a system for selecting potential parrots from among his 15,896 friends. He used three variables: how much they needed money ("Need"), how connected and respected they were ("Reach"), and how open they might be to selling that influence ("Corruptibility"). He chose a few people at random and ranked them in each category on a scale from 10 to 0, then graphed the results on his handset in three dimensions, looking for a cluster of dots where the three lines intersected. But in every case, scoring well in two categories meant a terrible score in the third: poor and highly corruptible people—his friend Finn, for example, a failed actor and quasi–drug addict who'd posted a recipe for speedballs on his page and lived mostly off the goodwill of his former Wesleyan classmates (Need: 9; Corruptibility: 10) had no reach (1). Poor, influential people like Rose, a stripper/cellist whose hairstyle changes were instantly copied in certain parts of the East Village (Need: 9; Reach: 10) were incorruptible (0)—in fact, Rose kept a rumor sheet on her page that functioned as an informal police blotter, recording which friend's boyfriend had given her a black eye, who had borrowed and trashed a drum set, whose dog had been left tied to a parking meter for hours in the rain. There were influential and corruptible people like his friend Max, onetime singer for the Pink Buttons, now a wind-power potentate who owned a Soho triplex and threw a caviar-strewn Christmas party each year that had people kissing his ass from August onward in hopes of being invited (Reach: 10; Corruptibility: 8). But Max was popular *because he was rich* (Need: 0) and had no incentive to sell.

Alex stared goggle-eyed at his handset screen. Would anyone agree to do this? And then it came to him that someone already had: himself. Alex graphed himself as he might appear to Rebecca: Need: 9; Reach: 6; Corruptibility: 0. Alex was a purist, like Bennie had said; he'd walked away from sleazy bosses (in the *music* business) just as he now routinely walked away from women who were drawn to the sight of a man caring for his baby daughter during business hours. Hell, he'd met Rebecca after trying to chase down a guy in a wolf mask who'd snatched her purse the day before Halloween. But Alex had caved to Bennie Salazar without a fight. Why? Because his apartment would soon be dark and airless? Because being with Cara-Ann while Rebecca worked full-time teaching and writing had made him restless? Because he never could quite forget that every byte of information he'd posted online (favorite color, vegetable, sexual position) was stored in the databases of multinationals who swore they would never, ever use it—that he was *owned*, in other words, having sold himself unthinkingly at the very point in his life when he'd felt most subversive? Or was it the odd symmetry of having first heard Bennie Salazar's name from that lost girl he'd dated once, at the very beginning, and now meeting Bennie at last, a decade and a half later, through *playgroup*?

Alex didn't know. He didn't need to know. What he needed was to find fifty more people like him, who had stopped being themselves without realizing it.

"Physics is required. Three semesters. If you fail, you're out of the program."

"For a *marketing degree*?" Alex was dumbfounded.

"It used to be epidemiology," Lulu said. "You know, when the viral model was still current."

"Don't people still say 'viral'?" Alex was wishing he'd had a real cup of coffee, not the swill they were pouring at this Greek diner. Bennie's assistant, Lulu, appeared to have had fifteen or twenty—unless this was her personality.

"No one says 'viral' anymore," Lulu said. "I mean, maybe thoughtlessly, the way we still say 'connect' or 'transmit'— those old mechanical metaphors that have nothing to do with how information travels. See, reach isn't describable in terms of cause and effect anymore: it's simultaneous. It's faster than the speed of light, that's actually been measured. So now we study particle physics."

"What next? String theory?"

"That's an elective."

Lulu was in her early twenties, a graduate student at Barnard *and* Bennie's full-time assistant: a living embodiment of the new "handset employee": paperless, deskless, commuteless, and theoretically omnipresent, though Lulu appeared to be ignoring a constant chatter of handset beeps and burps. The photos on her page had not done justice to the arresting, wide-eyed symmetry of her face, the radiant shine of her hair. She was "clean": no piercings, tattoos, or scarifications. All the kids were now. And who could blame them, Alex thought, after watching three generations of flaccid tattoos droop like moth-eaten upholstery over poorly stuffed biceps and saggy asses?

Cara-Ann was asleep in her sling, her face wedged in the slot between Alex's jaw and collarbone, her fruity, biscuity breath filling his nostrils. He had thirty minutes, maybe forty-five, before she would wake up wanting lunch. Yet Alex felt a perverse need to go backward, to understand Lulu, to pinpoint why exactly she disconcerted him.

"How did you find your way to Bennie?" he asked.

"His ex-wife used to work for my mom," Lulu said, "years ago, when I was a little girl. I've known Bennie forever—and his son, Chris. He's two years older than me."

"Huh," Alex said. "And what does your mom do?"

"She was a publicist, but she left the business," Lulu said. "She lives upstate."

"What's her name?"

"Dolly."

Alex was inclined to pursue this line of questioning back to the moment of Lulu's conception, but stopped himself. A silence fell, punctuated by the arrival of their food. Alex had meant to order soup, but that had seemed spineless, so at the last minute he'd gone for a Reuben sandwich, forgetting that he couldn't chew without waking Cara-Ann. Lulu had ordered lemon meringue pie; she ate the meringue in tiny flecks off the prongs of her fork.

"So," she said, when Alex failed to speak up. "Bennie says we're going to make a blind team, with you as the anonymous captain."

"He used those terms?"

Lulu laughed. "No, those are marketing terms. From school."

"Actually, they're sports terms. From . . . sports," Alex said. He'd been a team captain many times, though in the presence of someone so young it felt too long ago to really count.

"Sports metaphors still work," Lulu reflected.

"So this is a known thing?" he asked. "The *blind team*?" Alex had thought it was his own brain wave: reduce the shame and guilt of parrothood by assembling a team that doesn't know it's a team—or that it has a captain. Each team member would deal individually with Lulu, with Alex orchestrating in secret from above.

"Oh, sure," Lulu said. "BTs—blind teams—work especially well with older people. I mean"— she smiled—"people over thirty."

"And why is that?"

"Older people are more resistant to . . ." She seemed to falter.

"Being bought?"

Lulu smiled. "See, that's what we call a disingenuous metaphor," she said. "DMs look like descriptions, but they're really judgments. I mean, is a person who sells oranges *being bought*? Is the person who repairs appliances *selling out*?"

"No, because what they do is up front," Alex said, aware that he was condescending. "It's out in the open."

"And, see, those metaphors—'up front' and 'out in the open'—are part of a system we call atavistic purism. AP implies the existence of an ethically perfect state, which not only doesn't exist and never existed, but it's usually used to shore up the prejudices of whoever's making the judgments."

Alex felt Cara-Ann stir against his neck, and let a long fatty piece of pastrami slide down his throat unchewed. How long had they been sitting here? Longer than he'd meant to, that was for sure, and yet Alex couldn't resist the urge to brace himself against this girl and push. Her confidence seemed more drastic than the outcome of a happy childhood; it was cellular confidence, as if Lulu were a queen in disguise, without need or wish to be recognized.

"So," he said. "You think there's nothing inherently wrong with believing in something—or saying you do—for *money*?"

"'Inherently wrong,'" she said. "Gosh, that's a great example of calcified morality. I have to remember that for my old modern ethics teacher, Mr. Bastie; he collects them. Look," she said, straightening her spine and flicking her rather grave (despite the friendly antics of her face) gray eyes at Alex, "if I believe, I believe. Who are you to judge my reasons?"

"Because if your reasons are cash, that's not belief. It's bullshit."

Lulu grimaced. Another thing about her generation: no

one swore. Alex had actually heard teenagers say things like "shucks" and "golly," without apparent irony. "This is something we see a lot," Lulu mused, studying Alex. "Ethical ambivalence—we call it EA—in the face of a strong marketing action."

"Don't tell me: SMA."

"Yes," she said. "Which for you means picking the blind team. On the surface it looks like you might not even do it, you're so ambivalent, but I think it's the opposite: I think the EA is a kind of inoculation, a way of excusing yourself in advance for something you actually *want* to do. No offense," she added.

"Kind of like saying 'no offense' when you've just said something offensive?"

Lulu underwent the most extreme blush Alex had ever witnessed: a vermilion heat encompassed her face so abruptly that the effect was of something violent taking place, as if she were choking or about to hemorrhage. Alex sat up reflexively and checked on Cara-Ann. He found her eyes wide open.

"You're right," Lulu said, taking a rickety breath. "I apologize."

"No sweat," Alex said. The blush had unsettled him more than Lulu's confidence. He watched it drain from her face, leaving her skin a jarring white. "You okay?" he asked.

"I'm fine. I just get tired of talking."

"Ditto," Alex said. He felt exhausted.

"There are so many ways to go wrong," Lulu said. "All we've got are metaphors, and they're never exactly right. You can't ever just *Say. The. Thing.*"

"Hoo dat?" Cara-Ann asked, her gaze fixed on Lulu.

"That's Lulu."

"Can I just T you?" Lulu asked.

"You mean—"

"Now. Can I T you now." The question was a formality; she was already working her handset. An instant later Alex's own vibrated in his pants pocket; he had to jostle Cara-Ann to remove it.

U hav sum nAms 4 me? he read on the screen.

hEr thA r, Alex typed, and flushed the list of fifty contacts, along with notes, tips on angles of approach, and individual no-nos, into Lulu's handset.

GrAt. Il gt 2 wrk.

They looked up at each other. "That was easy," Alex said.

"I know," Lulu said. She looked almost sleepy with relief. "It's pure—no philosophy, no metaphors, no judgments."

"Unt dat," Cara-Ann said. She was pointing at Alex's handset, which he'd been using, unthinkingly, mere inches from her face.

"No," he said, suddenly anxious. "We—we have to go."

"Wait," Lulu said, seeming for the first time to notice Cara-Ann. "I'll T her."

"Uh, we don't—" but Alex felt unable to explain to Lulu the beliefs he shared with Rebecca about children and handsets. And now his own was vibrating again; Cara-Ann shrieked with delight and speared the screen with her chubby pointer. "*I do dat,*" she informed him.

Litl grl, U hav a nyc dad, Alex dutifully read aloud, a blush promptly staking a claim on his own face. Cara-Ann pounded keys with the hectic fervor of a starving dog

unleashed in a meat locker. Now a blooper appeared, one of
the stock images people sent to kids: a lion under a sparkling
sun. Cara-Ann zoomed in on different parts of the lion as if
she'd been doing this since birth. Lulu T'd: *Nvr met my dad.
Dyd b4 I ws brn.* Alex read this one in silence.

"Wow. I'm sorry," he said, looking up at Lulu, but his
voice seemed too loud—a coarse intrusion. He dropped his
eyes, and through the blender whir of Cara-Ann's pointing
fingers, he managed to T: *Sad.*

Ancnt hstry, Lulu T'd back.

"Das *mine!*" Cara-Ann proclaimed with guttural indigna-
tion, stretching from her sling and stabbing her pointer at
Alex's pocket. Inside it, the handset was vibrating—had been
almost constantly since he and Cara-Ann had left the diner
hours before. Was it possible that his daughter could feel the
vibrations through his body?

"*Mine* lolli-pop!" Alex wasn't sure how she'd arrived at
this name for the handset, but he certainly wasn't correcting
her.

"What do you want, honeybunch?" Rebecca asked in the
oversolicitous (Alex thought) way she often spoke to their
daughter when she'd spent the day at work.

"Daddy lolli-pop."

Rebecca looked quizzically at Alex. "Do you have a lollipop?"

"Of course not."

They were hurrying west, trying to reach the river before
sunset. The warming-related "adjustments" to Earth's orbit

had shortened the winter days, so that now, in January, sunset was taking place at 4:23.

"Can I take her?" Rebecca asked.

She lifted Cara-Ann out of the sling and placed her on the sooty sidewalk. The girl took a few of her stuttering, scarecrow steps. "We'll miss it if she walks," Alex said, and Rebecca picked her up and walked more quickly. Alex had surprised his wife outside the library, something he'd begun doing often to avoid the construction noise from their apartment. But today he had an extra reason: he needed to tell her about his arrangement with Bennie. Now, without further delays.

The sun had dropped behind the water wall by the time they reached the Hudson, but when they climbed the steps to the WATERWALK! as the wall's boarded rampart was exuberantly branded, they found the sun still poised, ruby-orange and yolklike, just above Hoboken. "Down," Cara-Ann commanded, and Rebecca released her. She ran toward the iron fence along the wall's outer edge, always jammed at this hour with people who probably (like Alex) had barely noticed sunset before the wall went up. Now they craved it. As he followed Cara-Ann into the crowd, Alex took Rebecca's hand. For as long as he'd known her, his wife had offset her sexy beauty with a pair of dorky glasses, sometimes leaning toward Dick Smart, other times Catwoman. Alex had loved the glasses for their inability to suppress Rebecca's sexy beauty, but lately he wasn't so sure; the glasses, along with Rebecca's prematurely graying hair and the fact that she was often short on sleep, threatened to reify her disguise into an identity: a fragile, harried academic slaving to finish a book while teaching two courses and chairing several committees. It was Alex's own role in this tableau that most depressed him: the aging music freak who couldn't earn his keep, sapping the life (or at least the sexy beauty) from his wife.

Rebecca was an academic star. Her new book was on the phenomenon of word casings, a term she'd invented for words that no longer had meaning outside quotation marks. English was full of these empty words—"friend" and "real" and "story" and "change"—words that had been shucked of their meanings and reduced to husks. Some, like "identity," "search," and "cloud," had clearly been drained of life by their Web usage. With others, the reasons were more complex; how had "American" become an ironic term? How had "democracy" come to be used in an arch, mocking way?

As usual, a hush enclosed the crowd in the last few seconds before the sun slipped away. Even Cara-Ann, in Rebecca's arms, went still. Alex felt the lees of sunlight on his face and closed his eyes, savoring its faint warmth, his ears full of the slosh of a passing ferry. The moment the sun had gone, everyone moved suddenly, as if a spell had broken. "Down," said Cara-Ann, and took off along the Waterwalk. Rebecca ran after her, laughing. Alex swiftly checked his handset.

JD nEds 2 thnk
Yep frm Sancho
Cal: no f-way

At each response, he experienced an alloy of emotions that had become familiar in the course of one afternoon: triumph marbled with scorn at the yeses, disappointment with an updraft of admiration at the nos. He was just beginning to type a response when he heard stamping feet, then his daughter's longing cry: "Lollllllli-POP!" Alex flicked the handset away, but it was too late: Cara-Ann was tugging at his jeans. "Mine dat," she said.

Rebecca sidled over. "So. That's the lollipop."

"Apparently."

"You let her use it?"

"One time, okay?" But his heart was racing.

"You just changed the rules, all by yourself?"

"I didn't change them, I slipped. Okay? Am I allowed to have one goddamn slip?"

Rebecca raised an eyebrow. Alex felt her studying him. "Why now?" she asked. "Today, after all this time—I don't get it."

"There's nothing to get!" Alex barked, but he was thinking: How does she know? And then: *What* does she know?

They stood, eyeing each other in the expiring light. Cara-Ann waited quietly, the lollipop apparently forgotten. The Waterwalk was nearly empty. It was time to tell Rebecca about the deal with Bennie—now, *now!*—but Alex felt paralyzed, as if the disclosure had already been poisoned. He had a crazy wish to T Rebecca, even found himself mentally composing the message: *Nu job in th wrks—big $ pos. pls kEp opn mind.*

"Let's go," Rebecca said.

Alex lifted Cara-Ann back into the sling, and they descended the water wall into darkness. As they made their way through the gloomy streets, Alex found himself thinking of the day he and Rebecca had met. After trying and failing to run down the wolf-headed purse snatcher, Alex had coaxed her out for beers and burritos, then had sex with her on the roof of her building on Avenue D, to escape her three room-mates. He hadn't known Rebecca's last name. And in that moment, without warning, Alex abruptly recalled the name of the girl who had worked for Bennie Salazar: Sasha. It came to him effortlessly, like a door falling open. *Sasha.* Alex held the name carefully in his mind, and sure enough, the first intimations of memory followed it skittishly into the light: a hotel lobby; a small, overwarm apartment. It was like try-ing to remember a dream. Had he fucked her? Alex figured he must have—nearly all those early dates had concluded with sex, hard as this was to fathom from his communal bed awash in the smell of baby flesh and a chemical tinge of bio-degradable diaper. But Sasha refused to give ground on the question of sex; she seemed to wink at him (green eyes?) and slip away.

u herd th nUs? Alex read on his handset late one night, as he sat in his usual spot by the window.

yup i herd

The "news" was that Bennie had moved the Scotty Haus-mann concert outdoors, to the Footprint, a change that would require more outreach from Alex's blind parrots (for no additional pay) so that any potential concertgoers would know where to go.

Bennie had told Alex about the venue change earlier, on the phone: "Scotty's not wild about enclosed spaces. I'm thinking he might be happier out in the open." It was the most recent in an onslaught of escalating demands and special needs. "He's a solitary person" (Bennie, explaining Scotty's need for a trailer). "He has a hard time with conversation" (why Scotty refused to do interviews). "He hasn't spent much time with children" (why Scotty might be troubled by "pointer noise"). "He's wary of technology" (why Scotty refused to narrate a stream or answer Ts sent to him by fans via the page Bennie had created for him). The guy pictured on that page—long-haired, jaunty, grinning a mouthful of porcelain and surrounded by a lot of big colorful balls—caused an itch of aggravation in Alex every time he looked at him.

wat nxt? he T'd Lulu back. *oystrs?*
only Ets chInEs
!

...

tel me hEs betr in prsn
nevr met
4 rEl??
shy
#@♂*

...

They could meander indefinitely, these conversations, and in the pauses Alex monitored his blind parrots: checking their pages and streams for raving endorsements of Scotty Hausmann, adding truants to a "violators" list. He hadn't seen or even spoken to Lulu since their meeting three weeks ago; she was a person who lived in his pocket, whom he'd ascribed her own special vibration.

Alex looked up. The construction now covered the bottom halves of his windows, its shafts and beams a craggy silhouette beyond which the prong of the Empire State

Building was still just visible. In a few days, it would be gone. Cara-Ann had been frightened when the structure crawling with men had first made its jagged appearance outside their windows, and Alex had tried desperately to make a game of it. "Up goes the building!" he would say each day, as if this progress were exciting, hopeful, and Cara-Ann had taken his cue, clapping her hands and exhorting, "Up! Up!"

up gOs th bldg, he T'd Lulu now, remarking on how easily baby talk fitted itself into the crawl space of a T.

. . . bldg? came Lulu's response.

nxt 2 myn. no mOr Ar/lyt

cn u stp it?

tryd

cn u move?

stuk

nyc, Lulu wrote, which confused Alex at first; the sarcasm seemed unlike her. Then he realized that she wasn't saying "nice." She was saying "New York City."

The concert day was "unseasonably" warm: eighty-nine degrees and dry, with angled golden light that stabbed their eyes at intersections and stretched their shadows to absurd lengths. The trees, which had bloomed in January, were now in tentative leaf. Rebecca had stuffed Cara-Ann into a dress from last summer with a duck across the front, and with Alex, they'd joined a mass of other young families on the skyscraper corridor of Sixth Avenue, Cara-Ann riding on Alex's back in a titanium pack they'd recently bought to replace the sling. Strollers were prohibited at public gatherings—they hampered evacuation.

Alex had been debating how to propose this concert to Rebecca, but in the end he hadn't needed to; checking her handset one night after Cara-Ann was asleep, his wife had said, "Scotty Hausmann . . . that's the guy Bennie Salazar played for us, right?"

Alex felt a tiny implosion near his heart. "I think so. Why?"

"I keep hearing about this free concert he's giving on Saturday in the Footprint, for kids and adults."

"Huh."

"Might give you a way to reconnect with Bennie." She was still smarting, on Alex's behalf, over the fact that Bennie hadn't hired him. This made Alex writhe with guilt whenever the subject came up.

"True," he'd said.

"So let's go," she'd said. "Why not, if it's free?"

Past Fourteenth Street, the skyscrapers fell away, and the slanted sun was upon them, still too low in the February sky to be shielded by any visor. In the glare Alex almost failed to spot his old friend Zeus, then tried to avoid him—Zeus was one of his blind parrots. Too late; Rebecca had already called his name. Zeus's Russian girlfriend, Natasha, was with him, each of them carrying one of their six-month-old twins in a pouch.

"You going to hear Scotty?" Zeus asked, as if Scotty Hausmann were someone they both knew.

"We are," Alex said carefully. "You?"

"Hell yeah," Zeus said. "A lap steel guitar with a slide—you ever heard one live? And we're not even talking rockabilly." Zeus worked for a blood bank and, in his spare time, helped Down syndrome kids make and sell printed sweatshirts. Alex found himself searching Zeus's face for some visible sign of parrothood, but his friend seemed the same right down to his soul patch, which he'd kept all these years since they'd gone out of fashion.

"He's supposed to be really good live," said Natasha, in her strong accent.

"I heard that, too," Rebecca said. "From, like, eight different people. It's almost strange."

"Not strange," Natasha said, with a harsh laugh. "People are getting paid." Alex felt a blaze of heat in his face and found it hard to look at Natasha. Still, it was clear that she spoke without knowledge; Zeus had kept his role a secret.

"But these are people I know," Rebecca said.

It was one of those days when every intersection brings up another familiar face, old friends and friends of friends, acquaintances, and people who just look familiar. Alex had been in the city too long to know how he knew them all: clubs where he'd deejayed? The law office where he'd worked as a secretary? The pickup basketball game he'd played for years in Tompkins Square Park? He'd felt on the verge of leaving New York since the day he'd arrived, at twenty-four—even now, he and Rebecca were poised to spring at any time, should a better job come along in a cheaper place—but somehow, enough years had managed to pass that he felt like he'd seen every person in Manhattan at least once. He wondered if Sasha was somewhere in this crowd. Alex found himself searching the vaguely familiar faces for hers without knowing what she looked like, as if his reward for recognizing Sasha, all these years later, would be finding out the answer to that question.

You going south? . . . we heard about this . . . not just for pointers . . . live he's supposed to be . . .

After the ninth or tenth exchange of this kind, which happened somewhere around Washington Square, it became suddenly clear to Alex that *all* of these people, the parents and the kidless, the single and the coupled, gay and straight, clean and pierced, were on their way to hear Scotty Hausmann. *Every single one.* The discovery swept over him in a surge of disbelief, followed by a rush of ownership and power—he'd done it, Christ he was a *genius* at it—followed by queasiness (it was a triumph he wasn't proud of), followed by fear: What if Scotty Hausmann was *not* a great performer? What if he was mediocre, or worse? Followed by a self-administered poultice that arrived in the form of a brain-T: *no 1 nOs abt me. Im invysbl.*

"You okay?" Rebecca asked.

"Yeah. Why."

"You seem nervous."

"Really?"

"You're squeezing my hand," she said. Then added, smiling under her buttonhole glasses, "It's nice."

By the time they crossed Canal and entered Lower Manhattan (where the density of children was now the highest in the nation), Alex and Rebecca and Cara-Ann were part of a throng of people that overwhelmed the sidewalk and filled the streets. Traffic had stopped, and choppers were converging overhead, flogging the air with a sound Alex hadn't been able to bear in the early years—too loud, too loud—but over time he'd gotten used to it: the price of safety. Today their military cackle felt weirdly appropriate, Alex thought, glancing around him at the sea of slings and sacs and baby backpacks, older children carrying younger ones, because wasn't this a kind of army? An army of children: the incarnation of faith in those who weren't aware of having any left.

if thr r childrn, thr mst b a fUtr, rt?

Before them, the new buildings spiraled gorgeously against the sky, so much nicer than the old ones (which Alex had only seen in pictures), more like sculptures than buildings, because they were empty. Approaching them, the crowd began to slow, backing up as those in front entered the space around the reflecting pools, the density of police and security agents (identifiable by their government handsets) suddenly palpable, along with visual scanning devices affixed to cornices, lampposts, and trees. The weight of what had happened here more than twenty years ago was still faintly present for Alex, as it always was when he came to the Footprint. He perceived it as a sound just out of earshot, the vibration of an old disturbance. Now it seemed more insistent than ever: a low, deep thrum that felt primally familiar, as if it had been whirring inside all the sounds that Alex had made and collected over the years: their hidden pulse.

Rebecca clutched his hand, her slim fingers moist. "I love you, Alex," she said.

"Don't say it like that. Like something bad is about to happen."

"I'm nervous," she said. "Now I'm nervous, too."

"It's the choppers," Alex said.

"Excellent," Bennie murmured. "Wait right there, Alex, if you wouldn't mind. Right by that door."

Alex had left Rebecca and Cara-Ann and their friends in a multitude that had swelled into the many thousands, everyone waiting patiently—then less patiently—as the starting time of the concert came and went, watching four jumpy roadies guard the raised platform where Scotty Hausmann was supposed to play. After a T from Lulu that Bennie needed help, Alex had snaked his way through a gauntlet of security checks to Scotty Hausmann's trailer.

Inside, Bennie and an old roadie were slumped on black folding chairs. There was no sign of Scotty Hausmann. Alex's throat felt very dry. *Im invsbl*, he thought.

"Bennie, listen to me," said the roadie. His hands shook beneath the cuffs of his plaid flannel shirt.

"You can do this," Bennie said. "I'm telling you."

"Listen to me, Bennie."

"Stay by the door, Alex," Bennie said again, and he was right—Alex had been about to move closer, to ask what the fuck Bennie thought he was trying to do: put this decrepit roadie on in Scotty Hausmann's place? To *impersonate* him? A guy with gutted cheeks and hands so red and gnarled he looked like he'd have trouble playing a hand of poker, much less the strange, sensuous instrument clutched between his knees? But when Alex's eyes fell on the instrument, he suddenly knew, with an awful spasm in his gut: the decrepit roadie *was* Scotty Hausmann.

"The people are here," Bennie said. "The thing is in motion. I can't stop it."

"It's too late. I'm too old. I just—I can't."

Scotty Hausmann sounded like he'd recently wept or was on the verge of weeping—possibly both. He had shoulder-length hair slicked away from his face and empty, blasted eyes, all of it amounting to a derelict impression despite his clean shave. All Alex recognized were his teeth: white and sparkling—embarrassed-looking, as if they knew there was only so much you could do with this wreck of a face. And Alex understood that Scotty Hausmann did not exist. He was a word casing in human form: a shell whose essence has vanished.

"You *can*, Scotty—you have to," Bennie said, with his usual calm, but through his thinning silver hair Alex caught a shimmer of sweat on his crown. "Time's a goon, right? You gonna let that goon push you around?"

Scotty shook his head. "The goon won."

Benny took a long breath, a flick of eyes at his watch the only sign of his impatience. "You came to me, Scotty, remember that?" he said. "Twenty-some-odd years ago—you believe it was that long? You brought me a fish."

"Yeah."

"I thought you were going to kill me."

"I should've," Scotty said. A single hack of laughter. "I wanted to."

"And when I hit bottom—when Steph threw me out and I got fired from Sow's Ear—I tracked you down. And what did I say? You remember, when I found you fishing in the East River? Out of the blue? What did I say?"

Scotty mumbled something.

"I said, 'It's time you became a star.' And what did you say to me?" Bennie leaned close to Scotty, took the man's trembling wrists in his own, rather elegant hands, and peered into his face. "You said, 'I dare you.'"

There was a long pause. Then, without warning, Scotty leaped to his feet, upending his chair as he lunged for the trailer door. Alex was fully prepared to step aside and let him pass, but Scotty got there first and began trying to muscle him out of the way, at which point Alex realized that his job—the sole reason Bennie had placed him there—was to block the door and keep the singer from escaping. They grappled in huffing silence, Scotty's desiccated face so close to Alex's that he was inhaling the guy's breath, which smelled of beer, or the aftermath of beer. Then he refined his opinion: Jägermeister.

Bennie seized Scotty from behind, but it wasn't much of a hold—Alex made this discovery when Scotty managed to rear back and head-butt him in the solar plexus. Alex gasped and doubled over. He heard Bennie murmuring to Scotty as if trying to calm a horse.

When he could breathe again, Alex made an effort to consult with his boss. "Bennie, if he doesn't want to—"

Scotty swung at Alex's face, but Alex darted aside and the musician's fist smashed the flimsy door. There was a tannic smell of blood.

Alex tried again: "Bennie, this seems kind of—"

Scotty wrenched free of Bennie and kneed Alex in the balls, which made him crumple to the floor in fetal agony. Scotty kicked him aside and threw open the door.

"Hello," came a voice from outside. A high, clear voice, distantly familiar. "I'm Lulu."

Through his roiling pain, Alex managed to turn his head and look at what was happening outside the trailer. Scotty was still in the doorway, looking down. The slanted winter sun ignited Lulu's hair, making a nimbus around her face. She was blocking Scotty's path, one arm on each of the flimsy metal railings. Scotty could easily have knocked her over, but he didn't. And in hesitating, looking down for an extra second at this lovely girl blocking his way, Scotty lost.

"Can I walk with you?" Lulu asked.

Bennie had scrambled to retrieve the guitar, which he handed to Scotty over Alex's prone form. Scotty took the instrument, held it to his chest, and inhaled a long, shaky breath. "Only if you'll take my arm, darling," he replied, and a ghost version of Scotty Hausmann flickered at Alex from the dregs that were left, sexy and rakish.

Lulu twined her arm through Scotty's, and they moved straight into the crowd: the addled geezer carrying the long, strange instrument, and the young woman who might have been his daughter. Bennie hauled Alex onto his feet, and they followed, Alex's legs watery and spastic. The oceanic sprawl of people shifted spontaneously, clearing a path to the platform where a stool and twelve enormous microphones had been positioned.

"Lulu," Alex said to Bennie, and shook his head.

"She's going to run the world," Bennie said.

Scotty climbed onto the platform and sat on the stool. Without a glance at the audience or a word of introduction, he began to play "I Am a Little Lamb," a tune whose childishness was belied by the twanging filigree of his slide guitar, its gushy metallic complexity. He followed that with "Goats Like Oats" and "A Little Tree Is Just Like Me." The amplification was fine and powerful enough to eclipse the chopper throb and deliver the sound even to the distant reaches of the crowd, where it disappeared between buildings. Alex listened in a sort of cringe, expecting a roar of rejection from these thousands he'd managed secretly to assemble, whose goodwill had already been taxed by the long wait. But it didn't happen; the pointers, who already knew these songs, clapped and screeched their approval, and the adults seemed intrigued, attuned to double meanings and hidden layers, which were easy to find. And it may be that a crowd at a particular moment of history creates the object to justify its gathering, as it did at the first Human Be-In and Monterey Pop and Woodstock. Or it may be that two generations of war and surveillance had left people craving the embodiment of their own unease in the form of a lone, unsteady man on a slide guitar. Whatever the reason, a swell of approval palpable as rain lifted from the center of the crowd and rolled out toward its edges, where it crashed against buildings and water wall and rolled back at Scotty with redoubled force, lifting him off his stool, onto his feet (the roadies quickly adjusting the microphones), exploding the quavering husk

Scotty had appeared to be just moments before and unleashing something strong, charismatic, and fierce. Anyone who was there that day will tell you the concert really started when Scotty stood up. That's when he began singing the songs he'd been writing for years underground, songs no one had ever heard, or anything like them—"Eyes in My Head," "X's and O's," "Who's Watching Hardest"—ballads of paranoia and disconnection ripped from the chest of a man you knew just by looking had never had a page or a profile or a handle or a handset, who was part of no one's data, a guy who had lived in the cracks all these years, forgotten and full of rage, in a way that now registered as pure. Untouched. But of course, it's hard to know anymore who was really *at* that first Scotty Hausmann concert—more people claim it than could possibly have fit into the space, capacious and mobbed though it was. Now that Scotty has entered the realm of myth, everyone wants to own him. And maybe they should. Doesn't a myth belong to everyone?

Standing next to Bennie, who watched Scotty while frenetically working his handset, Alex felt what was happening around him as if it had already happened and he were looking back. He wished he could be with Rebecca and Cara-Ann, first dully, then acutely—with pain. His handset had no trouble locating his wife's handset, but it took many minutes of scanning that section of the crowd with his zoom to actually spot her. In the process, he panned the rapt, sometimes tearstained faces of adults, the elated, scant-toothed grins of toddlers, and young people like Lulu, who was now holding hands with a statuesque black man, both of them gazing at

Scotty Hausmann with the rhapsodic joy of a generation finally descrying someone worthy of its veneration.

At last he found Rebecca, smiling, holding Cara-Ann in her arms. She was dancing. They were too far away for Alex to reach them, and the distance felt irrevocable, a chasm that would keep him from ever again touching the delicate silk of Rebecca's eyelids, or feeling, through his daughter's ribs, the scramble of her heartbeat. Without the zoom, he couldn't even see them. In desperation, he T'd Rebecca, *pls wAt 4 me, my bUtiful wyf,* then kept his zoom trained on her face until he saw her register the vibration, pause in her dancing, and reach for it.

"It happens once in your life, if you're the luckiest man on earth," Bennie said, "an event like that."

"You've had your share," Alex said.

"I haven't," Bennie said. "No, Alex, no—that's what I'm saying! Not even close!" He was in a prolonged state of euphoria, collar loose, arms swinging. The celebration had already happened; champagne had been poured (Jägermeister for Scotty), dumplings eaten in Chinatown, a thousand calls from the press fielded and deferred, the little girls ferried home in cabs by the joyful, exultant wives ("Did you hear him?" Rebecca kept asking Alex. "Have you ever heard anything like him?" Then whispering, close to his ear, "Ask Bennie again about a job!"), closure achieved with Lulu at the introduction of her fiancé, Joe, who hailed from Kenya and was getting his Ph.D. in robotics at Columbia. Now it was well after midnight, and Bennie and Alex were walking together on the Lower East Side because Bennie wanted to walk. Alex felt weirdly depressed—and oppressed by the need to hide his depression from Bennie.

"You were fantastic, Alex," Bennie said, mussing Alex's hair. "You're a natural, I'm telling you."

A *natural what?* Alex almost said, but stopped himself. Instead he asked, after a pause, "Did you ever have an employee . . . named Sasha?"

Bennie stood still. The name seemed to float in the air between them, incandescent. *Sasha.* "Yes, I did," Bennie said. "She was my assistant. Did you know her?"

"I met her once, a long time ago."

"She lived right around here," Bennie said, beginning to walk again. "Sasha. I haven't thought about her in a long time."

"What was she like?"

"She was great," Bennie said. "I was crazy about her. But it turned out she had sticky fingers." He glanced at Alex. "She stole things."

"You're kidding."

Bennie shook his head. "It was kind of a sickness, I think."

A connection was trying to form in Alex's mind, but he couldn't complete it. Had he known that Sasha was a thief? Discovered it in the course of that night? "So . . . you fired her?"

"Had to," Bennie said. "After twelve years. She was like the other half of my brain. Three-quarters, really."

"You have any idea what she's doing now?"

"None. I think I'd know if she were still in the business.

Although maybe not"—he laughed—"I've been pretty out of it myself."

They walked in silence for several minutes. There was a lunar quiet to the streets of the Lower East Side. Bennie seemed preoccupied by the memory of Sasha. He orchestrated a turn onto Forsyth, walked a bit, and stopped. "There," he said, gazing up at an old tenement building, its fluorescently lit vestibule visible behind scuffed Plexiglas. "That's where Sasha lived."

Alex looked up at the building, sooty against the lavender sky, and experienced a hot-cold flash of recognition, a shiver of déjà vu, as if he were returning to a place that no longer existed.

"You remember which apartment?" he asked.

"4F, I think," Bennie said. And then, after a moment, "Want to see if she's home?"

He was grinning, and the grin made him look young; they were co-conspirators, Alex thought, prowling outside a girl's apartment, he and Bennie Salazar.

"Is her last name Taylor?" Alex asked, looking at the handwritten tab beside the buzzer. He was grinning, too.

"No, but it could be a roommate."

"I'll ring," Alex said.

He leaned in to the buzzer, every electron in his body yearning up those ill-lit angular stairs he now remembered as clearly as if he'd left Sasha's apartment just this morning. He followed them in his mind until he saw himself arriving at a small, cloistered apartment—purples, greens—humid with a smell of steam heat and scented candles. A radiator hiss. Little things on the windowsills. A bathtub in the kitchen—yes, she'd had one of those! It was the only one he'd ever seen.

Bennie stood close to Alex, and they waited together, suspended in the same precarious excitement. Alex found he was holding his breath. Would Sasha buzz them in, and would he and Bennie climb those stairs together to her door? Would Alex recognize her, and would she recognize him? And in that moment, the longing he'd felt for Sasha at last assumed a clear shape: Alex imagined walking into her apartment and finding himself still there—his young self, full of schemes and high standards, with nothing decided yet. The fantasy imbued him with careening hope. He pushed the buzzer again, and as more seconds passed, Alex felt a gradual draining loss. The whole crazy pantomime collapsed and blew away.

"She's not here," Bennie said. "I'm betting she's far away." He tipped his gaze at the sky. "I hope she found a good life," he said at last. "She deserves it."

They resumed walking. Alex felt an ache in his eyes and throat. "I don't know what happened to me," he said, shaking his head. "I honestly don't."

Bennie glanced at him, a middle-aged man with chaotic silver hair and thoughtful eyes. "You grew up, Alex," he said, "just like the rest of us."

Alex closed his eyes and listened: a storefront gate sliding down. A dog barking hoarsely. The lowing of trucks over bridges. The velvety night in his ears. And the hum, always that hum, which maybe wasn't an echo after all, but the sound of time passing.

th blu nyt
th stRs u cant c
th hum tht nevr gOs away

A sound of clicking heels on the pavement punctured the quiet. Alex snapped open his eyes, and he and Bennie both turned—whirled, really, peering for Sasha in the ashy dark. But it was another girl, young and new to the city, fiddling with her keys.

Acknowledgments

For their inspiration, motivation, and superb guidance, I'm indebted to Jordan Pavlin, Deborah Treisman, and Amanda Urban.

For editorial insights and support, or the right idea at the right time, thanks to Adrienne Brodeur, John Freeman, Colin Harrison, David Herskovits, Manu and Raoul Herskovits, Barbara Jones, Graham Kimpton, Don Lee, Eva Mantell, Helen Schulman, Ilena Silverman, Rob Spillman, Kay Kimpton Walker, Monica Adler Werner, and Thomas Yagoda.

For their patient attention to getting the book made, thanks to Lydia Buechler, Leslie Levine, and Marci Lewis.

For their expertise in fields of which I knew little or less, thanks to Alex Busansky, Alexandra Egan, Ken Goldberg, Jacob Slichter (for his book, *So You Wanna Be a Rock & Roll Star*), and Chuck Zwicky.

For their fine reading company over many years, thanks to Erika Belsey, David Herskovits (again and always), Alice Naude, Jamie Wolf, and Alexi Worth.

Finally, I'm grateful to a group of peers whose exceptional talents and generosity I've leaned on heavily, and without whom there would be no *Goon Squad* (as they know better than anyone): Ruth Danon, Lisa Fugard, Melissa Maxwell, David Rosenstock, and Elizabeth Tippens.